THE
CANTICLE
KINGDOM

THE CANTICLE KINGDOM

Michael Young

Bonneville Books
Springville, Utah

ISBN 13: 978-1-59955-362-7

Published by Bonneville Books, an imprint of Cedar Fort, Inc., 2373 W. 700 S., Springville, UT 84663
Distributed by Cedar Fort, Inc., www.cedarfort.com

LIBRARY OF CONGRESS CATALOGING-IN-PUBLICATION DATA

Young, Michael, 1984-
  The canticle kingdom / Michael Young.
    p. cm.
  Summary: Two brothers create a magical music box which causes people to
disappear into a parallel world when they touch it.
  ISBN 978-1-59955-362-7
  1. Fantasy fiction, American. 2. World War, 1939-1945--Fiction. I.
Title.
  PS3625.O9673C36 2010
  813'.6--dc22
                                    2009043201

Cover design by Megan Whittier
Cover design © 2010 by Lyle Mortimer
Edited and typeset by Megan E. Welton

Printed in the United States of America

10 9 8 7 6 5 4 3 2 1

Printed on acid-free paper

DEDICATION

To my wife Jenny
For now and always
My queen.

CONTENTS

PROLOGUE

ཉཉ

IDAR-OBERSTEIN, GERMANY, 1939

The lights in the workshop glowed brightly, even though the shop had been closed for hours. From the clock near the door, a single chime echoed, signaling the early hour. Even though the candles had nearly burned themselves into puddles, the two brothers huddled over the workbench remained wide-awake as ever. With a tool in each hand, each brother worked frantically over their piece, eyes glistening with excitement like children opening a long-awaited present. Several minutes more passed in the flickering candlelight with only the scraping of metal on wood to break the silence.

All at once, the taller man, muscular, with dark hair and a bristly beard, dropped his tools and gave his brother a hearty pound on the back. His brother, of leaner build and fairer complexion with a smooth boyish face, grinned broadly back. Then, slowly, one after the other, they let their tools drop to the table, clattering with a satisfied finality. Starting with a low chuckle, their mirth grew contagious and swelled until both brothers bellowed with triumphant laughter.

"It is finished, Jorgen! Our masterpiece!"

Jorgen nodded jovially. "Right, my brother. All except one thing."

The older brother picked up their handiwork and etched the familiar inscription on the underside with his ancient tool:

J und K Müller
Frankfurt, Deutschland

Setting their masterpiece on the table, they sat and admired it, the product of many painstaking hours of labor. For many years, the brothers had earned a living with their woodwork, but this piece was something much more special than their usual fare.

"Well, my brother," muttered Jorgen. "I think we should turn in for the night. We can give it a test run in the morning. We wouldn't want to disturb the others."

They finally blew out the pitiful candles and retired to their respective rooms. For a long while afterwards, the darkened interior of the shop remained still and silent. A chill winter wind rustled the shutters, whistling and howling like a band of ghouls.

Long after the brothers had retired to bed, a quiet creak sounded, and a shadow slunk down the stairwell, taking each stair individually. As the form reached the bottom, he dared to move a little bit faster, emboldened by the nearness of his prize. With carefully measured steps, the figure reached the table and brooded over it.

"You're mine," he whispered.

ᖚ

FRANKFURT, GERMANY, 1940

A heavily bearded man sighed as he entered the bank, carrying a tightly wrapped bundle under his arm. It had been a long, hard month of travel, and his muscles ached from the strain. He'd been up to a Nazi rally in Berlin, down to the University of Zürich in Switzerland, and over to Vienna to attend a number of concerts. By his estimation, he had sampled the best and brightest the German-speaking world had to offer and had gone away with everything that he had come for.

He smiled and hummed a jaunty waltz tune to himself as he stepped up to the teller at the first window he saw. The teller looked up, disinterested, and droned, "Welcome to the First Bank of Frankfurt. How can I help you?"

The bearded man glanced furtively from side to side, as if to make sure that no one else was watching him. He lifted the bundle and placed it in front of the teller.

"I would like to place this in my special safe-deposit box. Here are my papers confirming my account number and identity."

The teller took the papers and examined them slowly, his eyes lingering on each line as if scrutinizing each letter for mistakes. Finally, satisfied, the teller returned the papers and grunted. "Yes, yes, everything seems to be in order. Right this way, please."

The teller led the man down a dimly lit corridor, stopping at the end of the hallway in front of a heavy metal door. The teller removed a key ring from his pocket, rifled through the assortment of keys, and selected the correct one. The door swung open to reveal a completely empty gray room. The teller ushered the bearded man in. "Take as long as you like. I'll escort you out when you're finished."

The bearded man nodded and closed the door behind him. The teller stood outside and waited as the minutes quickly piled up to over an hour. The teller impatiently tapped his foot, wondering silently what on earth could be taking him such a long time.

After another twenty minutes had elapsed, he finally lost patience and rapped sharply on the door. "Sir, is everything all right in there?" He received no response. Suspiciously, he knocked again, and when no one answered, he reinserted the key and slid open the door. The teller gasped. The bearded man was gone. Only his strange, rectangular parcel remained in the center of the floor, still wrapped tightly in a dark cloth. Sweat broke out across the teller's brow. Should he report this? Was the man trying to steal something from the bank? Frantically, he tapped on the floors and walls, trying to find some alternate route of escape that the mysterious man could have used. His search *revealed nothing. He glanced down at the package and made up his mind. He would get rid of the evidence and forget the incident.*

Hastily, he snatched up the package, clumsily fumbling with the wrappings. He took one glance at the object inside and bit his lip in confusion. Why had the man gone to all the trouble to protect this? His questions lingering unanswered in the air, he stuffed the package under his arm, exited the room, and locked the door. He returned to his window, concealing the parcel in the shadows by his feet. Perhaps today was not such a bad day after all. The package might come in handy. At the very least, it would fetch a good price.

ന്റ

THE CANTICLE KINGDOM

The chamber window burst open, flooding the room with icy air and eerie shadows. Lightning roared from the open window, striking simultaneously with the clattering shutters. The feeble woman shot up in bed, clasping her chest as if her heart threatened to give up its life-sustaining labor.

"Your Majesty!" cried the man, Rufus, by her side. "You must remain calm! You are safe here."

The queen's breathing slowed, and she slowly reclined to her previous position on her back. From the corner, Camilla, the queen's calico cat, jumped up on the bed and snuggled up next to the pale woman. Camilla was the queen's favorite pet, and only rarely were they ever seen apart. The cat had been Rufus's only supporter during these midnight vigils.

"Thank you, Rufus. I know I am safe. My sleep was troubled enough without these storms."

Rufus nodded solemnly and removed a small vial of red-brown liquid from the night-stand adjoining the bed. "Here, your Majesty," he whispered, holding up the vial to her pale lips. "Drink this. It may not help as much as it used to, but at least it will do something."

Her lips trembling softly, the queen slowly sipped the liquid until the entire contents were gone. In desperate anticipation, the young chamberlain gazed at the queen's wrinkled face, looking for any signs of relief. None came.

Nothing made sense. Only a week before, the queen had been the epitome of health: young, fair, energetic, and hopeful.

"My lady, I don't understand! Cornelius prepared the draught as he always has. He's the best there is! I don't know why—"

A feeble gesture from the queen silenced Rufus's futile speculation. For several seconds, only the fierce pounding of the raindrops could be heard. The queen once again opened her sunken eyes and began to speak, her voice barely audible. "I am afraid we must do what—" A fit of coughing wracked her flimsy frame. Rufus placed a hand on her shoulder to steady her until the fit subsided. "—What we have worked so hard to avoid all this time."

Rufus's gaze darkened, his face lined with worry. "No, my lady! You will recover! You will remain . . . ," Rufus let his words trail off into nothingness. He did not believe them himself.

Silence reigned for a few moments more, and then the queen continued. "No, Rufus. Your faith is admirable. Your loyalty is unsurpassed. But it avails us nothing. I do not understand why this great change has gripped me so suddenly, but . . . ." She gazed wistfully into the distance. "I can feel the life leaving me. I have tried in vain too long for something that I cannot obtain. In a matter of days I will be gone, and there seems to be little else we can do to stop that."

Rufus's eyes filled with tears. "But with that option, you will be lost—forever."

The queen's eyes closed in resignation. "I am afraid that cannot be avoided."

CHAPTER ONE

ᡣᡩ

THE HIDDEN DOOR

THE CANTICLE KINGDOM

"Johann! If you don't come down to breakfast this instant, I'll—"

Young Johann was not interested in hearing the rest of his mother's threat. Instead, he muffled it with a pillow over his ears. Then, thinking better of his protest, he slipped grudgingly out of bed and into his brown tunic and tied it off with a forest green belt. There was no use in waiting to find out whether her threat was shallow.

"Coming!" Out of his bedroom window, he caught a quick glimpse of the gleaming white castle atop the distant hill. It glistened invitingly in the early morning light, the sun having finally peered out through the storm clouds. From the highest tower of the castle, a series of bells chimed—a low tone, followed by a high one and a descending scale—signaling that it was eight o'clock.

Johann had just celebrated his thirteenth birthday, and as such, he was still caught in that awkward stage in which the body cannot seem to make up its mind whether to move on to adulthood or to remain a child. He was not the strongest of boys, and his arms and legs had often been compared to things like willow wands and fire kindling. However, his pleasant smile and glistening brown eyes more than made up for his lack of strength when it came to disarming his opposition. Wavy light-brown locks that showed no desire of ever being tamed shot out from all over his head, much to his mother's dismay.

With several great leaping strides, Johann bounded out his bedroom door and down the stairs into the kitchen. There, his grandfather was already devouring his portion of bread and cheese while his baby sister toyed nosily with her porridge.

At seeing him, his mother gave an exasperated sigh and pointed severely to a bowl on the table, which had long since stopped steaming.

"Eat," she commanded. "Brutus wants you in the shop in a mere fifteen minutes, and it is not my fault if you have to bear the brunt of his displeasure if you're late."

Now, it was Johann's turn to sigh. Brutus was the blacksmith to whom he was apprenticed, and his muscular arms were not the only thing that caused sparks to fly in the shop.

As Johann made quick work of the portion in front of him, his grandfather looked up, his eyes seemingly gazing past the boy. "Quite the storm last night, eh, Johann?" he drawled.

"Uh-huh," replied Johann, his mouth still full of porridge. Grandpa leaned back in his chair, his wispy hair falling randomly along his temples.

"I can't recall a storm so fierce since Lady Ellis was the queen around here and Lord Balthazar came to power. Yes, times were different then . . . ."

Johann's mother stopped what she was doing and whirled around to face his grandfather. "Watch your tongue, you fool! You know full well it's forbidden to speak of such things! What if you were to be overheard?"

Grandfather wrinkled his brow in consternation, his lower lip jutting out. "No use in acting like the past doesn't exist. It's utter nonsense."

Johann saw his mother flush a deep shade of purple as she brandished her serving spoon like a bludgeon in the old man's face. "Listen, you loony, old codger. The only reason you are still alive is that the soldiers believe you are too senile to be of any threat to them. Unfortunately, I know better. You best keep up the act and keep your mouth shut." She stormed back to the stove. "Especially around my son," she added with venom.

Grandfather shrugged his shoulders, brushing aside her comment. "The boy will learn someday, Maria. Might as well be from us."

Maria sighed with a look of resignation. "I know. I just don't want him flying off places like his father . . . ."

Johann, though curious, had more pressing matters on his mind than grandfather's old stories. In his haste to gulp down the last of his porridge, he left generous portions spackled across his face. Finishing with a flourish, he leapt from the table, slipped on his shoes, and ran a hand through his hair all at the same time.

"Good-bye," he cried hastily and rushed out the door in the direction of the blacksmith's shop.

ॐ

As Johann timidly approached the Brutus's shop, he could already hear his uncle's rapid hammer strokes, and he caught a glimpse of the flying sparks shooting off violently in all directions. This was not a good sign. Then, as if possessing a sixth sense, Brutus suddenly stopped his hammering.

"You're late, boy," he growled, his face lit with the flames.

Johann gulped. This could get painful.

"S-so sorry, Uncle," he stammered. "I was—"

A sudden, ringing hammer stroke cut the boy off.

"Quiet. Excuses are about as effective as tempering metal over a match-stick." Brutus's smoldering eyes bored into Johann for several long moments. Then, his mood shifted, a twinge of worry suddenly entering his voice. "Have you seen Brigitta?"

Brigitta was Johann's partner in all his exploits. She was almost exactly Johann's age, and like Johann, she was slight of frame. However, unlike him, she was pure muscle. Most accused her of being a tomboy, an accusation that she never refuted. Her shoulder-length blonde hair was usually unkempt, and her bright blue eyes, more often than not, carried a very mischievous gleam.

Johann was not sure whether his uncle's words held a veiled accusation. "No, I haven't seen her since . . . lunch yesterday."

The blacksmith stepped closer, weighing the boy's words. "She wasn't in her room this morning. I figured that she snuck out with you. Perhaps I should have listened to your excuse after all."

Johann sighed, wishing he had something more exciting to say. For once, he had no idea what she was up to. "No, I really haven't seen her. She always lets me know about her, er, adventures. She's probably fine."

The gruff, bearded blacksmith wasn't convinced. He stood there in silence for a few seconds, his taut muscles glistening in the firelight. "You stay here," he grumbled, setting down his hammer and wiping the sweat from his brow. "I am going to look for her." Without another word, Brutus disappeared through the doorway.

Still a bit dazed over his good fortune of not being punished, Johann gazed around the room, trying to decide how to occupy his time until his uncle returned with Brigitta.

Immediately, Johann realized an additional lucky break—in his haste to leave the shop, his uncle had left the fires burning brightly. Usually, Johann was not allowed near the flames and was confined to menial tasks and remote observations. However, with his master gone, he would have time to make some progress on the project he had been secretly planning.

More than anything, Johann wanted a sword of his own. Unfortunately, this idea did not fare well with his uncle, and it fared even worse with his mother. Thus, Johann had to resort to practicing his budding swordsmanship with blunt sticks. In the meantime, he had saved—well, pilfered—enough scrap metal from the shop to make an attempt at swordmaking, should such a chance present itself.

Seizing this first opportunity, Johann ran eagerly to the flames to use what precious time he had. His uncle's hammer, which lay next to the flames, was a formidable tool. It was obviously much too large and heavy for his stripling arms. Needing only a few seconds to think, he stepped away from the flames and headed toward the back of the shop.

The back closet contained most of Brutus's spare tools. Johann knew that it contained hammers of various sizes and at least one that would fit his purpose. Trembling a bit with anticipation, Johann slipped open the door and squinted into the darkness. The closet was positioned so that the flames did little to offer him any light

Fully expecting his uncle to return any minute, Johann stretched out his hands and felt his way into the darkness. At first he felt nothing, but eventually his persistence was rewarded with the feel of cold metal on his fingertips. However, as he took another step into the darkness, his foot caught on an object lying on the floor, causing him to lose his balance. Hands outstretched, he tumbled farther into the closet with a yelp, bracing himself to land on something either very hard or very sharp. The impact was nothing like he expected.

Johann felt his hands hit the back wall, but instead of standing firm, the wall gave way like a trap door. His hands landed in loamy earth, and he couldn't see a thing. Stunned, Johann lay there for a good minute before trusting himself to stand again. When he did, he became immediately aware of a faint glow emanating from the center of the room, soft and constant, very different from the flickering firelight he was used to.

In the glow of the light, Johann was able to make out the details of the room. It was fairly small, only about three or four times the size of the closet he had just exited. Metal boxes lined the entire perimeter of the room. In the center of the room lay a compact metal table cluttered with various scraps of dark metal. In the center of the table, a faintly glowing yellow orb sat propped up on a squat pedestal supplying light to the room.

Johann brushed the dirt from his clothes and crept curiously toward the table. *What in the name of the Queen is my uncle* doing *back here?*

As he approached the table, he saw that one of the metal boxes lay open. Squinting in the dim light, he reached in the box and removed a lightweight piece of metal. The piece appeared perfectly square and was grooved along the sides. In the center of the sheet was a solid, squat cylinder of metal, perfectly smooth and polished. Gawking in amazement at its fine craftsmanship, Johann mulled the sheet over in this hand, wracking his mind for what use it could possibly have.

Replacing the sheet in the box, he searched around the rest of the table and found various pieces of metal, mostly sheets and cylinders in various stages of completion. However, it was what lay beneath the metal pieces that caught Johann's attention.

Spread out on the entire length of the table was a diagram in a layout that Johann had never seen before. The diagram was composed of a large rect-angle in which many horizontal lines had been drawn. At seemingly random intervals lay black dots strewn across the paper like a colony of motionless insects. At the top of the diagram lay a line of ornate text in a language that Johann could not understand:

> *Muster: EIN LIED DES HERZENS*
> *Komponiert von dem Herrn Jung*
> *Es lebe die Musik!*

Johann ran his hands up and down the lines several times, trying to make some sense out of the seeming randomness of the diagram. Unfortunately, before Johann could contemplate this strange inscription any longer, he turned his head at a distant noise. He heard heavy footsteps in the shop and an unmistakable, irritated grumbling. Brutus was back.

CHAPTER TWO

❧

FORAGING in the FOREST

DACHAU, GERMANY, 1943

The overcast skies set a perfect tone for the dismal scene. Inside the dirty confines of the barbed-wire fence, the prisoners were lined up in a row, shivering from the lack of warmth provided by their meager and tattered clothing. The guards paced up and down the row, carefully observing each prisoner through narrowed eyes.

The Nazi captain was an especially austere man, known for his brutality and seeming lack of conscience. At a meager 5´6˝, he made up for his lack of height with his use of muscle. As he inspected the prisoners, he sometimes lashed out with the butt of his rifle at any one that particularly displeased him.

However, this time his methods were somewhat different. Suddenly, he halted and let his eyes rest particularly long on a certain prisoner. She was a young gypsy woman, very slight of build, with deeply colored skin and delicate features. In happier times, she could have been considered beautiful, but the war had taken a savage toll on her appearance. However, the innate beauty was still manifest in her manner. She was beaten and despised, but still she held her head high and her gaze firm.

It was this very quality that both intrigued and disgusted the captain of the guard. He gazed menacingly at her, furrowing his brow and baring his teeth. She held his gaze for several tense seconds, emitting quiet determination.

Seeing that his gaze did not intimidate her, he crumpled his face in rage and slapped her hard across the face with his gloved hand. She flew back at the blow, but did not completely fall. Expertly masking the pain, she slowly rose again to full stature.

"You," spat the guard, "need to be broken."

Later, in the guard's quarters, the young gypsy tried hard not to show her fear as she waited for the captain to return. She was taken for what had been termed "interrogation," but what was more like a senseless beating. New bruises formed on her arms and legs, which throbbed with constant pain.

The guard stepped out for a smoke and promised her that he would return shortly.

He stomped out and left the door locked securely behind him. Searching desperately for any means of escape or defense, the young gypsy rummaged around the room but found hardly anything useful.

Just as she was about to give in to despair, she uncovered a small bundle that had been hidden cleverly behind the desk in the shadows under a stack of papers. Curious, she unwrapped the bundle to reveal the beautiful object inside. For a few short moments, she forgot about the throbbing pain in her skull and the ache in her side.

Suddenly, she heard the fall of approaching footsteps. The time for preparation was over. The guard fumbled a few seconds with the keys and then burst menacingly into the room, brandishing a hard rubber hose and emitting an almost wolf-like growl.

This time, however, it was the guard who recoiled in fear. The gypsy girl was nowhere to be seen. His eyes darted rapidly around the room, almost bulging out with confusion. There was absolutely nowhere to go—no closets, no drawers, and no hiding places. The room was silent, except for a faint tune sounding from an unseen source.

Reaching for his pistol, the guard stormed out of the room, beads of sweat beginning to form on his brow.

They would have his hide for this one.

ත්ව

THE CANTICLE KINGDOM

Johann trembled in the semi-darkness, wondering how he might escape his uncle's wrath. He couldn't let Brutus know that he had discovered the secret door. But if he stayed hidden, he would be punished for being absent from the shop. Pressing his ear up against the wall of the closet, he strained to hear the conversation taking place on the other side, hoping that maybe his absence would go unnoticed.

"I can't find her, old man! And if I don't find her soon, everything will be ruined! I can't believe she would run off on a day like today!"

The first voice was clearly his uncle's. However, the second voice surprised him. "Calm down, Brutus. We have many hours yet. The queen . . . ."

The second voice trailed off. It was his grandfather's.

"I know. The queen doesn't have much time left," added Brutus finishing Grandfather's sentence. "You've seen and heard of all the strange happenings. People disappearing, the crazy weather. Why, just yesterday there was the business of that man who was crushed by a falling tree that was sturdy as could be."

Grandfather lowered his voice, and Johann strained to hear. He only picked up the last sentence or two.

". . . Just keep your wits about you, Brutus. I'll help you look for her. I'm not expected anywhere until nightfall."

With that, Johann heard two sets of footsteps trailing off until there was silence once again. Crawling cautiously, he found the passageway in the wall and carefully slipped out of the closet, being sure to grab a suitable hammer on the way out. It was a minor miracle that no one had noticed his conspicuous absence. Something was dreadfully wrong.

Johann had not heard his grandfather sound so in control of his mental faculties in years, and things were quickly becoming very strange. His first impulse was to rush out the door to aid in the search for Brigitta, but he decided that he had risked enough for one day and that he better not assume that he was going to have any more lucky breaks.

Retrieving the scrap metal from under the cabinet where he had stashed it, he ran to the fire and began heating it.

ℵℵℵ

The better part of an hour later, Johann proudly mulled over his creation, tossing it from one hand to the other. It was not a weapon worthy of the royal knights, but it was a start. The blade extended the length of his arm and was about as shiny as could be expected for scrap metal. The hilt was a deep gray with a tarnished golden ornament that Johann had attached to the center. It would take a bit more time to put on all the finishing touches, but to Johann, Excalibur itself could have never looked so regal.

For a few minutes, Johann lost himself in his own world, battling invisible villains that leapt from the shadows. He swung his sword around roughly, parrying and returning invisible blows until the sound of approaching voices lifted him from his fantasy. Quickly, he thrust the sword under the cabinet where he had originally hid the scrap metal and returned to his workbench, trying to look busy with a menial task.

A few seconds later, Brutus sulked in through the door, his eyes blood-shot and his gaze downtrodden. This disturbed Johann greatly. As far as he knew, his uncle only had three emotions: anger, rage, and flying sparks. For a while, neither said anything until Brutus briefly raised his eyes to Johann and muttered. "Leave."

Only too eager to do so, Johann put down his things and quickly scrambled out of the shop.

The icy air outside the shop hit Johann harder than Brutus's hammer ever hit glowing steel. True, it was always a bit of an adjustment after coming out of the sweltering smithy, but this was downright strange. It was nearing the middle of summer, but cool temperatures were more common for a brisk, winter morning. Almost immediately, he began to shiver beneath his thin tunic, and he picked up his pace in order to get the blood flowing to his exposed legs. He had gone a few blocks before he stopped to assess the situation. By Brutus's reaction, it was apparent that Brigitta was still nowhere to be found.

Despite the goose bumps forming on his skin, Johann stood still and contemplated his next move. His mother would surely be expecting him home sometime soon, but then again, the thought of his cousin still missing did not sit well with him either. Brigitta rarely did so much as latch her shoes without letting him know first.

It did not take him long to make up his mind. His mother could wait. Holding his arms around him tightly for warmth, he scanned the horizon, searching for ideas of where to begin his search for Brigitta. To the north lay the castle; its white stones weren't gleaming nearly so brightly now that the sun had ducked behind the clouds. The rest of the town stretched out to the east and west, and to the south lay the heart of the Dunkel Woods. Brutus would have surely found her in town, and since there was no way that she would be roaming around the castle, that left only—

He shook his head. Brave as she was, Brigitta didn't have the courage to go roaming around the woods by herself. Not even the royal knights did so lightly. Many returned from the heart of the woods, but few came back unchanged.

A small object fluttering on the wind caught his eye, disturbing his thoughts. At first, it whipped around so fast that he could not quite tell what it was, but then another gust of wind carried it so that it snagged on a shrub only a few feet away. The chilling wind continued to blow, taking some of the shrub's leaves along with it. However, the object remained caught fast in the branches, billowing like a flickering blue flame.

Johann's eyes widened. He knew that ribbon. Though she was a bit of a tomboy, Brigitta was fickle about her hair and always tied it up with the same ribbon that matched her azure eyes. Panic rising in his chest, Johann frantically removed the ribbon and rubbed it gingerly between his fingers. Then, stuffing it into his pocket, he took off in a gallop down the trail toward the woods. Johann felt the chill leave him as his feet pounded the uneven ground. Snow flurries swirled around him, but he paid them very little heed—his current task absorbed all his attention. He deftly maneuvered around the other pedestrians, eliciting more than one angry outburst. He only once allowed himself to be distracted as he caught a whiff of the savory sausages and rolls being sold by street vendors near the marketplace. As much as his rumbling stomach tempted him, he decided to delay the indulgence until he could share one with Brigitta.

Halfway to the forest, his scrawny legs nearly gave out, and he collapsed in a heap, panting like the smithy's bellows working overtime. Wiping the sweat from his brow, he noticed the snow flurries for the first time. They lighted on his face in troops, melting instantly as they came in contact with his flushed face. He sighed, muttering to himself. "What do you think you're doing?"

He rose to a sitting position and gazed back the way he had come. He had a half a mind to abandon his crazy pursuit and go back home, where at least it was warm. Reaching into his pocket, he retrieved the ribbon and twirled it around his fingers. Perhaps he was on a wild goose chase, but again, maybe not. It was not a risk he was willing to take. Brigitta was his best friend—his only real friend. Catching his breath and dusting off the flurries, he continued down the trail as quickly as his tired legs would take him.

Reaching the edge of the forest some minutes later, he paused once again. The townsfolk spoke about the woods in hushed whispers, sharing fanciful stories about how the woods were possessed by demons that preyed on unwary travelers. The village had been rocked by reports just that week of a man found dead in the forest, pinned hopelessly under a tree. The man had been the soldier in the queen's guard, so his death had caused quite a stir.

Staring into the darkness created by the thick canopy of overlapping branches, Johann drew a deep breath and let it out forcefully. "If the woods don't kill me, my mother just might."

Johann jogged cautiously into the woods, glancing around him every few seconds. The woods were eerily quiet, except for the rustling of the wind through the trees and the footfall of Johann's cautious steps. The snow fell harder as Johann drew deeper into the forest, coating the path and leaves alike with a smooth blanket. Despite the snow, Johann could see no sign of footprints, which did nothing to calm his uneasiness.

Undaunted, Johann continued his pace, hugging his arms around him in a futile attempt to ward off the growing chill. "This place is cursed," he mumbled to himself, every moment regretting his decision to come in the first place. The snowy path gave way to a large clearing. The change was so sudden it caused Johann to gasp. The snow stopped abruptly, and the wind no longer howled. It was as if the clearing was contained in a bubble apart from the rest of the forest. For several moments, Johann simply stared into the clearing, unable to make sense of what he saw.

At a snapping sound from his left, Johann whirled around and was met instantly by a set of gaping, snarling jaws, set in stone. To his side stood an alarmingly lifelike sculpture of a werewolf, claws outstretched and jaws ready to strike. Trembling, Johann placed a hand on the statue, assuring himself that the horrific visage in front of him was indeed crafted of stone. At once, Johann felt a strange sinking feeling in his stomach, leaving a hole there as if he had not eaten in days. For a brief moment, his eyelids drooped, and then shot back up. Dazed, Johann turned his attention to the rest of the clearing.

As Johann surveyed the clearing, he counted more than a dozen statues, all depicting hideous creatures that ranged from gargoyles to lions, to oversized snakes.

"This place is definitely cursed," thought Johann aloud. He stepped up to a gigantic snake, marveling at the craftsmanship. Each scale was carefully carved, much more lifelike than any other statue he had ever seen. He kept a safe distance, just in case.

From across the clearing, a howl rang out in the stillness. Johann spun on his heel to face the sound. "Definitely not the wind," he muttered frantically to himself. Johann broke into a dash, heading away from the clearing without looking for the source of the sound. As he burst back into the woods, the snow and wind started again. Fighting for traction in the snow, he glanced back to see a grizzled mass of fur heading quickly in his direction.

Johann pumped his legs as quickly as he could manage, but even then, he knew he didn't have a chance. The monster was too fast. He searched the area frantically for cover but found only one possibility: a gigantic uprooted tree that lay across the road some hundred feet ahead. The path dipped at that point so that a small gap was created between the tree and the road. Not much of a plan, but better than nothing.

Just before Johann reached the tree, he tumbled forward as he was tackled from behind. Claws dug into his back, tearing his tunic as if it was nothing but wafer-thin parchment. Suppressing a yelp, Johann tumbled and fought with both hands and feet, convinced that he was now meeting his final moments.

Fortunately for Johann, the combined momentum carried them forward on the slick road, heading for the giant tree. At the last moment, Johann, who found himself at the bottom of the scuffle, slipped under the gap in the road, slamming the wolf into the side of the tree. However, instead of the thud of an animal against the wood, there came a shattering of stone, as the werewolf exploded into hundreds of shards.

Panting hard, Johann could barely move from the pain. Warm blood oozed down his back, as well as from his cheek and nose. Luckily, the tree shielded him from the flying shards of the shattered wolf.

His head spinning, Johann tried to extricate himself from the gap. His first two feeble attempts met with painful failure, but on the third, he was able to hoist his leg over the side of the gap. Moving excruciatingly slowly, he pulled the rest of his body up before collapsing again in the snow, which he immediately stained scarlet with his blood. The remains of the werewolf's claw lay inches from his face, still damp from the blood it had drawn. Johann reached out, and brushed his fingers across the claw, assuring himself for the second time that it was indeed stone.

He stared at it for several moments, mulling over in his mind the insanity he had just been through, when another howl sounded in the distance. Deciding the time had come to leave, wounded or not, Johann made his way around the fallen tree, He limped forward as fast as he could, his body still aching and groaning for him to stop. The howls grew louder, and Johann forced himself to ignore the pain and run faster. His heart beat a furious march in his chest, and his lungs stung from the frigid air.

Seeing a dense growth of trees ahead, he decided that the best strategy was to take his chances hiding again. Running at full speed, he practically dove into a patch of underbrush.

The impact knocked Johann right out of his senses. Meeting a very solid object just beyond the brush, Johann flew back and landed unconscious on the forest floor.

ॐ

"Guten Morgen, du Schlafkopf! Steh mal auf! Zwei Minuten noch, und die Ungeheuer kommen zurück!"

Johann blinked his eyes, trying to clear his blurry vision. A dark figure stood above him, speaking in a strange language that he could not understand.

The figure reached down with one hand, which Johann took, unsure if it was a friendly or hostile gesture. The figure helped him to his feet, while his vision slowly cleared.

The voice, distinctly a girl's, spoke again. *"Mensch! Was ist mit dir los? Du siehst so aus als ob Blitz dich geschlagen hat!"*

"I . . . I . . . ," Johann stuttered. "I don't understand what you're saying." He could see a bit of the girl's face now, which suddenly turned quizzical.

"Was? Du bist der Johann, nicht wahr? Wieso kanst du mich nicht verstehen?"

All of a sudden his vision cleared completely. The blond hair, the clear, blue eyes . . . "Brigitta! What in the world are you doing here? I'm surprised those monsters haven't eaten you alive yet!"

She shrugged. Johann noticed that her face looked flushed and that her eyes were glowing strangely in the light. *"Na, ja, ich bin ja stark genug. Ich kann mich selbst verteidigen."*

Taking her by the shoulders, Johann shook her forcefully. "Stop playing games, Brigitta! You're speaking gibberish! Snap out of it!"

Brigitta continued to smile strangely, sprouting off unintelligible words. Having had enough, Johann slapped her soundly across the face. At once, the color from her cheeks drained, and her eyes returned to their normal luster.

Dazed, she shook her head as if she had just been awoken from a dream. Considering Johann for a moment, recognition finally flashed in her eyes, and she blurted out. "Johann! What's going on? Where did you come from?"

Johann's eyes opened wide in an incredulous stare. "Where did *I* come from? Where did *you* come from? One minute, I'm running for my life through the forest, and the next, you're standing over me, spouting gibberish! Where have you been? Brutus has gone insane looking for you!"

Brigitta narrowed her eyes. "I . . . I'm not sure. I remember meeting a stranger in town this morning. He said that he came from the castle and that he had an errand for me to do. He handed me a few gold coins and sent me into the forest to fetch something for him."

Johann cocked his head to the side. "Well, who was it? Didn't he tell you? What did he want you to get?"

Brigitta squinted even harder. "I . . . I don't know who he was. He was dressed really funny, but he looked important. He said he needed somebody small, who could fit into tight spaces. He told me that he lost something and that I'd have to crawl under a fallen tree to retrieve it. Said it was the tree that fell on that poor man last week."

Johann moved in closer, his voice dropping in volume. "He didn't tell you what it was you were supposed to retrieve?"

Brigitta shook her head. "Nope. Said it was pretty valuable though—gold, and all that. I figured we could use the money."

Johann sighed. "Why didn't you tell me about this? I'm convinced that this place is just as cursed as they say. You could have been killed coming out here by yourself!"

"You came alone too," replied Brigitta curtly.

Johann's cheeks grew red. "Well, I . . . I just . . . I did that to save you, you crazy girl!"

Brigitta's hands flew to her hips. "Oh, crazy am I? Or is it just because I'm a girl?"

"No!" Johann retorted. "I—" His reply was cut off by a distant cry, a roar that echoed through the woods. Frozen in their places, they both tried to keep as silent as they could. "I vote that we settle who's to blame some other time," whispered Johann, as he began heading in the direction he had taken before.

"No!" whispered Brigitta. "We can't go that way. There's some sort of massive wall there. It looks like it's made of wood, but I can't even see the top, it is so huge. We better go back the other way."

Brigitta took off, and Johann followed grumbling to himself. "Yeah, great idea. Right back into the lion's den . . . ."

Brigitta and Johann made fairly good time making their way back through the woods. Johann stole glances behind them every few seconds to make sure they weren't being followed.

"Did you see the tree?" asked Johann. "I think I might have seen it back that way."

Brigitta shook her head. "No, I came a different way. Is it very far?"

It was Johann's turn to shake his head, his face grave. "No, but I don't think it's a very good idea to head back that way. Let's just say that the cuts on my back didn't come from your father."

Brigitta slowed, and then stopped, noticing the cuts for the first time. "Oh, Johann!" she exclaimed. "What on earth happened to you?"

Johann grunted. "Nice of you to notice. Some crazy fur-ball in a really bad mood attacked me right around that huge fallen tree. I think all of those stories about curses and demons must be true."

Brigitta's shiver had nothing to do with the cold. "Sorry, Johann. I don't know what's come over me. I haven't been quite myself today. Those are some nasty gashes. How are you going to face your mother with those?"

Johann rolled his eyes. "One obstacle at a time. Let's just worry about getting out of here first. We might have to forget about that mysterious man for now."

Brigitta nodded heartily. "Though I'm accused of being your twin, I'm not fond of the idea of getting matching scars."

Surveying the scene one last time, Johann decided that the coast was clear. He gestured with his right hand to Brigitta to follow, and they both took off down the snowy trail.

Neither Johann nor Brigitta looked back even once. The falling snow became thinner and thinner as they made their way back through the woods, until it had disappeared completely. With a generous helping of snowflakes caught in her hair, Brigitta looked like a sugar-dusted pastry.

As soon as they reached the perimeter of the woods, they allowed themselves a moment to breathe, collapsing hard on the grass. After several moments of deep, labored breathing, they both sat up and glanced around.

"So," muttered Brigitta. "What now?"

Johann grunted. "If we're going to go running errands for your mystery man, we need to do it before either of us goes home. Brutus is frantic. Once he sees you, he won't let you out of his sight for a month."

She nodded. "Neither will your mother if she gets a glance at those gashes on your back. But we can't go back in there without a little more protection."

"Right," Johann agreed. "What did you have in mind?"

Brigitta wrinkled her face, deep in thought. "Well, I did leave a little stash of ammunition under the bridge. Do you have anything?"

Johann nodded, thinking of his unfinished sword back at the shop. "Yes. It's not much, but it will have to do. When did you tell the stranger you would meet him?"

"I'm supposed to meet him in the castle gardens by sundown," she replied. "He told me of a side entrance where I could sneak in."

Johann shuddered with delight. That alone was a dream come true. No matter how this turned out, the knowledge of a secret passage into the castle grounds would pay big dividends in the future. He glanced up at the sky. It was still mid-afternoon, and they had several hours of sunlight left. "All right," he said. "You go down to the bridge while I go to Brutus's shop for my swor—er—my supplies. It's better that you stay out of town." Grinning broadly at his cousin, he hurried down the path. "Last one back here has to fight the first demon!"

"*Tschüss*, Johann!"

Johann turned and eyed this cousin through squinting eyes. "What did you say?"

Brigitta's face appeared no less puzzled. "I . . . it means 'goodbye.' My grandpa . . . um . . . used to say it to my grandma all the time."

Confused by the partial explanation, Johann let the matter drop. There were more important things to worry about.

Making it a point to stay out of sight, Johann crept toward the smithy. As he peered into the shop's window, it appeared that the fires were still glowing, which meant that Brutus was still working. *This complicates things*, Johann thought. He needed to create a diversion without wasting too much time. For once in his life, Johann decided to tell the truth . . . sort of.

Tousling his already wild locks, he rushed into the shop in a breathless panic. "Uncle! Uncle, I just saw Brigitta!"

Brutus, who was meditating in the corner, suddenly sprang to life. "What? Where is she? Speak up boy!"

Johann pointed frantically into the distance. "I saw her headed toward the east forest. I tried to catch up with her, but she was just too fast! I have no idea what she's thinking!"

The blacksmith's eyes burned with intense heat. "Out of my way, boy! I'll not see that little girl whisked away by demons! You head home this instant, and don't you dare try to follow me!"

Johann put on his best terrified face as his uncle tore out of the shop, clutching a sizeable hammer.

As soon Brutus was out of sight, Johann scurried across the shop and retrieved his sword from its hiding place. Stuffing it in his belt, he set off to meet Brigitta. *If I survive this*, he promised himself, *I'll give up this blacksmith's apprenticeship for one with the local acting troupe.*

Brigitta looked very pleased to see Johann back in such quick time.

"Johann! Do you have what you went for?"

Johann grinned and unsheathed the sword at his hip. Brigitta was unsure how to react. It was a sword all right, but it was the shoddiest specimen she had ever laid eyes on.

Not wanting to hurt his feelings, she simply shrugged and said. "Great. At least it's sharp. I'll handle the long range, and you'll take the short range."

"Did you have any trouble at the bridge?" Johann asked.

Brigitta rolled her eyes. "I met up with Bruno and his gang. You might imagine his surprise when he got a snowball in the face."

Johann laughed. Bruno and his gang were a group of kids whose goal in life was to cause as much trouble as possible.

They kept mostly quiet as they made their way back to the woods. This time they did not follow the main path to provide an extra element of stealth. Reaching the edge of the woods, they paused only momentarily.

Johann glanced over at Brigitta. "Okay. We get in, we get . . . whatever it is, and we get out. No time for sight-seeing."

Brigitta smirked. "No problem. I saw enough the first time around. I've never really liked snow."

Without another word, they bounded off into the forest with Johann leading the way. His path was not hard to follow as his footprints were still very visible in the snow. The same ghostly howling echoed through the forest as before.

As they approached the clearing, Johann hesitated. The last time he was here, he almost lost his head. He motioned to Brigitta to be silent. He held up his sword, cautiously, and signalled Brigitta to arm herself as well, which she did without question.

The second they entered the clearing, Brigitta could not suppress a yelp. Acting on instinct, she loaded her slingshot and released a jagged stone at the nearest statue, a tiger with its fangs bared. The impact permanently disfigured the tiger, erasing most of its facial features.

With their cover compromised, Johann grabbed Brigitta by the arm and dragged her behind him. It was simpler than trying to explain.

Stealthily, Johann crossed into the clearing, followed by Brigitta, whose eyes bugged out in disbelief. "What is this place?" she whispered.

Johann shrugged. "Nice shot," he muttered. "We might need a few more of those."

Johann scanned the clearing in hopes that nothing had changed. At first everything appeared as before. However, just as he was about to relax, an awful thought crossed his mind. *Where's the snake?* The reptile was nowhere to be seen. Johann wasn't sure whether to tell Brigitta, but in the end, he decided that he should keep his mouth shut for now. After all, it could be nothing.

Nervously, he grinned and continued. "This isn't somewhere we want to be long. The thing that attacked me started out as a statue here. Some sort of sorcery."

Brigitta's hand still clutched her weapon. "Perhaps we ought to destroy them all now," she suggested.

Johann pondered the proposition for a moment and then shook his head. "No, we don't have time. There must be dozens of them, and I don't know about you, but I don't want to be around when—I mean, if—one of them wakes up."

She agreed quickly, still considering her handiwork with the tiger. Without another thought, they stole into the woods on the other side of the clearing, following the path Johann had used before.

Up ahead, the fallen tree loomed large. Bloodstains still stood out on the snow even though the clouds still belched forth a steady stream of flakes. Johann shuddered at the sight, not daring to think what might have become of him had luck not intervened.

Standing side by side with Brigitta at the tree, Johann was able to get a good look at it for the first time. Before, his mind had been too occupied with survival to see much of anything.

"Johann!" Brigitta cried in disgust. "Look!" She pointed to a spot right before the gap in the road. Sticking out from underneath the tree was a human hand, which was a shade whiter than even the snow around it. The cold had preserved it completely from decay.

Johann suppressed a lurch in his stomach. *No one bothered to remove the body?*

The pair hunched over the hand with morbid curiosity. From the looks of it, the hand belonged to full-grown man buried in the snow.

But what was he doing in the forest in the first place?

For several moments, they both remained stone silent. "Brigitta, perhaps this man has what you're looking for," Johann ventured.

But before she could reply, something hard smacked her from behind, and she fell face-first into the snow.

CHAPTER THREE

❧

SUFFERING for HIS ART

THE CANTICLE KINGDOM

Rufus sighed as deeply as death. The visage that stared back at him through the mirror looked ghostly enough. His light brown hair was frazzled, flying off in all directions as if drawn by some powerful magnetism. His eyes were sunken pits, and his cheeks were gaunt and hollow.

At this rate, he thought, *I won't last much longer than the queen.*

Rufus ran his fingers through his hair, trying to restore some semblance of order. It was useless, like so many things he attempted. He sighed again as he glimpsed a faint streak of gray in his tousled hair.

He had stayed by the queen's bedside all night without so much as a wink of sleep himself. Terrible exhaustion combined with awful anxiety rendered Rufus on the verge of collapse.

The queen's sleep had become more and more disturbed. Most nights, she would mutter strange, mostly unintelligible things. Last night, however, she had repeated the same word over and over: lost. Sometimes she reached out into the darkness or clutched her chest in delirium. He had tried to make sense of it all but had not been the least bit successful. The once beautiful queen had been reduced to a raving lunatic.

Just then, another face appeared in the mirror next to him, a raven-haired man with a long pale face. He was dressed in deep blue robes tinged with silver streaks.

"Rufus," he began in a low, resonant tone. "How is she?"

Rufus did not turn but stoically replied. "Not good, Cornelius. Not good at all."

Cornelius stepped closer, observing the young chamberlain with pity. "That upsets me greatly," he solemnly began. "I am doing all that I can. You know that I . . . *care* for the queen as well."

Rufus still did not turn but lowered his head, averting his eyes. His fists clenched tightly by his side. "Why isn't your potion working anymore?" he seethed, trying to keep his emotions from flaring up. "It *used* to work. You call yourself an accomplished wizard . . . ."

Cornelius smiled knowingly, seemingly unphazed by the chamberlain's insult. "Now, now, Rufus. You mustn't let your temper get the best of you. I *am* doing the best I know how. The problem is that we don't know the exact nature of the problem in the first place—just the symptoms. This is unlike any other case I have ever dealt with."

Rufus released the tension in his taut muscles. Cornelius was right. "Why are you here, Cornelius? Just to relearn the obvious?"

The wizard shook his head. "No, not entirely. I also came to see if I could borrow your sketchbook. I am still making progress on creating statues for the castle garden, and I heard that you have quite a knack for drawing mythical figures. I was wondering if I could use some of them as a template."

Deeply annoyed that the wizard would bring up such a trivial matter at such a time, but wanting also to be alone as soon as possible, Rufus clenched his eyes shut. "Fine," he replied, barely restraining his frustration. "The sketchbook is lying open on my desk. Just return it to me in one piece, or no amount of magic in the world will protect you from my wrath."

Cornelius grinned almost childishly. "By the Queen! It must have been a very long night. My most humble thanks. Your services to the kingdom will surely be remembered for generations to come."

Without another word, Cornelius strode over to the table and lifted a thick, leather-bound sketchbook from the table and immediately began leafing through the contents as he exited the room. With each successive drawing, the excited gleam in his eyes intensified, and his pulse quickened until he was sure his heart would burst from his chest. Then, as he came to the final page, his eyes grew as wide as full moons, and he broke into a delighted run.

Back in his study, Cornelius mulled over his spell books. His eyes blurred from staring at the pages, searching desperately for the answer to pop out at him. It was no use. Everything remained as obscure as before.

Before him stood an unfinished statue of a cougar in mid leap, seemingly out of solid rock. The details were shaping up nicely, and he could picture in his mind the place he wanted it to occupy. However, he had encountered a roadblock. His magic refused to go any further, and he had no idea why, since this had never happened before.

Finally, the wizard sighed and tossed the book aside. This minor statue was nothing. He still had his greatest work to complete, and the unveiling was scheduled in two days. Not only would his magic need to be in top form, but it would also have to be sustained. At this rate, things were going to be a major disappointment.

Well, it wouldn't be the first time in recent memory.

Glancing around the room, his eyes fell on a tiny hammer and chisel, which lay unused on the desk. His troubled mood deepened. Stepping over to the table, he picked up the tools, eyeing them sadly. "Well, I guess there is always the old fashioned way."

ಬಿ

Rufus's hands worked quickly, flying over the sketch like a fowl across water. Beside him lay the sleeping queen, her hands folded serenely across her chest, which rose and fell in deep breaths. The chamberlain scarcely took his eyes away from the queen, only pausing once or twice to glance down at the parchment.

The door creaked, and Rufus raised his eyes from the parchment. It was only Camilla, the queen's cat. The cat strode gingerly over to the chamberlain who gently stroked the fur on her back, eliciting a contented purr. Rufus narrowed his eyes, sensing that something was amiss. The cat's normally brightly colored fur showed ugly gray blotches and speckles that had not been there the previous night.

Odd. She looks as bad as the queen.

Then, as he glanced down at the parchment, his eyes found something amiss. He rubbed his finger against a certain piece of the parchment, first gently, and then harder. Try as he might, a glaring flaw refused to leave. With an exasperated grunt of frustration, he threw up his hands and stormed out of the room, leaving the parchment to flutter noiselessly to the floor.

Rufus struggled to curb his frustration as he wandered the halls of the castle, slowly making his way toward the chapel. The sketching, he reminded himself, was really just a minor diversion. He had much more important work to accomplish, and he needed to have his wits about him. The portrait could wait.

He sighed. If he did not do something soon, it might be the queen's death portrait he was sketching. The thought struck him, and he quickened his pace. Taking the chapel steps down two at a time, he was glad to find no one in his way.

Pushing back the ancient door, he stepped into the quiet room. He paused briefly to admire the streams of sunlight filtering through the stained glass, which cast brilliant patterns of color across the floor. He glanced about and, finding himself alone, approached the altar.

Rufus knelt, folded his hands, and gazed up at the red and gold stained-glass window depicting Mary and the Christ child under the star of Bethlehem that provided a backdrop to the altar. Light streamed gently through the window, projecting its patterns onto Rufus's face. Silently bowing his head, he muttered an earnest prayer. His world was caving in, and there had been many such vigils in the past weeks. With the fate of the Canticle Kingdom resting on his shoulders, he savored these brief moments of solitude and contemplation.

This evening's mission would be crucial, and if he failed, he would be out of other options. Having not left the castle in some time, he felt an anxious pain gnawing at the pit of his stomach. However, as he breathed deeply and focused on his prayer, a familiar peace washed over him.

This is not my errand alone.

Completing his prayer, he stood and reverently sang a passage that he had learned as a child. The chapel lay far below the castle, ensuring his solitude. Within the chapel, the sweet tones echoed off the smooth walls, enveloping the space in sound. Reverently, he took out a delicate piece of parchment from a pocket in the folds of his robe and reread its words written in the fine hand he knew so well. He had found the message attached to his door that very morning smelling faintly of perfume, and he knew that it took precedence above all other things. It had not been the first time he had received such a note from the queen, but it was by far the most important task she had ever asked of him.

Having completed his daily ritual, Rufus stood and turned to go. However, before he left, he paused for a few moments to admire the sculptures at the back of the chapel. In one of the alcoves, the sculptor had depicted the Nativity, complete with shepherds, animals, and a manger. The scene, however, was conspicuously incomplete. This particular set was missing all of the three kings. The neighboring set from the Book of Acts was also missing one of its statues, leaving the Apostle Paul alone, looking on and presenting his message with outstretched hands, his stone face unaffected by the fact that his audience had deserted him.

The four missing statues had been stolen, and after the entire chapel was protected by magic, people surmised that the thief was a powerfully dark wizard. Why anyone would want to steal statues out of a church was a question that baffled most. Even stranger, each of the statues had been stolen seventy-five years apart, to the very day. It had been almost exactly seventy-five years from the last theft, and the queen had ordered Cornelius to increase the protective magic around the shrine. Small signs, written in bold letters were set in front of each display to deter would-be thieves: "*Warning! Do not attempt to touch any of the statues—powerful jinxes employed. Violators will be added to the display as statues.*"

Rufus grinned and wondered silently whether any of the current statues were actually unfortunate art connoisseurs. He shook his head at the notion.

He'd seen the same statues there every day for years.

The tower chime toned four o'clock. Broken from his reverie, Rufus left the displays and made his way up the stairs at the back of the room. He had much work to do.

He made his way silently through the castle's corridor toward one of the lesser watched side entrances. Before he made it far, he heard the queen's familiar voice cry out. "Rufus! Rufus! Come quickly!"

The queen's voice was laced with alarm. Breaking at once into a sweat, he glanced nervously down the hall and then back the other way. Struggling within himself, Rufus growled in frustration. "Not now! This can't be happening now!" Her voice called again, but he continued toward the castle entrance and broke into a dash, cursing his luck. "She will have to wait."

Pulling his cloak more tightly around his head, Rufus slipped out one of the many secret passages that led from the castle. To his luck, the night was starless, overwhelmed by a thick blanket of clouds. Walking at a steady pace, he made his way toward the glowing lights of the town below.

This evening's venture was his absolute last resort. Had the queen not requested it, he might not have gone at all. He had not left the queen's side for days. Each moment was rife with terror, not knowing when, or if, she would simply slip through his fingers.

"Richard," he muttered. The name of his target came to the forefront of his mind. It seemed a far stretch to ask for his help, but no better options had presented themselves. Even if this did not work, he would still feel better having tried.

Reaching the outskirts of town, Rufus paused momentarily and scanned the scene to get his bearings. He did not venture into the town often, so he was a bit confused about which road he should take. Seeing an old man with a crutch sitting by the side of the road, he approached him and said in a low tone, "Where might I find the Buchmuller house?"

The grungy man shrugged and gestured toward his ears, indicating that he was deaf. Rufus sighed, tossing the man a shiny, gold coin. "They say that money can work miracles. Is that true?"

"They live on the other end of town, past the pond and right on Baum Street," said the bum.

Rufus smiled and rushed off without another word, leaving the man to ponder his good fortune. The poorly lit side streets provided ample cover for Rufus as he made his way toward the other edge of town. Rufus peeked out of a dark alleyway to make sure the street was clear of onlookers. Satisfied, he made his way out into the street, keeping himself close to the houses.

He found himself outside St. Molly's, an impressive stone church on the south end of town. It was well known for its architecture, and it was the queen's favorite. Rufus paused for a moment to admire the structure. It was crafted out of marble and granite and kept to a high polish. Stained-glass windows ran up either side and a lofty bell tower adorned the top. A variety of statues adorned the exterior, mostly depicting knights and saints with an occasional animal. An impressive mural above the entryway depicted a boy bathed in heavenly light withdrawing a sword out of a pedestal.

Suddenly, Rufus wrinkled his nose. Right above the entryway stood a statue he had never seen. The grotesque form of a gargoyle carved out of dark stone stood out horribly amidst the many other pleasant light-colored statues.

"Odd," he muttered under his breath. Returning to the task at hand, Rufus turned from the church and continued on his way. The chill in the air seemed to intensify, and Rufus wrapped his cloak tighter around him. He hadn't gone far when suddenly he was tackled from behind, and he fell hard. There was a ghastly growl and then blackness.

ʕ๏ʔ

When Rufus finally came to his senses, he was sitting by a campfire by the edge of the woods. No one else was around the fire, and for several moments, his mind reeled for an explanation.

A voice spoke from the darkness. "I have waited all my life for this moment."

Rufus shot up straight, searching in vain for the source of the sound. He groped around for his knife and found it gone. "Who are you? Show yourself!"

The voiced chuckled coldly. "I think not. It heightens the justice of the situation. For many years, I did not know who you were, either—just your crimes."

Rufus reeled around, bringing his fists to bear. "Crimes? I haven't a clue what you're taking about," he yelled into the darkness.

"Indeed," spat the voice. "The guilty rarely do. Would you like to try explaining yourself after all these years?"

Rufus shook his head in disbelief. "I haven't the foggiest idea—"

"Don't try playing ignorant with me, Rufus. You remember those times as well as I do, though perhaps you'd like to suppress those memories. You know of what I am speaking—the Ellis uprising."

Rufus's eyes turned up in exasperation. "Are you one of those old, intolerable rebels? You must be ancient by now!"

"Not just *a* rebel, Rufus. *The* rebel."

Rufus's heart began to pound, unable to comprehend how this was possible. "What? You couldn't be him! You're bluffing! He was killed in the uprising."

The reply was almost instantaneous. "No, no—not killed. You might say I was ripped from everything I held dear, mutilated, and left for dead perhaps, but not killed."

Rufus's mind reeled, searching for connections. "I don't understand—I never met him. I was just a young soldier then. I barely saw any fighting!"

"You saw enough. Your poor decision crushed me. If you don't remember, it makes you that much more the monster."

Rufus honestly did not remember. "What do you want from me?" Rufus pleaded.

For a long moment, there was silence, marred only by the rustle of leaves tousled by the wind.

"You must atone for your crimes." The mysterious voice was quiet. "But death would be too sudden, and I am not a murderer like you and your kind. I will spare your life if you will come and help me repair the damage you have done. If not, I will smite you here as you stand."

Rufus gulped, feeling an unseen gaze fixed upon him. "I'll go," he muttered. "I'll do whatever you ask."

A faint chuckle floated from the darkness. "Good."

As a free man, Rufus walked swiftly out of the forest. All things considered, Rufus felt that he had gotten off fairly easily. After being attacked and held hostage, he was released with little more than a pounding headache. The mysterious man's demands hadn't been so steep either. He only demanded that Rufus play the part of spy on a certain person inside the castle—not too difficult for someone in his position.

Rufus glanced at the skies. It was late, but not too late to complete the errand he had set out for that evening. Glancing around to make sure that he was not being followed, Rufus stole toward his destination.

CHAPTER FOUR

GOOD KNIGHT
and GOOD LUCK

DACHAU, GERMANY, 1945

The British brigade stormed into the camp, brandishing their weapons in preparation to strike. The precaution, however, was usually unnecessary, as most of the German soldiers had already fled, and those who remained gave up with little resistance. Moving more cautiously throughout the camp, the British soldiers began their grisly search for survivors. Hundreds of wraith-like prisoners meandered aimlessly throughout the camp, scarcely able to comprehend their newly found freedom.

Lieutenant Miles Rupert was torn by a variety of emotions. At first he sighed in relief at not having to take any more lives for the time being. Almost the next moment, he recoiled in horror and about lost his breakfast at the grim sights that assaulted him from every direction. The dead and dying were everywhere, and the stench was overwhelming. The place possessed a tangible aura of evil.

Lt. Rupert thought of his own sweet daughter as he passed by a battered, little Jewish girl about Molly's same age, and tears sprang immediately to his eyes. Taking the little girl up in his arms, he cradled her for a few moments, overcome with grief. Walking solemnly, he carried the girl back to the outer boundary of the camp where the medical trucks were gathering.

Returning to the compound, he began his methodical work of searching each room for survivors or items of interest. His search turned up very little, until he approached a certain office near the end of the hall in the main building. Faint music wafted through the corridors, and the lieutenant figured that someone had left the radio on.

As he opened the room, however, he discovered something quite different.

LONDON, ENGLAND, 1945

Christmas Eve dawned cold and cloudless. Already, little Molly Rupert felt like she was about to burst from suspense. Her father had been teasing her all month that he had found the absolute perfect gift for her, but he refused to giver her so much as a hint as to what it was. She had asked for a variety of things, but she had a hunch that the gift from her father was even better than anything she could imagine. She thought perhaps her father had purchased the King Arthur storybook she had asked for, but the package didn't seem to be the right size.

The hours ticked by incredibly slowly, like water dripping tediously from a faucet. At first she tried helping her mother prepare the Christmas cookies and candies, but she was so distracted that she spilled the sugar, knocked the eggs off the counter, and dumped molasses all over the floor. After that, her mother decided that she didn't need any more "help."

Although the Christmas goose and trimmings were as delicious as ever, she barely noticed. Her attention was caught by a particular package under the tree. It was about the size of a small shoebox and had been meticulously wrapped in shiny red paper. She just knew it had to be hers. She stole a glimpse at it whenever she could, trying not to look too distracted.

After dutifully finishing her meal, she wandered slowly into the living room and sat down in her little rocking chair by the fireplace. Her parents and brothers soon joined her, each taking their respective places around the hearth. Her father opened the dusty family Bible and started to read the second chapter of Luke, the account of the first Christmas. Even the wonderful, familiar story failed to capture her interest. Neither gold, nor frankincense, nor myrrh could possibly be as exciting as what her own package contained.

As her father finished with the biblical account, he closed the Bible and announced. "Time for bed, children. If Santa catches you away from your bed, there's no telling what he'll do . . . ."

At this announcement, most of the children scrambled from the room, eager to let visions of sugarplums dance in their heads. However, Molly stayed behind, a woeful grimace painted on her face.

This look was not wasted on her father. "What's the matter, little miss? You look like it's the last day of summer holidays rather than the night before Christmas."

She sniffed and then sighed. "Oh, Daddy, it's nothing. I just . . . I just can't wait any longer. That beautiful red package has been calling to me all day."

Her father smiled knowingly and nodded ever so slightly. Silently, he crept over to the tree, stooped down, and retrieved the package. He then placed it gently in his daughter's expectant hands.

"But Daddy, it's not Christmas yet! Father Christmas will know! I—"

Her father raised a finger to his lips. "Don't worry. Father Christmas and I are good friends. I promise I won't tell."

Her eyes brimming with delight, Molly reached for the edge of the paper and carefully unfolded it, not wanting to tear the shiny surface.

As the object came into view, she suppressed a shriek of delight. Carefully, she lifted the lid completely to get a better view. "Oh, Daddy! It's perfect!"

Molly clutched the package tightly as she bounded up the stairs that led to her room, trying hard to suppress a gleeful giggle. She figured that her brothers would already be asleep, so she tiptoed down the hall past their rooms and into her own. Turning on the light on her nightstand, she settled down cross-legged on her bed with the gift laid out in front of her.

Practically shuddering with delight, she lifted the top of the gift to get a better look. She grinned widely as she gazed at the tiny figures of the beautiful music box. "They're perfect!" she whispered. "I shall have to make some more friends for them."

She glanced at her shelf across the room. Several dozen tiny figures stared back at her. The figures varied as widely as her imagination. From peasants, to kings, to pets, to fanciful creatures, all were the wooden handiwork of Molly and her father.

Seeing the layer of dust that had accumulated on most of the figures, she took a deep breath and exhaled forcefully onto the dusty figurines. A flurry of dust flew everywhere, causing Molly to cough several times. As the dust cleared, a very strange sensation gripped Molly, as if she were falling, tumbling in slow motion. The room around her became a blur and started spinning around her. She tried to scream, but no sound came out. Everything was drowned out by another sound . . . a song.

All of a sudden, everything became very calm. The song gently tinkled around her, calming her frazzled nerves. Blackness gathered around her, as she gently shut her eyes, enveloped in a cushion of peace.

∽∾

"Molly! Molly!"

Rupert rapped forcefully on his daughter's door, eliciting no response. With it being Christmas morning, this was extremely odd. He tried the door and found it locked— also very strange. She was usually down the stairs before the rest of the children, most often more eager to present her siblings with their gifts than to receive her own. He had already searched the rest of the house before coming back to her room.

Rupert tried to tell himself that it was nothing, that she had probably accidentally slept in and had the covers over her head. However, a certain fatherly instinct told him otherwise. Panic swelling up inside of him, he resolved to put his girth to use. In his younger days, he had been an accomplished rugby player, and the military had gotten rid of whatever excess fat might have accumulated in the years since. Slamming his shoulder squarely into the door, he grunted as it fell away almost without a struggle. Only the lamp on the nightstand, which cast strange shadows on the opposing walls, illuminated the room.

Rupert drew his breath in sharply: Molly was nowhere to be seen. The Christmas bundle lay opened on the bed, but other than that, nothing was out of place. Not even the sheets on the bed were wrinkled.

"Molly?" At first it was a whisper. "Molly!" His voice rose frantically.

"MOLLY!" As tears filled his eyes, he glanced over at the shelf where the tiny figurines lay. Last year, he had helped her craft a miniature nativity set, which was displayed in the middle of the shelf. With tears obscuring his vision, Rupert walked over and gently caressed each small figure, ending with the small child in the manger.

Slowly, he slipped to his knees, bowed his head, and clasped his hands. "There is still hope."

ᖾᖰ

THE CANTICLE KINGDOM

Brigitta scrambled to her feet and turned to face her attacker. "So, you ain't the witch I took ye for!" exclaimed an obnoxious, all-too-familiar voice.

A lanky, brown haired boy a little younger than Johann stood in the snow, grinning.

Johann almost lost his jaw in the snow. "Get out of here, Bruno! It's dangerous!"

Brigitta glowered at both of them, her entire body coated with a thin layer of flakes. "Oh, so now you're concerned about *his* safety."

Johann bristled. It was true—they were all probably in considerable danger, and this wasn't the most opportune time for an eavesdropper. He could think of only one course of action; he drew his sword. "Get lost, Bruno! You're not welcome here!"

He tried not to let his nervousness show, but the trembling sword was a dead giveaway. Bruno's expression was a mixture of shock and amusement.

"You steal that from the scrap heap? Ya couldn't stick a pig with that toothpick!" His voice betrayed only the tiniest hint of nervousness. For several moments, the two boys just stared at each other, unsure of who would make the first move. Suddenly, Bruno's eyes grew round as saucers at a king's table. "What in the name of Queen Molly is that?" His finger pointed behind Johann.

Johann rolled his eyes. Even he wouldn't fall for that. Sensing the drop in defenses, Johann shot toward his opponent. "Nice try," he said coolly.

Fortunately for Bruno, Johann never made it to his intended target. A piercing scream from behind him shattered his resolve in mid-dash. Johann swirled around to find that Bruno, for once, had told the truth. However, this was no time to mark the momentous occasion on the calendar. Brigitta was in trouble.

From under the fallen tree, there emerged a great and terrible creature: a huge snake, its scales constantly shifting color to different shades of red, yellow, and orange. Although it looked like a plume of flame, the creature did nothing to melt the snow. It had given Brigitta her second unpleasant surprise in the last five minutes, wrapping itself tightly around one of her legs.

Frozen by fear, Bruno looked on blankly, as though his brain was unable to tell his feet to run. Johann, however, simply redirected his aggression for Bruno toward the new threat. Changing the direction he was dashing, he lunged at the snake and brought his sword down as hard as he could somewhere near the snake's middle. The result was quite unexpected. Instead of resulting in a bloody gash, the impact resulted in a splintering of stone, sending small shards flying in every direction. The area just around the gash lost its fiery color and reverted to a deep, stony gray.

Seeing his new victim, the snake loosened its grip on Brigitta and turned its attention toward Johann. For a terrible moment, the snake simply gazed at Johann with its lidless eyes of flame.

The strike came as if in slow motion. However, instead of lunging forward, the snake spewed a jet of flame at Johann, barely missing him. The wave of heat knocked the boy aside and completely singed the hair off his arms. The snow around him evaporated instantly, leaving him no cushion to land on. The snake then returned to its original victim.

As the snake whirled around, Brigitta pelted it with a barrage from her slingshot. Several of the projectiles met their mark, chipping off flakes of stone wherever they hit the snake's long body. Instead of deterring the snake from its course, Brigitta's efforts only served to aggravate the stone reptile even further.

With lightning speed, the snake coiled around both of Brigitta's legs, closing in tighter and tighter. She fired for as long as she could, but too quickly, the snake had her arms pinned to her sides.

Rising slowly to his feet, Johann rushed again toward Brigitta, his head swimming and muddled. Though his heart was pounding wildly, he knew this was no time to be timid.

The stone snake continued spewing plumes of flames from its nostrils and mouth, all the while coiling tighter around Brigitta as the color drained slowly from her face. Johann rushed forward in a frenzy, brandishing his sword wildly over his head. His attempt, though courageous, was short-lived. The snake violently swung its head around, impacting Johann squarely in the gut. He was sent sailing, the breath knocked completely from his lungs.

Johann landed hard in the snow and teetered on the edge of consciousness. With blurred vision, he saw the monster looming high above him, leaving the inevitable moment of strike in suspense. He barely registered Bruno fainting in the snow, finally yielding to his fear.

Bearing its awful fangs, the snake reared up ready to strike. As the snake raced toward his target, Johann closed his eyes peacefully, a single word forming on his lips. "Brigitta."

A glowing arrow sailed from the forest, impacting the snake in mid-strike, cleanly removing its head from its body. The head sailed away, landing in the snow accompanied by a shower of stones. Flames spouted from the broken neck of the snake's body, which flopped around like an untamed water hose. The flames swept the surrounding snow away, and the nearby trees burst into flames, causing the remaining snow to glisten brilliantly.

A second arrow shot out from among the trees, snapping the snake in half. The snake exploded in a final burst of flame and stone, and then lay still. Only the crackle of flames broke the silence of the forest. A dark figure emerged quietly, maintaining the hushed silence. He stooped over the unconscious Johann, pressing his hand to the boy's forehead. After muttering a few words, a warm glow washed over Johann's face, and his body relaxed. He then attended to the fallen Brigitta, repeating the process. Approaching the third child, he did not see any superficial wounds and decided that it was best simply to let him sleep.

ಊಂ

Johann was the first to come to his senses. Sitting up slowly, he rubbed his blurry eyes and then the crown of his head, surprised at how little pain he felt after his violent encounter. As he stirred, he noticed an ancient man standing over him.

"How do you feel?" asked the stranger, his voice deep and smooth.

"Uh, fine," replied Johann. "To whom do we owe thanks for saving our lives?"

The stranger bowed slightly. "I am called Siegfried. I am a knight of Lady Ellis and a wizard of weaponry," he announced, "and you are lucky to be alive."

Siegfried's tall and solid frame was covered mostly by armor, which looked at least a hundred years old. Though lightly peppered with rust, it appeared to be of sound quality and once was probably most impressive. Siegfried's head was crowned by only a thin wisp of hair whose whiteness rivaled the surrounding snow. The deep crevasses around his eyes gave him the appearance of being the only thing older than his ancient armor. His chestnut eyes, however, radiated an unmistakable youthful energy. Strangest of all, the man only had one arm.

"But . . . you killed that snake with arrows! A *stone* snake no less. Can you shoot with just one hand?" Johann asked incredulously.

The wizened knight smiled. "No, not in the conventional sense. But, like I said, I am a wizard of weaponry and thus have been able to overcome my physical limitations." To demonstrate what he meant, Siegfried removed an arrow from his quiver with his hand. Tossing the arrow into the air, he then thrust his hand forward, uttering a command. As if released from an invisible bow, the glowing arrow shot forward faster than Johann had ever seen an arrow fly. The arrow pierced clean through a thick tree, leaving a gaping hole.

Johann's eyes grew wide in disbelief. "That was incredible! What else can you do?"

The knight chuckled quietly. It had been sometime since he had been asked to show off his tricks. "There will be a time for more demonstrations later. As for now, we better leave this place. I would be willing to wager that our friend the snake was not the only monster lurking in these woods."

Johann nodded, and then turned sharply, remembering his fallen comrade. "Brigitta! Is she—"

Siegfried nodded. "She's fine, lad. Probably a bit shaken up, but there shouldn't be any lasting damage."

Johann ran over to his friend, who was slowly coming to her senses. Shaking the snow from her hair, her eyes grew wide as she caught a glimpse of the towering knight.

"It's all right," reassured Johann. "He's the one who saved us."

The knight again bowed slightly. "Brigitta, it's a pleasure. I am glad I saw you in time. But I must say I *am* confused as to why you are here in the first place. Not many children wander so deeply into the forest."

Johann grimaced and decided on the truth. When dealing with a wizard, you couldn't be sure they were not reading your thoughts anyway. "We were . . . looking for something."

Johann explained the mysterious circumstances of their journey to the knight, who listened gravely without interrupting. When Johann finished, the knight turned his gaze to the fallen tree.

Siegfried drew his eyebrows together in a contemplative expression. "Brigitta, could you describe the man that wanted you to retrieve the object? What did his voice sound like?"

Brigitta shrugged and grinned ruefully. "I couldn't see much of him because of the cloak and hood he was wearing. I don't think he wanted me to see his face. And now that you mention it, his voice *was* a little funny. He pronounced things strangely, and it sounded like he had something caught in this throat."

Siegfried digested the information and nodded gravely. "I am sorry to say, children, that you may already find yourselves involved in matters that are well beyond your years." Without another word, the knight strode toward the tree, considering it carefully. Reaching the side of the tree, he stooped down beside the gap in the road.

"Look out!" Brigitta cried, as a large fissure appeared in the ground.

Another tree, almost as mighty as the one on the road, cracked and tumbled toward the knight in a direct collision course. Whirling around to face the tree, his hand shot up, releasing a pulse of blue energy. With a resounding crack, the tree reversed its direction, landing loudly in the snow. Scarcely able to breathe, Brigitta and Johann stared on in disbelief.

The knight spoke first. "It is as I expected. There is a curse surrounding this place and only an amulet can break the curse. I cannot retrieve it . . . but I believe," he turned his gaze to meet Brigitta's, "that you can."

Brigitta looked incredulous. "Me? You must be crazy! I am not going anywhere near that tree!"

Siegfried placed his large hand on her shoulder. "There is nothing to fear, young one. The curse prevents anyone but children from taking the object you've come to retrieve. Unfortunately, this poor fellow must have been too old.

Brigitta still seemed less than convinced. "Don't worry," he reassured. "If anything happens, I will be here to protect you."

Seeing that Johann was confident in the old man' prowess, Brigitta had no choice but to trust his judgment. Creeping slowly toward the tree, she made her way to the hole. When the surrounding trees made no move to assault her, she began to relax, and she slipped into the hole. Several seconds later, she reappeared, clutching a golden object that gleamed in the remnants of the snake's fire.

In her hands Brigitta held a large, multicolored and multifaceted jewel that was attached to a thin, golden chain.

Brigitta tried to give the pendant to Siegfried, but he recoiled.

"Stay back!" he said loudly. "Keep a good distance from me, and we shouldn't have any trouble."

Brigitta eyed the object in her hand suspiciously. "What is it?" she asked. "It just looks like a piece of expensive jewelry." But they all knew that it was more than just an expensive piece of jewelry. None of them could quite take their eyes off it.

A strange sense of well-being settled over the group. "I am not sure," replied Siegfried. "But I can see that it possesses a great deal of magic. Come, we must get out of the open."

The knight gestured for the group to follow him. He hefted the still unconscious Bruno over his shoulder, and the others followed. Brigitta was sure to keep a safe distance.

Winding off the trail, they followed the knight through the snow for several minutes, speaking very little. Suddenly, Siegfried halted and signaled for the rest of the party to do the same. "Good," he said. "We are nearly there."

Johann glanced nervously at Brigitta. He saw nothing but trees for quite some distance. Chuckling quietly at the look on the boy's face, Siegfried raised a hand and uttered a command in a language that Johann did not understand. Where once stood only trees, a small, stone cottage materialized in the middle of the woods. The children gasped, and the knight could not fully contain his laughter any longer.

"I'd almost forgotten how the appearance of my home affects the uninitiated. Come, let's get you all out of the cold. Brigitta, you can leave the pendant outside in that hollowed tree trunk. It will be safe there for a while. Only a child could retrieve it anyway, and you seem to be the only children brave enough to venture into this neck of the woods."

After showing Brigitta the hiding place, he guided her inside. He laid Bruno out on a mat on the floor, since he was still unconscious. Moving with the dexterity of a man several decades younger, he quickly boiled water and prepared hot cider for each of the children. Lastly, he pulled an ornate wooden mug carved with hunting scenes around it and filled it to the brim for himself. He sipped at the top, sighing in contentment.

When he was satisfied with his beverage, he turned his attention back to the children. "I am sure my presence raises many questions, and if I tried to answer them all today, we'd be here until the wee hours of the morning. I am sorry that I cannot explain everything, but I do believe that we can help each other."

Brigitta set down her mug, her cheeks turning very rosy. "What do you mean? How could we possibly help you? My only real talent is marksmanship, which you seem to have a knack for already."

"Yeah," Johann agreed, "and my sword was nearly useless against that snake . . . thing."

The knight's face brightened. "Ah, your sword. Not a bad piece of work for a first blade. Did you make it yourself?"

Johann's cheeks flushed even deeper than Brigitta's. "Uh, yes. I know it's not much. I was still working on it, but I had to use it today because . . . well, because Brigitta was in trouble." Brigitta grinned widely, displaying her less-than-perfect teeth. Johann had more than made up for his previous cowardice.

"That was a very brave deed, Johann. A bit foolhardy, but brave. May I see your sword?" Nervously, Johann handed the sword to Siegfried who turned it over and over in his hands. He felt the hilt and tested the weight, stabbing at invisible villains in the air. Finally he strode over to the fire and gestured for Johann to follow him.

"Johann, in honor of your valor today, I am going to help you with your blade. Though I wouldn't deprive you the satisfaction of completing it yourself, I will aid you in the process. When I give you the signal, I want you to start pounding on the blade with this hammer."

The knight gave Johann a small, silver hammer from above the fireplace. Johann held the hammer in his hands, and found that it was surprisingly lightweight. Siegfried stretched the sword over the flames and began muttering under his breath. The flames jumped up higher and caught the sword, turning it white hot with uncanny speed. Almost as quickly as they had come, the flames receded, and the knight gave the signal to Johann.

Swinging as hard as his bruised and weary arms could manage, Johann struck the sword multiple times sending blue sparks flying in every direction. As he continued to pound, a light blue aura enveloped the blade. At another gesture from Siegfried, Johann ceased his strokes and fell promptly on the floor, exhausted.

Siegfried took Johann by the hand and raised him from the floor. Gently, he placed the sword in Johann's hand. "You will find that your blade is considerably stronger, but not complete. Tempering this blade will be a longer process—difficult, but rewarding."

Johann gazed at the blade and found that it was true. Many of the rough edges had been smoothed out and the edge of the blade had grown much sharper. Johann also thought he could see a remaining blue tinge in the metal of the blade.

Siegfried lowered his voice and leaned in so that only Johann could hear. "Your blade is very special. It has been endowed with some magical properties, which are yours to discover, but I will tell you this: if you are ever in great danger, simply stab the sword into the ground and yell the word "*Hilfe*." The sword will then protect you. I must warn you, though, only to do this in desperate circumstances and only as a last resort. Doing so takes a lot of energy, and either you or your sword might not survive the attempt."

Johann stared solemnly into the wizard's ancient eyes. He could sense both deep wisdom and sadness therein. "How do you do this? Where did you learn all this magic?"

Siegfried gazed earnestly at the boy. "It is a craft that runs in my family. It can be taught to those who have a propensity for it, but it is both a blessing and a burden." The knight seated himself on a low stool by the fire. "The use of magic takes a lot of energy and therefore requires a lot of endurance from the user. Magic is intended to do good, and as a person uses his magic for good, his capacity increases."

Siegfried averted his gaze to the flickering flames. "However, as with any good thing, magic has a dark side. Over the years, many dark wizards have abused their gift and brought terror to the hearts of many. It was once my job to root out these dark wizards and bring them to justice. But that was long ago, at a time when there was still justice to be found."

The children kept silent, unsure of what to say. They were now part of an adventure they could have never imagined, and it was still a bit surreal for the both of them.

Siegfried suddenly snapped out of his reverie. "Anyway, that is another story. We must now focus on current matters—your meeting with that strange, hooded man this evening."

Brigitta gulped, trying to dispel the large lump in her throat. "What should we do? If this amulet is as powerful as you say it is, I don't know if we want to hand it over to someone we know nothing about. For all we can tell, he could be one of the evil wizards you mentioned."

Siegfried slowly stroked his beard. "Yes. Those were my thoughts exactly. Only someone with some magical experience would know its true worth. Regardless, it's size alone is enough to make it a worthwhile item for almost anyone."

"True," added Johann. "It makes me wonder who that fellow was who was crushed under the tree."

Brigitta wrinkled her brow. "I didn't see much of him, but by the looks of his clothes, it seems that he was somebody important. They were not common peasant clothes."

"Which would point us to the palace," commented Johann.

Siegfried stopped rubbing his beard and glanced absently around the room. "The very fact that you are supposed to meet him in the castle garden already points to that. They don't usually allow children to run around in there."

Brigitta glanced out the window and gazed in horror at the darkening sky. "The garden! We'll never make it at this rate! What are we supposed to do now?"

The old knight smiled knowingly, seemingly unaffected by the apparent crisis. "Relax. I am a wizard, remember? Surely you don't imagine that I spend all my time pulling animals out of hats to amuse children?"

Brigitta still looked puzzled. She had never seen such a trick. "Then you think we should still go?"

Siegfried nodded. "Yes. It may be our only hope to discover the identity of this mysterious person. Only then can we decide on a further course of action."

"Are we to go alone, then?" asked Johann, exhibiting very little confidence.

"Yes," replied Siegfried reluctantly. "This person must not be led to suspect anything. No matter what happens, don't try any heroics. We have absolutely no idea what we are dealing with here. Just get in, do what you need to, and get out."

Doubt gnawed painfully at Brigitta's stomach. "Are we to give him the amulet, then?"

Siegfried hesitated ever so slightly. "Yes. Not without leaving ourselves a back door, however." He stepped to a cupboard near the back of the room.

Opening one of the top drawers, he reached in and produced a small, shiny object. "This little device," he explained, "emits a very strong magical signal that I can detect. If all goes according to plan, I should be able to figure out where this person takes the amulet, which will help us figure out who he is."

Johann nodded, obviously impressed. This was sounding less and less like a wild goose chase. "Great! When do we go?"

Siegfried's actions told him that the answer was something like "right now." They left the cottage immediately, and Siegfried explained to Brigitta how to attach the small device, which appeared to be no more than a metallic metal oval with one surface flattened out and the other rounded. Brigitta retrieved the amulet from its hiding place and attached the device, which immediately blended in to look like the rest of the metal.

The knight led the pair through the woods. Suddenly, Brigitta stopped in her tracks and glanced frantically back at the cottage. "What about Bruno? Are we just going to leave him there?"

The knight raised a hand in consolation. "Don't worry. I will see that he gets back home. He will wake up firmly convinced that he has had the most fanciful dream."

This seemed to satisfy the two children, and they continued through the woods until they reached a small clearing that contained nothing but an old, bronze fountain. The fountain was raised up on a pedestal with a round basin atop it, and the bronze had greened over time. No water, frozen or otherwise, filled the basin. In all respects, the fountain appeared quite plain. Siegfried approached the fountain and beckoned for the children to join him. "This is our stop, children."

Siegfried remained at a safe distance while both Johann and Brigitta moved closer. They glanced at each other, both thinking the same thing: Siegfried might be senile, after all.

As if reading their thoughts, Siegfried started to explain. "Very well. This ordinary-looking fountain is actually a very cleverly disguised secret entrance. Once you grasp the basin with both hands and utter the key word, it will reveal a tunnel. Simply step inside, and let magic do the rest. This particular tunnel connects to a spot very near the castle gardens and should get you there quickly. This isn't the nicest tunnel, nor is it the only one of its kind, but it *is* the fastest way to the castle, given our circumstances."

"So, we just need to place our hands on it like this?" Johann grasped the frigid rim of the fountain.

"Yes," replied Siegfried. "Brigitta, you join him, and I will supply you with the key word. Remember, once you are finished in the gardens, go straight home. Your parents are probably beside themselves with worry already. I will contact you later tonight."

Brigitta joined Johann in grasping the fountain. "How will you know where we are?" she wondered.

Siegfried grinned broadly. "I have my ways. Are you ready to go?" They both nodded, grasping the edge of the fountain a bit tighter.

"Good luck." The knight then drew in a deep breath and shouted a word, which to Johann sounded something like "geh-yah." Instantly, the fountain rotated, dragging the children with it, and then plunged into the earth. Neither of the children even had time to gasp.

For a moment, all was dark and still. Then a faint light, like that of a firefly, appeared in front of them, dancing in the darkness. Others joined the glow until there was an entire school of dancing lights. The lights surrounded the two children making their bodies feel strangely lightweight. Suddenly, the lights jerked forward, taking the children with them. In an incredible burst of speed, the children rocketed through the underground tunnel.

It's too bad that nobody else but Brigitta is going to believe my story, thought Johann.

CHAPTER FIVE

ᘄ

DEALING with DARKNESS

THE CANTICLE KINGDOM

When the dizzying ride finally halted, Johann and Brigitta found themselves staring up at the fading sky. It took them several minutes to realize where they were and what had just happened.

Coming to his senses first, Johann reached up his hand and hoisted himself out of the hole they were standing in, then, he offered Brigitta his hand and lifted her out as well. No sooner had they cleared the hole than a fountain, almost identical to the one in the forest, shifted over to close up the opening.

Interesting, thought Johann. *I will have to keep my eyes out for these things around town. They could prove useful.*

Glancing around, Brigitta located the tall, orderly hedge that marked the entrance to the castle gardens, which lay on the base of the hill on which the castle perched. Trying to keep as quiet as possible, she motioned to Johann to follow her and to remain silent.

The two approached the hedge and found that a small section on the part closest to them had been cleared away, allowing easy access to the garden beyond. Brigitta shot a nervous glance at Johann. "Almost as if someone was expecting us," she whispered.

Johann nodded but said nothing. Careful not to rustle any leaves, he first peered through the hedge and, on finding that the coast was clear, stepped cautiously through. Brigitta followed close behind, her hand unconsciously finding her weapon as she did so.

A remarkable scene met their eyes. Bushes had been formed to almost every shape and style imaginable, accented with vibrantly colored flowers. There were about as many statues strewn about, some in the strangest places, such as in the middle of a walkway or sticking halfway out of a bush. Though most of the statues resembled humans, many of them looked rather like the creatures he had seen in the forest. The twilight caused the statues to cast eerie shadows over the walkways like flickering phantoms.

All of the cobblestone pathways in the garden led to its center, where an imposing statue stood: a great hooded figure, his fingertips placed together right below his face. His robes flowed around them as if tousled by the wind, and his face lay completely concealed. Behind the figure, a towering obelisk of black stone shot up into the darkening heavens. Tiny specks of light gleamed on the surface of the obelisk, giving it the appearance of a star field.

The sight filled the children with an odd mixture of wonder and terror. The edifice appeared smooth and unblemished, unlike any statue they had ever seen.

Making sure that there was no one else in sight, the children approached the statue, believing it to be the obvious meeting point. Reaching the statue, they both studied it for a few moments and then uneasily turned away in order to watch for the coming of the mysterious man.

Several tense, silent minutes passed. Johann turned to Brigitta. "He didn't say anything else about exactly where to meet him, did he?" he whispered.

Brigitta opened her mouth to reply but was interrupted by another voice, ominous and deep. "Oh, this place suits me just fine."

Both children whirled around and let out pronounced gasps. There had been no one there just seconds before. As they looked, there was still no one there.

The voice came again, from within the hood of the statue. "I don't think I told you to bring anyone along. I might forgive you—if you indeed have the item."

Brigitta gulped and grasped for the amulet in her pouch. Finding it, she held it aloft in front of the statue. "I have it. Where do you want it?"

"Place it at the base of the statue, touching the stone."

Brigitta did as she was told, trembling slightly. This was not what she had expected.

It was Johann who built up the courage to speak next. "You have what you want. At least tell us who you are."

The sound coming from the statue was something of a mix between a scoff and a chuckle. "Pretentious little boy. My identity is not important. But if it is a name that you want, you can call me the Many-Named One."

Suddenly the amulet disappeared, seeming to melt into the stone. Johann mustered his courage and opened his mouth again. "Well, I think we're finished here. You said something about a reward for us. We went through a bit of trouble getting you the amulet."

The chuckling returned, more ominous this time. "But of course! Behold!"

In much the same manner that the amulet disappeared, a small chest materialized from the surface of the statue. The wooden chest was inlaid with carvings and trimmed with shiny brass. Brigitta stepped over to the chest and popped the lid. Her eyes widened in disbelief as she surveyed its contents—a mountain of gleaming gold and silver coins. With a trembling hand, she reached out to pick up one of the coins, rubbing it between two of her fingers to assure herself that it was real.

"Th-thank you," she stammered. "If you ever need our help again—"

"I will not," replied the statue curtly. "Consider yourselves lucky. I do not often enlist the assistance of others." Johann gaped at the treasure as well, calculating in his head all the things and adventures they could now afford.

"Now go," commanded the voice, "and tell no one of this meeting."

Anxious to comply, Brigitta scooped up the chest, cradling it in one arm, and turned to go. All thoughts of stealth now banished, both children sprinted forward at full tilt, wildly rustling leaves as they raced by. As they ran, the wind picked up behind them, howling through the garden. Shadows danced rapidly as trees and bushes flailed around in the wind.

Suddenly, Johann glimpsed the exit in the hedge where they had come in. Like a horse with its blinders on, he dashed straight for it, anxious to make this a place he visited again only in his memories. Dripping sweat and panting for breath, he leapt through the hole and on to the other side of the hedge.

He turned back to see how Brigitta was faring. "Whew, that was strange, huh? I—" But as he glanced back, only an empty garden greeted him. Johann's breathing quickened as panic swelled up in his chest. Had she not followed him out of the garden?

"Brigitta!" he yelled at the top of his lungs, but his cry was mostly drowned out by the wind. Bringing his sword to bear, he turned back to the hedge and bounded through. "I lost you once today," he yelled at the wind. "I won't lose track of you again!"

Reaching the garden once again, he glanced around, frantically Brigitta's name. Retracing his steps, he made his way back to the central statue. Strangely, its surface had changed to a plain, gray stone with no sign of stars.

Suddenly, Johann sensed a tingling in his hand and realized that his sword was vibrating. He turned it over in his hands, searching in vain for the cause. Something whizzed past Johann's ear, causing him to whirl around. Brandishing his sword, he inadvertently deflected a second shot, causing sparks to fly with a loud ring, as metal glanced off metal. Certain that he'd be felled by another projectile at any moment, Johann cast his eyes toward the direction of the shot. The sight was unlike anything he had ever encountered.

Three figures that appeared anything but human hunched a small way off. Each creature possessed the body of a primate. The largest possessed the head of a crocodile, while the other two resembled a panther and an eagle.

Each creature clutched a blowgun in menacing claws, the largest one having just removed it from its lips. It turned to its comrades and promptly started beating the panther on the head with its blowgun. "You fool! You couldn't hit a mountain with a cannonball! Come on!"

What's going on? Johann though. *Did I fall on my head back there?*

Just then, all three creatures leapt toward Johann. He raised his sword, instinctively, hardly allowing fear any time to kick in.

The panther came within range first, leaping with claws outstretched. Ungracefully, Johann swung his sword at his attacker, his timing woefully off. *Great,* Johann thought. *I'm about as useful as a toothpick in the face of a tornado.*

Regardless, the moment the creature came in the vicinity of the sword, the sword let forth a cloud of blue tendrils and grasped the creature, which fell instantly, paralyzed. Gaining courage, Johann swung at the creature again, and even before his sword found its mark, a second swath of blue tendrils enveloped the creature. Johann saw that the creature had reverted to stone.

The second creature let out a deafening screech and bolted faster toward Johann. The screech temporarily deafened Johann so that he could not bring his sword to the ready. In a moment the creature pounced upon him, driving his claws into his tunic. As they tumbled, the sword grazed the eagle creature and worked its deadly spell. The creature skidded across the path, nothing more than a mere statue.

Obviously a bit smarter than the other two, the third creature paused in its tracks. Hesitantly, it glanced both directions and suddenly bolted off into the distance. Johann breathed an audible sigh of relief, letting his sword swing by his side, but his relief was short lived.

"They must have taken her," he mumbled, his voice trailing off in the midst of the calm. He noticed he had to concentrate to keep from falling over in exhaustion, and for several moments, he noticed very little of what was going on around him.

As if on cue, two wolf statues embedded in the hedge sprung to life. A figure of a knight in armor leapt into life behind him, and several gargantuan crows sprang from their perches on the side of a fountain. Every second, a new creature came to life and joined in circling Johann. Strangely, they all kept their distance but wasted no time intimidating Johann, growling, howling, hollering, and clawing at the ground.

Trembling, Johann brought his sword up and kept it extended toward the gathering crowd—the odds were stacking completely beyond his grasp. Johann found it strange that instead of the crushing terror that should have gripped his mind, his only thought was a prayer that his mother often recited—the same line flowing through his mind over and over: "Deliver us from evil."

Johann tensed for the moment of attack. He swung his sword repeatedly at the fringes of the crowd, which recoiled at the sword's approach. Once in a while, blue tendrils leapt from the end of the blade, and a creature would drop to the earth. Still, it seemed like evaporating a single drop in an angry ocean.

With a rusty squeak like the twisting of door hinges in need of oil, the crowd of creatures abruptly halted their awful dance. A nearby hedge burst into flames, revealing a tall suit of armor as the leaves burned away. The suit was much taller than any normal man and polished to the point of almost glowing. The strangest trait, however, was its lack of a helmet, or head of any kind for that matter. Presently, the armor opened up a panel near its middle revealing a furnace of flickering flames. Reaching inside, the armor pulled out a stone head of a fox with horns protruding out of its head. The armor placed the head squarely on its shoulders, which elicited a burst of flames around it. When the flames fell, the head was no longer stone but as real as could be imagined.

The fox gave a mischievous grin and turned his attention to Johann. "Welcome to my garden, Swordslinger. It is a pity that I can't show you the lovely labyrinth downstairs as well. Your friend was lucky enough to enjoy that pleasure."

A howl from the crowd broke the mob out of its silence. "So," continued the fox, "do you still insist on resistance? Or shall you accept the inevitable?"

"What do you want from me? I only wish to return home! I won't bother you any further if you just let me go!"

The fox bared its gleaming teeth. "Foolish little boy! Your type is always the same! I ought to know!"

The fox reached again into its panel and retrieved another head with one hand while pushing down the old head with the other. This time the head that appeared on his shoulders was distinctly human.

"Does this look familiar to you by chance?" glowered the former fox. "It should."

Atop the suit of armor sat a man's face with deep brown eyes, thick, wavy chestnut hair, and a generous mustache. Immediately, Johann was struck by the uncanny feeling of recognition, though he could not place who the man was. He stared unblinkingly at the tall figure, desperately trying to make sense of it.

"I don't know what you're talking about," he replied truthfully. "You are just playing tricks on my mind."

The man laughed sinisterly. "A little dense, are we? Oh, well. I tire of this meeting. Kill him." He waved his hand as if brushing aside an annoying pest and disappeared back into the bushes.

The creatures did not leap all at once into the fray, but left their task to the boldest ones. Immediately at the pronouncement, a tiger sprang toward Johann, only to be cut short by a swing in his direction. Two gigantic hounds, that looked like they had been crossed with a reptile, quickly followed him. Bearing its teeth, one lunged and caught hold of Johann's foot, tearing the boot clean off before Johann could bring the sword around to fend him off. While Johann fought off the dogs, the crows had circled their prey and dove in for the strike. One slashed Johann's shoulder with its talons while the other lacerated his back.

More and more, the creatures threw themselves wildly in his direction as Johann whipped the sword around him with all his might. He no longer sought a specific target—he simply lashed out in all directions in a crazed attempt to mount a sufficient defense. However, as one statue fell, another two came to take its place. His consciousness hovered just on the border as the world melted into a melee of sight and sound around him. As he reached the brink of abandonment, he suddenly recalled Siegfried's advice by the fireplace. Jerking the sword swiftly down into the earth, he gathered his strength and yelled the command with as much gusto as he could muster. *"Hilfe!"*

Time froze for a split second, and Johann captured the entire scene upon his mind: claws in mid-strike, frozen faces of contorted rage. However, the frozen faces soon gave way to faces of astonishment as a shock wave of energy shot from around the sword with the force of an avalanche, blowing the entire crowd in the air and reducing all but the heartiest creatures to shards. The shock wave rumbled into the distance, and Johann's world faded to black.

ෆ

When Johann awoke, it was under a vast field of brilliant stars. For a good while, he remained totally mesmerized by the scene. It seemed to him that he could feel his body floating toward them, embracing the vast expanse, wide as eternity.

Just as he felt he was about to fly off into space, his thoughts came rushing back to him, accompanied by a wave of crushing pain. Suddenly, he bolted upright, trying to convince himself that he had not perished. The possibility that he had survived was simply too good to be true.

Night enveloped the garden, leaving it shadowy and silent. All around him, Johann glimpsed half-ruined statues and shards, strewn all about like toys in the playroom of a giant two-year old. His thoughts immediately turned to Brigitta. The guilt from his loss nearly crippled him, and at once he nearly keeled over again with nausea.

Though he had miraculously made his way out of this scrape, he knew that he could not count on another such escape. If he was ever to see his cousin again, he would need help, and Johann knew exactly where he might turn. Turning smartly on his heels, Johann shook his aching muscles and broke into a weary jog.

ⁿℓ

Johann's mother feared the worst. Earlier that morning, Brutus had blown through the house in a frantic search for Brigitta. Then, Johann had turned up missing after being released from Brutus's care. To top it all off, Brutus himself had gone missing. Despite the townspeople's best efforts, he was still nowhere to be found.

Unable to attend to her usual daily tasks, Johann's mother instead had spent the time stewing and pacing. She had offered to join the search but was reassured that she should stay home, just in case some sort of foul play against the family was at work.

Night had fallen, and she was the only member of the household still awake. With a single meager candle, she kept her vigil by the window, hoping to catch some news as soon as it was available. She had not received any word in hours and assumed the search parties had turned in for the night. Nevertheless, her vigil continued.

Surprise nearly overwhelmed her as she glimpsed Johann himself running up the block. She had to rub her sleepy eyes several times before she convinced herself that she was not dreaming, nor hallucinating. Instantly on her feet, she burst through the door and out onto the street, not sure whether she wanted to hug or slap him. She decided on the first and embraced him tightly, tears streaming down her cheeks.

"Mother," he spoke softy. "I have so much to tell you."

CHAPTER SIX

ဢ

A LIGHT in the LABYRINTH

LONDON, ENGLAND, 1945

The snowy streets of London offered no comfort to a stricken father. His drab wool scarf concealed most of his face, a scanty coat draped over his body, and his arms cradled around a knapsack. Spotting his destination, he hurried to the door, working the knob clumsily with his gloved hands.

A burst of warmth slammed him as he entered the heated room, causing him to feel a bit drowsy. Without interruption, he walked up to the counter, removed his gloves, and put the sack down in front of him.

The clerk, noticing he had a customer, left his work arranging the shelves on the back wall and approached the front counter. "What have we got today, ol' bloke?" Rupert carefully emptied the bag of its contents. The clerk looked only mildly impressed. The clerk took the item and studied it in his hands. " 'Made in Germany,' it says. What is it, a war trophy?"

The customer shook his head. "No . . . it was just a gift. It was for my daughter, but . . . ." Rupert had to struggle to keep back the flow of tears. ". . . She's gone now. I can hardly bear to look at it."

The clerk nodded, his brow furrowed in concern as he placed a consolatory arm on Rupert's shoulder. "Sorry to hear that, mate. I'll give you a good price for it."

Mr. Rupert nodded weakly. "Just get it off my hands." Silently, the clerk took a small stack of notes and slipped them into Mr. Rupert's hand. As Mr. Rupert turned to leave, the clerk placed the package on the back shelf.

ဢ

THE CANTICLE KINGDOM

When Brigitta awoke, she found herself encompassed by darkness. The ground beneath her felt cold and damp, the air musty and oppressive. She attempted to rise to her feet but was stunned by a spell of dizziness. *A bit too fast*, she thought to herself. Steadying herself, she slowly rose to her feet, crouching under the low ceiling. She pulled her arms around herself to preserve her warmth.

With nothing else to do but explore her surroundings, Brigitta inched her way along, gratefully arching her back as the tunnel expanded. She paused, startled, when she noticed someone hunched over a meager candle, constantly mulling his hands over one another, his whole body trembling. The firelight flickered off his face, giving it a wild and maniacal glow.

He looked to be an older man, diminutive in size. Coarse black hair covered his face, and his eyes gleamed wild in the firelight, which also glistened off his tear-stained cheeks. She could still not understand most of the words, but after a minute or two she could discern a certain phrase that slipped time and again from his lips. "The struggle . . . the struggle . . . it is lost . . . ."

Unsure how to proceed, Brigitta watched the man suffer for several moments. The man hardly seemed rational, but her curiosity got the best of her like it always did. Creeping within the glare of the candlelight she raised her hand and said meekly, "I beg your pardon, but could you tell me where we are?"

The man immediately shot upright, his eyes as wide as a predator's before striking its prey. "If I knew, I would find some way to leave." He shook his head curtly. "There is no way out."

The man kept the silence for several moments, his eyes boring into Brigitta's. "My name is Dolf. I was born to suffer. There is no way out." Something in the man's voice convinced her that she should not argue, and Brigitta wandered back the way she had come, but stayed close enough to see the light.

After a few hours, Brigitta awoke again in darkness, her body chilled to the core. She didn't remember falling asleep. Dolf's candle had burned down, but still emitted a faint glow. He continued to rant, but most of it was completely incomprehensible. Almost unconsciously, she moved toward the light, if for only a shred of warmth. Seeing her approach, Dolf ceased his drivel and gazed up at her with a scowl that rivaled the air for chill. "I see you survived the night. Pity."

At any other time, Brigitta might have been sorely offended. However, her strength had completely left her and with it her fighting spirit. "Nice to see you too, Dolf." After a few moments' silence, she tried to make conversation. "Dolf. That's an interesting name. Where is it from?"

His signature scowl was back in full force. Surprisingly, he answered. "I don't know. I don't remember anything before I was thrown in here. I woke up here with no memory of how I got here or where I was before. I found this paper in my pocket. I figured that it was my name on it."

Feebly, he extended a tattered scrap of paper, which had been torn in several places. Under a faded picture, she could just barely make out the word "dolf." It looked like part of the document had been destroyed around the name. She managed a sympathetic smile and handed the paper back to him. "It's a nice name."

After several moments of silence, Brigitta tried again to start a conversation. "So, Dolf, how long have you been here?" she managed. She didn't think it was possible, but his expression soured even more.

"I don't know, and I don't care, blast it!" Dolf barked. "If I die in here, I'll count myself lucky!" He waved the girl away. "Why don't you go bother someone else for a change?"

Brigitta had started moving back toward her niche in the darkness, when she turned, confused. "There are others down here?" she ventured weakly.

"Of course. In fact, they just threw someone new in this morning. A woman, even. Go bother her." He gestured in a general direction and promptly withdrew back into his own world, leaving Brigitta completely alone once more. Not knowing what else to do, she blindly crept off in the direction Dolf had indicated.

Tentatively, she groped through the darkness, losing her balance several times on the slick stones. She kept her hands outstretched at all times as to avoid any unpleasant surprises. She thought a good deal of time had passed, but there was no way to tell for sure in the darkness. The light of Dolf's candle had faded in the distance, and the chill became more and more acute.

Dejectedly, Brigitta plopped down in the darkness. Unbidden, hot tears trickled silently down her frozen cheek. "Curse you, Dolf!" Brigitta yelled back. Her arms flailed out wildly, and her thoughts spiraled out of control with panic. Her scream echoed into the darkness, briefly filling the oppressive silence before all was quiet once again.

Brigitta closed her eyes. Her strength was almost entirely spent, and her will was fading fast. She sat down in the darkness and started contemplating what it would be like to die, when suddenly something tugged at her foot. Startled, she pulled her foot away and let out a little yelp.

"Who's there?" Brigitta cried. After several seconds of silence, she heard a scurrying noise from behind her, followed by another in rapid succession. Another tug, this time at her sleeve, tore a small portion of the fabric away from her shirt. Terrified, she flailed her arms around, frantically trying to ward off her invisible assailant.

Her hand struck something alive, small, and furry. It squealed and flew away into the darkness. The scurrying and squeaking intensified, and Brigitta felt more and more tugs at her clothing and skin. Tiny claws and razor teeth scraped her arms and legs, drawing blood. She screamed as loud and as long as she could in the darkness, but still, no one came.

Just as pain and fear threatened to push her over the brink of insanity, a brilliant flash of light shot through the corridor. For an instant, she caught a glimpse of large, mangy rodents with coarse, black fur and beady yellow eyes before being blinded by the intensity of the light. The rodents scattered, retreating to their dark corners and crevasses. Brigitta fell to the ground, her hands held firmly over her smarting eyes.

A woman's voice, soft and comforting, spoke from the darkness. Squinting, Brigitta was only able to make out the woman's eyes, which glinted palely in the light. The woman placed a hand on Brigitta's forehead. "Are you all right, little one? Those awful creatures may be desperate, but I think I've scattered them for now. Let's get out of here."

Brigitta rubbed her eyes, suddenly becoming aware of the pain all over her body. For the first time, she realized the source of the light that filled the tunnel—a brilliant globe of blue light hovered near the woman's hand. With assistance, she managed to stand, gradually regaining her balance. The woman's hand felt smooth and soft, as thought it hadn't ever seen a hard day's work.

What is a person like her doing here?

Gradually, Brigitta found the courage to address the stranger. "Thank you," she said timidly. "I . . . I'm Brigitta. Who can I thank for my rescue?"

The woman wrinkled her forehead, as if trying to find the right answer to a difficult riddle. When her voice came, it was barely above a whisper but very pleasant and soothing to hear. "I . . . can't say. I woke up in this filthy place, and I can't remember a thing about how I got here or even who I am. It is the strangest thing. I can remember"—she moved her hand from side to side and the blue orb followed as if on a string—"how to use my magic but I can't seem to remember who I am or how I got to be here. It's almost as if it's on the tip on my tongue, but"—she paused for a moment of sorrowful silence—"everything is just a bit cloudy."

Brigitta could imagine nothing worse than adding memory loss to the terrors of the dungeon. Being in physical darkness was bad enough. However, the woman's words had given her hope. "Was that magic you used to scatter the rats? That was pretty amazing."

The woman sighed. "Yes, that was magic. I remember all sorts of tricks but nothing else. What about you? What can you remember?"

Brigitta wrinkled her nose, confused. "Everything . . . I think."

Frantically, she wracked her brain for the events of the past day. The forest, the garden—

That had all happened yesterday, right?

The stranger shook her head. "Well, that's not important," she said with a regal wave of her hand. "What I would really like to know is if there is any way out of this awful place."

Brigitta shook her head sadly. "I don't know. I haven't been here that long, and it's just been too dark, well, until you came along."

"Would you like a little more light?"

The light of the blue orb intensified so that it filled the entire corridor.

Shielding her eyes, Brigitta saw her benefactor's face clearly for the first time. She was a middle-aged woman, very slender, with golden hair and piercing blue eyes. Though her eyes seemed youthful, her face was riddled with care and worry, making her seem much older.

Brigitta took in their surroundings. Their prison appeared to be more of a cave than anything else, complete with jagged, wet rock formations, various colors of moss, and stalactites. The cavern stretched out in both directions and Brigitta was unable to see either end. Despite the darkness, the light gave her an immense amount of hope. At least now they could explore. Brigitta glanced around the room, relishing her ability to see.

The musty chamber did not seem nearly so imposing now. Brigitta turned to the woman, her newfound hope lighting her eyes. "I don't know about you, but I'd like to see the light of day again, and soon. What do you think our chances are of getting out of here?"

The woman shrugged. "It is certainly worth a try. Anything would be preferable to rotting down here. Is there anyone else that you've seen? Perhaps they could help us."

Brigitta gazed back the way she had come, debating whether to tell the newcomer about Dolf. She had felt uncomfortable in his presence, but she couldn't put her finger on why. Perhaps it was the fact that he'd sent her on her way to becoming rat food. "There was an old man"—Brigitta pointed back the way she came—"but I don't know that he'll be much help."

The woman smiled, the lines in her face making her appear very tired. She coughed deeply several times, causing the light above her hand to flicker. She set out in the direction Brigitta had indicated, taking her by the arm. After only a moment, Brigitta stopped and glanced up at the strange woman. "Until you get your memory back, what should I call you?"

The woman paused and bit her lip. Then suddenly, a look of realization washed over her face. "You can call me Gwen. I'm not sure why, but I fancy that name."

Brigitta nodded and redoubled her pace toward Dolf's hideout. Gwen spoke a soft command, and the blue orb shifted position to above her head, leaving both her hands free.

They made good time with the help of the light, and quickly reached the place where Dolf had been sitting. Brigitta called his name, but no one answered. Puzzled, Brigitta looked around. She was under the impression that Dolf didn't leave his spot much.

"Are you sure he was here?" asked Gwen softly. "These tunnels all look the same to me."

Brigitta nodded as she bent down to pick up one of Dolf's pictures, meaning to show it to Gwen, but bolted suddenly upright as a savage cry rang out from behind her. A swift shadow sprang from the darkness and tackled Brigitta, pinning her to the ground. The creature clawed at her face with its hands snarling and growling fiercely.

Gwen responded instantly, yelling commands as blinding bolts of yellow light erupted from her fingertips in rapid succession. The bolts nearly singed Brigitta's skin, but they had the desired effect of driving off her attacker, who fled in the opposite direction with a howl.

Stopping only to help Brigitta to her feet, Gwen dashed off in pursuit to take out Brigitta's attacker. They ran for what seemed like miles, but soon Gwen had to stop because of a terrible coughing fit. Brigitta collapsed gratefully to the cold ground while Gwen fumbled about in her pockets to see if she had a handkerchief. She only succeeded in pulling out an old mirror. She studied her face in the dim light, trying desperately to recall a useful memory. Nothing came. She replaced the mirror, looked around, and found Brigitta curled up in a ball, sound asleep. She had finally succumbed to her terrible exhaustion. Gwen smiled and sat down next to the sleeping girl. With a word, the blue light vanished, and Gwen fell fast asleep as well.

ಬಌ

After a few hours' sleep, Brigitta and Gwen started on their search for an escape from the caverns. However, just as they had decided to leave, an object on the ground caught Brigitta's eye. Stooping low, she retrieved a tattered piece of parchment, which lay just to the right of the place where Dolf had previously been living. She flattened out the piece on the ground and squinted to read the scrawling words. The language in which they were written was not her usual one, but strangely, she found that she could understand it easily.

" 'Do you know the story of Hansel and Gretel?' " she read. " 'Follow the bread crumbs, and they will lead you home.' "

She approached Gwen and showed her the parchment. The older woman shook her head. "It looks like gibberish to me."

Brigitta stared at the paper a second time to make sure that her eyes were not playing tricks on her. "It's strange," she said. "I've never seen anything like this before, but my mind is making sense of it somehow. I can understand the words, but I don't understand what they mean. What do bread crumbs have to do with anything?"

"It seems that whoever left this note left some sort of trail for us to follow."

Brigitta studied the note, trying to confirm her suspicions. "I'm pretty sure this is Dolf's handwriting. I saw it on some other things he had on him. Who else could it be?"

The older woman shook her head. "I don't know. Who can say what other poor wretches are stuck down here?"

Brigitta wrinkled her face in mock offense. "What? Doesn't that make me a poor wretch too?"

Gwen smiled genuinely for the first time since waking up in the tunnel. "No, I'll let you be the exception. Why don't we just look around for that trail?"

Standing where she found the note, Brigitta soon spotted a trail of white blotches on the ground. A closer inspection revealed them to be small patches of melted candle wax that formed a trail down the corridor.

Brigitta and Gwen followed the wax trail, carefully glancing about and behind them in an attempt to avoid any other surprise guests. They walked in silence for several minutes, both of them shivering from the cold, which was deep enough to turn each breath into a frosty cloud in front of their faces.

After a good while without incident, Gwen attempted some quiet conversation. "So, Brigitta, tell me about your family. I'm sure your parents are missing their daughter by now."

Brigitta nodded, not quite sure how to reply. She often found it difficult to talk about her family. "Yes—Brutus is probably going crazy looking for me. He's the one who takes care of me." Her voice trailed off, leaving the corridor quiet. "I don't really know much about my parents. Brutus never really talks about them. He's always scurried off the subject faster than a jackrabbit. I've always wanted to know . . . so badly that I often have dreams about who they are and what they look like. Usually, I imagine they're brave and important, but I just don't know. They could be the most ordinary people ever. I don't think that would bother me, if only I knew."

Gwen had been looking for a drop of information about Brigitta's life, and instead, she had tapped a well. The proper response proved difficult. She decided to keep on the same vein. "Do you have any brothers or sisters, then?"

Brigitta shook her head. "If I do, I sure don't know about them either. I've just lived with Brutus for as long as I can remember. He didn't have any children either, so I think he liked that I was around to be like his daughter. I do hang around with Johann, though. He's sort of like a brother to me."

Gwen attempted a smile, but another fit of coughing cut her short. They stopped momentarily to let her catch her breath before continuing. "So," Gwen managed between coughs, "is Johann just a neighborhood boy, or do you know him from school?"

Brigitta grinned in a painful mixture of mirth and regret. "Johann is Brutus's nephew. We go to school together, but I think some of the teachers prefer we didn't."

Gwen raised an inquisitive eyebrow, and Brigitta responded. "We have a knack for finding, well, I like to call them adventures, but no one else thinks of them that way. We like to have fun, and that means missing school once in a while, maybe pulling a few pranks, but nothing dangerous." Brigitta sighed. "I bet he's really worried right now. It wouldn't be the first time I've made him worry."

She let the comment hang in the silence. The thought of Johann made her sad; she just didn't know whether they would ever see each other again. But at the same time, thoughts of him gave her a reason to live, to resist succumbing to the awful darkness of the dungeon. "Do you think he's looking for me?" Brigitta finally managed, her voice cracking despite her efforts to remain brave.

Gwen placed a soft hand on her shoulder as they continued to follow the trail. "Well, I don't know him, but if you are as close as you say you are, I can't imagine that he's sitting home staring at the wall."

Brigitta smiled and swallowed the lump in her throat. "Yeah, he's probably planning something. Ever since he made that sword for himself, he's been trying all sorts of crazy things. You'd think he was a dragon instead of a kid."

They both chuckled softly but stopped abruptly as they both realized that the path of wax they were following suddenly left the floor, climbed up the jagged wall, and continued onto a ledge suspended at least three times above Gwen's height. The girl and the woman both frowned at the new development.

Tentatively, Gwen walked over to the rock face and ran her fingers over it. "Well, there seem to be plenty of niches in the rock. We could probably climb up it if we could find enough of them."

"I'll go up first," Brigitta volunteered. "I am lighter, and it would be easy—" Another thought struck her. "Wait, isn't there some kind of spell you could use to help us up there? It would be a lot simpler than risking broken necks."

Gwen's face fell. "I wish I could, but I feel so weak. Just keeping this light aglow is drawing on strength that I barely have." Another fit of coughing appropriately accented her words. She struggled for several moments, her entire body trembling with the exertion. "I . . . agree," she croaked out. "I think you should go first and have a look around. I'll follow close behind."

Brigitta watched the frail woman practically double over with the wracking coughs. Something terribly wrong was happening to Gwen, and she needed to get her out of here as soon as they could manage it. After quickly rubbing her hands together, Brigitta ran her hands over the wall until she found a suitable foothold. Assuring herself that the stone would hold, she hoisted herself up and onto the wall. Before long, she traversed the rock face and was out of sight.

After a few minutes without seeing or hearing anything, Gwen called up to the girl, a note of panic entering her voice. "Brigitta! What do you see? Should I come up?"

Brigitta replied with an air-rending scream.

Without a second thought, Gwen raised her hands, uttered a syllable, and shot up along the rock's face. Reaching the top, she leapt onto a surface of the precipice. She landed forcibly on her knees and stayed there. The effort drained her completely. Darkness gathered around the corners of her vision, and her head swam with dizziness. Summoning a deep-rooted resolve, she pressed her hands into the ground, attempting to propel herself forward. She managed to go only a few feet and collapsed, hitting her head against the jagged ground. Trying to shake off the bright lights clouding her vision, she reached for her last resort.

"I'm sorry, Brigitta."

Gwen muttered a soft syllable, and a faint glow appeared around her. She leapt again to her feet and dashed fearlessly down the corridor.

The tunnel closed in around her, but with a concerted effort, she managed to squeeze herself through. The tunnel then opened up, revealing a domed chamber, filled with choking, oppressive air. A smattering of primitive torches lined the wall, adding to stifling air and casting an ominous ambience. The floor stretched out for several feet, ending in a sharp drop into a pit, which took up most of the room. As she glanced about the strange room, the firelight revealed a series of maniacal scribbles, which covered almost every free space on the wall. A certain cross-like symbol dominated most of the scribbles, but she also glimpsed a variety of different scenes: rough representations of people, animals, and decrepit buildings.

Her gasp echoed throughout the chamber. On the very edge of the pit, on a slightly lowered platform lay Brigitta, asleep. Her arms and legs revealed nasty cuts as well as a ghastly gash near her left temple. She did not stir. "Brigitta," she gasped. "Wake up! It was all a trap . . . all a trap."

Brigitta still did not stir. Gwen stooped down in order to lift Brigitta off the ledge. She stopped halfway when the contents of the pit came into view. Jagged bones lined the bottom of the pit, many of them broken to expose their edges and then placed pointing upwards. This created a field of ugly spikes like the mouth of a great creature waiting to swallow its victims and cut them to shreds. She barely suppressed a scream by clamping her hand firmly over her own mouth.

What kind of monster lives here?

Shifting her whole focus to Brigitta, she stooped the rest of the way and took Brigitta in her arms. Holding her close, she detected only shallow breathing. They did not have much time. Bringing Brigitta around, she stopped and stared at the exit in frustration. Her first trip through the tunnel had given her many of her wounds, but she did not see any alternative of escape. She glanced down into the listless face of the young girl in her arms. "I can't draw on her energy again. It just might kill her if I tried."

The irony did not escape her. She had to put the girl at greater risk in order to save her. She had taken a portion of Brigitta's energy after spending her own to mount the wall, but now she regretted her choice.

She shook her head. It had been the only option. If not for that, she would be just as unconscious outside the cave, and of absolutely no help to Brigitta. She glanced again around the room. "If only there was another source of energy." Her train of thought was interrupted by a feral growl rumbling from the darkness, and in the tunnel, a pair of bright, frenzied eyes peered toward them.

Gwen felt as if those eyes penetrated right to her soul, searching for any weakness the dark creature might exploit. Raspy breathing rattled from the tunnel, echoing eerily in the enclosed chamber. Before she could raise her hands in defense, the creature pounced. Almost on a reflex, Gwen flung herself over Brigitta, shielding her from the attack. The creature's claws tore at her flesh, ripping large gashes in the back of her dress, and sending lances of pain throughout her body. She cried out in agony and tried to lash back, but she felt utterly helpless against the savage, unknowable thing from the darkness.

The creature struck again, howling like a banshee and clawing ferociously. She warded it off the best she could, but felt as if she were scraping the parched bottom of a dry well for life-giving water.

If only I had strength . . .

Suddenly, as if in answer to her pitiful plea, she felt a great surge of power well up from somewhere deep inside. She let out a great cry, not in pain this time, but in exhilaration. The call conjured up a glowing, green cage of light around the two. The creature flew back, singed by the light, and for the first time, its form came into view. The creature appeared humanlike, hunched over, and covered with an armor made entirely of bones. A mask made of an animal skull concealed the face from which the otherworldly eyes peered out. The creature growled and snarled ferociously, circling the cage of light, causing an aching Gwen to tremble in the low light.

She glanced out from the cage, gauging their situation, and pondering their good fortune. One thought kept racing through her mind, *The first axiom of magic,* she repeated to herself. *"Benevolence begets influence."* Her selfless choice to save Brigitta's life had saved them both by granting her an extra store of strength.

The creature did not take its eyes off of its victims. Realizing that it could not advance, it contented itself to pace back and forth in front of the cage, waiting with cool calculation for an opening in their defenses. Then to Gwen's surprise, the creature started to murmur and mutter, scarcely above a whisper, and in a language that she could not understand.

Concentrating her thoughts to one aim, Gwen began to mutter herself, causing a faint glow to appear between her hands. As she spoke, the glow intensified, accompanied with a low buzz, which continued to rise in pitch. Beads of perspiration formed on her wrinkled brow at the effort of weaving the incantation. The light between her hands flickered wildly, the buzz now a steady whine, growing and growing until it finally leveled off. Her hands now shook intensely as if trying to contain a volcano on the verge of erupting. She managed a terse smile and glanced toward her opponent. *I'll have at least five shots. This won't exactly be subtle . . . .*

With a single command, she dissolved the shield around her and flung three brilliant bolts of light in rapid succession at her foe. The first two flew wide of their intended target, but the third bolt grazed the creature's arm, soliciting an ear-rending shriek and a scattering of bones.

Unexpectedly, her foe countered with a spell of its own, flinging a plume of flame from his fingertips. Gwen ducked but could not prevent the flames from licking at her dress, which quickly caught fire. Panicked, she fired off two more bolts to fend off her attacker and hit the ground, rushing to extinguish the flames before they spread. Her attack bought her only a few seconds, as she ended up on her back, having very little strength remaining.

The creature took this advantage and sprung again, conjuring a trail of flames behind him. The creature gloated over his prey with fiendish glee, extracting a ghastly bone knife from his side, which blended in with the rest of its armor. With a swift kick, it turned Gwen over to face him. Raising the knife, it glared down at Gwen, its eyes smoldering with an evil blaze. "Auf Wiedersehen."

The knife shot down—Gwen's hands shot up in a last feeble gesture of defense. Much to her surprise, a brilliant flash of light accompanied the motion, catching the creature square in the chest. The knife clattered to the floor and the creature stumbled toward the edge of the precipice. *Hm . . . six shots. Maybe my memory isn't as good as I thought . . .*

With a final groan of defeat, the creature's eyes rolled back in its head and it tumbled over the edge. At the last possible second, the creature's hand latched onto Brigitta, dragging her with it into the perilous depths.

CHAPTER SEVEN

ෞ

A BRUTAL END

LONDON, ENGLAND, 1945

From the moment the man stepped into the shop, the clerk could tell that he was an American. Judging from his clean-cut appearance, he was probably a GI on leave. One word out of his mouth confirmed the clerk's suspicions.

"Excuse me, sir. I am looking for a present for my daughter. I'm on my way home from Germany, but I won't make it in time for her birthday."

Although the clerk was not usually too keen on tourists, the man's earnest brown eyes and gentle manner melted through his barrier. "I might be able to help. What does your daughter enjoy?"

The man wrinkled his brow for a second, biting at the corner of his lip. "Let's see . . . well, she is especially fond of music."

Moving swiftly among the shelves, the clerk surveyed the contents. Several times he paused, examined an item, and then placed it back on the shelf with a wag of his head. As he was almost ready to give up, he hesitated on a shelf located behind the counter. The parcel still lay there from all those months before, untouched and unopened.

For a moment, the clerk stood in indecision. He had a bad feeling about this one. Even though it was a beautiful item, it gave him a strange feeling in his gut to handle it. Especially after the way the man who had sold it to him had talked about it. However, his sale's sense finally got the best of him, and he retrieved the package from its resting place. "Here, this just might do the trick."

Pulling back the covering, the clerk presented the object to the American. The soldier's eyes suddenly grew wide, with a grin to match. "I'll take it."

ෞ

THE CANTICLE KINGDOM

The next morning dawned cold and gray. As he slowly woke, Johann realized he couldn't remember how he got to his bed. A dull ache pulsed through his body, making it very difficult to rise. He lay there for a long time after his eyes had fluttered open, staring at the warped boards that composed his ceiling. His eyes ran up and down the grain, tracing the frantic pathways aimlessly through the wood. The house was unusually silent and still, save the unpleasant sound of his mother's muffled weeping.

Exerting all his effort, Johann finally succeeded in swinging a foot over the side of the bed. Unfortunately the action of standing proved too much, and he lost his balance. He broke his fall with his elbows, which only partially absorbed the impact. Grunting in frustration, he rose slowly to a sitting position.

He attempted to walk and made it to the door. He glanced down at his arms and gasped as the strange sight met his eyes. His skin was speckled with flecks of gray, some tiny and others larger patches. Running his fingers over his arm, he found it cool, hard, and unusually stiff.

His mother's whimpering grew louder. Peeking down the stairwell, he could see her seated at the table, her face in her hands. Slowly, he crept down the stairs, taking them one at a time, careful to avoid the creaking spots he knew so well. About halfway down the stairs, he stopped cold at the sound of a man's voice.

"I'm so sorry. There wasn't much we could do once we found him. I don't know what possessed him to go there in the first place." No response from his mother—only tears. "That place is cursed, I tell you. You think he would have learned after what happened to his brother."

He heard a loud sniffle and then a tart reply from his mother. "You're not making this any easier."

The other person sounded truly penitent. "I *am* sorry. He is still alive . . . though I wouldn't count on Johann learning much more about being a blacksmith from him anytime soon. Perhaps he'd be suited for another trade—"

"Leave!" His mother spat, her voice full of venom. Johann's head reeled with realization. *What's happened to Uncle Brutus?* he wondered. At the sound of the door closing, Johann's head swirled with confusion and shame. *This is all my fault.*

Sensing his presence, his mother bolted upright from the table and stared at him as if he had woken up with blue hair. "Johann! You are all right!" she exclaimed, throwing her arms around him. "You passed out in my arms last night! I had to carry you inside and up to your bed—you were barely breathing. You kept babbling the strangest things in your sleep. I thought you had gone completely mad! And where did you get that sword?"

Johann's own eyes filled with tears, as much as he tried to keep them back. "Oh, Mother! What's happened to Uncle Brutus?"

His mother appeared as cheery as a mortician. "It doesn't look good,

Johann. He went out chasing after Brigitta and got stuck in the woods. They found him late last night in a terrible condition. It looked like he had been attacked by something with awful claws. They have him holed up in the inn, and it looks like—" Her sentence was interrupted by a burst of tears. "Oh, I can't bear it, Johann! Why must fate forever frown upon this family? Swear to me, Johann, that you will never go within a league of that awful forest. Do you hear me? There is nothing but death there."

She continued to sob into a handkerchief as Johann sat dumbfounded, unsure of how to respond. He knew he couldn't make such a promise and that something had to be done. *I've got to talk to Siegfried,* Johann thought. *He's the only one that can help me now.*

"Mother," he said softly, placing a tender hand on her shoulder. "I'd love it if you never had to cry again, and I'll do everything I can to make sure that happens. You still have Grandpa and me, and who knows? Brutus might still recover." It was the best his struggling conscience could manage.

His mother looked up, her bloodshot eyes glistening in the low light. "Ah, yes. Your grandfather. We best let him know. You'd better wake him. He'll want to go see Brutus."

Johann nodded solemnly. "He's a bit late in getting up, isn't he? He's usually a better timekeeper than our cuckoo-clock." Johann went to his grandfather's bedroom. The door lay slightly ajar, and a strange odor wafted from within. "Grandpa? Are you awake?" When no one responded, he tentatively opened the door a little farther. "Grandpa? We need to—"

Johann's knees buckled as he saw the scene within, and for the third time in a twenty-four hour period, he lost all consciousness.

When Johann finally regained his senses, it took him several minutes to comprehend the grizzly sight that lay before him. The room had been completely overturned, its contents flung about and smashed. Portions of the room had been charred black and were still smoldering, emitting an acrid smell. The floorboards and walls were streaked with blood, which appeared fresh. The old man was nowhere to be seen.

Johann blinked his eyes and tried to wrap his head around this impossibility. Surely they would have heard such a struggle. Hearing Johann stumble, his mother rushed to the door and stood silently next to her son, taking in the awful scene. "It can't be," she gasped, falling to her knees.

Johann felt as if he were dreaming. Nothing made sense. Taking his mother by the arm, he led her up to her bed and helped her lie down. Her eyes clamped shut and refused to open. Her brow was streaked with sweat, and her face was flushed. Johann stooped beside her, placing his hand on her shoulder. "Just rest, Mother. I think I know someone who can help. I'll be back."

Stopping only to retrieve his sword his mother had left by the front door, he dashed out the door and in the direction of the inn. Johann ran as quickly as his spindly legs could carry him, in spite of the stiffness of his body. The inn lay near the town center and consisted of a pub on the bottom floor and guest rooms on the other two. He flung open the front door and ran inside, startling a few patrons as he passed down the hall.

All at once, the surprised innkeeper spotted him and grabbed him by the shirt as he passed by. "Waddya doin', lad? Ye bin' chased by ghosts or somethin'? Cause if so, I hope ye shut the door behind ye."

Johann's breaths came rapidly as he attempted to explain himself. "I was . . . I just . . . I'm here . . . to see Brutus."

The innkeeper eyed him warily. "Is that so? And who exactly might ye be?"

Johann's breath slowed slightly. "I'm Johann. Brutus is my uncle."

Gradually, the innkeeper released his grip on Johann and eyed him keenly. "Ye don't say," he drawled. "In that case, we should get ye in there. He's been callin' yer name all night. That and 'Brigitta.' But I warn ye—he's not in good shape, lad. Ye best prepare yerself."

The innkeeper led Johann through the pub, up a set of stairs, and down a dimly lit hallway, the floorboards creaking in protest as they went. Finally, they halted before a decrepit wooden door. The innkeeper turned the knob, opened the door a crack, and motioned for Johann to enter.

"There ye are lad. He'll be glad to see ye." The innkeeper turned to leave down the hallway but turned at the last moment and glanced back at him. "Give me best regards to yer mother." He then disappeared down the dark stairwell.

Johann gulped and pressed gently on the door, causing it to creak open the rest of the way. The room was dimly lit, and from within, Johann could hear the sounds of shallow breathing. The room was sparsely furnished, with a simple table, a low bed, and a nightstand. His uncle's enormous girth took up most of the bed. His arms, legs, and torso were heavily bandaged. Even in the dim light, Johann could see that the damage was extensive.

Cautiously, Johann approached the bed and stood at his uncle's side, quite unsure of how to proceed. The decision, however, turned out to be out of Johann's hands. As if sensing Johann's presence, Brutus' eyes fluttered open. They smoldered softly like dying coals.

"Johann," he wheezed. "I lost her. I couldn't . . . couldn't find Brigitta. I knew I was close, but then . . . the creatures . . . they came from everywhere. I . . . . I couldn't find her!"

Johann placed a hand on Brutus's shoulder, an act that felt supremely awkward. "I know. But I'll find her. I promise."

Brutus lay silent with only his labored breathing to break the silence. "Johann," he finally managed. "There is something that I need to tell you."

Johann nodded solemnly, his guilt burning a hole in his stomach. "Yes, Uncle, there is something that I need to tell you as well."

Brutus continued without acknowledging Johann's remarks. "There is a reason we needed Brigitta last night. She was the only one who could help us on our mission."

Johann's eyes bulged out, suddenly becoming even more alert. "What mission? What are you talking about?"

Brutus breathed deeply, as if preparing himself to speak. "The kingdom is in danger, Johann, and strange as it sounds, we—our family—are the only people who can save it." Johann tried to speak but was cut off. "Johann, try to understand! I don't have much left in me! You must continue what we have started, or we'll all be made to suffer! My father will help you!"

With surprising swiftness and intensity, Brutus reached under the bed and retrieved a small stack of papers bound loosely together with string. He wasted no time in handing the book to Johann. "I have always kept this close to me. It's the record of our family's mission. We have been called to do it many times over the years, but the current queen has oppressed us to the point of near extinction." Brutus's eyes flared up momentarily. "This task must not die with me, Johann! You are the only one left that can carry on! Don't let those royal brutes win! They don't know it, but they are only stabbing themselves in the foot."

Sweat formed on Brutus's brow as his lungs heaved under immense strain. Exhausted, he sunk back on to the bed, breathing in gasps. "You'll . . . find the necessary materials in my workshop . . . go through . . ."

Johann nodded, his eyes welling up with tears. "I know, Uncle, I know."

Brutus smiled ever so slightly. "Should have known. You're too curious for your own good. You'll also need Brigitta if you want to succeed. She's the only one who can speak—" Brutus could not manage anymore. He clutched his chest, a pained expression etched into his face. "Oh, my Lady, I have failed you! I am so . . . sorry . . . ."

The last word trailed off as Brutus let out one last labored breath. His body finally lay still, the stiff muscles relaxed, and pain trickled off his face. In utter disbelief, Johann stayed on his knees gazing into space. The tears flowed silently. He had never had especially affectionate feelings for his uncle, but not in a thousand years did he wish this fate on him. There was so much Johann wanted to tell his uncle, but the chance was gone forever. As he sat there, he could feel the awful weight of responsibility crushing down on him.

"No!" he cried. "I can't do this! I don't want any of it!" The oppressive weight would not relent. His sword lay at his side on the floor, glowing with a bluish tinge in the low light. Wearily, he grasped the handle and hoisted it, standing as he did. "Brutus, I will not disappoint you." All he could do was try to make right what had happened to his family.

Reverently, Johann placed the covers over his uncle, blew out the candle, and walked silently out of the room. There was only one person in the world who would understand his plight. Unfortunately, he had no idea how to reach him.

When Johann arrived back at his house, he found his mother in almost the exact position at the table in which he had first found her that morning. As he entered the room, she looked up apprehensively, as though he was yet another bringer of bad news. As her eyes met Johann's, the question hung in the air without any words needing to be said. Dejectedly, Johann shook his head sorrowfully, avoiding her gaze.

Johann's mother's head returned to the table, her muffled sobs the only sound in the room. Johann approached his mother and tried to offer a bit of comfort, but as he stretched his hand out, his mother batted it away, indicating that she would rather be alone. Honoring her request, Johann slipped past her and up the stairs, clutching the papers from Brutus under his arm.

Collapsing on his bed, he noticed that on his nightstand sat a rounded earthenware jar about the size of his fist, painted with various colors and patterns. A solid cork sealed the opening. The jar vibrated slightly, moving back and forth on the table by its own accord. At times it hovered near the edge, but just as a plunge seemed imminent, the jar reversed its direction, buzzing off in the other direction. Perplexed, Johann rushed over to the table and picked up the jar, which continued to vibrate. As he grasped the jar, the patterns on the surface swirled and reorganized themselves into words:

> I'm a little teapot, short and stout.
> Here is my handle, here is my spout.
> When I get all steamed up hear me shout.

Johann wrinkled his brow. *What on earth was a nursery rhyme doing on the jar?* It had neither handle nor spout. Johann rolled the jar over in his hands, searching for more writing. The only legible markings he could find were the words of the nursery rhyme. Johann squinted at the writing, reading it once again. Suddenly, a thought came into his head. "The last line is missing," he muttered. "Tip me over and—"

Johann grinned at the simplicity of the clue. Wresting the cork from its place, he tipped the jar over and poured out its contents. Any other time, he might have been concerned by what his mother's reaction would be if she saw him dumping things on his floor, but in this case, he figured she had other worries that far eclipsed housework.

The last drop of liquid fell from the jar, and Johann replaced the cork. The liquid looked like water, but it congealed in a semi-circular puddle in the middle of the floor. The edges of the puddle constantly shifted, but never exceeded certain invisible boundaries. As Johann watched in amazement, vivid streaks of color passed through the liquid giving it a very pleasant and hypnotic appearance. Johann looked into the puddle and saw his own reflection. However, in the next split second, his reflection faded away to be replaced with the face of Siegfried. Johann hopped back in amazement.

"Surprised to see me, boy? I told you I would be in touch."

"Siegfried!" Johann gasped. "How . . . how is this happening?"

The face in the puddle grinned broadly. "A little transport charm. I tried contacting you earlier, but it seems you were away. I'm glad you got the clue."

Johann grimaced. "Yeah, I haven't heard that silly rhyme since I was a little boy, but it worked well enough."

The knight looked puzzled. "Aren't you still pretty young? Goodness, it's a bit difficult for us older folks to tell."

Johann smiled. "No offense taken. Just curious, how old are you anyway?"

"Two hundred and fifty-two," he proclaimed proudly, "and not a day younger."

Johann's eyebrows shot up in surprise. "That's impossible! No one lives that long! I thought if you lived to a hundred, you'd be lucky."

The knight bobbed his head. "Yes, that is the age of normal men, but this is a subject for another time." Siegfried looked up very earnestly into Johann's eyes. "I need you to tell me exactly what happened. I haven't been able to contact Brigitta."

Johann lowered his gaze. "There's a reason for that. She's been captured, and I don't know where they have taken her."

"I feared something like this might happen," Siegfried mumbled, frowning deeply. "However, the good news is that I might have an idea where she is. But first, you must tell me everything."

Johann related the events of the previous night and tried to contain his feelings when he spoke of his uncle's recent death. When he looked back at Siegfried, Johann saw that the old man's face appeared even more lined and worried than usual, his brow set in a thoughtful furrow. "This is serious, indeed," said Siegfried. "It also confirms my suspicions. Someone from within the castle took both the pendant and Brigitta, and whoever it was must know a good deal of magic. The exact location of my probe has been obscured because of all the additional magical influence surrounding it."

Johann shuddered, gazing intently into the puddle. "What are we to do then? My uncle died because of me, and who knows how long Brigitta still has? And I still don't understand this mission that my uncle conferred on me. What does this book mean? What I am supposed to do?"

The knight thought for a moment. "Open the book. What does it say?" Fingering the yellowed pages, Johann opened the book to its first page and perused the contents.

The words did not make sense to Johann. The letters still resembled the ones to which he was accustomed; however, the words themselves seemed completely foreign. Just to be certain, he thumbed through the remaining pages but found nothing but strange writing. He glanced back into the puddle in despair. "I can't read them, Siegfried! The words don't make any sense!"

The knight wasted no time in his reply. "Hold the book up to the puddle so that I can see it." Johann did as he was told, and the old knight smiled. "My intuition is two-for-two today. The book has writing in the ancient language spoken by the first queen. It's no wonder you can't read it. There are few left who can. Lucky for you, I happen to be one of them. Bring the book to me."

Johann sighed. "How? I am not going back to those woods! Enough of my family have met their end there, and I don't intend to add any to that number."

"You won't have to," came the soft reply. "I shall come meet you—but not in your house and not in the town. There are still some who seek my demise and I must remain as invisible as possible. I shall meet you under the bridge that crosses the river before it enters the forest. Make haste. I fear our time is limited."

"Yes," Johann agreed. "I'll meet you there soon." He turned to go, but then glanced back at the puddle in dismay. "Siegfried, what do I do about this puddle? My mother's at the end of her wits as it is."

The knight gestured with his hand. "Not to worry, my boy. Simply take the jar and place the opening near the puddle."

Johann followed the instructions and watched in amazement as the liquid flowed back into the jar. He replaced the cork and set the jar again on the night stand beside his bed. Picking up his sword, he fastened it to his tunic with a leather belt. Then, wordlessly, he threw open his door, ran down the stairs, and dashed out of town toward the bridge.

༄༅

Johann reached the bridge in record time. When he first arrived, he noticed no one. He stood under the bridge, thinking how recently he had been there with Brigitta. Longingly, he glanced into Brigitta's stash of loot and ammunition, seeing what she had left there. Only one bag remained, bulging from its contents. Curious, he poked his hand into the bag. Immediately, he recoiled, realizing why Brigitta had probably left this bag

untouched. It was brimming with inky blogseeds, the height of the prankster's art. Once they struck their target, they exploded in an inky, stinky,
sticky mess. Though they were potent weapons, they were also known to
backfire on their owners. Too much pressure and—

"What have you got there, boy?"

Johann jumped up suddenly, scattering the seeds across the ground. The
smell of rotten fruit assaulted his nostrils. Johann whirled around to face
Siegfried, who had appeared as if out of nowhere. Johann wrinkled his face in
consternation. "Please, don't startle me like that. I have had enough surprises
for a lifetime."

Siegfried appeared contrite. "I *am* sorry, Johann. It's true—you don't
deserve that. Do you have the book?"

Johann retrieved the book from his leather pouch, which he had slung
over his shoulder. The pages crackled under his fingers as he handed it to the
old knight.

Squinting to read the faint characters, Siegfried studied the book for several
minutes, carefully turning over the pages as he went. Several times he raised his
eyebrows and grunted softly under his breath. Johann grew restless and paced
back and forth, trying to gather the unbroken seeds back into their bag.

As he finished rounding up the seeds, the sun finally peered out from
behind the clouds, and Johann took full advantage of it. Stepping out from
under the bridge, he basked in the glow of the morning, for a moment forgetting the awful events of the previous day. He closed his eyes and thought
of his cousin's face. She had always been able to look after herself. With any
luck, she would be just fine. After what seemed like an age, Johann once
again felt a hand on his shoulder. Pivoting around, he almost tackled the old
knight. "What did I tell you about—"

Siegfried sighed and threw up his hands. "It's not my fault you have some
healthy reflexes. Come back here out of the open. This is interesting material." Johann did as he was told, following Siegfried under the bridge and as
deep into the shadows as they could manage. Once there, Siegfried sat down
and opened the book on his lap. Opening to the first page, he began to speak,
his voice low and hushed, as though he feared his voice would carry on the
wind to unscrupulous ears.

"Listen, Johann. It is written in a very old dialect, even for me, but I
think I managed to suitably decipher it." He lowered his voice even lower, his
face solemn as a church statue. "Johann, your family's work is very dangerous. I hate to burden one so young . . . ." His voice trailed off, his eyes deep
with concern. "I can help you with this task, but I won't be able to take your
place. You're the only one who can do it now."

Johann stared back, a cold chill rushing over his skin, causing his hairs to prickle. When his voice came out, it sounded brittle, as if a wisp alone would crack it. "If you think I am ready, then I'll try—that is, if I am the only one."

Siegfried brought his eyebrows together, the lines on his face becoming canyons. "Johann, you have it in you, I know, and I would not ask you if there was another. In this case, it is up to us to prevent an awful fate from overtaking the kingdom. Let me explain." He offered the page to Johann. "It says here that the fate of the kingdom is unalterably linked to the life of the queen. It is thus imperative that a new queen is found before the old queen dies. The book sets forth this process and indicates that this task is the responsibility of your bloodline: Buchmuller. There is only one way that this can be accomplished. It points to a chamber deep beneath the castle in which a new queen can be called. It sets forth a plan by which a person of this bloodline can speak the necessary words in the ancient language in order to start this process. It appears to involve a fairly complex piece of machinery, but I would have to study it more in order to understand it completely."

Siegfried stopped speaking, letting the words sink in. "Most of the book describes specific directions . . . where to go, what to do. However, the basic task is clear. We must find the route deep beneath the castle. If your uncle was worried about this enough to entrust you with this task then the time must be desperate."

Johann shook his head, trying to clear it. "I don't understand. Do you think this has something to do with the amulet? We still don't know what makes it so special."

"Not yet," muttered Siegfried, wrinkling his nose. "But we will, if we wait. In the hands of a powerful sorcerer, that pendant won't be used for philanthropic purposes, I can tell you that. I would just as well stop him before he has the chance to demonstrate what it does."

Johann clenched up his face, trying to fight back the frustrated tears. The situation grew bleaker every moment, and his new responsibility weighed on his shoulders like a ball and chain around his neck. "How are we going to do that?" blurted Johann, trying to mask the fear he felt. "Haven't you dealt with this guy before?"

Siegfried stared wistfully off into the distance. "As a matter of fact, I have. But I was much younger and more capable back then. I've been able to cheat time, although not completely, as you see. I also had more help back then. *Four* others, to be exact. Back then, we presented a formidable force."

Johann gazed up at Siegfried, hope rushing in and flooding his eyes. Perhaps they would not be alone in this after all. "Well, where are they now? Can't they help us?"

Siegfried's response dashed Johann's tender hopes. "No, they can't. One is dead, one sent himself into retirement, one betrayed us and hasn't been seen since, and the other . . . well, no one knows about the other one. I won't say he's dead, but I haven't seen him in many, many years," offered Siegfried in a hushed tone. "It wouldn't bother me so much if I only knew why."

Siegfried suddenly snapped back into the matter at hand, dismissing the old topic with a swipe of his hand. "It doesn't matter now, Johann. They cannot help us, nor can we expect help from inside the castle, as they may be in league with the enemy. We have no choice but to find a new queen ourselves."

Johann felt as if his head had been cinched between molten blacksmith's tongs. A healthy appetite for adventure and mischief was one thing, but this was real conflict. Every ounce of bravado he had ever possessed seemed to be melting out his ears. "Well, that's easy for you to say," he protested. "You're a knight! I am hardly even worthy to be called a sidekick or a pageboy. If you hadn't put that enchantment on my sword, I would be mincemeat already! I can't do this!"

The knight stared back knowingly, his gaze level as a patch of newly fallen snow. "You're right," he observed coolly. "You can't. Not yet."

Siegfried rose to his feet and glanced back toward the forest in the direction of his cottage. He beckoned to Johann with his one hand. "Come on, lad. Though I like keeping the secret, I think it's finally time for someone to learn how I manage to defy time so easily. It may be just the break we both need."

Tentatively, Johann stood but didn't follow the aged knight. "I can't. I can't go back in those woods. I'm sure it'll be the death of me!"

Siegfried stepped toward Johann and clasped the boy by the shoulders, his face a mixture of sternness and concern. "I know how you feel about the forest, Johann, but now you must swallow your fear. All hope depends on this." The knight's eyes searched his, probing deep beneath the surface. "I know I am asking a lot. I have my doubts as well. Why do you think I hide myself there all the time? There are many who seek my life, and I don't live a day without a bit of anxiety. But if I let that get the best of me, I'd be dead already."

Johann stood still, feeling oddly at ease for the first time that day. His thoughts swam around in his brain, trying to conjure a reply, when another voice, maddeningly familiar, broke the spell. "Eh, Johann! If ye don't wanna go, I'll go instead!"

Both Johann and Siegfried whirled about to see the grinning face of Bruno, his hands on his hips. He had apparently been lying low in the underbrush out of sight but had suddenly blown his cover. The knight sprung to his feet in an instant, his face suddenly brimming with fury. "Foolish little mutt! How long have you been lurking there? What have you heard?"

The boy could not have replied even if he had wanted to. At over two centuries old, the knight's face could still inspire both admiration and fear. Bruno trembled mightily, grasping desperately for words. "I . . . I 'eard it all, sir! I saw Johann 'eaded for the bridge and I . . . I followed 'im, sir. Then things got . . . interesting. You don't see him 'anging out with grown-ups much."

The lines on Siegfried's face receded as he replaced the cork on his bubbling anger. "You've heard many things you should not have been privy to. You're a common garden snake, and that doesn't impress me much. I'd just as soon go on without you, but we don't have much choice now."

Siegfried grabbed the boy by the scruff of his neck with his one enormous, gnarled hand and started off in the direction of the forest. "Come, Johann, before we discover any other unwelcome company. It seems I should teach both of you a lesson."

The three headed quickly into the forest. Siegfried glanced around nervously, suspicious that there might be additional onlookers. In a mere matter of minutes, they had plunged into the heart of the forest. Johann struggled and panted to keep up, the heavy snow quickly soaking his feet and clinging to his garments. They skirted around the clearing containing the statues and headed past the road with the fallen tree to the place where he had found Brigitta deliriously wandering around just the day before. Reaching that point, Siegfried took a moment to get his bearings and then dashed off to the east, running parallel to the spot. Abruptly, he stopped and sat a terrified Bruno down in the snow. His eyes gleamed wildly, like an animal that knows it's being pursued by a vicious predator.

"Watch the young rascal, Johann. Keep him here no matter what you do. Though, I don't see that there is much use in trying to escape. He'd never make it out of the forest without my protection."

Johann did as he was told, keeping one eye on Bruno and another on the knight's strange activities. Seeing the logic in Siegfried's words, Bruno sat still as a statue in the snow.

Siegfried now used his arm to search rapidly through the trees, looking over his shoulder every few seconds as if dreadfully concerned about pursuit. He moved frantically, obviously not finding what he sought. His chest pumped up and down with exertion, and his teeth clenched in frustration. "Has it been so long? Only a matter of days . . . ."

He mumbled frantically as he searched. As Siegfried cleared the trees away, Johann could make out a dark, smooth barrier, which stood on the other side. He could not see above or around it.

"That must be what I ran into earlier," Johann muttered to himself. He glanced around, wondering who was responsible for the barrier. He saw nothing but empty forest and Bruno, who was doing his best to impersonate a statue. He ran his hands quickly over his arms in a pitiful attempt to keep warm.

"Aha! There it is!" Siegfried's exclamation startled Johann so that he jumped and spun back around. Not even Bruno's determination to stay still prevented him from jumping in response. However, he quickly resumed his former position, the look of a condemned prisoner on his face.

The knight's efforts revealed a break in the barrier through which a brilliant white light shone. Immediately transformed from berserker to explorer, the knight beckoned to the two children. "Come Johann, follow me! You'll be safe, I promise." Siegfried then beckoned to Bruno. "You can come too, my slithery friend."

A moment later, Siegfried slipped into the crack and disappeared from view. Seeing little choice, the two children followed the knight, feeling the light envelop them as they stepped into its embrace.

Nothing prepared Johann for what he saw next. He found himself in an enormous room, which seemed to stretch out endlessly in all directions. Everything, even the gleaming floor tiles, were composed of a brilliant white. Light filled the room, nearly blinding Johann, though he could not discern a source. Bruno stood just a little way off, also staring at the strange surroundings. Without turning his head, Johann whispered just loud enough to be heard. "Bruno, are you seeing what I am? We aren't just dreaming, are we?"

Bruno did not turn either. "I think so. I ain't never seen anything so white. Ye think we landed ourselves in heaven? Maybe we're dead."

Johann shook his head slowly. "Trust me, this isn't heaven. There's no way you'd be here if it were." Johann paused, lowering his gaze. "Or me for that matter," he added

"Heh," Bruno laughed nervously. "Yer one funny bloke. Ye shoulda done shows, you know that? Where d'ya figure that old man is anyway?" It was clear from his tone that he sincerely hoped they had lost him.

Johann took several cautious steps forward. "Let's look around—he might still be here. I'll admit that this place isn't heaven, but it's better than the alternative."

CHAPTER EIGHT

ಬಌ

RECOVERED

St. Louis, Missouri, 1945

Mrs. Edison dropped what she was doing and responded quickly to the knock at the door. "That will be the package," she muttered to herself. True to her prediction, the door swung open to reveal a uniformed mail carrier, a large brown-wrapped parcel in his hands.

"Are you Mrs. Edison?" he asked courteously. Mrs. Edison nodded, taking the clipboard on which she signed her name. With a friendly nod, the mail carrier retrieved the clipboard and went on his way with a tip of his hat.

As she shut the door, Mrs. Edison grinned so broadly it almost hurt. The package arrived just in time. She was putting the finishing touches on the birthday cake, and little Kate's friends would be arriving at any minute. She heaved a sigh of relief. Mail was slow these days, and her husband had forgotten in the past, but this time he came through brilliantly.

Attempting to hide the package under the small pile of presents that was beginning to accumulate on the table, she was caught by an excited, brown-haired little girl.

"Mommy!" Kate cried. "Is that from Daddy?"

Mrs. Edison nodded knowingly. "Yes, dear. Daddy sent you a present . . . all the way from Germany!"

Little Kate let out a squeal of delight. "Let me open it now!"

ಬಌ

The Canticle Kingdom

Rufus came home and collapsed on his mattress and didn't wake until a servant entered with a tray of food the next morning. In the course of his long night, Rufus had spent very little time tending to the queen. His mind raced as he played out dark scenarios that might have befallen the queen during the night. He dashed toward her room, unceremoniously flinging the door aside.

Befuddled, Rufus gazed at the scene that met his eyes. The queen was sitting up in bed, her eyes wide open. Her face was no longer wrinkled; in fact, she appeared as if she had just awoken from a long, refreshing nap. Even her golden hair, which ran down her shoulders, looked immaculate, as if she had spent the morning in front of the mirror. As he entered the room, she smiled widely at him, causing his heart to flutter wildly. "Your Majesty, you—" He could not finish his statement for joy.

Her blue eyes glittered in the early morning light. "Yes, I am feeling much better. It is as if I have had the most hideous of nightmares. I am ravenously hungry. Would you be able to fetch me something to eat?"

Rufus nodded wildly, unable to take his gaze off of the queen. "Of course, your Grace. Is there something that you would prefer?"

She shook her head slyly, stretching her arms high above her head. "No, just about anything would do at this point. I feel like I'm going to have to learn to use my teeth again after all this time!"

More than eager to please, the chamberlain rushed out the door, his robes flaring and flapping out behind him. "Where is that blasted cook now that I need him?" he shouted to nobody in particular. Practically screaming from a mixture of pent up emotions, he made his way back toward the main kitchens. "Anything for her," he muttered under his breath.

Finding the kitchen seemed to take an age. Usually he knew the castle like his own chambers, but the shock of seeing the queen had seriously clouded his judgment. Finally stumbling into the kitchen by sheer chance, he located a cook and hurriedly barked a command. "You there! I need a plate of your tastiest fare! The queen is famished and does not want to be kept waiting!"

The command had the desired effect. The cook and several of his comrades jumped into action. Scurrying furiously, they put together an impressive plate of breads, cheeses, meats, and fruits in record time. Rufus took the completed tray from the head cook giving him a curt nod. "I would like to deliver this myself. Your help is appreciated."

Rufus's heart pounded wildly as he made his way through the corridors back to the queen's quarters. *I must be dreaming*, he thought to himself. *She was so ill just yesterday. It's nothing short of a miracle.*

He stopped for a second, out of breath. His face flushed with emotion. "I mustn't be too optimistic," he muttered out loud. "I must still be on my guard. Her descent was so sudden the first time. It could happen again." Even as he said the words, he knew that nothing could extinguish his new hope. There was still a chance that everything would work out exactly as he had planned, and the whole kingdom would be none the wiser. Regaining his breath, Rufus continued his way toward the queen's room.

He found the queen sitting up in bed. The smile on her face outshone the sunlight filtering through the open shutters. Seeing Rufus enter, she turned her gaze to him, causing his hands to sweat and his face to flush even deeper.

"Your Majesty," Rufus managed. "I have your breakfast. I hope I did not keep you waiting too long."

The queen nodded gracefully, indicating the small oak table by her bedside. "Set it down there, Rufus. It looks delicious."

Rufus started toward the bed and almost stumbled as a hard object met his path. Teetering dangerously, he struggled for balance and eventually steadied himself. To his relief, the contents of the tray remained unharmed. "A thousand pardons, your grace, I—"

He glanced down to see what had been the cause of his near disaster and wrinkled his brow in astonishment. There in the middle of the floor stood a stone cat, carved to appear in mid-step. The statue strangely resembled Camilla, the queen's personal pet. He shook his head in disbelief. The queen could be a bit pretentious at times, but this was reaching a new level. "That's a lovely piece of work you have there, your Majesty. I'll know to look out for it in the future."

She said nothing as he placed the tray on the bedside table and stepped back from the bed. The queen eyed the food hungrily and chose to start with a string of grapes. After a few bites, she turned to Rufus, who was still standing attentively, as if he wished to add another statue to the décor of the room. "Hungry as I am, there is no way that I could finish all of this. Would you care to join me?"

Of course you would! screamed the voices in his head. However, he could not form the words to comply. Instead, his insubordinate mouth came out with a dreadful substitute phrase. "No, thank you, your Majesty," he muttered, mentally cursing his spinelessness. "I have many other things to attend to in order to see that the festivities proceed on schedule. Since you are feeling better, there will be much to celebrate."

She smiled knowingly, and bit off the end of a crescent roll. "Do what you must. I shall prepare for the day, and let you know if I need your assistance." Rufus bowed quickly and took his leave of the room, his face flushed in shame. He had not the foggiest clue what it was that he actually needed to do. Suddenly, he remembered the task, which had been interrupted by the queen's call. Doing some quick calculations in his head, he selected a direction, and made off down the hall as quickly as his legs could manage.

ॐ

Cornelius sighed in relief as the queen entered his chambers. Everything was finally going according to plan. The queen was now the spectacle of health and the very epitome of beauty that she had been before. His heart seized inside of him, and he had to fight it back, reminding himself of the circumstances. He bowed deeply in reverence. "My lady, it is an honor. Have you seen the progress we have made on the preparations for the celebration?"

He gestured out the window and onto the fairgrounds behind the castle. Dozens of workers scurried about at their various tasks, erecting tents and pavilions. In the center, a massive red and white center tent already stood. The queen glanced at the progress and smiled warmly, obviously pleased. "Excellent, Cornelius. I know why I keep you around. This kingdom needs your expertise—you're truly irreplaceable!"

Cornelius nodded his head. *You have no idea,* he thought. *Now if only I could get you to think the same thing at a more personal level.*

"You flatter me," he said instead. "Remember, Majesty, your generosity makes this all possible. Is there any other way in which I may serve you, my lady?"

The queen smiled, masking the concern in her eyes. "Find out what happened to my cat. She's missing, and now all I have is a statue. I pray that it's merely a coincidence or some sort of cruel prank, but I am not sure. I do know that you're just the person to help."

So that's it. A visit over her stupid cat, Rufus seethed internally. *Why can't it ever be more than trivial matters?* However, his answer reflected none of his internal conflict. "Of course, your Grace. I'll use my means to find out what happened. In fact, I'll start right now."

He bowed again for show and scurried out of the room, barely glancing back to observe the queen. When he was sure that he was not being watched, he dashed off in the opposite direction of the queen's bedroom. He didn't know why he bothered with so much show. "Someday soon," he muttered, "people will show me the respect I deserve." He stopped cold in mid-stride, clutching his chest and wincing in pain. He placed a hand on his forehead and felt that the skin had gone clammy and cold. Lowering his hands, he noticed how much they resembled the color of freshly made bread dough. All at once, a thought struck him, and a wicked smile crossed his face. "But until then, I'll just have to pray."

CHAPTER NINE

෴

THE SPACE BETWEEN

ST. LOUIS, MISSOURI, 1945

Captain Edison drove a bit faster then usual down his residential street. Getting pulled over was the least of his concerns. He was finally going home.

Pulling up into the familiar driveway, he killed the ignition and paused for just a moment. He struggled briefly and then gave in, letting tears flow down his cheeks. Soldier or not, it was good to be home, especially in one piece.

Drying his eyes on his sleeve, he opened the door, and stepped out on to the lawn. He sauntered up to the door as if in a dream, ascended the front steps, and rapped thrice on the white front door. A flutter of footsteps approached and the door burst open, revealing a beaming Mrs. Edison in a blue, spring dress. Immediately, he caught her up in his arms and kissed her longingly.

After several tender seconds they released and gazed at each other in disbelief. It had literally been years, with no promise of safety. Mrs. Edison looked him up and down, nodding approvingly. "It looks like the army has done you some good."

He grinned wryly. "Perhaps to my waistline, but not to my heart."

He pecked her gently once again and turned his gaze to the stairs. "So, love, where's our little girl?"

Mrs. Edison grinned. "She's upstairs playing with the birthday present you got her."

Edison grinned and bounded up the stairs toward his daughter's room. A soft music floated from behind the door. Edison gripped the knob and turned.

The door swung open revealing the quaint bedroom of a little girl. A trundle bed with a canopy stood up against the wall, piled high with stuffed animals of various sorts. A hand-crafted doll-house with its tiny inhabitants stood off to one side, and on the other sat a small table with several children's books strewn across it. The wallpaper showed a tiny rose and stripe pattern very similar to the light color of the carpet.

Little Kate sat on the floor, propped up against the bed, her curls wrapping around her head like a bouquet. The door creaked open, and Kate's head popped up, her curls bouncing freely. "Daddy! You're home!"

The child leapt to her feet and bounded toward her father, embracing him with all the strength her little arms could muster. Her father held his daughter firmly, being careful not to squeeze too hard.

After several moments, they released, and Kate turned back toward the bed her hand outstretched. "Daddy, thank you for the present! You even got it here for my birthday!"

She scooped up the gift and presented it to her father who opened the lid and gazed inside. "You're welcome, sweetie! I found—"

Suddenly, the gift burst to life, vibrating and emitting a sweet mechanical music. Startled, Capt. Edison dropped the gift, which fell toward his daughter. "Kate!"

There was a blinding flash of light and total silence.

ϿʘϾ

MIDDLESPACE

The more Johann ran around the empty room, the more nothingness he saw. He firmly clamped his eyes shut, certain that staring at the whiteness any longer would drive him to complete insanity. His thoughts focused on Siegfried's face. *I'd do anything to have him show up right now. I sure don't want to be stuck here forever.*

No sooner had he thought this, then he heard a noise from behind. Cautiously, he turned around to meet the smiling face of Siegfried, seated at a table with a huge roasted drumstick in his hand. Upon seeing Johann, his face brightened. Siegfried set the meat down and beckoned for him to sit. Johann noticed a chair next to the knight that was the ideal size for a person his age.

"Johann! Good for you! I was hoping you'd find me quickly. Not that time really matters here."

Unsure of whether he was more excited to see the old man or a break in the monotonous white, it took Johann several minutes to respond. However, he eventually gathered his wits about him and joined the knight at the table. As he sat in the chair, he noticed that another plate of food was set out on the table for him. Unsure of what else to do, he dug in to the victuals. The hearty meat, bread, and cheese revived his tired body and did his heart good.

Finally, when he had consumed the last crumb, he turned his attention back to the knight, his eyes inquisitive. "What are we doing here, Siegfried? Where is 'here' anyway?"

The knight reclined in his chair, exhaling gradually. "I wish I could explain that as well as I would like. I'm not sure it really has a name, but I've taken to calling it the 'Middlespace.'"

Johann was no closer than before to understanding their plight. He glanced around the table. Beyond it lay only whiteness. The knight sighed.

"I know it will be difficult to understand, but this is my great secret. This is how I cheat time, for time has little meaning here."

Johann's eyes nearly bugged out of his head. "You mean time doesn't pass here?"

The knight shook his head. "I wish it was that simple. Let's just say that the river of time does not stand still here—it just flows much more slowly. We can spend many months here and find that only a day or two has passed back in the village. It's a very handy system."

Johann shook his head, his mind unable to comprehend what was happening. Dozens of questions tumbled around in his mind, each vying for the front of the line. He decided on one and went with it. "Why did you bring us here?"

The knight leaned back in his chair, appearing almost a different person than the frantic one he had seen in the forest. "Because it is safe, because there are few distractions, and mostly because time is something we could use a little more of at the moment. If we are to make a difference, we need a little more preparation before dashing headlong into the fire."

Johann leaned forward in his chair, listening intently to the knight's words. "How are we supposed to prepare? There's nothing around here."

"On the contrary," the knight replied. "It's a whole new world here. There's an incredible store at our fingertips, Johann. You will understand in time. As to our preparation, I plan to pass on to you everything I know. Even with such a retreat as this, I am in the twilight of my life and power. If we do succeed, it will only be enough to win one victory. We must prepare you so that you can defend the kingdom for good once I'm . . . gone."

The silence seemed even more profound in such an immense empty space. Siegfried's words thrilled Johann to his core, but at the same time they caused such terror to well up in him as he had never before experienced. Johann quickly sought to change the subject. "Is Bruno okay? I saw him at first, but I don't know where he's run off to. Then again, I didn't see you for awhile either."

Siegfried rolled his eyes. "That insolent little rooster? Yes, he is still here. However, he doesn't realize that we are here with him yet. You can't see anything here that you don't want to see. Sure, he wants to find us, but he hasn't focused enough on the fact yet."

Johann shook his head again. All this speaking in riddles was giving him a headache. Siegfried relieved Johann of the burden of speech. "Just go find him and tell him about this table. Once he wants to come and eat, he'll be able to see it just fine. Bring him back here so that we can get started. There are different rules here than those to which you are accustomed, but I think you'll catch on."

Siegfried turned back to his meal, gnawing contentedly away at the bone as if Johann no longer existed. Seeing no other alternative, Johann pushed away from the table and turned his sights on the vast whiteness all around him. He trotted away from the table and glanced around for the other boy. For what seemed like ages, he ran back and forth in various directions, calling out Bruno's name, but received no answer. Finally, he fell down on his knees, exhausted, and became as frustrated as if he were trying to find his home in a blizzard.

How did I find Siegfried in the first place? Johann thought to himself. *There has to be a way.* Then another thought struck him. He had found Siegfried not merely by thinking of him but by desiring his presence. *Could it really be that easy?* he mused. Getting to his feet, he stretched and spoke words he never imagined he would utter. "I wish Bruno was here." In an instant, Bruno appeared close by. Both boys jumped as they suddenly noticed each other.

"Waddya tryin' to do, ye blockhead! Ye scared me 'alf tuh death!"

Johann steadied his breathing and replied, his voice laced lightly with annoyance. "Be grateful it was only half. I spent forever looking for you. Just come with me, or I'll let Siegfried send you the rest of your way."

Bruno started to shake his head but changed his mind. The utter nothingness of the room was enough to drive any rational man to the brink of insanity. "Fair enough," he conceded. "Show me the way."

Johann wrinkled his brow in concentration. It was difficult to explain a system that he did not understand. "It's not that easy," Johann began. "Things work a little funny around here. I found him the first time by wishing I could see him. It's hard to believe, but I found you in the same way. If I understand correctly, we might as well not move an inch. If we both wish to see him—that should be enough."

At first, Bruno wrinkled his nose at such an absurd notion. However, as he glanced around at the vast nothingness, he apparently conceded that perhaps it would be better to try Johann's suggestion than waste the rest of his life insisting that Johann was crazy. He clasped his eyes shut, muttering to himself. "I sure hope you're right, because if this is some sort of stupid joke, I'll—"

"You'll what?" interjected another voice. "Challenge him to a duel? What a splendid notion!"

Bruno's muscles tensed as something sharp crept up the back of his neck. He turned slowly to face the knight, who in turn lowered his sword, not intent on doing any real harm. The scrawny boy gulped, his face a mixture of rage and annoyance. "Why ya gotta sneak up on a bloke like that? This place is already creepy enough as it is!"

The knight gave no reply, but gestured to the table, which had also reappeared. "Eat up. You'll need your strength. I'd like to get started right away."

Bruno started to protest, but the sight of the food overcame any other urges. He swiftly sat himself down at the table and began devouring the food set before him. Johann's attention, however, rested on the sword, which Siegfried had used to frighten Bruno. In every way, it appeared exactly like his own, except for one detail—the blade was black. In all the months at his uncle's smith, he had never seen such a strange, ominous-looking metal, and the thought caused his full stomach to spin. He decided it was best to simply let Siegfried explain the blade when the time came.

Siegfried looked on in silence until Bruno had licked his plate spotlessly clean. The boy examined it carefully, making sure there weren't any spare crumbs he might have missed.

"Enough," Siegfried barked, a hint of annoyance in his voice. "You'll get more later, you greedy little grub. Stand up and take your place."

As the boy stood, the table and chairs vanished, causing Bruno to jump. In their place appeared a raised platform surrounded by a rope barrier. Bruno took a tenuous step onto the platform and found that it conformed to the shape of his foot. Johann followed suit, still very confused about what was going on. Siegfried cleared his throat. "Here we shall begin your training. If we are to be of use to this kingdom, we cannot do so in our present state. Johann, you will use your sword, and Bruno will use this one."

He handed the black blade to Bruno, who took it with shaking hands. When he managed to speak, it came out trembling. "Waddya think yer doin'? I'll kill 'im with this thing, or he'll—"

Siegfried cut him off. "The second part of that sentence would be much more probable, but lucky for you, there will be no killing on my watch. I have enchanted these swords so that they will do no harm. Now raise your swords, and I will guide you."

Both boys did as they were instructed, nervous grins on their faces. At a gesture from Siegfried, they stepped toward each other and swung their swords up briskly to meet each other. They met with a loud clang, and a small flurry of blue sparks. They sparred on, leaping around clumsily and swinging around their swords haphazardly. Often they caught each other on the arms or legs with their swords, which, true to Siegfried's word, did no damage to their skin or clothing. The fight, however, was not completely fair. Bruno's style of fighting reflected his underhandedness, often resorting to trickery and striking Johann when he did not expect it. However, Johann had a slight advantage in his agility, which allowed him to easily skirt away from many of Bruno's blows.

From the sidelines, Siegfried uttered subtle commands, speaking to one boy and then to the other. Before long, their brows swam with sweat and their muscles lagged under the exertion. At last they could take it no longer, and they collapsed nearly simultaneously on the soft surface of the platform. Their chests heaved like tiny bellows, giving the only sound to the bleak environment.

"Not bad," muttered the old knight. "You're better than I thought. Still, it's a good thing we have a literal lifetime for you two to improve." He beckoned to two small chairs, which had appeared next to him. "Come and sit. Best to train both the body and the mind. You need to know what we are up against and why."

The two boys gratefully collapsed in the chairs, content to sit still and absorb the old knight's words.

Quietly clearing his throat, the knight began. "Like I told you earlier, Johann, our kingdom has always been ruled by queens because it was a powerful woman who founded our kingdom. The very prosperity and survival of the kingdom is said to rely upon the health and life of the queen. Thus, when a queen begins to age, or falls ill, it is necessary that a replacement be found before she dies, or great evil will befall the kingdom. Since the queen has always been replaced, no one is sure exactly what would happen, but it is recorded that the death of a queen would cause this kingdom to cease to exist."

He let the gravity of his words hang in the air. Though slumped haphazardly on his seat, Johann still gave the knight his rapt attention, while Bruno, who was also slumped deep in his chair, bordered on sleep.

"During the reign of the first queen, the kingdom was attacked by a horrible dragon-like creature with two heads. One head spat poison, and the other spewed flames. There was also the issue of its fearsome claws and teeth. The knights of the kingdom could do little against the threat until a stranger appeared one day from the forest. Instead of running from the beast, the stranger confronted it, and with the help of powerful magic, he slew it.

"The queen was so grateful that she gave the man a high position next to her in the palace, even adopted the man as her own son. He continued to defend the kingdom with his mighty spells and became beloved of the people. However, the queen developed a grave illness and fell into a deep sleep. No one could wake her, and this stranger claimed the kingdom for himself. Many of the people did not accept his rule, and a bitter conflict ensued between those loyal to this wizard and those loyal to the queen. Many lost their lives in the conflict, but eventually the wizard and his forces were driven back by another powerful wizard. This was the beginning of the dark wizard, who fancied himself the 'Many-Named One.' For although he was thought to be dead, he returned time and time again, always in a different form and under a different name so that people did not recognize him until it was too late. He has appeared during the reign of every queen, and always, the people have defeated him. But he always comes back, each time more powerful."

Johann glanced up, worry flooding his eyes. "So he's back again, stronger than he was the last time? How do we even know he can be defeated again? How did they do it last time?"

The knight gazed into the vast nothingness, his gaze blanker than his surroundings. He sat there for some time, saying nothing. Suddenly a quiet rattling sounded from somewhere on Siegfried's person, breaking the silence. Startled, he felt around on his belt with his arm, trying to determine the source. Just as quickly, the buzzing ceased. Siegfried rose to his feet, and finally gave an answer. "That is a topic for another time. Suffice it to say that it is fitting, Johann, that you are to take part in this endeavor because it has always been your family's concern. Now, you two need some proper rest. Sleep as long as you want, and then find me again. Remember, whatever you wish to find here will be granted, but be careful what you wish for—it is all an illusion. The chairs, the fighting ring, the very food you eat, will only sustain you as long as you are here in Middlespace. You cannot take anything away."

Suddenly, Siegfried vanished, as if he too were just an illusion. The boys were too exhausted to care. Johann glanced up first and looked around. "Well, I'll like nothing more right now than to sleep in my own bed." He had barely finished the words when a bed appeared before him, which appeared exactly like his own. Delighted, he slipped under the blanket and closed his eyes. "Ah," he sighed. "If this is an illusion, maybe I've never known reality . . . ." Before he could follow the train of thought any further, Johann fell into a fitful sleep.

Though his body and mind were completely exhausted, he had terrible trouble staying asleep for longer than a few minutes. The complete absence of sound or smells made even his own bed seem foreign. At least back at home, he had the music of the crickets and owls to fall asleep to, but here, even a single cricket would have sounded like a symphony. The Middlespace, as Siegfried called it, was neither light nor dark, which disturbed him even further.

He experimented with the system and eventually found working solutions to most of his problems. First, he wished for a large, dark canopy over his bed, which cast a deep shadow that helped his body acclimate. Next, he wished for crickets, which first turned out to be quite uncomfortable as they appeared in his bed instead of outside of it. However, he quickly changed the image in his mind to have the crickets jumping around outside of the canopy, which at least brought some of the familiar sounds back to him.

Johann finally decided that he could live without the smell of his own room and was drifting off to sleep when the dark curtains surrounding his bed parted and Siegfried's face poked in. "Johann, I'm sorry to disturb you, but I need to talk to you while Bruno is still sleeping."

At mentioning Bruno's name, another bed appeared a way off emitting the most obnoxious snoring sounds imaginable. Johann covered his ears in protest. "That's only so we can keep an eye on him," Siegfried whispered. "If the snoring stops, then we'll know to be careful."

His face suddenly turned stern, as if he had come to Johann bearing a very unpleasant message. "Johann, I have come here to answer your question, but I didn't want Brute-o to hear. I told you earlier that I was part of a group of five knights. It is we who have driven off the dark wizard every time he has appeared in the kingdom. We all trained to become brilliant mages ourselves, and with our combined force, we were always able to stand against him. However, after this last time, we were irrevocably scattered, and now the dark wizard comes to us in yet another form. I fear that alone, I will be unable to bring him to bay, but it was not by chance that I met you so recently, Johann. You see, two of my companions were brothers—one was named Brutus and the other . . . ," he hesitated, a strange streak of emotion creeping in to his voice. "The other was called Wilhelm."

As Johann took in the words, all thoughts of sleep suddenly left his eyes. When he attempted to speak, he stuttered slightly. "Th–that's my uncle's name, and . . . my father's."

Siegfried nodded gravely. "Yes, and not by coincidence either. We were all born in the ancient times when the kingdom was first formed and made a covenant after the first attack to live here in seclusion as long as we were able in order to defend the kingdom. For hundreds of years, we were true to this oath, but time and fate have finally caught up to us, and I believe the time has come for others to take our place."

The implications of this were not lost on Johann, and his curiosity plagued him even more. The pieces did not yet fit snugly in his mind. "I don't see how that could be," started Johann. "I remember my father when I was growing up. He lived with us! And my uncle, what about him?"

The lines on Siegfried's face drew in and deepened. "That is the part that I most regret. After we had driven the dark wizard away during the time of Queen Ellis, we had reason to believe that we had gotten rid of him for good. We decided that we needed to make sure that we each had a family, so that we could have children to whom we could pass on our responsibility. We decided, however, that it would not be prudent that all of us should leave the Middlespace at the same time. I was the first to go. I eventually produced an heir and was living happily. However, true to my word, I returned here, leaving my child in the care of my wife."

He paused and sighed deeply, as if pausing to reflect. "She understood, but of course, it was—" his voice petered off, the pain in his eyes growing intense. "Anyway, the other four left in turn, but to my dismay, they never came back. After weeks of silence, they contacted me with dire news: the peace in the kingdom had been shattered. The current queen was gone, and a new queen had risen up to assume the throne. The only problem was that the new queen was little more than a child, so the old queen's counselors had gripped control of the kingdom, in the name of the queen. The people revolted and were brutally crushed by royal troops. Thinking that this might be the work of the Many-Named One, I made the decision to leave this place and join my comrades in the fight. However, for the first time, our group took different sides in the conflict. Your father, our captain, and I took up arms on the side of the people, and your uncle and his friend took up arms for the new queen. Thus divided, the conflict turned incredibly bloody."

His voice rose, the indignation flaring up in his tone. "In the course of the fighting, my child was captured, my wife murdered, and I was severely wounded. I barely escaped a burning building with my life. I had no choice but to return to the Middlespace. The queen's troops succeeded in taking control of the kingdom, and her ruthless counselors ruled in her name for years. I waited in vain for the others to return. I might have forgiven the wayward two for their lapse in judgment if they had just come back. Not even your father returned, and the curiosity burned at me day by day, driving me insane. At length, I decided to return briefly to the other world. I set up base in the forest because I knew that only the very foolish would find me there. I set out among the people, finding out what I needed to know."

His face calmed and his shoulders relaxed, as if rolling off a great burden. "Your uncle married, even had a little daughter, but then his wife mysteriously died, and he became more bitter than he had been before. The other man also had a son," muttered Siegfried, adding the sentence under his breath as if he spoke with a rancid taste in his mouth. "And your father . . . decided to stay with you and your mother."

Johann stared at the knight, looking sick, as though trying to stuff another course into an already full stomach. Tiny beads of sweat broke his brow as his brain strained to assimilate the overload of information. However, he could not stay silent for the question, which nagged at the forefront of his mind. "Siegfried, what happened to my father?"

Siegfried's face did not portray any emotion. "The fox, Johann, the agent of the dark wizard whom you faced in the garden. Your father was betrayed to him and murdered at his hands." Siegfried paused only for a moment and then continued, the words spilling out as if bursting over a punctured dam. "He was betrayed by the fifth of our number. You notice that I do not speak his name . . . I cannot bring myself to do it."

Johann had tried to remain outwardly impassive during the awful story, but now could restrain his emotions no longer. He collapsed in a fit of bitter tears, icy with loss and fiery with rage. "Who is this man who betrayed my father? Tell me!" The boy's face flushed bright with rage as the memories of his mother's grieving face flooded his mind. The loss of her husband had been the start of a lifetime of grief, and she had often told Johann that she could trace all her misfortunes back to that time.

The knight shook his head solemnly, his eyes glistening. "I wish that I could tell you, Johann. Sadly, I cannot. He has chosen exile." Siegfried rose. "I think that is enough for now. Try to get some sleep." Siegfried turned and walked away, his body seeming to dissolve into the surrounding whiteness.

Once again, it took Johann a long time to get back to sleep. He sat up digesting the strange story, which had so recently become *his* story. When he finally slept, it was fitful at best, and when he woke, he had the strangest sense of disorientation. He could not remember where he was, what day or time it was, and for an awful instant, who he was.

As he lay there, his memories trickled back to him, condensing on the sides of his mind. His thoughts pooled, coming to only one conclusion: *I want revenge, Father! I will find him! I will avenge you!*

Johann's thoughts continued to darken. He tried to put these thoughts away, but his rage and need for vengeance consumed his thoughts. *I will become strong! I will punish the traitor!*

Johann leapt from the bed, grabbing his sword, stabbing out into the darkness. The sword found its mark. Johann gasped, his nerves and brain frozen. The end of his blade protruded out of a man's armored chest, a thin rivulet of blood dripping from the wound. A deathly silence prevailed. Pain-fully slowly, the man's eyes rolled back in his head, and he slumped back onto the ground, where he lay very still. Johann glanced down at the body with dread. The armor looked only too familiar.

His mind raced so fast that he could not think clearly. A cold sweat trick-led down his brow as warm tears flooded down his face. No amount of water, however, could wash away the building shame.

Forcing his joints to work, Johann plodded over and knelt down next to the body, and immediately noticed something that again made his heart leap: the man's face was completely foreign to him. Johann gained some relief as he noticed that the man had both of his arms. Johann's heart pounded a drum roll in his chest. "If you're not Siegfried, who are you?"

The questioned remained unanswered. As Johann stared down at him, the stranger faded away into the whiteness around him, as if the man had been no more than a chalk outline swept away by a restless wind. Johann gawked in disbelief as the man melted away, leaving only his sword sticking out of the ground, the blade spotless.

CHAPTER TEN

⁊℧

IN A STEW

St. Louis, Missouri, 1945

When Capt. Edison awoke, he lay on his back staring up listlessly at the ceiling fan in his daughter's room. The room was silent, and a slight chill raised goose bumps on his arms. He sat up slowly and surveyed the room. There was no sign of his daughter.

"Kate," his voice came out gravely. Clearing his throat, he tried again calling his daughter. "Kate . . . are you there?"

Capt. Edison sat up and found his muscles were a bit stiff. The music box still lay on the floor right where he dropped it. The top of the lid now bore a nasty crack, scarring the artistically carved surface.

Picking up the gift, Capt. Edison turned it over in his hands. The rest of the box seemed to be intact. Flipping it over, he noticed an inscription. He could barely make it out due to the ravages of time, but as he squinted, the letters became clear.

> J. und K. Müller
> Frankfurt, Deutschland

Germany, *he thought.* I thought this thing was from England!
A bit disgusted, he tossed the gift down a bit harshly.
I've had enough of Germany for one lifetime.

⁊℧

Several hours passed, and there was still no sign of the girl. Mrs. Edison checked all her favorite places, and Capt. Edison even organized a search party to scour the neighborhood.

In despair, both parents returned home. Capt. Edison again related the strange tale to his wife, and once again, nothing made sense. Their joyful reunion had been grotesquely interrupted by this sudden separation.

Suddenly, Edison shot upright on the couch, a fresh, but daring idea creeping into his head. "We're going to Germany," *he stated coolly.*

His wife looked at him as though he had declared himself a space alien. "What? At a time like this? Why on earth would we want to go there?"

Edison furrowed his brow. "Because," he continued, "that is where that . . . thing is from. I know that box has something to do with Kate's disappearance! I found the names of the manufacturers on the bottom, and it says that they live in Frankfurt, Germany!"

Mrs. Edison wasn't convinced "Well . . . couldn't we just give them a call?"

Edison shook his head. "I don't think so. I would bet my purple heart they'll try to evade us. Who even knows if they have phone lines up again? I have a sneaking suspicion that we're not the only ones with this problem."

Mrs. Edison sighed, worry lines marring her youthful face. "So, when do we leave?"

Soon, *he thought.* We can't leave soon enough.

ෲ

THE CANTICLE KINGDOM

Gwen's eyes welled up with tears as she imagined the poor little girl's horrible fate, despite all of Gwen's best efforts to protect her. How long would it be before a similar fate befell her?

"Brigitta." Her whisper grew into a cry which escalated into hysterical sobs, echoing off the smooth walls in an eerie crescendo. Gwen conjured up a globe of light to see into the pit. The bleached bones shone even more grotesquely than before, but with the help of her light, she noticed a ledge protruding from the wall of the pit. On the ledge lay Brigitta, unconscious, or worse. Gwen's heart leapt in her chest. There was no way to tell whether or not Brigitta had survived the fall, or whether the danger had past, even if she did survive.

With no thought for her own safety, Gwen hoisted herself over the edge and found a foothold on the side of the pit. As quickly as she dared, she lowered herself down, swiftly losing control of her decent. Picking up speed, she landed hard on both feet, her knees instantly buckling on impact. Dual spikes of pain shot through her legs, causing tears to well near the surface. She fought them back and crept over to Brigitta, hoping to ascertain her condition. Pressing her face close to Brigitta's, she detected a faint breath, though barely enough to allow Gwen to cling to hope.

Suddenly, Brigitta shot upright, as if awakened from some hideous dream, only to find an even more hideous reality. "Gwen! Gwen, where are you?" Brigitta cried into the darkness, her voice drenched in panic.

Gwen caught Brigitta's arm and whispered in a soothing tone. "Don't worry. I'm here. That awful thing is gone now." Gwen sat herself down next to Brigitta, carefully wiping away newly forming tears.

Brigitta nodded silently, still trying to contain her feelings. She didn't cry often, but when she did the floodgates held nothing back. Still trembling slightly, she hid her face in her hands. "What are we going to do now?" she cried. "We're stuck down here in this nasty, old pit with no hope of a way out!" Her voice trailed off in sobs, and Gwen put her arms around the girl in a protective embrace. She sighed and cast a long look around the pit.

"There, there. You're not entirely right about that."

Brigitta sniffed and looked up quizzically at the older woman. "What?" she mumbled, her nose still stuffy.

"There *is* a way out."

Brigitta's eyes widened, glistening with a faint flicker of hope. "There is? You mean back up there?"

Gwen shook her head. "Can you see the tunnel?" Brigitta had to squint in order to see, but at last, she could make out the silhouette of where the passage continued, barely visible against the rest of the wall. She might not have been able to see it at all had it not been for the wisps of vapor which trailed around the outside.

With what little strength she had, Gwen lifted Brigitta, and they made their careful way toward the tunnel, doing their best to avoid the jagged bits of bone and rock that hindered their way and the noxious odor that permeated the cavern. Gwen did not hesitate when she reached the cavern, scarcely able to imagine that it contained any dangers more perilous than those they had already faced.

Gwen had to slump over in order to make her way through the narrow space, and thus they progressed very slowly. However, eventually she caught a glimpse of a faint glow ahead, not of sunlight, but light nonetheless. She continued with increased determination, though she could feel her feet cracking and bruising on the rough terrain. To her delight, she found that although the tunnel ended in an abrupt ascent, metal rungs jutted out of the wall, creating a rudimentary ladder.

"Brigitta, do you think that you could put your arms around my neck?" The weary girl nodded, but just then, they heard voices close by. At the sound, Gwen slunk back into the shadows, staying as close as she dared in order to hear the conversation.

The coarse voices came from two thickly accented men, who, luckily for Gwen and Brigitta, made no effort to keep quiet. The first man's voice sounded much deeper and about as intelligent as a wild boar. The second voice sounded higher with a touch of disdain in every sentence. Both men sounded muffled, as though they were speaking behind masks.

"I'm so bored," the first man complained. "When are we finally going to get to flip the switch? I swear, my finger's been itchin' for weeks!"

There was a dull crack, like the slap on the back of the wrist.

"You idiot," the second man hissed. "You flip that switch before its time, and the boss'll have your hide. You've got the patience of a teapot."

"I wouldn't really do it," the first man said, his pride injured. "It's just that this all seems kinda silly. Why do you think it doesn't work on kids?"

The second man paused briefly. "How the blazes should I know? I'm amazed that you even need that mask with your mentality! Then again, you forget things often enough as it is anyway, so who would know the difference?" The first man did not reply. A deep sigh echoed down the tunnel. "Come on, *dummkopf*, let's go. The tank's full, and so now we've got to check up on the old man . . . or did you forget that too?"

"No, sir!" came the swift reply. "That's my favorite part of the day! I love to see him sweat when I put on my menacing face. Maybe he'll get done tonight, and the boss won't need him anymore."

The second man sighed again, and Gwen could imagine the accompanying eye roll. The second man muttered sarcastically as their footsteps trailed away from the tunnel. "Sure, Hans, sure. Maybe. Let's go."

The footsteps grew fainter and disappeared. For the first time, Gwen became aware of a low hum like the constant grinding of a mill. Gathering her wits about her, she made sure Brigitta was secure on her back and hoisted herself up the ladder and into the room above.

An immediate blast of heat struck her face as they entered the room, and she nearly gagged from the humidity. The hot, acrid air flowed around her, and she felt suddenly dizzy as she tried to take in her surroundings. She turned around to determine the source of the wind and stood rooted to the spot, struck dumb by the sight that met her eyes.

An immense cauldron of sickly green liquid rose, bubbled, and roiled in the pit beneath Gwen. A roaring fire sent the fumes leaping from the cauldron. Behind the cauldron, an immense turning blade provided a hefty wind, which blew the fumes toward the opposite wall. Gwen turned around and glimpsed the opposite wall, which was riddled with tunnels and passageways into which the fumes vented.

As ominous as the first cauldron appeared, another detail caused her even more discomfort. In front of the first cauldron, slightly lower in the pit, lay a second cauldron full of black ooze, completely placid as if it had been a mirror. She had no idea as to what the cauldrons contained, but the very sight of them caused her to shudder.

Gently, Gwen propped Brigitta up against a boulder in such a way that it shielded her from the onslaught of the fan and the light. She walked away, looked back, and found the hiding spot completely satisfactory. She then glanced around cautiously to make sure that the two oafs had left and that there were no other prying eyes. Once she had assured herself, she made her way toward the exit on the other side of the room: a sleek metal door full of etchings, runes, and figures that she did not understand.

Holding her breath, she crept toward the door and gently slid it open a crack. Beyond the door lay a deserted hallway, which gave her courage to venture on slightly. She pushed the door the rest of the way open so that she could still keep an eye on the room Brigitta was in for as long as possible. Reaching the end of the hallway and turning the corner, she set herself up for her second big surprise of the day. Beyond the initial hallway, the passageway was completely framed out of mirrors, including the floor, ceiling, and all of the walls. The passageway immediately forked out in a wide spread of different smaller passageways with no indication where any of them went. Gwen groaned in frustration. They had escaped the cage only to be stuck in a maze.

Sighing deeply to herself, she returned to the fan room and checked on Brigitta. Slumping into the shadows next to her, she laid one hand gently on her forehead. "Well, my friend, it looks like we are not out of the woods yet. Then again, I'd take anything after that awful cave. At least if something wants to attack me here, it can't creep up on us in the darkness. Are you feeling any better?"

Brigitta gave no reply, but instead stayed fast asleep with only the slightest sound of snoring. Gwen sighed again. "I suppose I ought to get some rest too," she mused, chewing her lip slightly, "though that snoring might give us away." She ran her hands through her hair a few times, and stared off into space, when an idea dawned on her. "To think I can't recall my own name, but somehow I can manage a charm to quiet snoring. I hope I have enough for one more spell."

She muttered the charm softly, and with it, expended the last of her strength. She slumped to the floor and joined Brigitta in the blissful respite of slumber.

CHAPTER ELEVEN

ಌಌ

BROKEN SANCTUARY

THE CANTICLE KINGDOM

A flushed-faced pageboy burst into the room, causing Rufus to drop the cup he held loosely in his left hand. The pageboy saw the mess and offered to help while he managed a breathless explanation.

"Disturbance . . . down . . . in the chapel!"

Rufus only caught about every third word that the boy said. He helped the boy mop up the rest of the spilled beverage with a towel and placed a hand on the boy's shoulder. "Take it easy, boy! There's plenty of air in here. Take a few deep breaths and tell me—slowly—what's going on!"

The boy did as he was told and did not speak again until his breathing resumed a more normal pattern. "Sir, one of the knights sent me up to warn you! There's some sort of disturbance in the chapel! He said something about a hideous creature! We should alert the rest of the guard!"

Rufus sprang to life and bounded toward his window. There he found a thick rope made of deep red chords. With a mighty tug, the bells attached to the end of the ropes swung madly, alerting the rest of the castle guard to assemble immediately in the courtyard. He dashed over to the adjoining wall and yanked down his own sword. He paused a moment to consider the weapon, gripping it firmly. It seemed to endue him with energy, creeping up from his arm and spreading throughout his body. "I wonder if I still have it in me. The sword is strong, but I—"

Suddenly snapping back to his senses, he sheathed the sword at his side and dashed out into the hall. His robes billowed out behind him as he pumped his feet up and down like rapid drumbeats. As suddenly as the flurry of motion began, it halted, held back by a delicate hand. The queen stood before him, her eyes pleading, and her expression etched with deep concern. "Rufus! Thank goodness you're here! You *can* take care of this, can't you?"

Her hand lighted like a wisp of mist on Rufus's shoulder. A chill spread through his body, causing him to turn suddenly rigid. Facing soldiers and demons was one thing, but a lovely queen? He nodded dumbly.

The queen smiled brilliantly, drawing him deeper into her spell. "Wonderful. You'll never be a poet, but that's not why I keep you around."

Her voice trailed off, and, try as he might, Rufus could not take his eyes off the queen. Without warning, she turned away without another word and disappeared around the corner. He stood rooted to his place, his mind reeling. *She's never looked at me like that before . . . .*

Again, Rufus found himself struggling to regain his focus. He could not help but think how in the course of a single day, his world had turned completely upside down.

As Rufus reached the chapel, the main body of the castle guard had already arrived and was engaged in a fierce melee. Most of the pews were overturned or swept aside, and the priceless stained-glass windows were shattered.

A hideous creature circled the altar like a demonic predator gloating over its fallen prey. It had the general appearance of a lion, but instead of a mane, there was an awful mass of writhing snakes, growing out of its head as though transplanted from Medusa herself. The creature's fur gleamed ebony in the light that filtered through what was left of the windows. Several of the guards lay wounded on the floor, pieces of their armor smashed as if it had been no thicker than that of a water pail. The remainder of the guard hovered near the back of the room, trying to regroup and organize another attack.

The creature roared, accompanied by a chorus of hissing from his serpent crown. Rufus raised his sword to attack and was immediately struck down by one of his fellow soldiers. "Stay low!" the soldier yelled. "Those snakes spit venom! The creature nearly got you with that last blast!"

Rufus turned around and saw the soldier's words to be true. A dripping mass of purple and green venom oozed off the back wall where he had been standing only moments before.

Rufus nodded at the guard. "What are our options? Any other surprises I should know about? It doesn't breathe fire, does it?"

The solider shook his head and hunched lower. "No, it doesn't breathe fire. It's just nasty—and resilient. Arrows don't do much, and our swords have been largely ineffective. There has to be something we have not tried."

Rufus mused for several seconds, looking around the room. From his position on the floor, he noticed something glinting a few feet away. Sliding himself along the floor, he reached out his hand and grasped a large pane of glass, careful not to cut himself. He shot a glance back at the soldier who stared back in confusion. Rufus smiled reassuringly and mouthed the words, "Trust me."

The beast seemed preoccupied with spitting poison at as many soldiers as possible, and therefore, it did not notice Rufus as he slunk around the side of the chapel, clutching the pane of glass in front of his face.

From behind an overturned pew, he considered the creature. Gathering his wits, he counted to three and then leapt up from his hiding place with a powerful cry. *For you, your Majesty*, he thought, picturing her lovely image in his mind.

The creature reacted quickly, swiveling around and unleashing a deadly barrage of poison. As planned, the pane of glass halted the poison, causing it to slide noxiously down the front. Undeterred, the creature shot more slime in Rufus's direction, which again bounced harmlessly off the pane. Furious at its failure, the creature reared back on its hind legs and pounced toward Rufus, intent on rending him limb from limb. Rufus quickly parried the attack, jumping aside and slashing out with his sword as the creature passed. He managed to clip the creature ever so slightly, provoking its anger even more. The creature turned its attention solely toward Rufus.

Rufus darted nimbly around the creature, making sure to keep his distance. Occasionally, he seized the opportunity to sting the creature with the end of his blade, but he always quickly retreated, not causing any major damage. His own nimbleness surprised even Rufus—he felt young again, alive, full of fire, and more than a little reckless.

Imagining himself to have the upper hand, he did not count on his opponent changing tactics. The creature reared back to make another assault with poison, and Rufus raised his makeshift shield to counter the attack. At the last second, however, the creature instead swung its mighty paw at a statuette lying on the ground, sending a projectile careening toward Rufus. His makeshift shield was no match for the attack, and it shattered into a shimmering rain of razor shards. The shock and force of the attack left Rufus on his back, his face stinging from the embedded glass shards. His vision blurred, and as it cleared, he saw the grotesque visage of the creature glowering down at him, savoring its hard-earned victory. The serpents bared their fangs, threatening to strike at a moment's notice. Waves of rancid breath wafted over Rufus, sending his consciousness teetering perilously close to the edge.

With his one free hand, he groped the ground around him in a desperate attempt to make a last minute counter attack. *My queen . . . I've failed you . . . .*

The creature reared up on its hind legs and struck, descending like a plummeting comet. In the same instant, Rufus's hand shot up, stabbing the creature in mid-strike. A jagged shard of poison-stained glass protruded from the center of the creature's heart.

Rufus still clutched the end of the shard and pressed with all his might, driving the shard more deeply into its mark. Having given all his effort, Rufus collapsed, his bloodied face streaked with agony and triumph.

The creature staggered backwards several steps, growling slightly as it first teetered and then fell hard on the stones, its eyes rolling back in its head. The snakes around the creature's head twitched and writhed for several seconds more, and then, one by one, they fell limp and still.

The rest of the guard immediately rushed Rufus to the medical wing, where three nurses administered to his wounds. It was rumored that they had been tutored by Cornelius, and therefore mixed magic with medicine. Working constantly for several hours, they successfully bound up Rufus's wounds and prescribed several days of bed rest to recuperate.

Rufus lay in the darkness of his room, going over the battle in his mind. He was afraid to look into the mirror, anxious of what he might see. The nurses had tried to conceal their shock, but he could see it in their eyes—he would be scarred forever. He let his breath out in a long steady stream. *At least I did not disappoint my queen,* Rufus thought. *I think I would rather be dead than disgrace her.*

The nurses had ordered him to sleep, but he had little luck obeying. The cruel beast still haunted his subconscious. He saw it whenever he closed his eyes, still reaching for him, trying to take revenge on what Rufus had snatched from it. Rufus tried to replace these images with more pleasant thoughts, particularly those of the queen. Rufus finally drifted off to a nightmare-filled sleep, although it was not the creature, but another terror that haunted his dreams.

Rufus found himself dashing along a damp street in the evening, smoke in the air and fires leaping from nearly every window. His hand clutched a sword, and he carried a bow strung over his shoulder. Other men dressed in mail dashed around him hollering and beckoning after him. One who wore a particularly fancy suit of armor turned directly to him. "Come, this way! I saw him flee into that building! We have him now!"

Instinctively, he followed the man into a burning two-story brick building. The other man looked about frantically, as if searching for something extremely important. Finding nothing, he turned to Rufus and yelled at him above the roar of the blaze. "We can't let him escape now that we've got him cornered! You check upstairs and I'll finish down here. You know what to do when you find him!"

Obediently, Rufus unslung his bow and drew an arrow from his quiver. As if in a trance, he bounded up the stairs, flames licking at his heels, smoke curling up and choking his breath. At the top of the stairs, he came to a door, which lay slightly ajar. With a mighty shove, he slammed the door open and immediately sensed movement in the room beyond. Barely stopping to think, and running out of air, he cocked the arrow and took aim toward the sound.

Deliberately, he pulled the string back, closed his eyes, and—

A gentle rapping on the door roused Rufus from his fitful sleep. He shot upright in bed, his forehead dripping with icy sweat. After composing himself, he called for the visitor to enter. The door swung open, and the Captain of the Guard stepped in. The Captain was a tall, yet stocky man with thick black eyebrows and tan skin. His strong set jaw and prominent chin, coupled with his muscular physique, rendered him the epitome of a soldier.

"Rufus," he began in a gravelly voice. "How are you mending?"

Rufus coughed and shrugged. "As well as can be expected. I trust I won't be winning any beauty contests. Have you disposed of that awful creature?"

The captain nodded gravely. "Thankfully, yes, but we still have no idea how it infiltrated the castle. If you ask me, this is the work of terribly dark magic."

Rufus agreed solemnly. "I trust we had some casualties in all the havoc."

"Just one, sir. We found a body crumpled in the back of the chapel. It was Cornelius."

The color instantly drained from Rufus's face, his heart clinging to his chest. "But Cornelius never goes near the chapel! What in the blazes was he doing there?"

The captain shook his head. "We'll never know. And on the eve of the festival, too. It's tragic. No one else can brew potions as he did. Let us hope that the queen's present health holds true."

The two sat in silence for several minutes, the quiet click of a grandfather clock sullenly punctuating the silence. Overcome by emotion and exhaustion, Rufus collapsed back onto his bed. "Is there anything else to report, Captain?" he muttered dejectedly.

"Yes," said the Captain after a short pause. "The queen wishes to see you at your earliest convenience. She understands your situation, but I wouldn't keep her waiting too long."

"Thank you," Rufus muttered, his mind racing. "You may go." The Captain left quietly, leaving Rufus alone once again with his thoughts. He contemplated the consequences of what he had just heard. *Why must everything be so . . . complicated?*

When he could take it no longer, Rufus sprang from his bed, causing his side to burn with a sudden stab of pain. Recovering slowly, he sauntered over to his wash basin. Not wanting to face his wounds, he left the lights dim, and splashed some cold water over his face. Gazing into the water, he recalled his encounter the night before. *I am sure my blackmailing friend will find this quite interesting.*

CHAPTER TWELVE

A BITTER DRINK

ST. LOUIS, MISSOURI, 1945

Capt. Edison finally gave in to his wife's request to call his German contact. He had met Jonathan Kausen while stationed near the man's small village. Kausen worked as an interpreter for Capt. Edison's unit, and the two became friends when Capt. Edison showed a great interest in learning the local language. Mrs. Edison figured her husband's friend would be able to look up the strange men whose names they found on the bottom of their daughter's gift. Capt. Edison was less certain. Frankfurt is a big town, *he thought to himself as he dialed.*

The line was quiet for a moment, then he heard a few muffled rings. Finally, a voice picked up on the other end, a man with a thick German accent. "Hier ist Kausen!"

Capt. Edison responded. "Jonathan, you old Dummkopf. It's me, Edison!"

The line was silent for a moment, and the man on the other end responded jovially. "Ach! My favorite American! How is it to be home?"

Capt. Edison hesitated for a moment. "It's . . . fine, Jonathan, though I do miss a good bratwurst at times. Anyway, I have a question for you. Actually, there is someone in Frankfurt I need you to find for me."

"I'll do my best," *Jonathan responded politely.* "Who is it you're looking for?"

Capt. Edison fumbled with the scrap of paper on which he had written the name. "J. and K. Müller. I think that they make wood carvings and such."

The line fell silent for another moment, then Jonathan chuckled softly. "Capt. Edison . . . Müller is as about as common to Germans as Smith is to you Americans."

༈

IDAR-OBERSTEIN, WEST GERMANY, 1945

Despite his friend's reservations, Capt. Edison convinced Kausen to try to locate J. und K. Müller. Capt. Edison didn't offer many specifics initially, but he did promise to explain everything once they arrived in Frankfurt.

The next day, the Edisons packed their things and caught a plane Capt. Edison's nerves stayed on edge for every minute of the eleven-hour flight. They landed, rented a car, and drove to Kausen's home north of Frankfurt.

Almost immediately after their arrival, the Edisons found themselves being interrogated by Herr Kausen. "All right, my old friend, what is this all about? You don't just hop across the ocean to reminisce about old times."

Capt. Edison shook his head. "No offense to your country, but I told myself that I didn't really ever want to see Germany again—bratwursts or not. I came to ask you about this."

Reaching into his bag, he produced the music box and set it on the table in front of Jonathan. Wide-eyed, Jonathan studied the piece, paying special attention to the inscription on the bottom. Finally, he set the piece down, and looked earnestly back at the American. "Oh. You're looking for those Müllers."

ഗരു

THE CANTICLE KINGDOM

All lay still in the castle. Even the breeze had decided to comply and withhold its balmy breath. The torchlight barely flickered, and the Captain made scarcely a sound as he crept the corridors on his rounds through the castle. Turning a corner, he ran straight into a hooded figure coming from the other direction. In a flurry of motion, he drew his sword on the stranger, ready to strike. The man removed his hood, and the Captain at once saw his folly.

"Rufus! What are you doing out at this hour? And in such a disguise? To say that you scared me half to death is only half the truth!"

The chamberlain shook his head sorrowfully as he replaced the cloak over his eyes. "I couldn't sleep. That room feels like a tomb. I may look like a corpse, but I don't need to act like one just yet." He paused, unflinching, his eyes averted. "I'm trying to decide whether to present myself before the queen in such a condition. Such rare beauty should not have such grotesque company."

The captain placed a consoling hand on Rufus's shoulder. "Rufus, you've looked after her these long months while she's been ill. She owes you her life perhaps twice over after tonight. Maybe it's time you let her take care of you for a while."

"Beauty and the Beast," Rufus muttered under his breath.

The Captain raised his eyebrows but didn't say anything.

"Beauty and the Beast. It's a story she fancies. She tells all sorts of stories to that cat of hers . . . and that's one of her favorites. A beautiful woman must learn to love a hideous beast . . . ," Rufus's voice trailed off.

"How does the story end?" the Captain prompted.

Rufus shook his head. "I'm not sure. I felt guilty for listening. I've never heard the ending."

The Captain frowned. "Seems a bit out of character for her, at least it was before—"

"Before the illness," Rufus finished. Both men decided they had said too much. With only a few muttered words of parting, they both passed off into the night.

The Captain continued down the hall, trying to forget his strange conversation with Rufus. Just then, a flash of movement caught his attention. Someone was darting down the hall next to him, moving fast. He snapped to alert as if slapped in the face with icy water. His legs pounded the stones. "Stop! In the name of the Queen!"

The dark figure did not slacken its pace. Drawing his sword for the second time that evening, the Captain increased his speed. The chase led him downward through the palace, until he reached the chapel. The Captain hesitated slightly before descending the stairs. "I don't like this," he muttered to himself. "This place has been anything but holy today."

Gathering his courage, he gripped his sword more tightly and dashed down the stairs. "I've got you cornered," he called. "There's no way out."

Silent as an adder in the grass, the Captain slunk through the room, keeping low. He shuddered slightly, remembering the awful sight of Cornelius's broken body sprawled at the bottom of the stairs. He shook his head violently. *Focus!* he told himself. His eyes swept around the room, wary for any sign of movement. Out of the corner of his eye, he caught a glint of something off to his left. He lashed out with his sword, cleaving a bench in two and scattering glass. Nothing.

His chest heaved like an ox as sweat trickled into his eyes, blurring his vision.

"*Artus.*"

The Captain whirled around to meet the source of the voice, an ominous whisper that rippled through the silence, disembodied and strange. He clenched his teeth to keep them steady. He had never told anyone his name. His soldiers referred to him only as "the Captain," as did nearly anyone else. The only person who knew his name was dead.

Determined as ever, the Captain lit some fallen candles with his flint and tinder, hefted the candelabra in one hand, and stretched out his sword with the other. He stepped bravely into the darkness toward the back of the chapel, following the source of the voice. "If you are trying to intimidate me, it won't work, you scoundrel. Come out and show yourself, and I just might be merciful."

But the voice did not speak again. The Captain moved off in silence toward the back of the chapel and stopped when he reached the alcoves that held the kingdom's treasured statues. He stepped toward the scene from the Book of Acts, fearing what he might see. As the candlelight crossed the holy scene his worst fear was realized: the Apostle Paul had disappeared.

At this evil omen, the Captain trembled openly in the flickering light. Whatever had done this was not the type of foe that fell at the edge of a sword. Falling to his knees before the figure of the manger, he let forth a frantic prayer from his lips. "Deliver us from evil. Deliver us from evil."

Mustering his entire will, the Captain leapt to his feet. "Show yourself, or I'll flay you alive!" he cried, screaming like a banshee. "You pollute this holy place!"

Swinging his sword blindly into the darkness, he struck nothing but air. His candle tumbled to the floor and snuffed out in the darkness. Just before all went black, the light caught the gleam of another shiny statue, standing suddenly where once the wise men had stood. The Captain caught only a glimpse of a pair of fiery eyes before being engulfed in a brilliant plume of flame.

ଧୀ

Rufus hesitated just outside the queen's chambers. Light still filtered out from under the door, which usually indicated that she was still awake. Strangely, he had never seen candles in her room, which led him to believe the rumors that spread around that the queen dabbled in the magical arts. His hand hovered next to the door, deciding whether or not to knock. He pulled his fist back slightly, glancing back over his shoulder in the direction from which he had come. *I could use some magic right now,* Rufus thought. *Maybe a wizard could restore my face.*

Suddenly, almost without thinking, he struck his hand thrice firmly against the door. Panic swelled up in him until he was sure he would drown. There was no going back now. Presently, a gentle voice spoke from behind the door. "Come in. I've been expecting you for some time now."

He did what he was told—perhaps a little too eagerly. He swung the door open with such force that he nearly fell into the room. The brightness immediately blinded him, and he had to cover his eyes for a few moments while they adjusted. His hands also covered his reddening face. Not only did his black robe stand out like an inkblot on freshly laundered sheets, but he felt like a fool for his blundering entrance.

The air smelled strangely sweet, as if the breeze wafting in from the open window was laced with sugar. The queen sat poised on the edge of her delicate armchair in the center of the room and stood shortly after Rufus made his entrance. Rufus met her gaze, horrified by the awkwardness of the situation, and quickly averted his eyes. However, the queen only smiled reassuringly, her luminous eyes shaming even the purest of starlight.

When she spoke, it seemed to Rufus that he had never heard a songbird so lovely. "Rufus, you are a true knight. You don't need to hang your head in my presence."

Rufus cautiously raised his head, craning it to make sure that he had heard correctly. "My queen, I have done nothing to earn your praise. I am a fortunate man and nothing more . . . made even more fortunate to have your grace."

The queen shook her head, her smile never faltering. "Nonsense," she said. "You *are* a champion. Your wounds are a badge to your bravery. You have served my kingdom from the beginning. You protected me during those perilous times of rebellion when I first inherited the kingdom, and you have protected me again today. At first, I was too young to realize that I was in need of such protection, but now I know how much you should be commended. Cornelius would be very proud of you if he had lived to see this victory."

"Please do not speak of those rebellious days," Rufus said. "Though, in light of recent events, I fear that we have more dark days ahead."

The queen tossed her head to the side with a carefree laugh. "Yes, let's not dwell on such dark things. You will join me for tea, won't you?" She gestured to the table near the center of the room, which was already set with accommodations for two. She seated herself on one side, and Rufus took his place across from her, stepping carefully on the light-colored carpet. He settled down, silently poured two cups of tea, and began to sip silently. The queen took her first sip, and then hastily returned her cup to the table, raising her eyebrows in surprise. "I didn't think it was still that hot. We ought to add just a little bit of cold water."

She glanced around the room, but Rufus had already reached to his belt and unhooked the flask he carried there. Unstopping the top, he lifted the lid of the kettle and poured in a small amount of liquid, and then replaced it at his side. "Don't worry. I promise its only water."

His remark lightened the mood, but Rufus couldn't offer much more than small talk. He stared at the woman sitting across from him. Her face was so familiar—he spent countless hours by her bedside during her sickness, and even in the time before she fell ill, he helped with all the menial administration of the kingdom.

Tonight, however, her face seemed strange to him. Something had definitely changed about her, though, try as he might, he could not place it. Shortly before her illness, she was austere, unapproachable, and distant. Since her miraculous recovery, she was the carefree person of her youth. Whether this was just the result of recovering from the brink of death or some other reason, he could not say. Rufus finally relaxed and dared to glance over the table into the queen's eyes.

Beauty has the beast under her spell.

The evening passed by in a blur, and Rufus could barely remember what they discussed, only that he enjoyed the sound of her voice, her closeness, and her attention. As his eyelids drooped, she finally stood slowly and smiled sheepishly, as if they had been drinking wine instead of sipping tea.

"Thank you, Rufus, for honoring me with your presence. You've been . . . charming company." He could only nod, still a bit incredulous to the whole situation. She took in his silence for a moment and then continued. "If you don't mind, I must bid you good evening. Get some rest. Tomorrow I would like to confer with the Captain to insure that the preparations for the festival go as planned. I've already spoken with him, and he has informed me that he's planning a few surprises, fitting for a hero"—without warning, the queen stepped forward and embraced him tightly, her hands winding around his waist—"like you." Rufus's body went stiff as an arrow shaft, his mind reeling at the closeness, rocking back and forth between elated and horrified. Drawing back, she placed her hand in his, as if to give him something.

All at once, Rufus snapped to his senses and recoiled with a cry. Frantically, he bounded from the room and shot off down the hall. He shook his head, pulling the hood tightly around his head. "I can slay lions, but I am slain by the glance of a woman." As he slammed the door to his chambers behind him, he collapsed to the floor, his heart pounding a pattern into the front of his chest. "Not just any woman," he reminded himself.

As he sat there, Rufus realized that he was clutching something in his hand. Intrigued, he crept over to his bedside and lit the candle that sat on his bedstead. As the light brought the object into view, he had to squint to make sure that he was not seeing things.

In his hand lay a severed finger, smooth and gray, made of polished stone. Rufus's stomach did a somersault as he touched the finger. It was so lifelike, slender, and feminine looking. The graceful nail came to a point at the end just like . . . *hers*. He shook his head, it could not be.

He turned the object over and over in his hands, examining it from every angle. It looked like the finger of a statue, which had been lopped off by the careless application of a sculptor's chisel. Had the queen placed this strange token in his hand just before they parted? He had left in too much of a hurry to tell. Even if she had, what did it mean? He sighed and rubbed his chin, deep in thought. *I can't very well go back there tonight. Not after the scene I made.*

He placed the strange piece of stone in the money pouch he always carried around his neck for safekeeping and replayed the day's events. His eyes glazed over as he stared at the withering candle giving off its feeble light.

"What do I do now?" he muttered absently to himself. Strangely, as he tried not to think of anything at all, the answer struck him with such force that it nearly lifted him onto his feet again. Whatever it was propelled him, and he was suddenly on both feet again and sneaking out the door, even neglecting to fasten his cloak about him more tightly. *I can't pass up this chance*, he thought to himself.

At last he reached the door that he was looking for. The runes on the door signified that the room was private, but Rufus figured that its owner would not mind anymore. He reached out his hand for the blackened handle, and received such a shock that he instantly drew it back. Cradling his newly injured hand, Rufus winced in pain and frustration. "This entrance must be protected," he murmured. "Curse wizardry! I'll never understand it!" His tirade lasted only a few moments longer before he turned back the way he came.

As he dashed down the halls, he rounded a corner and stopped short as he glimpsed a man standing motionless by a window, looking out at the night sky. He approached with caution, and as he came closer, he recognized the armor. "Captain?" he questioned softly.

The man turned around to reveal the Captain's face, which wore a particularly worried expression. His hair was matted to his head with perspiration and great beads of sweat trickled down his brow. "Rufus," he responded stoically. "You must be really burning the midnight oil these days. Prowling around on the queen's request no doubt?"

At the mention of the queen, his face flushed hotly. No one was to know of this evening's encounter. "No, not the queen's idea. I still just can't sleep, same as earlier," he replied, thinking of something to change the subject. "Have you seen anything out of the ordinary tonight?"

The muscular knight just shook his head. "No. It's been very quiet, except for a little thief I found sneaking around the halls. Pretty scrawny little fellow. I could have tossed him out the window and landed him in the town square."

Rufus grinned at the thought. "Maybe with a tailwind," he admitted.

The Captain showed little reaction. "So," continued Rufus. "The queen mentioned that she wanted to see you about plans for the festival tomorrow."

"Yes," the Captain replied, never taking his glance from the window. "I was planning a military procession tomorrow for the beginning of the festival, and the queen suggested that you ride by my side at the front. I could not agree more—you do deserve the honor."

A gnarled lump formed in Rufus's stomach. The last thing he wanted now was recognition, but he wouldn't dare refuse a request from the queen, especially not now. "Thank you," he replied, trying not to let his voice betray his concern. "Is there anything else?"

"Yes," replied the Captain. "There *was* one more thing. We need your assistance with another project. If you meet me here tomorrow morning, we could contin—"

The Captain halted abruptly, and both he and Rufus swiveled around as a brilliant fireball blossomed from the roof of one of the castle's buildings into the town below.

CHAPTER THIRTEEN

꩜

FRACTURED SONG

IDAR-OBERSTEIN, WEST GERMANY, 1945

The old Volkswagen lumbered down the highway at such a speed that any American might have mistaken the blur for a passing sports car. Nothing could be further from the truth. The Edisons hung on for dear life, fully expecting the whole contraption to fly apart at any moment. I have to hand it to those German engineers, thought Capt. Edison grudgingly.

Over the rumble of the engine, Capt. Edison managed to make himself heard. "I've got two questions, my friend!" he yelled." Where are we going, and more importantly, will we arrive in one piece?"

The diminutive German laughed heartily, not taking his eyes off the road. "Relax! You worry too much. We'll get to Frauenburg in one piece. We should be through Idar-Oberstein any moment now."

True to his word, they reached the city—a strange cacophony of multicolored houses still damaged from the recent war. The strangest thing about the town was a church built right into the mountainside, which Mrs. Edison insisted on photographing as they drove past. Jonathan told them that a man who had pushed his brother over that cliff had built the church as penance. As they climbed through the mountainous terrain, Capt. Edison tried not to contemplate the steep inclines on either side, nor the story of the poor man plummeting to his death.

At last, the vehicle slowed, and the driver turned onto a path which seemed to lead into the forest. Jonathan stopped the car at the base of a hill, and the Edisons sighed with relief as they quickly piled out of the car. Jonathan gestured toward the top of the hill. An ancient stone tower shot up from the center of the forest. "That, my friends, is the last known location of Herr Müller!"

They entered the old ruins with a strange mixture of curiosity and anxiety. Capt. Edison had half a mind to ask his German guide if he was joking, but opted for a different approach. "Jonathan, who is this man supposed to be? A hermit?"

The German shrugged. "I suppose one could call him that. He used to be a skilled craftsman in business with his brother." He lowered his voice, as though he was telling ghost stories around a campfire. "They say his brother disappeared mysteriously one night and that our Herr Müller disappeared a few nights later. However, some years later, people started spotting him again, wandering around these woods like a vagabond, but no one dares to talk to him." He turned away, looking sheepish. "That is, no one but the two of you."

Capt. Edison rolled his eyes. Great, he thought. We might as well be chasing the Yeti or the Loch Ness monster. *"Okay,"* he said out loud. *"What now?"*

"We search!" replied Jonathan jovially. "If nothing else, I'll have some great pub stories after this, won't I?" Capt. Edison made no comment. Jonathan climbed the winding stairs, and Mrs. Edison reluctantly followed him. Capt. Edison looked around the bottom floor, going only on the meager light that the sun let in through the doorway. As he sipped some water from his canteen, he started to cough, causing him to drop his canteen, which scuttled into the darkness at the bottom of the stairs.

As he recovered from his coughing spell, Capt. Edison noticed that his canteen sounded as though it impacted stone several times, each impact sounding farther and farther away. His curiosity piqued, Capt. Edison hurried over to the darkness and stepped one foot into it. He felt his foot lower onto a step just a bit below. He stepped back and considered the darkness under the stairway. "Well," he muttered. "It's completely hidden from where I am standing."

His excitement outweighing his fear, he thrust one foot into the darkness and then the other, descending quickly. "Time to go see if Sasquatch is at home."

As Capt. Edison descended the stairs, he fell prey to more than a few second thoughts. Who knows what could be lurking down here? Even if he was just a craftsman, he did sound a bit off his rocker.

His curiosity urged him onward, despite his misgivings. The long stairway finally came to an end in front of a solid wooden door, which was dimly lit by a feeble torch. He hesitated in front of the door, feeling unsure more than anything. Do I just knock and see if anyone is home?

As he leaned in to examine the door, he could just barely make out an engraving near the middle of the wood. After straining and squinting his eyes for several moments, he was able to make out the word "Müller" etched in barely legible handwriting. Chuckling to himself, he raised his fist and rapped it soundly on the door several times. "Either I've stumbled into a fairy tale," he muttered under his breath, "or I've lost my mind. How do I know this isn't just some old Nazi fugitive with a vendetta against Americans? Jonathan did say Müller is a common name—"

His train of thought was interrupted after only a few seconds. The door slid ajar, but no sound came from behind it. With a trembling hand, he pushed the door open wider and stepped into the room.

After a short, dark entryway, the room opened up into a much brighter area. As his eyes adjusted, Capt. Edison could make out a man hunched over a large table covered with tools and instruments of every type. Shelves lined the room, full of fanciful carved figures, their frozen faces staring at him in the torchlight.

The wizened old man set down his tools, brushed the sawdust off his clothes, and looked up. When he spoke, the grating sound of his voice made it seem as if he too were only made of wood and was unaccustomed to speaking. "So, have you come for a carving?"

Capt. Edison blinked. The question had caught him completely off guard. "Come again?" he ventured.

The old man smiled, his wreath of frosty hair making him appear like an old lion. "I asked if you had come to peruse my collection of carvings. It has been such a long time since I have had any visitors, let alone customers."

Capt. Edison stepped a bit closer, so as to examine the old man better, more convinced than ever that this Herr Müller was crazy. "No . . . I didn't come about a carving, but I think you can help me. That is, if you are the Herr Müller I am looking for."

The man wiped a smudge off his glasses with an old rag and grinned, showing off his aging teeth. "Plenty of those about. But if you are looking for Karsten Müller, you've found me."

Capt. Edison thought about the initials that he'd seen on the bottom of the gift—J. and K. "I believe I've stumbled on the right place then," said Capt. Edison, removing his backpack to retrieve the fated item. "If you are the right person, then you should be able to explain this to me."

Herr Müller's eyes widened to a grotesque size behind the lenses of his glasses as he examined Kate's ill-fated gift. "Where," he gasped, holding his heart, "did you get that?"

ಎಲ

THE CANTICLE KINGDOM

The voices started as only faint echoes in her head. They were muffled to the point of unintelligibility, but she could tell from the tone that they were quarrelling. The harder she listened, however, the more and more she understood until at last she recognized the two men from before. "All right, all right—I was disappointed too. But he ought to be finished today at any rate. That is, if he can still work after what you put him through."

Fully awake, Gwen glanced over at Brigitta and found her fast asleep and safe, curled up in a ball. She seemed utterly oblivious to her awful surroundings, but from her appearance, it looked as if she had been through the gauntlet.

Staying low, Gwen peeked around the corner and was finally able to pin faces on the oafish voices from the day before. One man was clearly more muscular than the other. Though both wore masks, Gwen could see both had the same blond hair, blue eyes, and strong facial structure. They were dressed in dark, close-fitting clothing, which further displayed their excellent physiques. Both men possessed only one hand—the other had been replaced by a wicked looking metal device that remotely resembled the talons of a bird.

The shorter man glanced around warily and then turned his gaze back to his partner. "Okay, here's the deal," he said, lowering his voice to a hush. "We finally got the word. It's going down today, but—"

The larger oaf threw his hands in the air and let out a deafening whoop of victory. He practically danced around as if he had just found out that he had landed a night out with the girl of his dreams.

The smaller man clenched his teeth, shaking his head with disdain. "But!" he bellowed, immediately silencing the other oaf. "We need to wait for the signal. When it's time, the boss will make our emblem light up. Right now, we are just supposed to get things ready."

The larger man's face fell. Without another word, he let himself down into the pit. Gwen heard a loud hiss as the oaf threw water on open flame. Acrid steam filled the air, obscuring the rest of the room from Gwen's view. She held her breath and closed her eyes, listening carefully for the sounds of anyone approaching through the mist.

A hand reached out from behind her and grasped her back. Gwen stifled a scream and whirled around to realize that the shape behind her in the steam was much too small to be either one of the burly men. "Gwen, what's happening?" Brigitta's voice was weak and faltering.

Gwen put a finger up to her lips, and drew the girl in close. She craned her ear to one side, listening for the sounds of anyone approaching, but she heard only the scraping of metal as the large oaf dragged the cauldrons, presumably switching their positions. The two girls waited in tense silence until the scraping sounds stopped, and they dared to breathe again. Through the clearing mist, she saw the two men turning to go. Suddenly, an idea struck her. "Brigitta," she whispered, "we need to go. Hold on to my neck and do not let go, no matter what happens."

The night's rest had done Gwen good. She felt she had enough energy for another spell. She spoke a few hushed words and the mists gathered around them both, completely obscuring them from view. If the oafs looked back, all they would see was lingering mist. As the two men left the room, Gwen set off after them.

The two men sauntered down the corridor, down one of the paths, which led to a crossroads. The maze of corridors made Gwen's head spin. *What is this place?* she thought. *How do they know where to go? Surely they don't have enough brains between them to remember directions.* Not only were the mirrored walls incredibly confusing to look at, but they also shifted position from time to time.

She had to run in order to keep up with the men, hoping against hope that Brigitta could hang on and remain silent. At last, the men led them out of the blinding tunnels and into a large room, still formed in glass. At the far end of the room lay an exquisite spiral staircase that led to a room above. The two oafs stopped shortly before entering the stairway. The larger one looked so excited to ascend that he might sprout wings at any second and fly up. However, the shorter man turned around and paced the room warily, making sure no one followed. Satisfied, he and his partner started climbing the staircase.

Suddenly the stairs began to retract, starting at the bottom, and winding their way up behind the steps of the men. Panicking, Gwen leapt into the air with a boost from magic so that she barely caught a hold of the bottom most step. She clung tightly, her arms loudly protesting their exertion. Her sudden movement surprised Brigitta, and she just managed to grab hold of Gwen's ankles.

Gwen glanced down and met Brigitta's eyes, "Hold on," she mouthed. "I won't drop you." The exertion was causing another problem. The faint mist around them flickered and threatened to dissipate. Thinking quickly, Gwen let go one hand and reached up to grab the ankle of the oaf in front of her on the stairs. She jerked back with her hand and let surprise and gravity take care of the rest. The three of them tumbled toward the ground as Gwen used her magic to slow their decent, exposing them to view. Gwen took the brunt of the fall, with Brigitta landing hard on top of her. The brute landed on his back a few feet away, knocked out cold on the slick floor.

Sighing with relief, and attempting to regain her breath, Gwen turned first to Brigitta to make sure she was in once piece and then rose to her knees and studied the strange man. "He's still breathing. Thank goodness," she whispered to Brigitta.

Brigitta sat up groggily, rubbing her head. "So am I. My head hurts so bad, though, I wish I could pass out too." She looked at the unconscious oaf. "Now that he's down here, what are we going to do with him?"

Gwen crawled over to the unconscious man. The mask over his face produced strange breathing sounds, though he presented no other signs of life. His menacing metal hand gleamed in the artificial light of the room. She had no desire to find out what its purpose was, and she knew that if she did not act quickly, she might have to find out. She quickly made her decision and raised her hands in preparation to strike, not to kill, but to make sure that this oaf would not be troubling them ever again.

However, before the spell could escape her lips, she recalled the man's words from earlier as she stooped over and unfastened the mask covering his face. *It doesn't affect children* . . . .

Gwen assumed that they had been speaking of the noxious steam from earlier. The fumes obviously weren't lethal, but they were obviously affecting her in some other way. Balking a bit from the awful smell, she carefully strapped the mask across her own face. Suddenly, her entire body tingled with a renewed rush of magical energy. A smile crept to her lips as she shot to her feet. "Brigitta, it seems that I've made the right decision, sparing this man."

Gwen turned her gaze toward the ceiling, studying the place where the stairs had gone. She positioned herself under it and then looked earnestly at Brigitta. "Do you think you could stand up here next to me? I think you've been through enough today without getting cut by exploding glass."

With some effort, Brigitta managed to rise and scuttle over next to her. A moment later, a brilliant shaft of light burst from Gwen's outstretched hand, accompanied by a shower of stinging glass shards. Gwen produced a magical shield which protected them from the shower of glass that followed. As soon as the hailstorm subsided, Gwen shot a worried glance at Brigitta. "After that racket," she moaned. "I'm afraid every living thing within a mile will come rushing."

As she studied her handiwork, Gwen saw that shards of glass still clung tenuously to the side of the hole, threatening to teeter and fall at any moment. Since the stairs had disappeared, she realized her only option was to jump through the ceiling.

Taking store of her energy reserves, she realized that she probably only had strength enough for one attempt. However, as she gauged the distance and best path to take, she heard frantic footsteps and shouting as more blond-haired, blue-eyed men ran toward them. The nearest one raised his arm and with a shout, he launched a flaming projectile at them. It screamed past them, only a foot off its mark. Grasping Brigitta tightly, Gwen bent her knees and thrust upwards with all her might, screaming a magical command. They soared upwards as a volley of flaming weapons converged on the spot where they had been standing only moments before.

The burst of energy propelled them through the hole in the ceiling and into blackness. For a horrible, sickening moment, Gwen lost all sense of orientation, flailing helplessly through the darkness. She grasped Brigitta with all her strength, a terrified scream escaping her lips.

After a few stomach-churning moments, they landed soundly on the floor of the room above, breathless and trembling. The sounds of the scuffle below had all faded, leaving complete darkness and silence, as if they had stepped off the edge of the world. "Brigitta," she whispered anxiously. "Are you all right?"

"I'm fine," Brigitta said, the young girl's trembling voice indicating the contrary. "I'm getting used to being shoved around lately. I think I'm growing thick skin." Brigitta groped through the darkness until she found Gwen's shoulder and held on tight. "Why don't you give us a light? We'll never find our way in this darkness."

Gwen raised her hands and tried to summon the orb of light that had led them in the caverns. The orb flickered for a moment, and promptly disappeared. Gwen sighed. "It's no use! I can't even rival a firefly right now. That jump just now sapped the last of my energy store. I'm sorry."

They sat still in the darkness for what seemed like weeks. The longer they sat in the darkness, the less and less they thought about trying to move at all. A calm resignation crept over them, taking from them the need for words. After a good while, however, Brigitta started to speak, but then trailed off, as if embarrassed.

"What's that?" asked Gwen

"Oh, it's nothing. I think my eyes must have been playing tricks on me."

"No, go on," encouraged Gwen. "I could use any sort of idea right now. It seems we're stuck here, and I'm beginning to care less and less. My bones ache, and all I can think about is sleep. This place is swimming with evil magic. If we don't do something quickly, I'm afraid I'll pass out completely and who knows what will happen then."

Brigitta considered this. "Well, it's just that when the light went on, for a second I thought I saw something shiny not too far from here."

"Shiny? Like metal? Or a mirror?"

"Definitely like a mirror, like the rest of the maze. It only reflected off that one spot. Strange."

Gwen nodded in the darkness, pondering her options. "I could try again," she offered weakly. "It won't be for long, but it might give us an idea of which direction to go."

Gwen breathed deeply, concentrating intently on channeling her energy. She muttered softly, and for a few seconds, the orb of light reappeared. For a fleeting second, the light reflected off something close by. Seizing Gwen's hand, Brigitta towed her along quickly as the light faded, hoping that they could find their way in the darkness. Soon, however, Brigitta slackened her pace. "It can't have been this far. We must have passed—"

Her foot struck something hard, and she fell forward, reaching out with her arms to break her fall. When she landed, she found herself sprawled out at an upward angle instead of lying flat on the ground. The surface under her was smooth, slick, and cool to the touch.

"Gwen!" she exclaimed. "It's the stairs! They must come up here after they leave the other room."

Gwen followed the sound of Brigitta's voice until she found the slick stairs. Finding the guardrail, they clung to it as they ascended the spiral staircase until it leveled out at the top and met a wall. Feeling around a bit more, they discovered a door handle. Gwen hesitated as she gripped the cold metal in her hand. *Who knows what's on the other side?*

"On the count of three, we'll open the door together. All right?"

"Okay."

Gwen began to count. "One . . . two . . . ."

On three, they yanked the knob around, flung open the door, and found themselves blinded by a bright light. As their eyes adjusted, they noticed an old man standing nearby, staring curiously. Brigitta gasped in surprise. "Grandpa?"

His face and arms were covered in bruises. Soundlessly, he twitched his head to the right, as if trying to draw attention to something. Brigitta raised her eyebrows, taking a cautious step toward the stairs.

Unfortunately, the old man's meaning suddenly became all too clear. A hulking form stepped clumsily in front of the old man, casting a huge murky shadow across the stairs. Brigitta screwed up her face in frustration, *How could I have forgotten about the other oaf?* Thankfully, the large oaf appeared just as startled as Brigitta and Gwen and twice as confused.

"What are you doing here?" He mumbled, eying the mask on Gwen's face. "Did they send you up?"

"Uh, yes," Gwen replied slowly. "Yes, they did. We are supposed to bring the old man with us . . . to the boss."

The large oaf furrowed his brow. "What? Just as I was about to have some fun with him? That's not fair!" The man threw the equivalent of a temper tantrum, flailing his arms about, smashing his fists into the floor and walls, and throwing everything in reach. As the tantrum lost its wind, the oaf turned his attention again to the intruders, his face flushed deep with rage. "H-how . . . do I . . . know," he spat, so flustered that each word came only with effort, "that the . . . b-boss sent . . . you? What's his name?"

Such a simple question, but yet Gwen's mind reeled trying to scrape up a feasible answer. She breathed out forcefully, clearing her mind. Silence would only condemn her, so she might as well spit something out. "He has many names. You know that as well as I."

The man's face fell, his blue eyes sweeping the ground. "Yeah, that's what they always say. 'No reason to know his name,' they tell me, 'cause its always changing.' Curse him! Always ruining my fun! Having everyone push me around!" He considered his mechanical arm. "Nothing I can do," he said, suddenly quiet. "The boss said that he'd take the other hand off if I didn't do what he says. You're not going to rat on me are you?"

Gwen donned her best stern look, enhanced greatly by the awful mask on her face. "I have half a mind to, but you are a pathetic creature. I'm in a good mood today, so . . . I won't say anything."

The oaf lowered himself down on the stairs, a surly expression frozen on his face. "Fine," he grumbled. "Do what you have to. Just leave me alone."

And with that, the oaf slunk off into the darkness, silent and brooding.

Gwen and Brigitta both exhaled twin sighs of relief. The old man approached Brigitta, his eyes clouding slightly with emotion. "Such a welcome face in such a dark place," he whispered, hugging Brigitta, who gratefully returned the embrace. "I'm delighted to see you, but what are you doing here? Who knows who else they've dragged off?" He looked about expectantly. "Johann isn't with you, is he?"

"No," she muttered, fighting back emotion. "I don't even know if he is still alive. Oh, Grandpa, so much has happened, but you'd hardly believe me if I told you."

The old man threw up his hands, his gaze to the ceiling. "Dearie, after what I've been through recently, I'm bound to believe just about any tale, no matter how far-fetched it sounds. Why don't you start by introducing me to this lovely young woman you've brought with you?"

The three of them sat on the steps while Brigitta explained her plight in the forest with Johann and then later in the castle garden and finally about her dealings in the tunnels and how Gwen had saved her life. The whole time, Grandpa just nodded and grunted politely at the appropriate points. When Brigitta finished her tale, Grandpa rose to his feet and began to tell his part of the story.

"There I was one night, all bundled up for sleep and lying in my bed, just as comfortable as an old man can be, when all of a sudden this awful smoke comes pouring through the window. I start coughin' and wheezin', and I'm about to go find out what's wrong when suddenly there's this man in a dark hood standing in my room! I know the door was shut—I checked it three times before I settled down—so naturally I think he's a ghost or demon. So I started spoutin' off my prayers like a pious man, but let me tell ya. In a case like this, it might have been best to run first and pray later, 'cause I didn't last more than a minute.

"The man threw something else to the floor, and the smoke got worse, and I passed out. When I woke up, I was in this awful room with Fool and Bigger Fool gloating over me like a pair of bloodhounds. Somehow they got it into their heads that I was some sort of master at machinery: cogs and wheels and levers and stuff. They brought me up here, expecting me to fiddle with this huge contraption until I get it up and running again! Don't know how they got that idea in their dim-witted heads, no ma'am!

The old man, paused his ranting to take a deep breath. "I've been here long enough to sense that something sinister is going on."

Johann's grandfather gestured up the stairs for them to follow. "Come on. I'll show you the contraption. See if either of you can make sense of it."

Grandpa led them up the stairs and across a long, metal platform to a console next to a guardrail. Below them lay a gigantic metallic cylinder on its side spanning the length of the room. On the surface of the cylinder, at various intervals, lay dark patches of raised metal. On the far side of the cylinder, a line of long, thin rods stretched out across the entire length of the cylinder. The console, they noticed, was adorned with an assortment of buttons, levers, and knobs of various colors all in a horrible state of disrepair. Grandpa motioned toward the largest lever. With great effort, he forced the lever down, the device protesting all the way with a metallic moan. At once, a low rumble, like the advance of a mounted army, broke the silence and the massive cylinder creaked into motion, rolling slowly, like a cresting wave.

The cylinder picked up speed and at once the party discovered the device's strange purpose. As the bits of raised metal struck the bars on the far side, they produced the most glorious tones, ringing across the room like a chorus of angels heralding the sunrise.

After several melodious moments, however, the cylinder ground to an abrupt halt, and the song suddenly ceased. Brigitta stared at her companions, her face reflecting her yearning for the song to continue. "I know that song!" she exclaimed. "I've heard it every day of my life! It plays from the clock tower, but it doesn't sound like that."

Johann's grandfather nodded. "Yes, I noticed that too. But the strange-ness doesn't stop there." He gestured to another lever on the control panel surrounded by strange words. With another great effort, the old man pulled the lever. The scraping sound of metal on metal caused the others to clamp their hands firmly over their ears. "Try as I might, I can't change the lever to any position but this one," he said, wiping his brow. "The result, though, is very interesting."

Brigitta and Gwen watched the giant cylinder, which now buzzed with movement. Across the surface, some of the lumps of metal disappeared into the cylinder, leaving no trace of where they had been, while other new lumps emerged just as suddenly from other places on the surface. The site left them speechless.

"Watch what happens when I pull this other one again."

With less effort than before, Grandfather yanked down the other lever as he had previously done, and once again, the cylinder ground into move-ment. This time a different melody filled the room, very unlike the previous song. Minor, melancholy chords filled the room briefly. As the echoes died off, it left the three with such a profound weight on their shoulders that no one ventured to utter a word. The very lights in the room seemed to deepen as the somber mood blanketed everything.

It was several minutes before anyone could bring themselves to speak.

"Please don't play that one again," whispered Brigitta hoarsely. "It's a dark, sad thing. I'm glad it was broken." The others nodded solemnly, not meeting one other's gaze.

"Well," began Johann's grandfather, sliding the lever back to its original position. "That's what I am up against. For some reason they think that I can fix it, and truth be told, the only person alive who could fix something like this is your father, but unless they catch him too, we're pretty much stuck." He shrugged and grinned sheepishly. "I am open for ideas," he admitted.

Brigitta studied the panel for any other hints about the fascinating machine. Stepping closer, she scrutinized the strange words whose meaning she could not begin to understand. As she scanned the panels, Brigitta noticed something new, apart from the other buttons and levers. Spaced at even intervals were smooth black panels, each with the form of a hand drawn onto them. The two hands on the right side of the panel were a deep blue, barely visible against the background, and the other two were a deep red.

Curious, she reached out her hand and touched one of the blue panels. Nothing happened. She tried the other blue panel with the same result and then moved on to one of the red ones, her expectations low. However, she jumped in alarm as she placed her small hand on the first red panel. "Look here," she cried. "It's glowing!"

The red outline now stood out brilliantly against the background, emitting a quiet but pure tone. Brigitta smiled as the light sent a warm, tingling sensation throughout her fingers, which spread up into her arm. Curious to see what would happen, Brigitta finally removed her hand, and the panel plunged again into darkness. She experimented several times more, trying both hands and receiving the same effect each time.

"It's never done that before," muttered Johann's grandfather. "I've tried messing with those panels, and I've never seen so much as a flicker." He sank deep into thought, stroking his scraggly beard. "Maybe *that's* what he was talking about," he muttered ponderously.

Brigitta turned, her face inquisitive. "Who, Grandpa? Who was talking about this?"

Johann's grandfather sighed and looked wearily at his two companions, guilt written across his face. "I haven't been totally frank with you," he began. "It's true that I don't know how to fix this thing, but actually, I have known of its existence for quite some time and so has Brutus. We are far under the castle, in a secret vault. This machine has high significance to the kingdom, and it's said that in times of peril it is our only hope. Your father and I did some research. It turns out that the queen has been hiding this machine for years and forcefully imprisoning anyone who found out about it.

"This machine is essential in the selection of a new queen when the current queen draws near to death. It is said to have been operated by a certain family who has taken care of it since it came into being, and Brutus discovered that he is a descendant of that ancient line. A few days ago we decided to set off in search of this place, but for some reason, he wanted you to come along because he said it wouldn't work without you."

Gwen gazed at the old man, puzzled. "Do you think it has something to do with that panel she just touched?"

Johann's grandfather shrugged. "Quite possibly. It's hard to say."

"But, if you studied so much about it, how come you don't know how to fix it?" inquired Brigitta.

The old man once again flushed, looking terribly sheepish. "That's just the thing. I studied the lore, and Brutus studied the mechanics. My old brain is too full of wax to pick up that technical jumble. Besides, I seem to remember that he said it was more than just a matter of mechanics. Apparently, there's some magic involved as well."

They let out a collective sigh. Brigitta wished Brutus was there to help them. On the other hand, she did not wish on anyone else the fate of being trapped here.

Suddenly, the light in the room increased dramatically, and another tone sounded from the panel, in perfect harmony with the first. Looking over her shoulder at the others, Gwen managed a large grin, displaying two rows of brilliantly white teeth in stark contrast to her smudged and dirty face. "It appears that this device requires a woman's touch."

Brigitta stared at Gwen, flooded with the strongest sense of déjà vu she had ever experienced. She shook her head vigorously at the strange sensation. "Gwen?" she began timidly. "Are you sure we haven't met before? I just have the strongest feeling that we have . . . a long time ago . . . ."

Grandpa chuckled heartily. "A long time ago? Ha! You have no idea what that means, you little sapling! How long is a long time? A month?"

Brigitta rolled her eyes. "For your information, Grandpa, I can remember back many years. I know that only seems like a few minutes to an old, gnarled oak like yourself, but it's still something."

Grandpa threw up his hands in mock offense. "All right, settle down there, little ember. You're bound to catch the room on fire. Besides, it seems like we should direct all that energy into finding a way out of here while the guards are otherwise . . . distracted. Got any ideas?"

The two women removed their hands from the panels, and immediately, the room fell silent and still. Gwen put a thoughtful hand to her mouth. "I do want to get out of here, as soon as possible, in fact. But at the same time, I feel reluctant to leave this place. If we leave now, there is no guarantee that we'll ever be able to find this place again. I can't help wonder what would happen if we found others who could light up the other two panels."

Gwen's face darkened, as if deep in thought. After several seconds it lit up with the exhilaration of an excellent idea. "I think I know how we can get back here. I don't know if I have the energy to try right this minute. Could you keep an eye out for me while I rest?"

Grandpa's left eyebrow shot up. "Slow down, ma'am. I may be an old oak, but I still need things in plain terms. Why would we stay?"

Gwen shook her head, coming back down to earth a bit. "I'm sorry, sir. I can work a bit of magic. It takes a lot out of me, so I need a little time to build up the energy."

It was Brigitta's turn to speak. "Gwen, what would you do?"

Gwen sighed. "It's a bit complicated, but I think I could make a magical doorway of sorts. It would be very hard to see, but we could use it to come back here later."

Grandpa's eyes brightened. "Couldn't you work some of that hocus pocus to get us out of here?"

Gwen shook her head disappointedly. "Unfortunately, no. I could only leave a door here to use later. This particular brand of magic is like drawing the X on a treasure map. Once we're away from here, I'll be able to find it again. I can't do it the other way around, since I don't actually have any memories of being anywhere else. I know it seems crazy, but—"

Grandpa nodded, his disappointment apparent. "It's all right, dearie. I'll just have to trust you on this one. As to where you are going to stay, I know just the place. If you two would please follow me." He started off with uncharacteristic speed for one so old. He led them around to the right and down a ramp steep enough to make holding on to the metal railing a necessity. The ramp led them down to the floor in front of the massive cylinder. A dark narrow path led them to a plain metal door with a rusty handle. Without hesitating, Grandpa gripped the handle and pushed the door, causing a thin beam of light to filter in. He turned to the two followers. "Hurry in. I'll hold the door."

They scurried past, squinting their eyes at the increase in light. Beyond the door lay a cozy room, complete with a desk, a bed, and an area in which to prepare food. The covers on the bed lay disheveled, half of them having already tumbled to the floor. The room was many degrees warmer than the room outside and very stuffy. The ceiling was low enough that Gwen had to watch her head, while Brigitta found it ideal.

Grandpa glanced around nervously and then frantically began to tidy up the bed, sweeping off the debris and straightening the sheets. "It's not much," he muttered sheepishly, "but it will have to do. I can't say I was ever expecting any visitors."

Brigitta looked up at Grandpa, "What is this place?"

Grandpa took a seat at the desk, trying to straighten it up as well. "I'm not sure exactly. They've kept me in here since I arrived. All this stuff was already lying around, and if you think it's bad now, you should have seen it then. The dust nearly choked me when I first entered, and it took me hours to actually find the desk. One thing is clear: someone used to live here who wasn't overly concerned about housekeeping."

Gwen lay warily on the bed coughing quietly. "It'll do. Wake me up if there's trouble."

Gwen fell asleep almost immediately, and Grandpa also nodded off by the fireplace, his head propped up on a pillow. *It's either one extreme or the other,* Brigitta thought, ruefully. *Either I'm fleeing for my life, or I'm bored stiff in a stuffy, old room.*

She made her way over to the desk and looked at some of the old diagrams. Figuring this provided a better diversion than listening to Grandpa snore, Brigitta brushed some of the dust off the chair and settled into it. She noticed that many of the diagrams explained the workings of the giant musical device. Most of the words were written in the same strange language and in very poor, faded handwriting. Some of the diagrams made no sense at all; sheets with straight lines across them covered with scattered black dots, some with tails, some connected with arcs and lines. Leaning back, she scratched her head, wondering who in the world had taken the time to create such intricate drawings. She imagined a strange old hermit with a scraggly beard, cooped up in this little hovel, scribbling away at his parchment by candlelight.

A moment later she felt herself falling backwards as the chair reached its tipping point and toppled over. She only had a second to flair her arms before her head hit the ground hard, causing her vision to blur. Several bits of metal fell from the desk, and her last grasp at the desk unearthed several sheets of paper, sending up even more dust into the air.

As she lay on her back, her head swimming, she heard Grandpa stirring, but amazingly, he did not wake.

She groaned slightly as she looked around until she noticed a full color diagram on the ground directly in front of her, which in itself was odd because most of the others had been simply drawn with black ink. The parchment depicted the four hands on the control panel of the device in their respective colors. Underneath the drawing, a lengthy paragraph scrawled down to the bottom of the page in the same sloppy writing as the others. Curious, she picked up the page, examining it for anything important that she might be able to glean from it.

The words on the page made no more sense than before. However, as she stared at them, they seemed to leap out at her, and she understood their meaning. With anxiety welling up in her, she tried to pry her eyes from the page, but she found herself transfixed to the words and their strange and revealing message. Her eyes followed every line, moving faster and faster until they had swept over every word.

"I know how it works!"

Both Grandpa and Gwen shot up from their slumber, startled, and stared blankly at the little girl. "What did you say?" muttered Grandpa.

"I know how the machine works," she repeated, careful to pronounce her words with care, but the others comprehended as little as before.

Gwen furrowed her brow. "Brigitta, speak more clearly. I can't understand you at all."

But it was no use. The more Brigitta spoke, the less her companions understood. She tried speaking quickly and then slowly, varying her pitch, but to no avail. The words out of her mouth sounded to them like nonsense.

Grandpa and Gwen glanced at each other as frustrated tears formed in Brigitta's eyes. In a last ditch attempt at getting her point across, Brigitta picked up the diagram and began pointing at various sections, trying her hardest to explain.

"I think she's figured out something," Grandpa said to Gwen, "but I don't think it's just my old ears that are having trouble understanding what it is."

Brigitta nodded fervently, renewing her efforts. Gwen shook her head in disbelief. "I've never seen anything quite like this. Maybe she should lie down—" Before Gwen could continue, the sound of approaching footsteps echoed outside the door. In panic, Grandpa extinguished the light and motioned for everyone to get down. Gwen slid under the bed, and Brigitta hid under the table.

A second later, the door swung open with a creak, and a burly guard stepped across the threshold. A second later, the rather stupid oaf they had outwitted earlier limped in contritely behind them. "So you say there were two others besides the old man?" the tall guard asked the other. "Or were you sleeping on duty again and just dreamed them into existence?"

The oafish guard shook his head resolutely. "No, sir. They're real all right. Said they came for . . . uh . . . you know whom. There was a little girl and a woman, looking like they had just run out of a thorn bush or something the way that—"

The taller guard raised his hand to silence the other and turned his gaze to the old man. "You, prisoner. Where are you hiding the others? If you value your feeble life, I suggest you speak quickly."

Grandpa glanced around innocently, shrugging his shoulders. "I . . . ah . . . don't know anything about that. You see, I was just feeling ill and thought I'd turn in for a spell, take a little nap."

The tall guard faltered for a moment, glancing back at his dense companion who had been known to make up stories. However, he decided to continue pressing the matter. "Do you take me for a fool?"

Grandpa only shook his head and muttered incoherently. With a single savage shove, the guard shoved Grandpa aside, stirring up latent clouds of dust as the old man landed ungracefully on the floor.

Brigitta shrank farther back under the desk scrounging for something, anything she could use as a defense. Praising her luck, she wrapped her fingers around a particularly aerodynamic looking paperweight. Straining to see through the dust, she swallowed hard, took aim, and let the object fly.

The object hit the offender directly in the forehead. With a groan, the guard fell forward, clutching his injured head. His companion, unsure of what to do, took off in the other direction without as much as a glance behind him. Brigitta rushed out from under the table over to the old man who lay panting on the floor. "Grandpa, are you hurt?"

Through a fit of coughing, Grandpa barely managed to answer. "Fine, haven't felt so good in ages," he hacked sarcastically. She helped him to his feet and dusted him off. Gwen came out from her hiding place and leapt to her feet. "We've got to get out of here—and fast. It won't be long before someone notices this missing guard."

Grandpa furrowed his brow. "Do you possibly have enough energy to cast that spell?"

"Perhaps," Gwen said after a few moments. "I've gotten all the rest I'm going to get, so I might as well try." She sank back onto the bed and stared at her steepled hands with great concentration. "Keep an eye on the door. This will only take a minute."

The other two did as they were told, keeping the door just barely open enough to keep watch while Gwen began her spell. Chanting and rocking back and forth, she held a bit of light in her cupped hands. The light grew steadily brighter, until with a sudden, brilliant flash, it subsided. At the same instant, Gwen collapsed in a heap at the floor with a muffled grunt. As she fell, her hand opened to reveal a small, shiny object. Brigitta saw that it was a tiny, gilded music box. Her thoughts, however, quickly left the box and focused on the woman lying on the floor. Sweat trickled from Gwen's forehead, and her face appeared as pale as a jug of fresh milk. Her breathing came in soft, shallow gasps, labored and painful. "I didn't think . . . it would be . . . so—"

Brigitta put a hand to her lips. "Hush. Keep still now."

Gwen obeyed, her eyes listless and glazed. Suddenly, both Brigitta and Grandpa doubled over as well. An icy stiffness webbed through their bodies, causing them also to crash to the ground. Brigitta glanced at her hands in horror to see that they had both turned a stony gray.

"I can't move my hands!" she wailed in fright. Grandpa gave no reply. He had fared considerably worse. Where Grandpa had been just a moment before, lay only a statue. She rushed toward him, but found her feet had also turned to stone.

Unfortunately, the guard was the first one to regain use of his limbs. Brigitta stood rooted to the spot powerless, as the groaning guard arose and swept the bed covers from off of Gwen in one quick motion. In a fit of stinging rage, he lashed out at her with his boot, striking her hard in the side, and eliciting a shriek of agony from his victim. Over and over he swung, his face twisted in fiendish glee. Too spent to fight back, Gwen took each blow in stride, her groans trailing off as she lost consciousness. Suddenly, before the man could deal another blow, his foot froze in mid-air; a streak of gray rippled through it until it engulfed his entire body. In an instant, the guard could have passed for any of the statues in the castle garden.

Brigitta watched in horror as Gwen's breathing became shallower and shallower. Powerless as she was, Brigitta could do nothing but stare into space, feeling all the while stiffer and stiffer. Her horror deepened as a menacing shadow covered the door, and an enormous man stepped in the room. The dark-haired man, clad in full armor entered the room, a satisfied smirk written all over his face. He seemed not to notice either Brigitta or Grandpa but turned his gaze directly on Gwen. With a mirthless laugh, he whispered, "Can't have you going just yet, your Majesty."

For the first time, he glanced around the room. His chilling laugh returned. "To think you almost got away only with the help of these two, the sapling and the firewood. Seems the incompetence of our guards has increased as of late."

The man turned to face the now frozen guard who had given Gwen a beating. The man made a movement with his hand around his navel and in a brilliant flash of light the statue crumbled and disappeared. Next, he turned his attention to Grandpa, studying him carefully. "Mr. Buchmuller, I presume. It's an honor," he crooned, bowing mockingly. "I must apologize for my frank manner, but I do not think we will be needing your services much longer. It seems we've found some suitable replacements for you. But, until their accommodations can be arranged, I suppose we ought to let you tinker a bit longer."

The man clasped both of his hands on Grandpa's brow and gradually, the old man's form began to loosen until he was fully himself again. Grandpa rubbed his eyes sleepily, shaking his head as if coming out of a dizzy spell. As his eyes focused on the form in front of him, the old man gasped in terror.

"It can't be you—I watched you die!"

The armored man appeared taken aback for a moment and then shook his head in agitation. "Ah, yes," he grumbled. "I almost forgot that you knew this face. I suppose I ought to change into something more . . . suitable."

With that, the man's features blurred grotesquely. Colors blended and separated in a colorful mass, completely obscuring his face for several seconds until a new form gradually became apparent: a hideous jaguar-like face with jet-black fur streaked with red, and haunting golden eyes. Grandpa nearly fainted from shock. "I don't understand. How can this be?"

The creature silenced Grandpa with a throaty growl. "I know what I did to your son, but the question now is what will I do with you? We know you've been less than . . . forthcoming with your assistance. I have half a mind . . . ."

The beast's voice lowered to an intense, menacing whisper, so that Brigitta could no longer hear what was being said. Suddenly, another voice spoke in her mind, *Brigitta*. It was Gwen's voice, resonating from deep within her, like a ripple of water from the drop of a stone. She understood the voice and strained her senses, aching for more, *Brigitta . . . run . . . go . . . find . . . Johann.*

She tried to reply in her thoughts, but couldn't seem to send back the same sort of communication. *Bring him here,* the voice spoke. *GO!*

In an instant, her body broke free from her invisible shackles, and she dropped silently to the floor. Glancing, briefly back at Gwen, she realized that, strangely, Gwen had a smile on her lips. She remained motionless and battered, but to Brigitta she looked almost . . . content. Seizing her tiny window of opportunity, she crawled across the floor and slipped out the open door.

Once free, she tore down the metal pathway as silently as she could, not daring for an instant to glance back to check for pursuers. Bounding up the stairs, she ran back toward the way she had come, finding rest in the dark corner for a few moments. Breathing heavily, she shook her head and wrapped her arms around her shoulders as panic welled up like a reservoir behind her chest. She needed to find a way out.

Just as the panic inside her threatened to boil over, she saw it: a series of metal gratings a good distance up the sheer walls. She shot madly toward the grating and, with an impressive but futile leap, proved that she would need help reaching it.

Hearing footsteps clanging toward her, she cast her eyes about for some way of giving herself a boost. The floor was almost completely empty, save a long stretch of thick pipes, which lay strewn about near the controls to the music maker. Snatching up the longest one she could find, she rushed back over to the grating. The pipe curved slightly at the end, and she was able to fasten the end of the pipe between the slats of the grating next to the one she wished to enter. Wrapping herself around the pipe and praying that it would hold long enough, she shimmied up the pole and toward her goal. She nearly lost her grip when a cry rung out from behind her. "There she is! Shoot her down!"

The guards wasted no time in priming their bows on her. Several arrows twanged through the air and impacted the walls around her with sickening thuds. The pipe wavered but did not fall. Her heart threatening to pound out of her chest, she ascended the last few feet of pipe and clutched the slats of the grating.

Her victory, however, was painfully short lived, as an arrow hit the pipe straight on and sent it careering out from under her feet. Brigitta yelped as her body fell and her arms went taut. Straining with all her might and motivated by the continued barrage of arrows around her, she pulled herself up and grabbed hold of the grate. After several swift tugs, the grate would not budge, and the muscles in her arms began to tremble from exertion. At that moment, an arrow embedded itself in the wall directly beneath her arm, jolting her senses, and providing the necessary surge of adrenaline. She deftly yanked the arrow out of the wall and positioned it as a lever behind the grating. Using almost all her of her remaining strength, she pushed down on the makeshift lever, and launched the grating into space.

Brigitta swung herself up into the crawl space with a valiant effort. The space was just large enough to accommodate her small body, and after crawling some ways into the tunnel, she stopped to catch her breath and promptly collapsed. The full-grown soldiers would have no way of following her for the time being, but that did not mean they could not devise some other method of capture.

Closing her eyes, Brigitta imagined Johann as she had last seen him: trembling and afraid. As good a friend as he was, what use would he be at a time like this? The two of them had only survived the past few days due to the miraculous intervention of other adults, and without them, Brigitta was not sure they could stand up for very long against any more awful things they should encounter.

However, as Brigitta kept her eyes closed, the pathetic, trembling image of Johann melted away to reveal a much bolder, stronger looking boy. The sword, which he clutched at his side, gleamed with energy—the same contagious energy that seemed to glow from the boy's face. All at once, Brigitta felt a wave of calmness wash over her as she sensed in her heart what she could not yet know with her mind—Johann had changed for the better, and together, they would make a difference.

CHAPTER FOURTEEN

ᴙᴓᴙ

REWRITING HISTORY

IDAR-OBERSTEIN, WEST GERMANY, 1945

The old man held his breath as he gazed at the box for several more tense seconds. Then, slowly, he extended his hand, his fingers trembling. Capt. Edison took the hint and placed the box in the man's fingers, which closed around the box as if he would never again release it from his grasp. "This was my greatest work," he began in an almost reverent tone. "Now it's my worst nightmare."

The enigmatic words hung in the air like an unpleasant stench. Karsten returned to his desk, setting the box on the surface, and started a careful scrutiny. "It's been through a lot, it would seem," he finally continued. "At least on the outside. But I wonder . . . ."

His fingers searched along the side of the box until he found a tarnished silver knob. Grasping the knob in his gnarled fingers, he rotated it several turns before letting go again. For a moment, a faint mechanical whirring and clicking sounded from the box, and Capt. Edison thought he heard the first strains of a lilting melody, which quickly died away in a grinding halt.

Karsten removed his glasses, wiping the first tears forming at the corners of his eyes. "It's worse than I thought. The damage is more than external, and it's not something I can fix . . . from out here. Why do you have it?"

"It was a gift for my daughter," Capt. Edison explained, beginning to display some of his own emotion. "But I don't know. She—"

"Disappeared? Suddenly?" Karsten finished his sentence with a knowing nod.

ᴙᴓᴙ

THE CANTICLE KINGDOM

By the time Rufus and the Captain reached the scene of the rooftop attack, the villagers and a few soldiers on duty were furiously battling the blaze, which had engulfed the inn in the center of town and was quickly spreading to some of the nearby buildings. Debris lay scattered across the square where the night air was mingled with shrieks from the onlookers and desperate commands from the officers. In awe of the inferno, Rufus quickly joined the brigade of men fighting the flames, making sure to keep his face concealed as much as possible. "What happened?" he asked the man working beside him.

The solider shook his head, calling over the roar of the blaze. "No one knows, sir! Everyone was asleep, and suddenly the whole place just went up in smoke. The innkeeper got out alive, and he claims that there wasn't even a fire burning at the hearth."

Rufus continued to battle the flames with the bucket he'd been given, moving as if he were on fire himself. "I saw it from the castle. It looked like an explosion!"

The soldier leaned in a bit closer. "People are already starting to talk . . . saying that this is the work of the dark wizard. We've never seen anything like this before. Do you think he really could be back?"

Though the man's face remained brave, his voice betrayed his uneasiness. Rufus was swift to answer. "I'm not sure. There's been no shortage of strange occurrences lately, but I wouldn't jump to conclusions. It's probably just—"

As if to counter his argument in mid-sentence, another explosion rang out in the night, this time from outside the town square. The crowd cast their eyes toward the sound and found that another building had fallen prey to flames on the outskirts of town. Mass panic ensued, some dashing toward the new blaze and others fighting the old one with renewed fervor. The shouts and cries intensified into a chaotic chorus of confusion, rubbing already frayed nerves raw.

The townspeople fought valiantly but ultimately could not save the doomed buildings. By the time they finally had the blaze under control, the inn and the surrounding buildings, as well as the house on the edge of town, were no more than piles of ash and soot. Dumbfounded, the soldiers set out on an immediate search of the town, combing through every house and business in search of a perpetrator or other incriminating evidence. Though the soldiers routinely stormed buildings in search of subversive material, the townsfolk could never recall such a thorough and brutal operation as this.

Rufus paced up and down the streets, disturbed by the images in his head conjured up by the dark, smoldering streets. The last time he had seen this, his enemy was clear and controllable. This time, though, the enemy was not even visible.

On one of his rounds of the smoky streets, one of the soldiers approached Rufus briskly, clutching a small bundle in his hands. "Sir, we found this when searching one of the houses on the street," he reported transferring the item to Rufus's hands. "We've taken the suspects into custody for questioning. We didn't think there were any of these left, but I guess the fire made them let their guard down."

Rufus glared first at the solider and then down at the object. It was an ancient, dusty volume, bound in leather with hundreds of yellow pages between the tattered covers. "How often do you conduct these searches?"

"Once a month, sir!" the soldier replied smartly. "By the order of the queen."

Rufus chewed nervously on the edge of his lip. "The queen, " he muttered, his heart sinking to his shoes. "I'll take this specimen in myself. I'm sure the queen will find it . . . interesting." With a smart salute, the solider carried about his business, leaving Rufus alone in the darkened streets.

With the conspicuous bulge under his cloak, Rufus dashed back to the palace with all the strength he could muster. He knew little about the book, other than that he should probably burn it, but something inside him drove him mad with desire to peruse its contents. Luckily, everyone else seemed so fixated on the pandemonium in the town that they hardly noticed the cloaked figure. He bounded up the stairs and reached his room in record time. After firmly securing the door and checking the windows three times, he sat down and propped the book open on his desk.

The tattered pages appeared as if a well-placed sneeze would disintegrate them. They were covered with blotches of yellow, and there were spots where portions had worn away entirely. Many of the pages clung together at points, and thus, Rufus handled them very delicately. As he managed to pry the title page away by itself, he could not shake the feeling that he had just set himself at the feet of an old sage in a rocking chair whose mind possessed an array of experience to share.

Rufus sniffed a bit as the book's dusty smell reached his nostrils. However, his slight discomfort disappeared as his eyes scanned over the first page. There, in painstakingly formed crimson letters, a title leapt from the page: *A History of the Canticle Kingdom*. Rufus scrutinized the page, his eyes fixed on it as if the book itself had captured them. With light fingers, Rufus turned over the first page and squinted at the carefully formed script. The text was arranged in two tight columns separated by a thin ebony line. He could understand the text on the right column; however, the text on the left remained completely foreign to him.

He mumbled the text as his eyes scanned the text. "In the reign of Gretchen, the first queen, the great palace rose over the sacred edifice below the earth. The town blossomed below in the valley, creating a haven of peace and safety for the inhabitants, who came from many lands to populate the kingdom. The noble family moved among the people, spinning sweet melodies and clothing them in gilded words . . ." He stared up from the book. This was not how the traditional histories began. No, this was unlike any story he had ever heard. The story continued on, detailing the rise and fall of each of the queens, the advent of the evil wizard during each reign, and the exploits of the five knights who had always risen to the kingdom's defense. Interestingly enough, it also continued to tell of the noble family who filled the kingdom with music, which played an integral role in finding and coronating each new queen.

Some tales were so fanciful that Rufus could barely believe that they were classified as history. One particularly wild tale told of a day in which the sky had broken up suddenly and a giant face had appeared. The giant face had produced a gale of such force that it had engulfed the entire kingdom in a cloud of dust and debris.

Although sometimes fantastic, the text was rich and full, nearly over-flowing the pages with beauty and meaning. His eyes leapt over the words, only pausing when swiftly turning the pages as he read deep into the night. Reading quickly, he skimmed through most of the contents, reaching the end of the text as the first inklings of sunrise peeked over the horizon. He noticed that the book contained many empty pages, yet to be written, and the account of the last queen remained terse, cutting off abruptly as if suddenly slashed by a guillotine blade.

"And in the day that Lady Ellis abruptly fell from life, there arose a gleam-ing, new terror—innocuous at first, but destined to poise the kingdom for ruin. The new queen, but a mere child, accepted the influence of those cor-rupted councilors who had served inauspiciously under the last queen. Willing to take any measures necessary to uphold their illegitimate rule, they ruthlessly crushed any who opposed them, slaughtering some and throwing the rest in their gruesome prisons. In this dark hour, the five knights, instead of oppos-ing the measure, fell also into rebellion amongst them and betrayed the trust of the kingdom in its time of greatest need. The coup succeeded, and evil ones placed themselves on the throne. The sweet child grew up around so much corruption; it cankered her soul, like a sapling raised in a swamp, turning her from a charming little girl into a selfish, petulant queen, with only the outward appearance of ruling the kingdom. As the kingdom rotted from within, her twisted councilors led her as a marionette. Now the people of the kingdom live in constant terror that at any time they could be the next lives snuffed out, taken by the hideous three: Artus the Cruel, Cornelius the Devious, and—" Rufus paused for a moment, his breath catching in his throat. He squinted to make sure that it was not a trick of the early morning light. "—Rufus the Heartless."

On impulse, he seized the book and slammed it shut in his hand, aban-doning all caution and flinging it across the room. In moments, he had dashed to the fireplace and kindled a mighty flame, which rose like a beast from its place, its molten teeth licking at the floor and at the face of its creator. With a cry of rage and confusion, Rufus hoisted the book above his head, intent on feeding it to the flames. To his horror, he was powerless to carry out the deed.

Rufus gazed into the flames, which seemed to have taken on a voice, mocking and taunting him, crackling and hissing accusations. The firelight seemed to reach out, intent on grasping him, to draw him in with the book into its fiery embrace. It was as if he truly possessed a gaping hole where his heart should have been, and he gave in to the despair that the flames spat out at him. His hand unclenched as he crashed to the floor, the book landing first with a dull thud. There he lay on the singed floor, his flushed face drenched with sweat and his mouth contorted in a whispered cry. "Heartless . . . ."

∽∾∿

Rufus awoke with the smell of smoke in his nostrils. He still lay on the floor, having passed out there the night before, the fire having burned itself down to embers. When his eyes finally came into focus, he was aware of a scrap of brightly colored parchment on the floor in front of him. Rubbing his eyes to banish the sleepiness, he first raised himself to his knees and groggily snatched the piece of parchment from the floor and held it close to his face.

He knew the writing well from many other such messages he had received in the past. However, unlike all those other times, the words filled him with trepidation instead of elation. The queen's notes appeared by seemingly magical means, and who knew if they were just the beginning of her power. Even though the queen's health seemed restored, something was still not right with her, though he could not say what. That and the book . . . .

The book! He shot up so that he was sitting completely straight and eyed the floor for the book. It still lay on the ground with its pages open to the air, and fluttering slightly back and forth with a slight draft. Rufus hoisted the book and lay it back on the table, contemplating its fate as with that of a prisoner. He still had half a mind to destroy it, but he decided that there still might be treasures to glean from its pages. He shoved the book deep under his bed, away from prying eyes, stood up, and promptly remembered his promise to meet the captain to discuss festival matters. He swiftly changed clothes, ran his hands several times through his hair and followed the familiar path to Cornelius's study.

To his surprise, he found the door already open and the Captain inside. "Come in, Rufus. I've been looking over things, and I can't seem to make sense of any of it. Perhaps it just needs a more . . . artistic eye."

The Captain gestured to a partially empty canvas at the center of the circular, torch-lit room. They both walked over to it and saw that it was stretched taut and covered with harsh black lines, which formed more chaos than anything Rufus could easily discern at first glance. In front of the canvas lay an assortment of paints and brushes, arranged in no apparent order on a short desk. The rest of the room was taken up by a maze of cupboards, full of various flasks and clutter, at whose function he could only guess. The room smelled of a strange musty combination of mold and chemicals.

Rufus took in every detail of the room with anxious fascination. This was not at all the errand he had expected. "What I am supposed to do here?" he inquired. "I've never even seen this place."

The Captain fixed his gaze on the canvas. "Cornelius was working on this project before he . . . died. Not many people knew it, but he was something of an artist himself. This was supposed to be showcased at the festival today, but unfortunately he left it unfinished. Knowing your obvious artistic talent, the queen has requested that you finish the piece as a tribute to our fallen comrade."

Rufus stared quizzically at the canvas, trying to figure out the original intent. "That's a touching sentiment, and I'm flattered, of course," he muttered impassively. "But I must admit that I haven't the slightest idea what it is supposed to be. He didn't leave any other indication?"

The Captain chuckled heartily. "Now why on earth would he have done that? He fully expected to finish it himself! You never wake up one morning and expect that you won't see the next one."

Rufus sighed, accepting his lot. "Well, I guess you're right. I'll do what I can." Rufus stooped down and lifted one of the thick brushes from the table. Its bristles were still saturated with paint, but surprisingly, the paint had not dried or caked into a hard shell. Curious, he surveyed the other brushes, and found the paint on them shiny and ready to use. He shuddered a bit. *Wizardry*, he thought to himself. *It's so unnatural. Why shouldn't his paints dry out like any normal man's?*

Shoving his reservations aside, he lifted the brush in his hand and applied the first stroke to the canvas. Strangely enough, as he began to paint, the patterns became familiar to him. His pace increased, and he found himself sloshing the paint onto the canvas at a more rapid pace than he had ever achieved before. Excitement welled up in him, as the picture took form from the dull surface of the canvas. In a flurry of motion, Rufus worked on, snatching new brushes and colors with the dexterity of a monkey swinging on jungle branches. Working feverishly, Rufus lost all sense of time and his surroundings, becoming entirely engrossed in his project.

At last, the frenzied movement halted, and the surrogate artist stepped back to contemplate his work. Smiling to himself, he turned to seek the Captain's approval. Instantly, his smile vanished: the Captain was nowhere to be seen. Rufus called out, his eyes wildly scanning the room looking for the passage from which he had come. He could see no means of exit. Desperately, he left the canvas and ran his hands along the walls feeling for the secret passage that had led him there. His hands met only a solid wall of mossy stones.

Rufus fought back panic as his fate became clear to him. It would be futile to call out and even more so to rub his hands raw while searching for another well-hidden door. Instead, he turned his attention to the room around him.

He first stumbled upon an ancient bookshelf stuffed full of dusty, yellowed volumes. He scanned the spines, reading a few of the titles to himself. "*Faust, Percival, Mein Kampf . . . .*"

He took the first few books from the shelf and flipped through the pages. He immediately noticed the sketches in the margins, which covered almost every single page. The sketches often came with notes, though Rufus found that he could not read a single word of them.

He scanned the entire row and did not see a single book he recognized or had even heard of. He left the bookshelf, shaking his head slightly. Obviously, Cornelius had been more of a bookworm and an artist than Rufus had ever given him credit for.

Rummaging through the other shelves and cupboards, he found mostly unlabeled vials and beakers at whose contents he could only begin to speculate. To make matters worse, the rest appeared to be nothing more than scraps of metal and worthless junk. With a sigh, he sat down on a rickety stool in front of his recently completed painting.

"Well," he mused to the painting, "what could be so important about you that they'd shut me up in here? You think they plan on taking me back once I'm done? They probably didn't think that I could complete it so quickly . . . ."

Rufus shook his head, suddenly realizing how crazy he sounded talking to a painting. Rubbing his temples to clear his mind, he stared at the painting more closely. As he did, a small detail popped out at him, which he in his haste had forgotten to finish. "Clumsy me," he muttered with a shake of his head. "How on earth could I have missed that?"

Dipping his brush into the still fresh paint, he completed the line with a tiny stroke. To his surprise, the seemingly insignificant action brought tremendous results. Suddenly, the entire room burst to life. Clear glass tubing suddenly emerged from the many vials and flasks, connecting to each other to form an intricate network, which led to the center of the room and disappeared into the wood of the easel.

The multi-colored chemicals bubbled and raced around the room in their glass tubing, flowing into the easel. As the chemicals flowed in, the colors on the canvas glowed brightly, growing more vibrant by the second. The entire canvas seemed to dance, as if infused with life. Sparks of various colors shot off in all directions as the quiet flowing of the chemicals increased to a roar. At last, the entire canvas shone with such a multicolored luster that Rufus had to shield his eyes, both from the light and the acrid, colorful smoke that quickly engulfed the room. Rufus dropped to his knees, with the whizzing of sparks overhead the only indication of what was going on. He buried his face in his cloak, gasping for breath as close to the ground as he could manage. For several awful seconds, he felt consciousness slipping from him as he struggled in vain to find a pure breath of air.

Then, just as suddenly as the bedlam had started, it ceased. With a final whirl like the roar of a tornado, the suffocating smoke disappeared through the ground at the center of the room as if being sucked in by an enormous nostril. Silence returned, as did normal consciousness to Rufus's mind. Weak from shock, he hoisted himself up onto the nearest cupboard and gazed dazedly around the room, his breath coming in greedy gasps. Most of the room appeared strangely the same as it had before; however, the center of the room where the canvas had stood appeared much different indeed. Instead of an easel and paints, a jagged hole dominated the center of the room. Smoke still rose from the hole and small patches of flame rimmed the edge, casting eerie shadows on the rest of the room.

Getting his bearings, Rufus staggered over to the hole to gaze into its depths. He could see nothing in the blackness. Choosing a spot without flames, he knelt and looked closer and immediately flew back as a ferocious roar emanated from the pit. The growl rose from the pit and reverberated off every stone of the chamber as if it would collapse on itself. His heart beating wildly, he backed himself against the wall as far away from the pit as he could manage.

Clutching his chest, he suddenly had a horrible realization. "I know what I just painted," he muttered. "Countless people are going to die, and it will all be my fault." Rufus could do nothing but stare into the great abyss before him. "There's no other way out of this," he muttered dejectedly. "I've turned this place into the dragon's lair and sealed myself in." He glanced back forlornly one last time at the wall through which he had entered and ran his hands along it. It proved to be no more than mossy stone. A calm resolution passed over his face as he fastened his hand to the hilt of his sword, closed his eyes, leapt into the jaws of the gaping hole in front of him, and was enveloped by the billowing darkness.

CHAPTER FIFTEEN

THE APPRENTICE DUEL

IDAR-OBERSTEIN, WEST GERMANY, 1945

Capt. Edison's jaw fell open and then clamped back shut, gritting his teeth. "You know what happened to my daughter?"

The old man stared back, his eyes brimming with sadness. "Yes, I do. It's the same thing that happened to my brother and . . . my own daughter. The good news is that they still live, and it is still possible to retrieve them. However, I'm afraid that it will take some doing."

The two stared at each other, Capt. Edison growing more impatient by the minute at Karsten's enigmatic responses. "So . . . I take it that the problem is that this music box is broken," he said.

The grinding had been unmistakable. The damage was not only to the casing. The old man's face grimaced as he ran his fingers over the smooth wood. He muttered to himself unintelligibly, paying no heed to his guest for several minutes.

At last, he set the box back on the table, his head bobbing resolutely. "Yes, it's broken, and that's the first of our problems, but luckily, it's not completely beyond repair. The outside damage does not concern me as much as what's within."

Karsten returned to silence, causing Capt. Edison to fidget uncomfortably. He could not begin to comprehend what the old man meant. "So, what can you do to fix it? You said you made it. If anyone knows how to fix it, I'm sure it would be you. I'm a bit anxious to get on with it if we can. I'll help you however I can, if it means getting my daughter back."

Karsten chuckled good-naturedly, thoroughly catching Capt. Edison off-guard. "Heh, very generous of you, but you don't know what you are asking, and I couldn't possibly explain it to you. If you'd like to start right away, it's up to you. What I can tell you is that the task would be perilous at best, and at worst, well"—he paused for dramatic effect—"I'll leave it up to your young imagination."

Capt. Edison was not sure whether to be insulted or frightened by this remark.

131

Gaining his composure, he smiled confidently and replied. "I'd do anything for my little girl. Just point me in the right direction, and I'll do whatever is necessary."

"Good!" chimed Karsten. "You never know what will be required in such adventures. Come, have a seat. Before anything else is to be done, I must repair the exterior damage." Stooping under his desk, Karsten removed an ancient wooden toolbox and placed it with a heavy clunk before him. He muttered nonchalantly as he rifled through the contents searching for the proper tools. "I suppose I could tell you a few things while we wait . . . like I said, you better sit down."

ന്ദ

MIDDLESPACE

Whether days or months had passed, Johann could not tell. Time seemed to have lost all of its meaning in such a way that he had simply ceased to care about it. Johann and Brutus simply slept when their bodies wore out and trained and learned once they were rested. Though Johann looked forward to the training, he dreaded sleep. Suppose there were other people wandering around. He hadn't yet told Siegfried about the man he fought that first night—the man he thought he had killed. It might have been a dream, but it seemed so real. Johann tried to push the unpleasant thought to the back of his mind by concentrating completely on his training.

There had been much more swordplay, which had increased in intensity with each progressive match. Now that Johann and Bruno had really got the hang of swinging at each other full kilter, they found that they progressed quickly. The sluggishness slowly wore off along with any baby fat that remained on their bodies.

Johann was pleased with the progress, though he remained cautious. He often found himself gripped by intense sudden flashes of anger, which he could not explain. They came always in the thick of battle, which meant that he directed the brunt of his rage on Bruno. Crying like a banshee, he would strike out with an intensity that often sent his opponent sprawling, which warranted Siegfried's intervention. Although he still cared very little for Bruno—he was still an obnoxious little twerp—the feelings frightened him nonetheless. Before entering the strange Middlespace, Johann had always been levelheaded and had hated when others displayed their anger, especially his mother. He would cringe at the sound of her raised voice, but now, he figured that he could put even her to shame.

To divert himself from fighting, he asked Siegfried to teach him some of what he knew about magic. Thus the knight added a regimen of magic spells to their training that, although not as advanced as Siegfried's complete knowledge, gave the boys a good overview about what spells to use to defend themselves. Johann spent many of his down moments throwing fireballs and sparks at targets, which he had conjured up from the Middlespace. He fancied himself to be quite good, a fact that showed as his lightening bolts grew in intensity every practice session.

Johann had not observed Bruno doing any magic, until one day he found him with his back turned, fumbling with his fingers and chanting softly. Johann approached cautiously, intrigued. Up to this point he had considered Bruno too dense to do much more than swing his arms around, but this was something completely different.

As Johann approached, he realized that he did not recognize any of the words Bruno was chanting. In addition, Bruno did not sound at all like himself. His voice growled out the words, deep and guttural as if they ground his throat on their way out. Wanting to break his nervousness, Johann decided on the path of a prankster. Muttering softly to himself, he released a tiny fireball directed at Bruno's pant leg. Luckily his aim was true, and the spark found its mark. He chuckled to himself as the corner of Bruno's clothing began to smoke, although it was nothing that the boy could not easily stamp out in a second.

However, when Bruno finally became aware of his problem, his reaction was one Johann could never have expected. Bruno whirled around with uncommon speed, flinging out his arms, his fingers spread wide. A cry escaped his lips as a dark mass of energy rushed toward Johann, threatening to envelop him. On impulse, Johann's fingers flew to his sword, raising it to face the oncoming blast as Siegfried had instructed him. Had the sword been ordinary metal, it might have been as useless as a tree branch. However, with the enchantment that Siegfried had given, it protected its owner, sending the dark mass flying off in another direction until it vanished in the vast whiteness of the Middlespace.

Deep in shock and breathing heavily, Johann started at Bruno with a puzzled expression. Bruno met his gaze with a cold indifference, with not so much as a glib remark escaping his lips. Then suddenly, his face melted into one of genuine contrition. He shook his head, as if someone had just splashed a bucket of cold water across his face. "Eh, whaddya doin' here? Sneakin' up on me again? Ain't ye got enough tricks when we're trainin'?"

Johann laughed mirthlessly. "Bruno, you just about took off my head, and that's all you've got to say? I didn't think you were that interested in magic!"

Bruno placed his hands on his hips, his lips curled up in a snarl. "Magic? What ye talkin' about? That stuff is creepy. Ah never could understand why ye were so fascinated wit' it."

Johann could feel a quiet spark of rage flitting around in his heart. "Don't mess with me!" he spat, his voice taking an edge. "I saw you chanting away like a little goblin; then you attacked me! I'm not making this up, and you know it, so don't play stupid!"

Bruno's scowl turned into a full-blown dirty look. "It's you that's messin' wi' me!" he retorted, picking up his sword, which lay on the floor beside him. "I never did any such thing, but the more you talk about it, the more it's soundin' like a good idea."

Without another word, he leapt forward, brandishing his sword like a madman. In horror, Johann brought his own sword around to block. "Bruno, stop!" he managed. "You forgot to activate the charm."

The clang of metal on metal punctuated the sentence. Apparently Bruno did not care that his blade could actually cleave his opponent in two. Johann parried the first blow easily, taking the defensive. With the sudden onset of the battle, there was no chance to the put the enchantment on his own blade, which he could now do by himself. He fought on, his rage intertwining with horror. There was no way he would run another person through, specter or not.

His passive stance, however, only served to infuriate his opponent, who spat epithets that he'd never known existed. Johann fought back desperately, attempting to do no harm. "What do you have against me anyway?"

Bruno did not miss a beat. "Ye think yer better than me, but you're not! You're the same sort of fatherless scum, crawled out of the same swamp!"

The comment only fanned Johann's rage, and for a moment he flared up against his attacker, landing three quick blows in succession.

"What do you know about my father?" he retorted. "He was a valiant man who died honorably! Who knows what can be said about yours?"

Bruno replied with a swift kick to Johann's abdomen, sending him sprawling across the floor. Taking advantage of his position, Bruno rushed forward swinging his sword wildly around and placing it less than an inch from Johann's face. "My father," he began levelly, "left when I was toddler. Never seen 'im again. I *hate* him, and I . . . hate . . . *you!*"

Johann held his breath, contemplating how far this crazed boy would go. He closed his eyes trying not to breathe too heavily. Trying to clear his mind, he surreptitiously lifted a few fingers on his right hand. "That's too bad, Bruno. But . . . I don't think you have the spine to—"

Suddenly, his fingers flared, and a burst of flame shot out, engulfing Bruno's sword. Bruno screamed, his fingers flying off the superheated metal. However, the sword never hit the ground. Towering over both of them, Siegfried cast an ominous shadow, a steaming sword gripped in his only hand. "Children, becoming like your fathers is often a noble thing, but in this case, I'd say this is a little too close . . . "

Siegfried glanced first at one boy and then at the other. Standing between them, he looked like a totem pole flanked by chipmunks. His expression was neither hot nor cold as he swept his gaze over them. Nevertheless, neither boy could meet his eyes. When he finally spoke, it was in a tone they had never heard him use before, deep and sober. "I don't usually discourage healthy rivalry. No, to the contrary, it can be quite constructive. Your fathers were rivals of sorts, and when it got out of hand, the results were unbearably tragic. However, it seems that we ventured into something even worse. You are both tampering with powers that you have no idea about—powers that nearly destroyed our kingdom many times. If you trifle with it, it will trifle with you. I must know Bruno, how did you learn that magic?"

Bruno's gaze remained impassive, staring straight ahead. "I can't tell ye, so I won't."

Siegfried's face registered a brief flash of anger. "I don't have time for insolent answers, boy! The magic you demonstrated today was supremely dangerous. If Johann had not been nimble enough, he probably would not be here now."

A wry smile crossed Bruno's face for the first time. "Why would a power like that be so bad? We need all the power we can to take on the blokes at the castle! Should we get rid of our advantages so easily?"

Siegfried's anger flashed strong this time. "It is not an advantage! It's a dangerous power that requires incredible restraint when it is used, if at all! A campfire is harmless when carefully controlled, but it also holds the power to consume a forest when not."

Bruno's face remained unrepentant despite the tirade. "And if I don't tell yeh, what'll ye do then? Beat it out of me? What business do ye have being scared off by some little kid like meself? Maybe yer just weak."

Surprisingly, Siegfried did not flare up again at this blatant provocation. Instead, he slowly gripped his sword and stared at the defiant boy below him. "Perhaps I am," he muttered half-mockingly. "There seems to be only one way to tell. You and I are just going to have to have a go at it. That way, we'll see what is stronger: the wisdom of experience or the craftiness of youth."

Bruno scrunched up his face, his lips forming a snarl. "Yeah, is that what you want? A brawl? Okay then. But I'm warning ye, I won't hold back like I did with this pathetic weakling here. You'll be sorry."

Siegfried's only reaction was a slight arch of his eyebrows. "It's settled, then. A duel of sorts. But what is a duel without something at stake? I say, if I am victorious, you will tell me what I want to know about your magic. If you, however, carry the day, I will divulge everything I know about your father."

Cockily, Bruno accepted the terms, shaking Siegfried's single out-stretched hand. Johann gazed on in disbelief. "Who do you think you are?" he interjected to Bruno. "Brigitta can keep you at bay with her sling shot.

You're pathetic! Are you trying to prove something?"

Bruno did not reply but turned his face toward the arena, which had suddenly appeared nearby. He entered the ring, his usual swagger replaced by the stance of a gladiator ready to slaughter lions. Johann just shook his head, unable to see where the old knight was going with this.

Siegfried mounted the other side of the ring, his face level as he gripped his sword in one hand, swinging it absently in the air. Bruno assumed a fighting stance, almost comical in its seriousness. David could not have looked more ridiculous in front of Goliath.

Suddenly, Siegfried leapt into action, lashing out his sword with a cry. Bruno lithely dodged the blow and retreated, skirting quickly around the edges of the arena. Siegfried continued his assault with a series of blows just like the first, which Bruno easily dodged at every turn. Johann wrinkled his brow. "I know Siegfried can move faster than that," he murmured. "It's like he's playing with him . . . ."

The elaborate dance continued for several minutes. As it drew on, Johann noticed that Bruno had begun to mutter, just like he had before striking out at Johann. "Siegfried!" he cried. "Watch him! He's going to use dark magic!"

But if the knight heard the warning, he made no indication. In short order, Johann's prediction came true. In mid jump, Bruno let out a shriek as bolts of dark energy streamed from his fingers and surrounded the knight. The old knight lifted his sword as the darkness swirled about him. The knight swiftly slashed out with his sword, dissipating the darkness where he struck. Sensing that his hold was slipping, Bruno renewed his attack, releasing more energy from his fingers. He continued his inhuman shrieks, more color draining from his face with each passing second. The darkness swirled more quickly around the knight, until it completely hid him from sight. Enveloped in darkness, the knight fell to the ground and lay still.

Johann rushed into the arena to aid his mentor but strangely, as he tried to cross the threshold, an unseen force propelled him backwards. Frantic, he leapt again to his feet, drawing his sword. However, no matter how he tried, he could not cross the barrier into the arena.

Grinning wanly like a lunatic, Bruno stopped his chanting and stood gloating over his defeated opponent. Cautiously, he nudged the fallen knight with his foot and, sensing no response, broke into haughty laughter. "Still think it's not an advantage, ye ol' fool? I'll have them bowing at my feet, and I don't need your help! Now tell me what I want to know!"

The darkness dissipated from around the knight like a cloud suddenly pierced by the sun. Slowly the old knight's eyes fluttered open, revealing the ancient eyes, bright as ever. "Yes . . . I shall tell you."

In a blur, the knight's hand shot up, thrusting toward Bruno's face. Bruno flew back as if carried by a cresting wave. Even before he landed, Siegfried sprung into the air, intercepting Bruno's flight, bringing his sword down hard, and driving the boy to the ground. The moment that Bruno hit the ground, Siegfried raised his hand, a sphere of the same dark energy forming at his fingertips.

Johann's jaw remained glued to the floor as he watched Siegfried bring down the sphere on Bruno forming a prison of roiling energy. To Johann's puzzlement, Siegfried appeared the epitome of health while Bruno could have passed for a plague victim. Siegfried calmly returned his sword to its sheath and stared down at his captive. "Do not worry, you foolish boy, I do not intend to cause you further pain. Think of this as an object lesson, one that I hope will not be necessary to repeat."

Bruno glanced out with glazed eyes, his voice raspy. "I don't understand . . . I had ye . . . I had ye . . . ."

Siegfried nodded slightly, his face grave. "Yes, it appeared so, but it is as I said. I was able to turn on you the same power you used against me. It's a good thing that you did not go much further, or you might have completely exhausted your strength."

Fire still smoldered in Bruno's eyes. "Why can't I control it? Why does it listen to you?"

Siegfried cocked an eyebrow. "Correct me if I am mistaken, but I believe it is you that should be answering the questions now."

Bruno hung his head in defeat. "Alright, I'll tell ye." Bruno sat up as much as the sphere would let him. The entire story came out at once, his accent even thicker than usual. "So, I was just wanderin' about one day, feelin' a bit sorry for myself and all. Johann 'ere had just given me a right proper thrashing, and I found myself wishing I had a way to get the upper 'and on 'im. Suddenly, there was this huge bloke in a big black robe standin' in front o' me. He told me 'e had 'eard my request and was willin' to teach me a few things that might give me the advantage I wanted. He told me that he was gonna be in charge of things around 'ere soon and that I could be part of 'is kingdom if I wanted. He said that he'd already drawn in great people from other worlds to 'elp 'im and that I could take me place with them if I was a good student. I called him every chance I could, and he taught me 'ow to do those spells and such. It made me feel powerful, and I was just waiting to bring it out at the right time. Johann spoiled it all by sneakin' up on me, and I think yeh know the rest."

Siegfried hung his head. "You have done some foolish things in the time I've know you, but that, Bruno, was by far the king of them all."

He turned and stepped quietly into the white void. Bruno's face contorted in panic. "Hey! Yer not gonna just leave me 'ere, are ye?"

Siegfried turned about, his face grim. "The spell will wear off in time.

Until then, you'll have plenty of time to think about your actions with absolutely no chance of getting in trouble." Before Bruno could protest further, the knight had vanished. Johann followed quickly thereafter, leaving the groaning boy alone in his personal prison.

ॐ

As Johann wandered out in the vast nothingness, feelings of loneliness crept up on him more intensely than they had ever before in his life. Unfortunately, in this bleak place, there could be no comfort. His mother had been the only one who could ever console this ache, but she was far away at the moment and conceivably in great danger. Not to mention Brigitta. He had no idea if he'd ever see her again.

Just as tears of frustration and hopelessness started to form in his eyes, he glimpsed something that made him pause: another person wandering aimlessly toward him. He had never seen her before, so he was sure he couldn't have wished her to him. He halted and considered the person, growing more confused by the second.

She was a pale little girl, with short golden hair, which flew out around her head in every possible direction. Her clothes were unlike Johann had ever seen. Intrigued, Johann rushed toward her, clutching his sword as he went. She did not look at all threatening, but he had learned not to trust any appearances lately. As he approached, the girl finally caught a glimpse of him, and terror spread immediately across her face. She broke into a run in the other direction.

Johann kept up to her pace and called after her. "Stop! I'm not going to hurt you! I can help you!" He did not really know whether this was true or not, but it was enough to make the girl turn and slacken her pace. Johann easily caught up and stood staring at the strange girl. Cautiously taking his hand away from the grip of his sword, he slowly extended it to the girl, who was trembling now like a cornered animal in a trap. "Hello, I'm Johann. Who are you?"

It was several moments before the girl mustered up the courage to speak. When she did so, her voice reflected her trembling body. "I-I'm Kate. I'm lost. This place is awful!"

Johann nodded, trying on his best reassuring smile. "Can't say that I like it here myself. I know how I got here, but I have a feeling that you don't."

Kate nodded, swallowing hard and fighting back tears of fright. "You're right. I was just in my room playing with the new present my daddy brought me. I remember some music and then a bright white light. Then I was here."

Johann fumbled for the right words. He had never heard of such a thing. Whatever it was, it sounded like a nasty sort of magic that he did not want to have anything to do with. "Well, Kate," he spoke softly, taking her by the shoulder "I think you may want to come with me. I think I know someone who might know how to help you. He may be able to get you back to where you came from."

"Okay." Kate sniffled and fell in step with Johann as they walked back the other way. Johann pictured Siegfried in his mind, and they found themselves quickly back to the circle of chairs. To his dismay, however, Siegfried was nowhere to be seen. He had Kate sit in one of the comfy chairs and then dashed about, searching for his mentor. Suddenly, in mid-stride, his foot landed in something wet. Both startled and annoyed, Johann leapt back, shook the moisture from his foot, and then glanced down to find the source. Before him on the ground lay a large puddle of water, still rippling from his recent footstep. Johann craned his ear closer as he thought he could hear sound emitting from the pool. As the ripples in the pool settled, the image of Siegfried came into focus. A wild look of terror marked the old knight's face, making Johann's heart seize in his chest. Only then did he understand the words emitting from the puddle. "Trapped, Johann, I'm trapped! What sort of devilry is this?"

Words failed Johann as he gazed into the puddle, which now more clearly showed his master's frantic shape. Desperately, he reached into the puddle, trying in vain to raise his master, but this only blurred the image without further effect. Eventually, he gave up and let the water settle again so that he could clearly hear his master's voice. He strained his ears, a tear beginning to form at the corner of his eye.

"Johann, can you hear me?" came the worried voice from the puddle.

Johann nodded swiftly, quickly swiping away the tear of frustration so his master would not see it. "I can, Master, what is going on? What's holding you in there?"

The knight shook his head. "I have no idea! I can barely move. It's all so blurry . . . ."

Johann's breathing grew rapid, and he motioned for Kate to sit. "What were you doing when this happened? Did you see anyone?"

"Not a soul," he replied in confusion. "Well, that is, not here. Perhaps I better explain. I was using the water jar that I used with you to communicate with another . . . ally. Everything looked normal as I poured the water out, but something strange started to happen as it pooled on the ground. The water began to bubble and a black inky stain spread slowly through it. Without warning, it leapt up at me with inky arms and dragged me down until I couldn't see anything but blackness. When I came to, all I could do was look up through this hole. I've never heard of anything quite like this before, but it's surely a sign of dark wizardry. I'm afraid it's a surer sign than ever that he's returned. "

Johann shuddered as the implications sunk in. The knight could only be referring to one person. Johann rubbed his eyes and shook his head. "What does this mean, then? What are we supposed to do? There must be some way to get you out of there!"

Siegfried cocked a rueful smile. "The only person I know who could dispel magic this powerful was your father. For a lack of better options, I'd say I'm stuck here for now."

Johann's face strained with frustration. The answer only served to remind him how alone he felt. He hung his head in despair. "But I can't do this alone! I don't have a chance without your help! If Bruno doesn't do me in, there's bound to be someone who will! I'm not strong enough and definitely not brave enough to—"

The knight cut him off in mid-sentence. "Johann. You do not have a choice. This problem is a wide gulf with only one bridge. Any other path leads to a long, dark fall with a painful ending at the bottom. The bridge may be rickety and perilous, but it's the only path."

Johann shook his head vehemently. "I can't do it alone. I have no idea how to go about it . . . no plan . . . nothing."

Siegfried's face finally took on a manner of composure. He looked directly at Johann, his brow furrowed earnestly. "Johann, you can do this. It is in your blood, and you are destined for greatness. You will finish the task for which your father strove for many years, and he will at last be able to rest. I still feel his tormented presence often, as if he is still near us, unable to leave, but powerless to intervene. This task is in behalf of more people than you could ever imagine, Johann. I know that it's a huge burden, and I also intended to help you carry it to the end." The knight lowered his head regretfully. "But I do have a plan, Johann. That much I can give you."

A calm resolve flowed over Johann's features. With resignation, he knelt by the side of the water. "Go on. I am listening." Siegfried breathed deeply and then began, speaking slowly and levelly. Johann listened intently, his eyes never leaving the pool, his jaw tightening. When Siegfried finished, Johann stood, closed his eyes and nodded gravely. Turning about, he found that a rift had opened in the whiteness, revealing a wintry forest scene. Glancing back one last time at his master, and indicating for Kate to follow, he gave a parting salute, and marched solemnly toward the opening.

CHAPTER SIXTEEN

ʓℚℚ

A WARRIOR
and a SCIENTIST

IDAR-OBERSTEIN, WEST GERMANY, 1945

After they had both taken their seats, Karsten began his account in the deep voice of a master storyteller. Capt. Edison could not help but think how much his daughter would love to be here, sitting in a European castle in a secret room and listening to an eccentric old man weave strange tales.

The thought weighed heavily on his heart as he struggled to listen. "My brother and I are artists by trade, and we love nothing more than to carve life out of a piece of wood. Though we mostly worked well together, he, as my younger brother, sometimes let his jealous side show. He resented my natural abilities, which far exceed his own, and thus he turned to other venues to enhance his skill." Karsten leaned forward, strain showing on his face. "He turned to dark paths, things of which I do not lightly speak. They quickened his hands but cankered his soul. But what could I do? He was my brother and still my best friend."

He picked up the box from the desk. "This project was meant to be our masterpiece. A very powerful man commissioned it on very short notice, and we stood to make a fortune for a job well done. We worked day and night for more than a week. Exhausted from the effort, I stumbled off to bed on the night we finally finished. However, when I awoke the next morning, both my brother and the box were gone."

Capt. Edison perked up at the mention of the disappearance. "So are you saying that your brother's disappearance had something to do with the box?"

Karsten nodded. "Yes, but I did not put two and two together for a long time. At first I thought he had simply betrayed me and had taken the box to deliver alone so that he could run off with the commission. But as weeks turned into months and years without hearing anything about the box's whereabouts, I began to wonder. So, I set out to find both my brother and the box. I quickly found out that neither of them had ever reached our wealthy patron and that the patron was still quite angry about the whole affair."

Karsten produced a flask of some dark liquid from beneath his desk and offered some to Capt. Edison, who declined. The old man poured himself a portion into an ancient, cracking glass and continued after a healthy swig. "The search spanned several years, but I was not to be deterred. Slowly, I pieced together my brother's dark path, which led me first to the box and then to the startling truth about his whereabouts."

Karsten leaned forward, the firelight dancing across his face, as if ready to divulge a great mystery. "The box had traveled across the entire country and had seen both the upper crust and dregs of society. When I found it, it still appeared to me the same as the day we finished it. Still, I knew something was amiss, for I had heard rumors of his true purpose: to be king."

Capt. Edison furrowed his brow. The story was not making any sense. "King of what?" he asked flippantly. "The box? That's not much of a kingdom."

Karsten wrinkled his brow and clamped his eyes shut, causing the lines on his forehead to deepen into crevasses. "You know," he said at last. "You're right. It's best that I show you instead."

Karsten turned a knob on the backside of the box, and music began to play. Capt. Edison's vision blurred suddenly, causing his head to spin. The colors of the room blurred and merged together like a drop of water striking a painting. Then, all at once, he found himself in a vast sea of white nothingness.

The whole process had taken place so quickly that Capt. Edison had no time to react. For several long seconds afterwards, he simply stood in shock, not knowing which way to turn or what to do. He felt panic rise up in his chest as he saw himself alone until Karsten appeared next to him.

The other man took a mere second to shake off his disorientation and a second later his lips broadened into a wide smile. "Ha!" he exclaimed. "We did it! It still works! It's not completely broken!" He danced around like a schoolboy doing a victory jig on the first day of summer vacation. "Edison, this is wonderful! If we hurry, we might even find your daughter soon!"

Capt. Edison grudgingly followed the man, who darted forward as soon as he could. Once again, Karsten's words had left him unsettled, and he decided to trust him, crazy or not. He followed for several minutes, until suddenly Karsten halted and stretched his hand out in to what seemed to be perfectly empty space. A chilly breeze blew forcefully into both of their faces, and the fresh smell of pine needles wafted into the space.

Capt. Edison stared skeptically at the opening. "I'm not stepping out there until you give me some idea of what is going on!" he asserted in a voice he had perfected as a solider.

His traveling companion sighed the only way an old man can at a young one. "Well, I guess there is no hurt in trying, though I don't think you'll be able to grasp it all in one sitting. Speaking of which, sitting is probably a good idea."

Two over-stuffed armchairs materialized behind them, along with a small table and a silver platter full of an assortment of pastries. Capt. Edison's eyes bulged out, but he took his seat without question. Karsten sat down as if a living room set appearing out of thin air was a very normal phenomenon. He snatched a pastry and shoved the whole thing in his mouth. His face wrinkling with delight, he began his explanation. "Don't be afraid. I won't go into detail, but this food is just as real in this place as the breakfast you had this morning.

"As I explained previously, my brother and I went into business together and created the most spectacular things. Life was good, but we never could seem to get over our greatest fundamental creative difference. I prefer to think 'inside-the-box' as they say. I'm a stickler for heritage, tradition, and rules, while my brother was more of the 'out-of-the-box' thinker, wanting to experiment and forage new territory. He would often accuse me of being stuck in the past, and I would note with discomfort that he would resort to any means possible to meet his ends. He could not meet his goals in our native world, so he decided to take a chance on this one. Ironically, he became the one to think 'inside-the-box,' albeit literally."

Capt. Edison glanced sidelong at Karsten. "What do you mean, exactly? No more word play."

Karsten raised his gaze to the heavens. "We are literally inside that music box you brought to me today, and so is your daughter."

Capt. Edison nearly choked on the cream puff he had just popped into his mouth. After a brief fit of coughing, he regained his composure. "What? You can't really mean that! We're in the music box?"

Karsten nodded gravely. "As surely as I sit here, we are. This place is a result of my brother's ambition. While this was once no more than a nicely carved chunk of lifeless wood, it is now a living, breathing kingdom—a kingdom whose inhabitants for the most part have no idea of its true nature. Some of them are from the outside world like you and me, while others are nothing more than works of art brought to life by the deep magic my brother practiced."

Capt. Edison stayed silent for some time, before finally concluding that he had no other choice but to believe the strange man. He could not think of any other logical course of action or explanation for the day's strange occurrences. Running his hands through his hair, Capt. Edison sighed. "Okay, I admit it sounds completely crazy, but I'm going to trust you on this. I'm still confused, though. What does he have to gain from all this? Maybe he just needed a nice vacation spot . . . ."

Karsten shook his head firmly. "I'm not entirely sure, but I know that he's always been bent on power and conquest. I think that he intends on bringing something—or someone—from this world into the outside world. I know that he has done the opposite on many occasions. There are many things available for him here, which he didn't enjoy on the outside. I've tried to stop him, but he's grown so powerful already that he's foiled even my best efforts."

Karsten furrowed his brow and sighed heavily. Capt. Edison could tell that he felt *the weight of all those heavy years, and he began to feel a twinge of pity for him.*

"He is still my brother," Karsten continued, "and I just keep telling myself that there's a spark of the man he used to be somewhere inside him. It's lost in a murky sea of evil, but I'm determined to bring it out. I can't tell you how many times I've tried."

Capt. Edison furrowed his brow. "So you mean you've been here—to this world—before?"

"Most definitely," replied Karsten gravely. "Take hope in that fact. It is possible to go back and forth, but unfortunately it's not that easy for the uninitiated. The important thing now is that the faster we move, the sooner we can find your daughter and bring her home. What do you say we get started?"

The chairs vanished almost before Capt. Edison had a chance to rise. Gaining his balance, he fixed his gaze on the opening. "Well, Karsten, I'm not sure this isn't the airline food from last night talking, but if it isn't, I don't want to waste any more time."

He motioned for Karsten to lead the way, and they started off with a brisk pace toward the opening. In a single leap, Karsten bounded through with uncommon agility for a man his age. Capt. Edison followed gingerly after, landing both feet firmly in the snow. To his delight, Karsten noticed a promising sign as soon as they entered the forest. "Look, Capt. Edison, two sets of small footprints leading from this entrance! I'd bet my beard one of them belongs to your daughter! Hurry now!" They both scampered off down the trail, their excitement making them oblivious to the icy air swirling around them.

෨෬

THE CANTICLE KINGDOM

Rufus plummeted through the darkness, still clutching his sword. Bright shapes and colors whizzed momentarily past him in the blackness, giving him the impression that he was falling very fast. *This was either very daring or very stupid*, thought Rufus ruefully. *I'll either be a hero or a corpse very soon.*

The fall, however, ended before too long when he landed in a lump of soft material. Smarting, but still able to stand, Rufus examined his surroundings. The object that broke his fall was a broken bed with a large, fluffy mattress. A search of the space brought the discovery of more shattered furniture—desks, chairs, cabinets, and other miscellaneous bits. Papers, books, and diagrams spilled out from various places in the ruined furniture, sprinkled with bits of broken glass.

"How strange," muttered Rufus aloud. "If I didn't know any better, I'd say I've landed in somebody's bedroom." To his surprise, his remark was answered with an anguished groan from somewhere behind him. Rufus swirled about to face the sound. "Who's there? Are you hurt?"

Stooping down, he caught a glimpse of white hair and realized an old man had been pinned under a fallen cabinet. With a mighty show of exertion, Rufus succeeded with moving most of it off the body of the man.

The man had a wrinkled face surrounded on either side by two tufts of unruly white hair and bushy eyebrows. His plain, coarse clothes were tattered and torn, revealing nasty bruises and burns. After taking a few moments to recover his wits, the man raised his head slightly and sighed.

"Thank you," he cried weakly. "I thought it might be the end. But of course, it still might be. I had always feared that something like this would happen—expected it really. I can't say that it's completely unwelcome. At least it means that my experiments have been validated."

The man rambled on in a listless voice, his head swinging slowly from side to side. Rufus could not quite place his accent. He bent down and studied the man closer. His body appeared frail, but his eyes were brimming with life and wisdom.

"I'm Rufus, the chamberlain to the queen. I don't believe we've met."

The old man shook his head. "Not a chance. I've only seen a few people since I've arrived three—could it be four?—years ago." He pulled himself up, his narrow eyes wincing in pain. Rufus moved to steady him and the man grinned gratefully. "I am Bert Stein, a man of science. I have been conducting my experiments here for some time, and after what I've seen today, I would say that my work has been a success, but at what price?"

Rufus surveyed the destruction. He had a very good idea what had caused it all, but he could still not fathom how it had been possible. "If you don't mind me asking, what sort of research were you conducting? This place looks like it has been hit by a meteor."

The man paused as he was overtaken with a fit of painful coughing and then continued slowly, an edge of pain entering his voice. "Art, my friend. The marriage of art and science. A fascinating and dangerous endeavor! I sought to breathe life into the imagination, but for years, I was met with nothing more than burned parchment and disappointment. My success has been intermittent at best, but after today, I know that I have not worked in vain. We worked so hard on our last experiment, but sadly, the subject was damaged before we—that is, my employer and I—could complete it. It would seem, however, that someone has succeeded in repairing it." The intensity of his stare bore deeply into Rufus. "Tell me, sir, was it you?"

Rufus froze. Could it be that the old man was referring to his painting? "It was mine to begin with, after a fashion. Someone borrowed the original sketch from me, and so it was familiar to me when I saw it again. I finished the painting, and then, all this happened."

Bert grinned broadly. "I do not blame you. It was a masterful painting—frightening, but majestic. You should never be ashamed of your work."

Panic welled up in Rufus's chest. "But the thing which we've brought to life is no harmless creature! Unchecked, it will lay waste to the entire kingdom, spreading carnage and terror wherever it goes! This is a disaster! Why did you want to bring such a horrible thing to life?"

The reply came swiftly. "Why did you want to paint such a thing in the first place? The exhilaration of creation, the thrill of discovery! It doesn't matter now. It is done. Perhaps it is still possible to undo . . . ." His voice trailed off with a tinge of regret. His eyes had taken a faraway look, and his face paled. When he spoke again, his voice was barely audible. "What have I done? I'm not a butcher! I'm not a madman. I'm a scientist, a creator! How could I forget that so quickly?"

Bert's eyes fluttered as he groaned quietly. Rufus put his hand to feel the man's pulse, which was now barely detectable. "Stay with me, Bert. You have to tell me more about your experiments. It might help me figure out how to stop this thing. Tell me, who were you doing this for?"

Bert's eyes glazed over as his voice crept out. "Well, my friend . . . the answer to that is . . . relative."

His muscles trembling, Bert stretched out his hand to reveal a small object. Then, in one mighty rush, he let out his last breath and was still.

ॐ

Rufus stood in shocked silence, instinctively bowing his head in reverence. He removed the proffered object from Bert's pale fingers and solemnly took a sheet from the bed, and laid it over the man's body. "May your genius be appreciated more in the life to come," he muttered, feeling an inexplicable sense of emptiness. As he walked away, he considered the small object. Spherical in shape, it appeared to be cast in tarnished gray metal showing two circular golden dials with various ascending numbers attached to either end. A clear band formed a stripe around the center of the object, allowing the viewer to see a tiny, rapidly spinning hourglass.

Unsure of what to do next, Rufus headed off in the other direction, stuffing the object in his pocket. As he cautiously crept through the darkness, he mulled things over in his head. "If only I could have found out who was putting Bert up to this. The Captain said that this lab had something to do with Cornelius, but now he's dead and—"

A low, menacing cacophony of growls, snarls, howls, and yelps unlike anything he had ever heard before sounded from the darkness ahead. It sounded as if an entire zoo had gotten loose. Rufus shivered as he pictured the abomination that lurked ahead. "I brought it into this world. It is my duty to take it out."

Rufus drew his sword and dashed ahead into the darkness, teeth clenched and nostrils flared. The animal sounds drew ever closer, egging him on. He increased his pace, his robes flaring out behind him like trails of smoke, when suddenly he found the level ground sloping steeply downwards. He grasped desperately but futilely at the ground, trying to find some sort of handhold to slow his fall as he barreled ever faster toward an unseen doom.

Just as he lost hope of ever slowing down again, the angle of his descent gradually decreased, and he began to level out. With a cry of relief, he skittered to a halt, feeling as though he had broken every bone in his body. For a long while, he lay on his back, barely clutching to consciousness and staring up into the semi-darkness.

As Rufus's eyes came into focus, he noticed that the room he had landed in appeared most like an enormous cavern of pale gray stone. Terraces connected by thin stone staircases rimmed the cavern walls at intervals. At certain points, a large gap loomed behind these staircases and terraces. Rufus noticed massive slabs of stone, which lay on carts and sleds at various points around the cavern. An assortment of sculpting tools, mostly hammers and chisels, lay strewn about the ground. Stone dust coated the floor, and he noticed that many of the blocks were still works in progress.

Trying to get to his feet, Rufus winced at a sharp pain in his side and cried out, his voice echoing eerily in the gigantic space. Gingerly, he felt his side and assumed he bruised some ribs in the fall. Returning to one knee, he glanced around, assessing his surroundings for danger. Though there was no immediate threat, the sight was nevertheless unsettling. On each floor and terrace stood intricately crafted statues. They represented every form and creature imaginable, from armored knights to grotesque beasts. Rufus's breath caught in his throat as he glimpsed a statue that looked exactly like the dreaded lion-like beast he had defeated earlier.

He wiped the sweat from his brow with his free hand. *This is the work of decades!* he thought in awe. *The details are exquisite! For once, though, I am not too keen on meeting the artist.*

Rufus attempted again to stand. Slowly, he paced around the floor, closely examining the statues. He stopped when he came to the statue of a decent-sized winged horse, complete with ram's horns. The features were so lifelike that he had to reach out and run his fingers over the surface of the smooth stone. No sooner had his fingers grazed the stone than his arm recoiled in a sudden shock. Almost all sensation left his arm. He watched the change occurring in front of him in disbelief. Gradually, the bleak colors of the statue were replaced by vivid hues. The horse's coat and mane were a brilliant white, streaked with a pearly blue.

No sooner had he moved his hand than a great commotion rang out from above, and a dark, immense figure descended from the ceiling. Grasping its reins, Rufus whipped the horse around and hoisted himself onto its back. Acting on instinct, he dug his heels into the horse's side and was greeted by a welcome leap into the air, a short impact with the ground, and finally flight.

He soared toward the beast, whose odor alone formed an effectual wall around the creature. Weaving in and out between the creature's melee of attacks, Rufus raised his sword and struck a lightning blow against the brow of the dragon, sending putrid scales flying off into space. The entire creature erupted in a flurry of motion, the echo of the deafening roar sending cracks through the walls of the room.

Rufus's brow glimmered with sweat as a cloud of spikes slashed through his robes, tearing streaks of pain through his skin. His steed whined in terror as red streaks shot up its side, tainting its otherwise flawless white coat. Rufus swooped down out of the range of the creature's menacing claws, finding shelter behind the largest block of stone he could see. Tumbling off the horse, he winced as he removed the end of a large spike from just above his kneecap. The pain seared through him like lava in his veins, and for a fleeting moment, darkness threatened to close in on him for good. Falling against the stone for balance, he could feel his stomach lurching as his eyesight blurred, his whole world careening out of focus.

He hit the floor hard, his bones feeling as fragile as fallen August leaves trodden underfoot. In his state of delusion, he felt something nuzzle up against his head. His vision cleared for a fleeting second, and a woman's face appeared in front of him, more beautiful than anything he could imagine. Her golden hair crowned her face like a wreath of starlight, and for a moment, Rufus thought he had already passed beyond this world. "Your Majesty," he muttered reverently. "Have you come for me?"

The angelic face shook her head regretfully, and when she spoke it was the voice of the a true queen, as he had not heard in years. "No, Rufus, not yet. It seems we are both in grave danger. I need you to live, and so I bestow in you my final strength. I am deep beneath the castle, and soon they will take my life. Follow my light, and it will lead you to me. Go now, brave warrior. Resist evil with your whole might—it is all we can do."

The light of the vision faded into the face of his white steed, nuzzling its face up against his. Rufus's body swelled with light and energy, renewed vigor coursing through his veins. He arose with sword in hand, ready to remount his steed, when he realized that the noble creature had once again become stone. He reached out to bring the creature back to life, but just as his fingers grazed the stone, he realized that it was the wrong thing to do. The creature had drawn energy from him to become alive and had returned his strength for a reason.

As he looked around, he noticed a small glowing shape flitting around him in the air. As he moved, the shape remained close to him. As he closed his eyes while looking at the shape, he caught a glimpse of the queen's face and remembered what she had said to him: her light would be with him.

Though he had not realized it at the time, she had meant this in a very literal sense, and the thought filled the emptiness in his heart where fear had hollowed it. *I might have to sleep my days away from now on, if this is what I'll see when I close my eyes*, he thought to himself.

As Rufus watched the dancing light, it flew over and rested on the large slab of stone resting on a cart a few feet away. Rufus hurried over to the cart, peered over the edge of the platform on which it stood, and saw that he was still a considerable distance from the ground. The fighting and sound waves had turned the once smooth stone into a minefield of cracks and crevasses. Rufus glanced back at the huge stone block, an idea formulating in his mind. He placed his hand up against the smooth surface of the stone, pressing lightly, gauging its weight. "If only I could get this over the edge," he muttered ruefully. "Then I might really be able to do some damage."

An arrow of pain shot up his leg, forcing his weight onto the other one. This action thrust his arm out harder against the stone. Strangely, the cart gave a lurch forward as if ten sets of hands stood behind him instead of one. The queen's light rested on the stone, swirling around its massive shape. Ignoring the pain in his leg, he thrust both of his arms forward, sending the cart careening off the edge. The vengeful projectile, hurtled toward the floor and landed resoundingly, sending shards of debris like angry hail into the air.

The creature responded in kind, unleashing a barrage of spikes and a plume of fire in his direction. Rufus dashed up toward the next cart, his long range protecting him from any damage. Frantically taking the next ladder up, he rushed over to an even larger slab of stone and sent it over the edge. The impact of the second stone proved even more impressive than the first. The resulting shock wave seemed to shake the entire room. Splinters rained down from the ceiling, ladders toppled, and debris clouded the air, shrouding the creature from view.

Creeping forward slowly, he found to his delight that the ladder to the next level had survived the impact. Glancing over his shoulder one last time, and not sensing any nearby motion or sound, he thrust his hands out and grabbed the lower rungs of the ladder. He hoisted himself up as quickly as he dared, his lungs filling with choking dust. A sudden blast of air sent the dust swirling anew, completely blocking his view. In the oblivion, Rufus felt himself suddenly falling backwards through space as the ladder fell free from the wall. His arms flailed out, floundering desperately for anything solid to anchor himself onto, but met only sickening emptiness. He fell for several more seconds before landing hard on his back at an angle, feeling the sickening crunch of his bones. Trying feebly to rise, he found that the fall had buried him in chunks of debris, pinning him to the ground. Gasping for breath, he sought desperately for the queen's light.

Fear swelled in his chest as a flash of flame erupted in front of him. The flames flicked to and fro over his head. The heat seared his lungs and singed his face. Bracing himself for the worst, he closed his eyes and pictured the queen's lovely face, in case this was to be his last thought. However, as his eyes flicked back open, he realized to his amazement that the flames had not spouted from the creature. Above him stood his faithful steed, whipping his head about, clearing the fallen rock with its horns and freeing Rufus.

In a flash of light, the horse returned to its stone state. It had reared up on its hind legs, creating an effective ladder to the next level. Praising his good fortune, Rufus wasted no time scaling the statue as quickly as he could manage. As he reached the top, he glanced backwards briefly to take one last look at the brave animal who had saved his life.

His pause lasted only a fraction of a second before he dashed up the incline, his legs inflamed with exertion. As he rose, the dust settled again, revealing the creature as terrifying as ever. The creature writhed, agitated and anxious for blood. The next block lay only a few yards off up the steep incline. Rufus's breath came in deep gulps with his lungs choked with dust, his eyes stinging and clouded.

Suddenly, his foot caught in a tiny crevasse, sending Rufus hurdling to his knees. Maintaining his momentum, he launched forward, barely pausing to register the pain. The stone blurred, becoming no more than a fuzzy blob. His fingers clawing at the ground, he dragged himself toward the stone, barely managing to place one finger on the surface before he collapsed.

The cavern shook again as the creature released its hold on the ceiling and swung down lower into the cavern. With a sickening bellow, the creature adjusted itself to the exact level as Rufus, bathing him with its foul breath. The dragonlike head swiveled around and with it all the others, hundreds of eyes boring into the chamberlain like a storm of needles. Rufus glanced up in despair, expecting his life to end at any moment. "Guess you only get to cheat death so many times."

The creature's head reared back to strike, but in the moment before the fateful blow, a light rose in Rufus's field of vision like a glorious shooting star. As the light rested on the rock, Rufus knew in an instant what he had to do. He thrust his finger forward. The light still rested on the stone and the push sent the massive stone toppling over the edge. The cavern shook with fury, the ceiling giving way in a calamitous avalanche. A thunderous roar drowned the creature's final bellow as the cavern folded in on itself, entombing the monster under a mountain of jagged rock. The tumult thundered for several minutes more as if Armageddon itself had broken loose over their heads, threatening to extinguish all life and consciousness. However, the clanking soon died away, replaced by an eerie undisturbed silence. Rufus closed his eyes, and at last, gave in to the darkness.

ನಿ

When he finally regained consciousness, Rufus stared into the darkness for an indeterminate length of time. His body ached everywhere, so much so that he could not focus his thoughts on anything. The pain was his only link to reality and the only thing that assured him that he was still alive. Once in a while, the queen's light passed in front of his eyes, offering him the faintest glimmer of hope. He tried to raise his arms toward it but was completely unsuccessful in moving them even a fraction of an inch. Slowly the words of the queen came back to him, barely perceptible. "Rufus, true knight. I wish to put an end to your suffering, but you must live a little longer." Rufus's lips formed the name of the queen soundlessly. The queen's voice continued. "I am weak, and the time is painfully short. It will only be minutes before they have sealed my fate and with it the fate of the entire kingdom and everyone who lives in it."

"M-Molly . . . ," Rufus managed.

"This last time, I will give you the power to save yourself, but after that I can do no more. By lending you my own power, I too am dying. Retrieve the source of my power."

Rufus could feel his strength coming back to him, though his dread grew, considering the queen's implications. Her voice began to trail off. "I'm afraid your only choice may be to use the device in your pocket. It is a terrible alternative, but I fear that my time may be numbered in seconds, not hours. Only once I am safe can we have a chance at defeating the dark wizard." Her words trailed off, ending with a ghostly, and barely audible "farewell."

"Molly!" Rufus cried in anguish, using the queen's name, as he had never done before. As the vision faded, the stones above him flew out of his way. Honoring the queen's wishes, despite his physical pain and mental anguish, he leapt to his feet and thrust his hand into his pocket to retrieve the item he had stashed there.

The spherical object appeared to still be in perfect condition, despite the rough handling it had received. Rufus's eyes darted over the object, searching frantically for any indication of how it worked. As he squinted his eyes, he noticed a small circular section on its surface. He ran his fingers over the place, pressed down lightly and was rewarded with a faint click as the area lowered slightly. Almost instantly, both of the dials whirred into life, and a clear voice emitted from the middle of the device.

Rufus immediately recognized it as Bert's voice. "You have activated the temporal borrower. Depress the button again to spin the dials. Both dials will spin and stop on a value, which will indicate the current exchange rate between current time and future time. The amount of current time will be indicated on the left dial and the amount of future time on the right. Once the exchange rate has been displayed, press the button one more time to accept the terms and initiate a borrowing. Do not attempt this procedure lightly, as the time will be subtracted from the end of your life in exchange for the time now. The device will automatically shut off in one minute, and will not be usable again for twenty-four hours."

Despite the unsettling terms, Rufus wasted no time. He immediately pressed the button, sending the dials spinning. They whirred for several seconds before coming to a stop and displaying two numbers. The left dial read "two hours" and the dial on the right read "two years."

Rufus's breath caught in his throat, not daring to make a move. He realized with horror that he had less than a minute to decide whether an extra two hours would be worth giving up two years of his life. The queen's words echoed in his ears. He had no idea what exactly was happening to her, but she had use the word "seconds" to describe her predicament, and unless he could magically whisk himself away to her, he was going to need more time.

Sweat pouring from his forehead, his finger hovered precariously over the button. He thought about the last two years of his life, how much joy and satisfaction they had given him. But then he thought of the queen's sweet face and her trust in him. The two thoughts struggled for prominence in his mind, driving him to the very brink of insanity. His finger remained frozen in the air, as if an invisible barrier inhibited him from making the final, fateful step.

Summoning up all his will power, Rufus closed his eyes and pressed the button. The device whirred to life, flashing and spinning rapidly in Rufus's grasp. At last, the device lay still once again, and a metallic voice announced, "Transaction complete."

Rufus opened his eyes, and found himself standing in the castle hallway not far from the entrance to Cornelius's lab. Sunlight streamed through the window and the hallway lay absolutely still. He heard voices approaching and realized in shock that they belonged to the Captain of the Guard and himself.

"It worked!" Rufus muttered to himself, ducking behind a pillar to stay out of sight. He watched with a sickening feeling as he saw himself being led into Cornelius's lab. After the door had shut tightly behind them, he shot out from behind the pillar and ran down the hallway. He could feel the queen guiding his steps and knew that he would still have to hurry in order to help her. He only hoped that it was not already too late.

CHAPTER SEVENTEEN

☙

THE MIRROR MAZE

THE CANTICLE KINGDOM

Snow scattered wildly as Johann dashed through the forest as quickly as he could mange while still clinging to Kate's tiny hand. The little girl's teeth chattered with fright and cold, which also prevented her from saying anything. An inhuman moan whistled through the trees, and the pair could not be sure if the voice belonged to the wind or to some other fell creature of the forest. Johann did not dare to look to one side or the other for fear of knowing what lurked in the shadows might be more frightening than not knowing.

His breath coming in greedy gulps, Johann led Kate all the way out of the forest and toward the town. When they reached the bridge, however, they paused and were finally both able to attempt to catch their breath. Tears rolled down the little girl's flushed face, and a pathetic whimper escaped from her pursed lips. Seeing the child's distress, Johann placed his arm around her and wiped the tears off the best he could. "Sorry about that, little one. That forest is downright spooky, and I don't want to stay in it a second longer than I have to."

Kate nodded her head in agreement, her locks bobbing playfully up and down. "When . . . when can I see my dad again?" she sniffled.

Johann searched for words and finally decided to take an even course. "I don't know, but I'm sure he's looking for you right now. He'll probably run into us soon."

Kate's eyes brightened as she raised her head. "Do you really think so?"

Johann nodded with a smile, feeling inwardly rotten because he was not sure at all. As Kate rested under the bridge, Johann removed Brigitta's stash once more and placed a bag of the sticky weapons and an extra slingshot in his belt. When he found Brigitta, it would be best that she would be able to pull her weight if they had to fight their way out of somewhere.

Johann glanced toward the town, and in the distance, he could just perceive the strains of jolly music and commotion. Heartened by this, he took Kate once again by the hand and led her toward the town, this time adopting a slower pace. A smile crossed Johann's lips as they trotted along. His master's theories about timing were falling into place nicely. Everything was going to go exactly as planned.

Johann rapidly approached his house and found to his relief that his mother had not yet left for the festival at the castle. The streets were already packed with citizens making their way toward the hill, lugging carts and families in tow. In all the commotion, no one seemed to pay Johann and his strange visitor any heed.

As they approached, his mother looked up with interest. "Johann, there you are! I thought you wouldn't show up for the parade and the festival . . . I was getting really worried." Her eyes turned from Johann to his little guest. She raised an inquiring eyebrow. "Oh, and who is this? Seems a little young to be one of your classmates."

Johann gingerly shook his head. "No, Mother," he muttered. "This is Kate, and she's been separated from her father. She's really frightened, and I thought we could take her to the festival to see if we could find him."

Johann's mother's eyes welled up with sympathy. She hoisted the child up in her arms and led Kate in through the front door. "Oh, you poor thing. Of course we'll help you. Let's get you cleaned up, and then we'll go look for your father. Everyone in the kingdom is bound to be there, so I'm sure we'll have a good chance."

Kate nodded mutely, and Johann's mother whisked the child upstairs to attend to her. Suppressing a tiny twinge of guilt, Johann cracked open the door and slid out again, heading back in the direction of the woods. He let his feet guide him as they crunched over the tranquil snow as he searched out a spot that he had visited only yesterday, but it seemed likes ages ago.

Sure enough, after a bit of wandering, he located the solitary fountain and walked up to it. The proper word of command formed on his chapped lips, and suddenly he found himself whisked away on a fantastic journey, under the earth and toward the castle gardens.

Johann emerged from the fountain to the familiar ominous sight of manicured bushes. He shuddered to think of the last time he had been there, and suddenly welled up with deep regret that he had lost track of Brigitta. He could not know for sure whether she was still alive; he simply felt that it was not yet too late to make up for his mistakes.

Approaching cautiously, Johann drew his sword and craned his ears for any indication of life. However, this time the garden seemed more like a graveyard than anything else. He slipped under another leafy arch and was greeted by the familiar sea of statues and cobbled pathways. Not a breath of wind blew across the yard, and the only sound was the clack of his own feet on the path.

On instinct, he followed the path toward the familiar fountain where he had seen Brigitta the last time. This time, however, the ominous hooded figure remained completely silent. It appeared to be no more than a statue, and Johann began to harbor silent doubts about what he was doing here. Had he really heard a rumbling voice emitting from it?

Johann shook his head and rubbed his temple. Of course he had. Brigitta was gone, and they were both trapped as pawns in the middle of an elaborate chess match. At least he had been a pawn back then, but then again, any chess player knows that pawns that go the distance can be promoted. Raising his sword in the stance of a knight, he commanded in a booming voice, "Tell me where you have taken Brigitta!"

No sound issued from the statue. Johann stepped up on the rim of the statue and called again, his sword pointed directly at the statue's face. "Tell me or perish!" he roared.

The statue did not reply, but before Johann could take action, a sudden sound penetrated the fabric of silence. Horse's hooves were drawing nearer at a frantic pace. Tightening his jaw, Johann swiveled around to the direction of the sound, bringing his sword to bear. *This is it,* he thought to himself, wishing greatly that he could count on the protection of his master in the coming battle.

Johann's breath froze as a tall armor-clad figure on a white horse came into view. The knight carried a fierce looking spear, raised and ready to strike. The rider did not stop as he glimpsed Johann, but galloped full-tilt toward the fountain where he stood. Focusing his energy, Johann waited with sweat pouring down his face for the knight to come within range. Johann gritted his teeth and seized the opportunity, releasing a withering bolt of flame from the tip of his sword.

His aim was dead on. The knight attempted to block the bolt with his shield, but the resulting impact swept him from his horse and into a clattering heap in one of the fountains. With difficulty, the knight hoisted himself out of the fountain, placing his dripping spear on the edge, and proceeded to drain the water from his armor. He removed his helmet to reveal a boy Johann's own age. Johann lowered his sword, and approached the boy cautiously, fully aware that it could all be a clever trick to get him to lower his guard.

"I really am a formidable fighter," the boy said nonchalantly. "I've slain mighty opponents with this spear, but . . . I don't know, I just can't today. I was promised that I could march at the head of the parade, but instead they got me doing this ridiculous duty. I almost wish you were a really dangerous enemy. I'd let you right in the castle and have my revenge. My name's Parval. What's yours?"

Johann narrowed his eyes slyly. This could be the key. "As a matter of fact, I am Sir Johann, a knight come to overthrow the court. Is that sinister enough?"

Parval's eyebrow's perked up. "If anybody inquires, I will tell them you were a mighty wizard who knocked me out with a sleeping spell. I'll throw in a bit about the fountain . . . It will make an intriguing tale. Follow me."

Leaving his armor behind, Parval gestured for Johann to follow him around the fountain and down an nondescript path to a seemingly dead end. The path ended in a hedge, which Parval now stood in front of. He suddenly dropped to his knees and examined the stones. "Blast, I know it's around here somewhere," he muttered. "Been a while since I tried this."

After scraping around for a while longer, he let out a cry of recognition as he pushed in the appropriate cobblestone. The hedge suddenly dropped away, revealing a dark downward staircase. Parval gestured quickly with his hands. "Hurry down there before someone else comes around. As far as sneaking in to the castle goes, this is the best place. You'll quickly reach a fork in the road . . . the left path goes into the main castle, and the right leads into the labyrinth."

Parval turned to go, as Johann obeyed his suggestion for speed. The strange boy turned back only once, stopping to call back. "Stay in one piece. I want a rematch someday!"

Johann grinned as he descended the steps and dashed into the darkness, praying silently to himself that he had not just walked himself into a clever trap.

Johann reached only the fork in the path when a brilliant light flooded the corridor, and he had to raise his hands to shield his eyes. As the light dissipated somewhat, he could make out the figure of a beautiful woman with blond hair, wearing a simple robe. Though first he feared the woman, his anxiety was quickly erased by an exquisite calm. The woman raised one slender finger and indicated the direction of the labyrinth, her face reflecting the greatest urgency. Johann stared for a moment, unsure of what to do.

Mustering up the courage, he asked the question nagging at the back of his mind. "Are you . . . an angel?" he asked reverently.

The robed woman shook her head but still said nothing. Once again she pointed in the same direction, her features already beginning to fade. Johann nodded and quickly obeyed, tearing off down the passage in the indicated direction. As he did, the figure vanished, replaced by a tiny speck of light, which shot out in front of Johann. He dashed after the light and found himself approaching a set of glass doors.

Strangely, as he approached, they opened on their own accord, though he could see no one to operate them. Not wasting time to ponder this bizarre occurrence, he bolted through them into an intensely bright corridor. The walls, ceiling, and floor of the corridor were composed entirely of mirrors. The tiny speck of light reflected off all available surfaces, creating a brilliant gleam. Johann squinted his eyes just enough to make the light bearable and followed it.

After only a short distance, Johann's world went fuzzy as he smacked into a wall, which had appeared out of nowhere in front of him while he was going at full speed. Though he felt terrible, the wall did not seem to have sustained any damage. Staggering to his feet, he swung his sword and struck the wall with a glancing blow aimed at his battered reflection. To his chagrin, the mirror did not even register a scratch on its polished surface. He glanced around anxiously for a sign of the light, but it had escaped his view. He stood still for several seconds, observing how the walls shifted around periodically to create new directions in which to travel. However, as he stared at the wall that he had run into, it refused to move again, and thus he decided to move on rather than stare dumbly at his reflection.

He started off again, this time taking care to watch for shifting walls. He could usually predict when they were going to move by a quiet whooshing sound, which happened shortly before the shift. Having discovered this, he easily avoided any further accidents. As heartening as this was, however, the more he wandered around the maze, the more confused he became. Each passage appeared as lifeless and flat as the next. He felt panic starting to take hold of his senses as he realized that he did not know either how to get back to where he had come from or how to move forward.

His step slackened, and he finally stopped. "Is anyone out there?" he cried, preferring any sort of unpleasant company to the maddening solitude of the maze. When no one answered after several tries, he quickened his breathing and clenched his teeth, trying resolutely to keep his emotions at bay.

Before he could get too worked up, however, he caught a glimpse ahead of the angelic figure. He dashed forward toward her, only to find that he had been chasing her reflection. He whirled around and, to his relief, glimpsed the light, hovering not far off from where he stood. To his dismay, though, as he dashed toward it, he heard the telltale whoosh as the walls prepared to shift. His panic suddenly reaching its full maturity, he sprang forward with outstretched hands just as the shiny wall began to slide. The world seemed to move in slow motion as he barreled toward the light.

With only inches to spare, his head and torso cleared the pane, leaving him on his face on the floor beyond. His victory was sadly short-lived as an excruciating pain shot through his body. Johann glanced back and realized that his foot had been wedged awkwardly between the two intersecting panes of glass. His mind fully registered the agony, and he let out a scream, one that should have shattered the surrounding glass.

This time, however, his cries summoned company. Only a few seconds later, a ridiculously muscular blonde-haired, blue-eyed guard strutted around the corner. He said nothing, but thrust a burly finger in Johann's direction as if he intended to impale Johann with it. Johann struggled with his aching foot, knowing that he might stand a chance only if he could dislodge it. Drawing his sword, he pressed it against the glass and began to chant softly, conjuring up a simple freezing spell. Johann stared anxiously at the glass as frost crept painfully slowly up the pane.

The muscular guard strutted closer at a determined, but unhurried pace. Johann could see now that the man only had one hand, and where the second one should have been, there was an ominous looking cannon fashioned from blackened metal. From the sinister gleam in the man's eye, Johann knew that he would be all too eager to use it. This gave Johann an idea.

"Hey, big guy!" he called tauntingly as if he were not the one that was stuck in a glass wall. "That's a pretty nice little cannon you have there, but I bet it's all for show. Sure you could hit me when you're standing right in front of me, but I bet if you backed up a few paces, you'd miss every time!"

The smug expression on the man's face vanished like steam wiped clean off a mirror. "I'm first sharpshooter in my division," he retorted haughtily. "I could stand ten paces back and still take you're head off with one shot."

Johann's chest tightened uncomfortably, hoping that the man's statement contained more bravado than fact. Masking his fear, Johann continued. "Now you're just making up stories. I'd like to see you try."

The man's pale face contorted with rage. He turned smartly on his heels, rubbing his cannon menacingly with his free arm and grumbling to himself. "It'll be the last thing you ever see."

Johann counted as the man took ten generous paces back, swung around, and set his sights on Johann. Though he could no longer see the features of the guard's face, he could imagine the macabre anticipation. For a moment, Johann closed his eyes, forcing himself to focus. "Why wasn't someone here to talk me out of this?" he moaned softly.

Johann's eyes darted open as a thunderous crack echoed through the smooth corridors, accompanied by a dazzling flash. The sound of the crack whizzed at amazing speed directly toward Johann's head. As nimble as a jackrabbit, Johann thrust his body down at the last instant, avoiding the crushing blow by hair lengths. The pane of glass, made brittle by the cold, shattered nosily, creating a tinkly cloud of debris, which carpeted the corridor like glimmering snow. Johann stifled a scream as the shards bit into his skin like a swarm of angry wasps.

Johann barely managed to stay conscious through the pain, but the sheer fact that his foot was finally free was enough to make him count his blessings.

He limped forward and caught a glimpse of the guard through the haze. Bringing his sword to bear on the startled guard, he pronounced the freezing spell, this time with more force. The guard barely had time to struggle as the tendrils of frost encased him in a frigid cocoon. Once out of immediate danger, Johann fell to his knees again, the pain nearly overwhelming the rest of his senses. "I'm a pretty good shot too, but then again, you should see my friend. She's even better."

He inspected his foot to find that he barely recognized it. The heavy pane had crushed it so severely that he was surprised that he had managed to get as far as he did on it. He started to think about a healing spell, when he was given another rude reminder of the desperateness of his situation. With a whoosh, another plane slide smartly into place directly behind him, cutting off the way from which he had come. He then realized that he could not afford to sit around any longer in the maze. His foot would have to wait.

Bracing himself on the nearest wall, he dragged himself slowly to his feet and managed to start creeping along the corridor in the direction that the angelic figure had been indicating. As he rounded the corner where she had been standing, he heaved a sigh of relief as a very welcome sight met his eyes—a ladder that seemed to stretch out of the maze. Letting his injured foot dangle off to the side, he drew in his breath and started his slow and painful ascent. When he reached the top, he was met with yet another very welcome sight: a corridor in which he could not see his reflection.

CHAPTER EIGHTEEN

༒

DOUSING THE FLAMES

THE CANTICLE KINGDOM

As Karsten and Capt. Edison entered the town, they immediately lost themselves in the crowd of jovial peasants. Capt. Edison clung to Karsten's heels like a shadow, sneaking furtive glances at his surroundings. The older man seemed completely energized, his face beaming with excitement. He chuckled and smiled contentedly for no apparent reason. "You are in luck, Captain," he said, laughing. "On any other day of the year, you might have drawn unwanted attention, but today, people will take your clothes to be some sort of strange costume! Careful, people might start throwing money at you, expecting you to do tricks."

Capt. Edison grunted in reply. He was not really in the mood to count his blessings. They snaked their way through the crowd, coming ever closer to the gleaming towers of the castle. Capt. Edison, however, largely ignored his surroundings, preferring to devote all of his energy to the search for his daughter. To his dismay, the crowd was full of blonde children.

They entered the fairgrounds but had still seen no sign of little Kate. The kingdom had spared no expense in setting up the grounds. Multi-colored tents, flags, and streamers, all trailing in the breeze, dotted the fields surrounding the castle. Behind the central tent stood a platform, which was similarly trimmed with elaborate flags and swaths of cloth. The crowd made its way toward this platform where a small group of guards, officials, and other dignitaries were assembled. A particularly strange looking gray-skinned man with a red feather protruding from behind his ear manned an ornate bronze cannon in the center of the platform, inspecting and scrutinizing it with the care of a master brooding over his pampered pet.

After Karsten and Capt. Edison elbowed their way up to the front of the crowd, the gray-skinned man withdrew a silver whistle from his robe and blew a long, shrill note bringing everyone to attention.

"Your attention, please," he boomed ceremoniously. "I am the great Phisto, and it is my privilege to be the Master of Ceremonies on this festive occasion. At the sound of the cannon, the parade shall begin, after which Her Royal Majesty, the Queen, will address us!"

A cheer rose up from the crowd, but Capt. Edison did not join in. Something about the grey man, perhaps his voice and manner, reminded him too much of the sleazy salesperson that had suckered him into buying his last car. He continued to scan the crowd but also kept an eye on the Master of Ceremonies as often as possible.

At a signal, one of the nearby guards handed Phisto a flaming brand, but instead of lighting the cannon immediately, as everyone expected, he began to juggle the torch, whirling it around expertly. To the delight of all assembled, the attendant periodically handed him extra torches, which Phisto handled just as effortlessly as the first, weaving a fabric of flame. In the end, he juggled six torches, not once allowing the flame to lick his skin. With a mighty cry, he tossed each torch high in the air in succession and caught them single handed as they descended to create a bouquet of flames. At last, he used the flames to light the fuse of the cannon.

With a thunderous crack, a plume of multicolored fire sprang from the cannon, scattering harmless sparks over the crowd, who cheered with delight. Far away, the line of the parade inched forward. It had begun. A hearty cheer erupted from the crowd as several figures stepped out onto the balcony.

 ಬಇ

Brigitta knew she had to keep moving. As she moved along the narrow corridors, she heard shouts and the scuffling of many pairs of feet from adjoining rooms. It was only a matter of time before someone found a way after her. Whenever possible, she tried to take the tunnels that would bring her closer and closer to the surface, but the tunnels all seemed to double back on themselves.

As she took a turn down a particularly dark tunnel, she gasped and jumped back, startled. A faint glowing light stood directly in her way. She stayed rooted to the spot, unable to draw her eyes away from its beautiful, comforting glow. As she stared at it, the light changed shape until it assumed the faint outline of Gwen's head and shoulders. Brigitta suppressed a cry of delight in fear of being heard, but she did allow a whisper. "Gwen! It's you! Are you all right?"

The ghostly figure shook her head. "No, Brigitta," the image whispered. "I am in grave danger, and I need your help. Follow this little bit of light, and it will show you the way you should go. If you follow it exactly, it will lead you to someone who can help you escape and help me in the process."

A smile as warm as a summer sunrise crossed Gwen's face. "I'm counting on you, my little friend. Be sure not to let that music box out of your care—I paid dearly for it! Farewell."

In an instant, the figure melted away, leaving only the sphere of light in its place. Brigitta followed her luminous guide as it moved down the passage. Before long, she desperately needed a rest, but the light never slowed. As she ran, she imagined how nice it would be to just be sitting in school, thinking up pranks with Johann and practicing her aim on anything that moved. She rolled her eyes at the irony of missing school. The situation really had become dire.

Suddenly, the light halted in front of a particularly dark passage. It hovered in front of the spot for several seconds, and in the light, Brigitta could see that the passage appeared to be a downward chute. The passage wound around to the side, so she could not see where it led or how far it fell. To her horror, the light jolted downwards, disappearing around the bend. *Why would she lead me down there?* Brigitta thought. The idea of going further down filled her with fear. *We need to go up, not down!*

She trembled slightly as she inched toward the chute, realizing that the light might not wait long for her. Swallowing hard, she pictured Gwen lying on the ground, beaten and dying, and knew she could not let her down, no matter the awful circumstances. Closing her eyes, she stepped into the chute and launched herself into the billowing blackness.

Luckily, Brigitta's fall lasted no more than a few seconds, but she landed in a pile of something very cold, hard, smelly, and altogether unpleasant. Sputtering and coughing as the choking dust filled her lungs, she blinked frantically to clear her vision. She soon realized that she had landed in a large bin of jagged coal and that she had a bird's-eye vantage of the room.

The room was full of machinery, the largest piece appeared to be a humongous clanking furnace, belching clouds of putrid green smoke. In front of the furnace, a broad stone walkway spanned the length of the room, stretching from one arched entryway to another. She craned to see over the top of the bin and noticed a huge vat of a black roiling liquid. Just being above the vat caused her vision to blur and her stomach to seize with nausea. Retracting her head, she seized her mouth, just barely suppressing the urge to retch. Her head swirled with terrible dizziness. *Why would the light lead me here?*

As she peered cautiously back over the edge, she glimpsed a figure lying prostrate in front of the furnace. The dim light made it difficult to be certain, but she knew deep down that it must be Gwen. Unfortunately, her vantage point was such that it would make getting down a risky and complicated process. If she left the bin she also risked coming in contact with the fumes of that awful black brew again, something which she wanted to avoid at all costs.

Her breath suddenly caught in her chest, but this time it was not because of the noxious fumes. A massive, ominous figure walked through the room, flanked by a handful of squat, muscular figures, which resembled the other guards who were chasing her earlier. The central figure wore armor that gleamed so brightly it seemed like it produced its own light. Her heart raced as she recognized the horned fox-shaped head from her encounter in the castle gardens.

As the group approached the figure on the floor, an awful cloud of sneers and deep-throated chuckles rose from the guards. The fox-headed man raised a hand, snuffing out the rowdiness like a candle. Even in the darkness, Brigitta could see the sinister grin that formed on the creature's face. When he spoke, his voice barely reached a whisper, but it was laced with such evil that it seemed to leave a stinging aftertaste like a concentrated acid.

Brigitta suppressed the urge to clamp her hands over her ears, for she had to hear what was being said. "Your Majesty," the creature crooned. "I have anticipated this day for eons, as it were. I know you won't give me the satisfaction of a last pathetic plea, but I *do* know you can hear me."

He stooped down and deviously ran his finger over Gwen's bruised cheek. Brigitta had to look away. The mockery was more than she could stomach. *What's all this about calling her "Majesty"? I know she didn't remember who she was, but she couldn't possibly be royalty. The only royalty around here is—*

Before she could ride her train of thought any further, a harsh grating sound captured her attention. She chanced a glance over the rim of the coal bin and saw the burly blonde men dragging the vat that had been burning in the furnace. At first, she thought they had done this with their bare hands, but as she looked closer, she realized that each guard used the wicked-looking metal clamp they had instead of a hand. The clamps snapped shut with an awful clank and a swiftness and strength that could have snapped tree trunks.

They placed the swirling vat to the side and again focused their attention on their master. "The time has come. Take care that you don't spill a single drop. The Many-Named One spent months brewing it just right, but of course, spilling it on yourselves would be its own punishment."

The fox-headed man walked over to the edge of the vat and plunged the arm of the nearest guard into the swirling, frothy solution. The guard's unearthly shriek echoed through the corridor as he retracted his arm, which was now wreathed in a ghastly mist. The guard writhed in pain as the mist cleared, revealing only a twisted stump where his arm had been. The man's once pale skin changed into a sickly gray, sprinkled with darker gray blotches.

Snarling like a ravenous wolf, the guard turned on the fox-faced man, pouncing at him with his remaining arm outstretched. Before he could land his blow, the fox-headed man tore open a hinged section in the middle of his own armor, releasing a bright plume of flame that swallowed the guard whole. With a smug grin, the fox-headed man nodded tersely, finally convinced that he had made his point.

The guards set nimbly to the task, but just as they hefted the cauldron, a brilliant streak of lightening bolted through the room, nearly blinding Brigitta. Despite their rather brutal object lesson, the guards dropped the cauldron in unison as electricity coursed instantly through their bodies. The froth splashed over, portions of it landing on the guards who immediately erupted into a chorus of agony.

Their leader whirled about to face the source of the sudden, ferocious attack. He sniffed the air cautiously, a wicked snarl marring his face.

"Stand aside, you monster!" Brigitta recognized the voice, but dared not trust her eyes. *Could it be . . . ?*

A very different looking Johann emerged from the dark end of the corridor. He walked taller than Brigitta had ever seen him walk, though she noticed right away that he seemed to be favoring one foot. He walked with his sword outstretched, glowing comfortingly in the dark place. It was all Brigitta could do to keep from leaping out of the coal bin to help her friend.

The fox creature cackled. "Do you know who I am, *Johann?*" he questioned. "I honestly don't think you do." The fox's features suddenly warped and blended together, swirling like a painting that had come in contact with an errant water droplet. The fox's face disappeared and was replaced with the face of a dark-haired man with a thick beard and bewitching brown eyes.

The man grinned wryly and drew his eyebrows together. "Do you not remember this face? Then again, you were so young."

"What do you mean? I know who you work for, and I know who that is on the ground. Quit your riddles and raise your weapon." Johann's blade crackled as he swung it around, threateningly.

The bearded man nearly fell over with maniacal laughter. "Johann, you fool. It isn't very chivalrous to speak to family so. I see your mother hasn't kept you in line as she should have. A shame . . . a laughable shame."

Johann's heartbeat rose as he gripped his sword hilt tighter. His breath came now in heaves. "What do *you* know about my mother?" he spat.

Mirth showed all over the bearded man's face. "Oh . . . just about everything. You see, I can claim the same for you as well. I was *there* the day you came into the world."

Johann shook his head furiously, rage building up in him like the pressure of a dam. "Liar! Draw your sword."

The bearded man sighed and produced a blade wreathed in undulating flame. "Suit yourself, my boy. But be warned, it never turns out well when a boy has to fight his father."

Johann leapt forward with a cry of rage, slashing with his sword like a crazed warrior. His opponent raised his sword, the red flames flashing blue and then green as they impacted Johann's. The resultant sparks scattered like a swarm of angry fireflies. The old man pressed down hard, driving Johann onto his injured foot. Johann's leg crumpled out from under him, and his head smacked the pavement, sending additional sparks swirling around in his head.

The bearded man leaned his head in oppressively close, his fowl breath aggravating Johann's dizziness even more. "Do you really wish to fight me?" he crooned. "I can tell the apple didn't fall far from the tree. Still, its foolish for the little sapling to think that he can yank its parent tree out by the roots."

Johann's face remained passive, though his eyes boiled with fury. Even if the creature's face was somehow familiar, it was only the hollow shell of what it once was. He inched his way back, avoiding the glowing blade swinging precariously in front of his face. "You're—not—my—father—" seethed Johann through clenched teeth.

"You don't have to believe me," the man said, sighing. "Allow me, however, to express my bitter disappointment. I won't hesitate to cut you off, root and branch, but at such a pivotal moment as this, I prefer to relish it, and finishing you off now would be like ending a book after the second chapter—just when things were starting to get good."

The bearded man stretched out his hand and pointed it at Johann's leg. With a sudden barked command, a blast of red light leapt from his fingertip to rest on Johann's ankle. Johann braced himself, but instead of the anticipated pain, a feeling of wholeness coursed through his leg, and he was sure that his leg had been healed. Puzzled, he met his opponent's stony gaze.

"Get up," the bearded man commanded. "Raise your sword and give me a decent attempt!"

Johann complied, harnessing his energy and lashing out with a more controlled stroke. His opponent responded, and in moments they were locked in a deadly dance.

Brigitta almost forgot to breathe as she watched the swirling battle below. Johann's limp had disappeared, and he was standing up admirably to his larger and more experienced opponent. Still, he only barely managed to keep up with his opponent's strokes. Using his enchanted sword, the bearded man spread flames across the floor, cornering Johann into an ever-shrinking space. Johann countered with bouts of ice, but he couldn't stem the flow of flames.

Johann coughed and wheezed at the acrid smoke. Sweat poured into his eyes, blinding him. As his senses dulled, however, his adrenaline coursed faster, driving him into a frenzy of slashing and stabbing. The bearded man skirted around the room with inhuman speed, lashing out with his weapon like a frog lashing out its tongue to snatch flies.

Soon the entire platform blazed with multi-colored fire, leaving only a tiny arena centered around the fallen woman. Each blow rang like a hammer and anvil, surrounded by a sizzling forge. In a final desperate attempt, Johann lunged forward with a mighty stab, connecting with his opponent's midsection. To his astonishment, the sword imbedded itself several inches into the armor and hung there. The bearded man's eyes rolled back in his head as he clutched his chest in an expression of dire agony. His lips curled as his entire face bunched up in shock before melting away to reveal the beady malevolent eyes of the fiery red fox. Fingers of hungry flame sprang from the opening in his armor, drawing Johann into their sweltering grasp until he had disappeared from view.

Brigitta could no longer suppress a pent-up scream. It rang through the corridors but was largely buried by the roar of the flames. The awful fox-faced creature simply licked its lips and paced around with a smug expression on its gruesome face. Brigitta blinked her eyes in a desperate effort to dispel the tears forming there and was able to make out something curious. Directly where Johann had been standing, a small satchel lay on the ground with a long, slender object poking out of it. As she stared at the object, a faint voice whispered in her mind. *That is exactly what you need—he dropped it on purpose!*

Brigitta did not second-guess the voice. All she knew was that if that cauldron reached the furnace, she would not survive very long in her current position. In the firelight, she noticed a narrow pathway, which led from the coal bin down onto the platform. Her heart galloping in her chest, she waited until the fox-faced man turned his back before hopping out of the bin, sending bits of coal tumbling everywhere. Down on her knees, she crept down the pathway, the metal unpleasantly warm from the nearby flames.

Meanwhile, the fox-faced man carried the cauldron single handed toward the furnace. Though he walked directly through the flames, he seemed unaffected by the intense heat. He set the cauldron down directly before the furnace and turned about, bringing his sword in front of him. His malicious grin displayed every one of his gleaming dagger-like teeth as he looked down at the fallen woman. "So, your Majesty, I suppose this finally means goodbye. This concoction should finish you off, but just to make sure—"

Flourishing his sword in the air so that the flames danced and crackled, he struck. A split second before the fatal blow connected, the sword suddenly stopped, suspended in mid-air by an unseen force. The creature's face contorted with rage, and he pressed down harder against the force, sending sparks spiraling off in all directions. The sword refused to budge.

Brigitta's eyes widened with awe as a figure materialized in front of the fox. An imposing man in tattered robes appeared, brandishing a mighty sword, which he held resolutely under the flaming sword. The man's hair billowed out wildly behind him, the veins in his neck bulging out like miniature mountain ranges.

Seizing the diversion, Brigitta rushed across the scorching ground and snatched Johann's satchel. As she ripped it open, her eyes grew wide, and a smile found her lips, its cheeriness in stark contrast to her surroundings.

A flood of memories struck her suddenly. She remembered one night, on the first day of summer, Johann and a group of boys from school had camped out in the field outside of town. They had built a bonfire and stayed up late, telling ghost stories. That night, Brigitta and a few of her friends, armed with a satchel of the sticky black exploding seeds like the ones she had hidden under the bridge, snuck out to the edge of the camp. Taking careful aim, she and her friends waited until a particularly chilling part of the ghost story and launched the black seeds into the fire, extinguishing it with loud explosions. The boys scattered with uncharacteristically high wails, and the girls made fun of them for months afterwards.

Johann must have found her hidden stash under the bridge. Carefully, Brigitta reached into the bag and extracted her slingshot and one of the ebony seeds. Taking quick aim, she launched the seed directly past the creature's head, immediately drawing his attention. In split second of distraction, the robed man slashed the sword hard at the fox-faced man's midsection.

The fox flew back with an angry grunt. "Rufus!" he spat. "Why won't you stay dead? You must have a regular guardian angel watching your back."

The fox's features melted away momentarily, only to be replaced by those of the Captain of the Guard, bearing the same smug expression. "Yes, Rufus," he toned in the Captain's voice. "I trust you enjoyed your stay in Cornelius's laboratory. Of course, he's not called that anymore. He sure does have a interesting way of selecting his persona . . . all those statues."

The man called Rufus gawked at the man, unable to take in what he was seeing. "The statues . . . the Nativity in the chapel . . . that was Cornelius?"

He stood frozen, unable to press the momentary advantage he had so preciously won. His opponent reached for the hinge at the midsection of his armor. "Goodbye, Rufus."

The fox tore the flap open, again revealing a furnace of glowing flame, just as another whizzing seed rocketed through the air, landing soundly inside the armor and bursting with a loud pop. The expected torrent of flames failed to gush from the opening as black goo coated the insides of the inferno. Again and again, Brigitta pulled back the slingshot and released her seeds, shouting furiously as loud as her smoke-choked lungs would allow. "This is for Johann, for Brutus, and for Gwen!"

She fired with such force that her slingshot nearly rubbed the skin right off her fingers. The loud pops continued with the impact of each bullet, landing in rapid succession and spreading the black goo until no trace of fire remained. The being's face contorted and rapidly underwent a series of changes, taking forms from beasts to people, to things she couldn't identify. The glowing armor, coated in the black goo, faded and suddenly fell apart, clattering nosily to the floor and releasing a great cloud of steam.

In the midst of the steam, Brigitta could make out lighted shapes, which swirled around like will-o-wisps in the fog and settled to the floor. For several minutes, she could see nothing through the mist, and she stood completely still in the eerie silence which had taken over.

Her heartbeat rose as a face materialized in the mist in front of her. The ghostly apparition floated toward her, saying not a word. Anxiously, she grasped her slingshot and readied another seed, though she was not sure that it would do her any good if her opponent turned out to be a ghost.

Brigitta drew in her breath sharply, but this time, not from fear. She recognized the face—she had known it since her earliest childhood. Grinning impishly back at her through the fog stood Johann, who rushed forward and caught her up in a fervent embrace.

ကက

The face of the queen came back to Rufus's mind. Almost immediately after entering this awful fiery place, he found himself lying flat on his back, barely conscious of anything. To his side lay the queen, her face still smooth as porcelain and her breath barely perceptible. Rufus realized that this time, it was not only the image of her face that came to his mind, but her actual face, smiling back at him though her eyes were shut. Her lips moved, releasing a voice that was barely perceptible. "Well done, Rufus. You came just in time."

"It was a dire price to pay," he whispered. "But one gladly given." Rufus groaned and breathed deeply, though each breath sent agony pulsing through his body. "Molly," he wheezed. "I—"

He was interrupted by a loud whirring noise from his left hand. The time borrower, the source of the sound, grew warmer, and then suddenly the noise stopped with a click. Bert's faint voice sounded once again from within. "Payment is due and will be collected in one minute."

Rufus sighed heavily, relaxing all his muscles in grim resignation. "I guess I only had two years to live anyway," he muttered. His countenance suddenly changed, taking on a peaceful sheen. His eyes turned to Molly, who opened her eyes ever so slightly. "Molly, I love you. I always have."

"I know," she whispered, her crystalline eyes filling with tears. "I return your love." She smiled, resignedly. "You needn't fear death, Rufus. This world is not what it seems, and your death here will not be the end of your existence. The curtain will close on this stage, and you will enter another"—she paused, her voice brimming with emotion—"and I shall join you there shortly."

She paused again, her eyes fluttering. "There is only one thing I ask before you leave . . . ."

She leaned closer and whispered in his ear. Satisfied, Rufus nodded. Then, silently, his rough, scarred hand crept over to find Molly's smooth fingers, and he wove his own through hers, praying that she could somehow feel the love that channelled through every part of his being. Then, gently, his eyes closed, and the warrior's spirit ascended from his broken body.

ඥ

The fog cleared around Johann and Brigitta. Neither could bring themselves to say anything for quite some time.

"Johann . . . w-what happened?" Brigitta finally managed.

"I'm not sure," he said, shaking his head in utter confusion. "It was the most unpleasant thing that's ever happened to me. I felt like I was tossed around in a river of fire, not able to control where I was going. There were hundreds of others there with me. How long was I in there?"

Brigitta shrugged. "Luckily only a few minutes. I can't believe you thought to bring the seeds . . . ." Her voice trailed off, and suddenly a wry expression snuck across her face. "Say, Johann, you remember that time you went camping?"

Johann's eyes grew wide, and he lunged forward playfully to silence the embarrassing story. They laughed and kidded for several minutes more, momentarily forgetting their woes, but they sobered as soon as the mists cleared, revealing a strange scene. Bodies, some people and some animals, lay everywhere. Many of them lay still on the ground, while others had risen to their feet or had propped themselves up on their knees. The sheer number of all of the fox's previous victims staggered both Johann and Brigitta.

Johann glanced up in time to see the flash of a crimson fox darting across the walkway, a set of tell tale horns jutting from its skull. The sight sent Johann's mind reeling at the implications. He glanced frantically around the room as the startling truth came to him.

Puzzled, Brigitta glanced around as well, unable to tell what Johann was looking for. "What is it, Johann?"

He paced around the platform, sweeping the room with a keen eye. "That fox," he replied. "Did you see it?"

"Yes," she admitted. "But what does that have to do with anything?"

"That fox was a prisoner inside that armor, and the creature was able to take its form. What if it was doing the same thing with my father? What if my father isn't really dead? He might have been a prisoner this whole time! He could be here right now!"

Brigitta joined the search in earnest. Many of the creatures victims lay facedown and did not stir, and neither Brigitta nor Johann decided that they wanted to chance flipping them over. Though the mist from the extinguished armor still hung in the air, it was mingled with something else—a sinister edge that caused their lungs to constrict uncomfortably. Brigitta turned anxiously to Johann. "The fire must have sent some of that awful potion into the air. We need to get out of here quickly. You weren't around when he showed what that stuff can do, but it's awful"

Johann's face contorted with worry. "We can't just leave! He's so close, I can feel it! Just give me a few more minutes."

Brigitta weighed the options, staring intently into Johann's eyes. "Keep looking," she agreed. "I'm going to see about Gwen—she's a friend of mine. We need to get her out of here too."

As Brigitta trotted back toward the furnace, Johann called after her, the worry lines on his face deepening. "Brigitta! Let's try to stay within sight of each other! I don't want to get separated again!"

"Right!" she called back, trying her best to keep him in her line of vision. She reached Gwen's side and stooped down over her. Next to her lay the man who had blocked the flaming sword, his hand still locked tight with hers. Gwen's eyes fluttered open slightly. "Gwen, wake up! We need to get out of here. Can you stand?"

Gwen's head shook so slightly that it was almost imperceptible. A single tear fell from her left eye and disappeared into the stones. "Brigitta, come closer—I can barely speak."

Brigitta did as she was told, and she realized immediately that her initial optimism had been completely unfounded. Gwen's face was pale as the full moon on a cloudless night.

"Thank you, my friend." Gwen started, her breathing labored. "I remember now who I am. My name is Molly, and I am the queen of this kingdom."

The queen wheezed painfully, her eyes taking a faraway look. "The very life of the kingdom is drawn from my strength. If I die now, the entire kingdom will fall unless I am replaced by another. The Many-Named One has taken most of my energy to create an imposter queen out of an expert statue."

The queen's gaze found Brigitta's, and for a moment, Molly's eyes became clear again. "I have sent someone to take care of the imposter, and I hoped to regain most of my power, but at the rate I am deteriorating, he will not have time.

"Brigitta, I can bestow life energy, and I can take it away. Sometimes the process is automatic when I become injured, but I am too far gone for that now. I can only receive new energy from a willing volunteer, and so I ask you Brigitta . . . may I borrow yours?"

A cold chill rippled up Brigitta's spine, and she could not tear her gaze away from the queen's. "What do you mean, Gw—your Majesty? What will happen to me?"

The corners of Molly's lips twitched slightly. "Please, call me Molly." She became serious. "If you allow this, your life force will temporarily be transferred to me, and you will become a statue. When my power is restored, I can return your life force to you, and you will be your normal self." The queen extended her hand. "The question is, Brigitta, do you trust me? Take my hand if you do."

"What if this person can't get rid of the imposter?" Brigitta asked, her voice trembling violently.

"Then," sighed the queen, "it will be the end for the both of us."

Brigitta stood stock still, staring at Molly's outstretched hand. Her heart rending in two, she glanced back at her friend, who was desperately searching for his father. "I'm sorry, Johann," she whispered, and she grasped the queen's hand.

Johann sifted through the sea of bodies, his desperation growing as the seconds slipped by, and still no face even remotely resembled the one of his father. His hands flew to his head, running them through his hair in an effort to think. He stopped cold as he realized that he did not feel much. The head that had once been full of hair now only clung to a few wisps. He withdrew his hand and saw that his fingers were coated with soot. Looking around, he noticed others were similarly singed.

The realization dawned on Johann. His trip into the armor had singed his hair, which meant that it probably did the same for the rest of the victims. He had been searching for a man with a full head of bushy hair and a full beard. He further realized that if his father was a knight, it stood to reason that his armor might resemble the style that Siegfried wore. Shaking his head, he rushed back toward the place where he had started his search, his heart pounding a steady and wild beat. "Brigitta! I know what—"

Johann sprawled face first to the ground, his arms flailing out in front of him. He hit the ground hard, but recovered quickly as adrenaline pumped through his system. Whirling about, he realized that he had tripped over a n unconscious body covered completely with tarnished silver armor.

Brimming with excitement, Johann knelt down beside the man and lifted his visor. The man's eyes slid open to reveal dark, brown eyes. He groaned softly and tried to raise himself up on his hands, fumbling several times before finally succeeding in maintaining a tenuous balance. Suddenly, as if he had been doused by a bucket of freezing water, he shot upright, his eyes bulging out. "Where is he?" he rasped. "Where's the traitor?" Madness grew in his eyes as he took in the gruesome scene around him. "Where am I?" he blurted out in Johann's direction. "How did I get here? Is the battle over?"

Johann shook his head in disbelief. Somehow, on a level deeper than memory, he knew he had found the right person. "I don't know what to tell you, er, sir," he said awkwardly, trying to conjure up the proper way to address his father. "I have to ask you one question, and it's very important. What is your name?"

"My name?" he muttered, gazing intently into Johann's eyes. "My name is . . . ah . . . well . . . ." He fumbled for several moments more, his consternation growing all the while, before it hit him like a welcome breath of fresh air. He attempted what seemed like a grin. "Wilhelm . . . yes, my name is Wilhelm."

Johann's heart soared. Wilhelm was his father's name. Letting his sword clatter to the ground, Johann leapt forward and enveloped the man in an enormous embrace. Startled, the man flinched at first, but accepted the gesture. "Do I know you?" he muttered hesitantly.

"Yes, you do," Johann said, reigning in his emotions. "Indeed, you do."

After a moment, the man withdrew, studying Johann's face and features. He stroked the stubble of what remained of his beard, a faint gleam in his eye. "You do look familiar, boy. What is your name?"

"I'm Johann!" he blurted out without hesitation.

Wilhelm nodded slowly. "I *do* have a son by that name, but it can't possibly be you. Johann is only—"

Johann placed a hand on his father's shoulder. "A few years old. I know. You have been trapped for years by that . . . that thing. Siegfried told me that one of the other knights betrayed you—"

A deep, ominous rumble below their feet sent them both to the ground. Johann picked himself up, wheezing as the black mist gripped his lungs like an iron vice. He extended a hand to his father, veiling his mouth with his other hand. "Come, Father," he wheezed. "If we don't get out of here soon, we might not have much quality bonding time in the future."

He helped his father to his feet and whirled about in Brigitta's direction. She was still hunched over the queen, with her back facing him. He trotted quickly toward her, calling her name to catch her attention. She did not move. Concerned, Johann quickened his step.

When he reached the furnace, his breath caught and his blood froze. Hunched over the queen like one of the statues from her garden stood Brigitta, her face frozen in an agonized wail.

CHAPTER NINETEEN

‚Äçúû

IF THE FINGER FITS

IDAR-OBERSTEIN, WEST GERMANY, 1945

Mrs. Edison and her guide reached the top of the stairs and looked out from the roof of the castle. The mountainous woods continued as far as the eye could see, interrupted only by a tiny village directly across the way from them. The sky was overcast, and the air tingled with tiny droplets of water. She shivered slightly, but not just from the cold. Something about this place unnerved her, though she could not even begin to give it a name. Her guide came up behind her and inhaled deeply. "Ah, the fresh German air. Good for the health. How do you like it?"

Mrs. Edison shrugged. "Hm . . . a little humid." She fidgeted in her spot, folding her arms against the cold.

"What's wrong, Mrs. Edison? Do you not like castles?"

"Oh no, castles are fine. It's just—" She paused in mid-sentence, bringing a hand to her ear. "Do you hear that? Where is that music coming from? It's beautiful!"

The other man wrinkled his brow, straining his ears to see if he could also make out the sound. He heard nothing. "Are you sure, Mrs. Edison? I don't hear anything. Are you sure you're feeling okay?"

She nodded silently and stepped lightly toward the stairs. Before her guide could protest, she had started back down the stairs at a steady pace, following the enchanting music, which sounded ever louder in her ears.

By the time she reached the bottom of the stairs, she was so entranced that she reached the hidden set of stairs without so much as a second thought. The door at the bottom lay slightly ajar, and from behind it, the strains of music floated out louder than ever. Her entire body tingled with delight as she basked in the glorious melody, and for just a moment, all of her worries and sorrows melted away. Trembling with delight, she gripped the door handle and slid the door open.

‚Äçúû

THE CANTICLE KINGDOM

In the queen's bedroom, a woman groomed her long, blond locks, gazing into the mirror. She grinned absentmindedly, humming a contented tune to herself. In a few moments, she would stand in front of the entire kingdom to greet the front of the parade as it met the castle. A sudden draft of air tousled her hair, and she quickly set down her brush and sauntered over to the window to draw the curtains. She frowned as she realized that they were already drawn. Suspiciously, she glanced around to determine the cause of the draft, and upon seeing nothing, she returned to her combing.

She finished straightening her hair and applied a few finishing touches of make-up. Satisfied with the result, she turned from the mirror and felt a cold shiver travel up her spine. Glancing frantically around the room again, she assured herself that she was indeed alone and settled back down in her chair to have a sip of tea to calm her nerves. "I'm just nervous about being out in front of the crowd, that's all," she muttered quietly to herself.

She raised the teacup to her lips and immediately let it fall as a dark, ominous shape passed through the corner of her vision. Cursing her luck, she stood up sharply, whisking the spilled tea from her dress the best that she could. She turned to survey the damage in the mirror when a familiar voice whispered softly from behind her.

"Your Majesty," it said mockingly. "Do sit down and have a spot more tea. I didn't quite get enough of it last time." The woman whirled about to find a ghostly figure in the chair opposite hers, already raising a cup of hot tea to its pale lips. "You know, I think we'll have a lot to talk about," he said, rummaging in the pocket of his robes. "I even think I have something that belongs to you."

The woman looked on in rapt fascination as the phantom withdrew his hand to reveal a thin piece of stone, which looked like a detailed sculpture. Reaching across the table, he plopped the bit of stone in her tea, and it bobbed strangely to the surface. Horrified, the woman retrieved the stone and realized that it was a portion of a stone finger, so realistic as to make her queasy.

"So, Cinderella," the man seethed, a dangerous note of menace creeping into his voice. "Why don't we see if the shoe fits?" Feigning confusion, the woman threw up her hands in surprise and revealed exactly what the phantom had wished to see: nine fingers. The phantom flew through the table, snatched up the stone finger and fastened it on the end of the stub on one of the woman's hands. With a soft pop and a tiny flash of light, the stone finger sealed itself to the rest of her hand, becoming once again flesh and bone.

A sly smile slid up the face of the phantom. "My, my, my . . . a perfect match!" He stood only inches from the woman's face and extended his hand. In one swift motion before the woman could react, he shot out his hand and caught the woman's hand, squeezing tightly.

The woman's face contorted in an expression of shock, and her jaw dropped in a soundless wail. Swiftly the color drained from her skin, her hair, and even her clothing. "Rufus . . . ," she gasped as the life went out of her, leaving a pristine statue where a woman had stood only seconds before.

Satisfied with his work, the phantom released his grip and studied the statue. It was a good likeness, and had it not been for the urgent matter at hand, he might have gazed at it for some time. Instead, the phantom drew a slender, pale sword from its sheath and raised it high over his head.

Solemnly, he spoke. "As my last act in this bitter world, I set you free!" The air swished as the sword flashed through the air, cleaving the statue nearly in two with only one blow. Again and again he struck, like a relentless adder striking its prey. In mere moments, the brilliant white slashes reduced the statue to mere rubble. A faint glow rose from the rubble, framing for an instant the outline of a woman before fading into nothingness.

The phantom's essence began to fade, and he glanced around frantically for the final part of his mission. In that brief moment, he glimpsed the small statue of a cat and hurled his weapon at it, snapping it cleanly in half. Once again, the figure of a person rose from the statue, and instantly, both figure and phantom vanished.

CHAPTER TWENTY

✥

WAKING THE DEAD

THE CANTICLE KINGDOM

Johann gazed at the statue of his dear friend. Choking back his emotion, he glanced back at his father to offer an explanation. "She was my best friend, and I told her that I would take care of her. I've failed miserably."

Wilhelm nodded solemnly. "I am sorry, but the time for mourning is not yet. If all is as you've said, we must leave this place, and you shall help me set things right as I had planned to in the first place."

Johann stood slowly, his knees threatening to buckle beneath him. He knew his father's words to be true, but this did not make them any easier to accept. "Of course. You're right."

Wilhelm nodded graciously. "From the looks of things, the Many-Named One has infiltrated our kingdom once more. If we are to banish him, we need to enlist the assistance of as many of the remaining knights as we can. You said that you had been in contact with Siegfried?"

Johann bowed his head as he related to his father what had befallen Siegfried and Brutus. Wilhelm's face darkened visibly, especially at the mention of his brother's death. He stroked his beard as he digested the information. "We will require Siegfried's assistance. If I can reach him in the Middlespace, I can help him. You, on the other hand, must determine the whereabouts of the knight named Peter, if indeed he is still alive."

Johann's eyes grew wide with shock. "Isn't he the one who betrayed you? He's surely working for the other side!"

Wilhelm shook his head. "It is true that he betrayed me to the wizard. But you must realize that the wizard is cunning and only wants the evil in an individual to serve him, so that he does not risk being double-crossed. He separates the good part of his servants from their evil part through a hor-rific magical spell. In this case, he created an awful, shape-shifting monster from Peter's evil nature, which admittedly has grown far stronger than Peter's good nature, which the wizard locked away in a statue in the catacombs deep beneath the castle, as is his custom. Since you have conquered his evil side, Peter's good side might finally have the opportunity to be set free. You must do this, Johann, and quickly."

Johann nodded resolutely, standing up as straight as he could manage. "Just tell me how, and I will do it."

Wilhelm's face remained grim. "I wish there was another way, but you are going to have to take the quick way down. I know every nook of this castle, and if nothing drastic has changed, there is a wide stone shaft near here that leads directly to the catacombs. It would be easier to take the stairs, but—"

"Are you trying to kill me?" Johann cut him off incredulously. "How am I supposed to survive a fall like that?"

"Patience," he replied, holding up a grubby hand. "Siegfried was not the only one with extraordinary powers. Let me show you."

Wilhelm clamped his eyes shut and began to mutter softly to himself. Almost instantly, the soles of his feet left the ground, and he stood suspended in midair. With a satisfied grin, he opened his eyes and looked at the amazed Johann. "It's a very useful trick—one that my friends were jealous of. Try as they might, they could never quite replicate it."

Wilhelm hovered closer to Johann and offered his hand, which Johann took. As his father pulled him up, Johann also rose into the air until he was standing level with his father.

"You, however, are my son, and it appears that I am right in supposing that these sorts of things get passed on." Wilhelm gazed sternly into his son's eyes. "Now, I can lend you this power for only a short time, so you must go find Peter quickly and fly directly out of the shaft, or you'll be stuck beneath the castle. I will fly with you to the entrance of the shaft, and there we must part ways for a time. Meet me back by the entrance to the castle gardens as soon as you can manage it."

When Johann nodded, Wilhelm did not waste another moment. He flew off down the smoke-filled corridor, dragging Johann in tow. At first, Johann's nausea threatened to betray him, but he soon grew accustomed to the sensation of flying. He grinned to himself as he thought of all the times his mother had complained that his father had always been "flying off someplace." He never knew why she always used those exact words, but it suddenly had become very clear she was being much more literal than Johann would have ever guessed.

They twisted around the dark tunnels for several minutes, saying nothing as Wilhelm concentrated on their route. They came to an abrupt stop at the end of a passageway. Gathering his composure, Johann noticed a massive metal pipe standing floor to ceiling. Wilhelm pried open a metal hatch. By the looks of the rust and corrosion, it looked like no one had used this passageway in years.

Wilhelm looked at his son and nodded grimly. "I'm sorry to say that I barely know you, son, but I am proud that you have made something honorable of yourself," he said. "When I let go of your hand, simply picture yourself moving forward in your mind, and your body will obey. You have an hour before the magic wears off. You should land in what is referred to as the Chamber of Queens. Make your way through that room to the Chamber of Knights. You will find Peter's statue there. Simply place your hand on the statue, call his name, and he will come to you."

Wilhelm briefly described Peter's physical appearance so that Johann might recognize him when he saw him. Without further warning, Wilhelm released Johann's hand, and for a tense moment, Johann floundered in the air. He began to sink slowly before he remembered to focus all his thoughts on rising. With a small salute to his father, he moved through the door and into the shaft.

"I will not let you down, Father," he cried, mustering up as much courage as he could as the blackness enveloped him. The hatch creaked shut, snuffing out the last meager remnants of light. With a deep, shuddering breath, he braced himself and plunged into the chilly blackness.

In a flash of inspiration, Johann concentrated and summoned fire to his fingers. He swiftly let the bolt fly and took off after it as quickly as he could manage, using the flickering firelight as his guide. Before long, he landed on the ground as lightly as stepping off a shallow stair onto the floor. After fashioning a torch out of a piece of scrap wood that lay next to his feet, he started down a dark tunnel.

Soon he came to an elaborate gold marker on the floor that told him he had arrived in the Chamber of Queens. The octagonal chamber's ceiling rose only about twice his height and featured several smaller adjoining chambers. In each chamber rested an elaborate stone sarcophagus, each with the figure of a woman carved into its lid.

Try as Johann might, he could not resist the curiosity and awe that tugged at him at the prospect of seeing what markers marked the graves of the queens of old. Johann studied the names on all of the cases and did not recognize most of them. The first read simply "Sabine." She appeared to be an austere woman with sharp, commanding features and a large frame. The second, "Ellis," was of much slighter build and dressed in an assortment of flowing robes and scarves. There were a few other statues, all with equally strange names and inscriptions: Minerva, Hildegard, Christine, and so on.

At last, he turned his attention to the center chamber where an open casket lay. Nervously, he crept up and read the inscription. "Molly," he muttered through chattering teeth, his breath forming puffs of vapor despite the warmth of his torch. Holding his breath, he stepped closer and peered into the casket. It lay empty.

"Oh, you won't find her here . . . yet."

Johann whirled about in alarm, nearly dropping his torch in the process. A ghostly figure who looked just like the statue called "Ellis" hovered before him. Johann raised his torch, brandishing it like a club between him and the apparition. "What do you want?"

To his surprise, the woman chuckled, her eyes wrinkling with laughter lines. "I could ask you the same question, if I didn't already have a very good idea of what it is you want. I am the shadow of her Majesty Queen Ellis. I'm here now because I believe that you know my daughter."

Johann shook his head in bewilderment, completely unable to believe his ears. He could not possibly have anything to do with this ancient queen. "I'm sorry, but I think you have mistaken me for somebody else," he muttered anxiously.

Lady Ellis shook her head, the smile refusing to fade from her face. "No, Johann, thankfully I have not. Normally, when a new queen is crowned in our kingdom, the old queen returns to the time and place from which she was taken. Before I can return, however, I must see things put back to their proper order. I had a husband and a beautiful daughter, and they have been separated from each other."

Johann arched his eyebrows. "I'm sorry, I'm afraid I don't follow."

"My husband is a knight," she began. "It has ever been the tradition that a queen's subjects never know who a queen's husband is. Traditionally, the queen produces a female heir, in case the normal pattern of bringing women from the outside world should be broken. My husband and I had a beautiful daughter, but soon my kingdom was overthrown in a murderous coup. The new queen erased all memory of my existence and proclaimed that she alone had always been queen. My husband believes his daughter died in that onslaught. He knows her, but does not recognize her for who she is and the role that she can play. Until they come to this knowledge, my soul is trapped here to wander the catacombs."

The phantom figure drew closer to Johann, her ghostly gaze penetrating his very heart. "I will lead you to what you seek, Johann, if you will promise me one thing in return: You must tell my husband the truth. Only then will I be free."

Johann gulped and nodded, trying to rally what courage remained in him. "Of course, your Majesty. Tell me how to find your husband, and I'll do all I can."

"That should not be a problem," Queen Ellis said, smiling. "You know them both already. My husband's name is Siegfried, and we named our daughter Brigitta."

This time, Johann did drop his torch, which flickered harmlessly on the ground. He stood there for several long moments trying to convince himself that it could not possibly be true. But every time he looked up in the ghostly smile of the ancient queen, he could not help but believe otherwise. Was it true that he could see something of his lifelong friend in her features, or was he seeing only what his mind was telling him to see?

"I . . . I don't know what to say," Johann stammered. "I'll do what you ask, but I'm not sure that they will believe me. I'm having a hard time believing it myself."

The ghostly queen reached into her robes and retrieved a locket held by a brilliant red ribbon. Tenderly, she placed it in Johann's hand. "Show this to both of them. Now, your time is short. I suggest that we continue to the next chamber."

Without further ado, the queen floated toward a rounded archway, which led to a path that slanted down toward the next chamber. Johann retrieved his torch and followed anxiously, still mulling over the new knowledge in his head.

After the relative confinement of the first chamber, the size of the next one startled him. It rivaled the largest of ballrooms. This room was peppered with stone caskets, each with a similar statue resting atop it. Johann jogged along, following the rapidly moving phantom as she weaved in and out of the maze of stone. Johann noticed with unease the number of open caskets, and was tempted once or twice to pause briefly to read the inscriptions but resisted the urge in the fear that he would lose sight of the queen.

She eventually stopped in front of an enormous coffin next to an elaborate statue depicting a man in full armor clutching a sword to his chest. Johann stooped to read the inscription, which simply read "Peter."

The queen turned to him and smiled gently. Though her voice was no more than a whisper, it echoed throughout the great hall so that it seemed to surround him. "Here is the one you seek, Johann. Now I must make the final preparations to leave this place, for I trust you will soon open the door for me. Thank you, brave one. You are, to me, a knight in every respect."

The queen vanished quickly from sight, and once again, he found himself alone in the cold, dusty dankness of the catacombs. Fearing he had spent too much time already, Johann quickly placed his right hand on the arm of the statue, and cried. "Peter, awake!"

The hall magnified his cry so that it rang freely and enveloped him in echoing sound. The sound gradually died away as the statue softened and took form, shrinking until it resembled the size of a man. With a mighty yawn, which also echoed through the cavern, Peter arose, his uncanny resemblance to his son immediately apparent.

"Bruno," Johann gasped as he studied the man's face. Johann raised his sword, mixed tributaries of emotions flowing together in his heart. To his horror, he realized that he already recognized the face. It was the one from his waking nightmare in the Middlespace. As Johann watched the man rise, the temptation to stab him nearly overwhelmed him. *This man stole my father from me.*

Trembling, Johann sheathed his weapon. He trusted his father's judgment, and if his father could forgive the man, he could try to as well.

The man's mousy brown hair fell limp at the sides of his face, and his piercing hazel eyes locked their gaze on Johann. "I thank you for that, good sir," he began, his accent very much like his son's, though his words did not suffer from Bruno's butchery. "I've been lying there for years, with only my thoughts for company. I'm sorry to say, they were a dull lot indeed. To whom do I owe the pleasure?"

"Johann. My name is Johann Buchmuller."

Peter's eyes widened. "Not Wilhelm's son? My, my, my, it's been longer than I had imagined. Tell me, is your father well?"

Johann had to bite his lip to keep his emotions at bay. "He is . . . now," he managed. "But I am surprised that you of all people don't know this."

Johann had no choice but to fill him in quickly with the details he knew about what had happened between this knight and his father.

"Oh dear. This is serious. Though I was immobile, my senses have all been keen, and I have heard many things. The Many-Named One has split many people, as he did me. He takes all sorts of prisoners, and believe it or not, many of them are from outside of the kingdom, especially when he needs a particular skill to carry out his plans."

Peter leaned in closer. "They also say that the wizard performed the spell on himself. He's pure evil to be sure, but somewhere down here rests the portion of him that is still good. I was searching this very place when his dark side attacked, so I'm sure that I must have been getting close."

Johann considered Peter's meaning. If they could find this good half of the dark wizard, it might be the key to overpowering their formidable foe. Unfortunately, Johann couldn't be sure how much time had passed since his father had cast the spell on him, and if they searched now, they might never have the chance to escape. He relayed his concerns to the knight. Peter frowned and glanced about.

"That is a problem," he muttered, "but I think it's a risk worth taking."

Johann relented uneasily, and they started off in a brisk jog. Peter led the way out of the Chamber of Knights into another passage. He spoke loudly as they ran, explaining his rationale. "I devoted my life to studying the dark wizard and each of his appearances. A single pattern emerged: the man appeared to be obsessed with art, particularly characters from classic works of literature. The chambers here are organized according to social class. For a long time, I searched the knights, chamberlains, and magicians. Everywhere but craftsmen and artisans. Even then, when I searched their chamber, my search turned up nothing. He is a sly one, and I'm sure that he's found some way to hide his good part around here somewhere.

Peter stopped under an archway, reading the inscription. Satisfied, he nodded briskly and announced. "We're here, Johann. Craftsmen and Artisans."

Johann set right to work, swinging his torch around to illuminate the dark corners of the chamber. His uneasiness grew as the seconds ticked mercilessly on. To assure himself, he hovered slightly above the ground as he searched the musty chamber. He was painfully unaware of what he was looking for, and even though he strained his eyes as best he could, he could not find anything out of the ordinary.

Out of nowhere, he could feel himself sinking, despite his father's gift. Panicked, he thought harder about keeping himself aloft, with only limited success. He glanced around and could not see Peter. *Had he been abandoned. after all?* "Peter! Come quickly! We have to—"

It was as if a lever had been flipped in Johann's brain, and all his effort to fly exploded outwards at once. He rocketed toward the ceiling at an incredible speed, with barely enough time to let out a cry. His mind reeled as he imagined his body falling broken and battered to the floor.

Instead of smashing against the stones, Johann flew straight through the ceiling, sending a shower of rock and timber clattering noisily onto the caskets below. He landed hard, his face pressing into dusty, rough stone. Coughing to clear his lungs, he slowly stood and futilely brushed at his clothes. He bent down and retrieved another brand of wood to replace the torch that he had just misplaced. He lit the stick and stood in awe of what the light revealed: a solitary coffin, much like the others, crafted completely out of shiny, ebony stone glimmering menacingly in the firelight.

Cautiously, Johann approached the edifice and stooped to read the inscription. "Peter!" he called down as loudly as he could manage. "Would the man we are looking for be named Jorgen Müller?"

In a moment, Peter leapt up through the hole with a superhuman swiftness. His eyes opened wide with excitement as they scanned the sarcophagus. "It seems the fates have smiled upon you. That was the Many-Named-One's original name."

Johann shrugged. "What do we do once he comes out? I mean, shouldn't we get on with it, whatever it is? Our time is very limited."

Peter smiled wryly in a way that made Johann a bit uncomfortable. It reminded him much too much of the fox-faced man. "It is as you say. Time *is* of the essence. We must bring him with us and present him to the other knights."

Through squinted eyes, Peter studied the ornate box, walking around it, but keeping his distance, as if afraid of a contagious disease. Johann looked on anxiously, hearing every second tick off in his head. "Peter—" he began impatiently.

Peter held up a single gloved hand. "Quiet. I'm looking for traps or spells. Chances are, the old blighter didn't just leave this place without some sort of protection."

After what seemed like half a lifetime, Peter finally pronounced his opinion. "Yes, there is a strong magical binding on the lid. Even if we were to try to wake him, we'd be in for a shock at best, and at worst . . . ." He shook his head, dismissing the thought. "I think I have the skill to break it, but I will need your help. Step around to the foot of the box and stretch out your hands."

Johann obeyed, figuring that any progress was desirable. Peter continued as soon as he had taken his place at the head of the coffin. "Good, now on my count, close your eyes, place both of your hands firmly on the coffin, and channel all of your energy into it. If it works, the lid should slide away almost immediately, and if it doesn't, well . . . you'll know that, too."

Swallowing loudly, but choosing not to voice any of his concerns, Johann closed his eyes and waited tensely for the count. "One, two . . . *three!*"

They plunged down their hands in unison. "Jorgen Müller, arise!"

As Peter had promised, the effect was instantaneous. In a blinding flash of light, Peter and Johann flew back against the outer walls, their hands scalded by the sudden heat. With a painful, ear-rending grinding, the lid of the coffin slid open, scattering spidery threads of light and shadows across the room. Johann clenched his teeth, suppressing a cry. Peter, who was much closer, shielded his eyes as the light grew much brighter and a ghostly figure materialized. The outline of a burly man with a full, dark beard appeared so faintly that Johann had to squint to make sure he was not just imagining something. The apparition waved its hands about wildly, as if trying to break the surface of a lake while in the act of drowning.

"Ach!" it wailed pathetically. "He who thinks freedom is sweet has never tasted of the nectar of sleep!"

Johann wrinkled his brow at the strange saying. It was about the last thing that he had expected from such a being. Cautiously, he took a step closer and addressed it, "Jorgen, sir. We're sorry to wake you, but we need your help."

The faint figure raised a hand. Johann could just barely see that he wore the gloves and apron of a craftsman. Directly around him, the air smelled faintly of sawdust. "Save the talk if there is work to be done. I am barely a specter of the man from whom I was formed, and I cannot hold my feeble form for long. If you are planning to take me along, I will have to inhabit something or someone for the journey. Choose quickly before I'm forced back into the coffin."

Returning to his feet with incredible swiftness, Peter lunged forward and grabbed Johann's sword. Swiveling around with the agility of a dancer, he thrust the shining blade through the phantom figure, which grimaced and immediately dissolved again into nothingness.

Peter extended the hilt of Johann's sword for Johann to see. He noticed that it now glowed slightly brighter, as if bathed in moonlight and trembled ever so slightly. Johann tentatively extended his hand as he grasped the sword, his hand tingling slightly, as if with electricity. He quickly stuffed it back in his belt and turned to Peter. "We need to go, now."

Johann tried to imagine himself rising, but to his despair, he couldn't move a single inch off the ground. "Peter! I can't fly anymore! What will we do?"

The older knight sighed, his face the epitome of calmness. "Never fear, young one. Though releasing the spell probably drained the last bit of magic out of you, I've had years of rest. "

Peter's face shone like the pale moon rising as he smiled, and he quickly disappeared back down the hole leading to the room below. Johann crept over to the side and peered down. To his relief, Peter stood there ready to catch him. Johann wasted no time, landing with only minor discomfort. Without a word, Peter led them back the way they had come and into the Chamber of Knights.

Johann's sword continued to vibrate against his side as he walked, a constant reminder of his phantom passenger. He wondered why he, of all people, managed to stumble on something that the knights had been seeking for centuries. *Perhaps the time had never been right*, Johann thought. *Until now.*

As they made their way swiftly through the chamber, Johann had to glance backward several times. He thought he heard a familiar voice whisper from the shadows. The first few times, he dismissed it outright, but as it continued, he could no longer ignore it.

He called for Peter to stop for a moment, and turned his head toward the sound. "Johann," whispered the voice. "I'm right here, just turn around."

As he did, Johann faced a person that he had been sure he would never see again. His third ghostly visitor that day carried a massive hammer, which he tossed leisurely up and down, as if he were handling nothing more than a twig.

His expression was much cheerier than the usual one he had borne in life.

"Hello, Johann," he began gruffly. "This is indeed an opportune meeting."

Without warning, Brutus glided over and placed the mighty hammer squarely in Johann's hands. Johann doubled over under its weight, threatening to keel completely over. He gazed down at the hardened hammer in puzzlement. It was the same one that he had seen Brutus use on any number of occasions while working at his blacksmith's shop. Johann could not decide how to feel, given the situation. Though ecstatic to see his uncle, it only brought home the severity of his own situation all the more. "Uncle, it's good to see you," he managed, "but this might not be the best time to tell me I need to go back to work."

Brutus offered a rare smile. "Actually, that is exactly what I am going to ask you to do," he said. "You see, Johann, before my untimely death, I was working on something of great importance. Our family has always been responsible for maintaining the great musical instrument beneath the castle. It's designed to play a variety of songs, and each has a different effect. Not only did our family maintain the machine, but we wrote the songs."

Brutus reached into his blacksmith's apron and retrieved a long scroll of paper, which he presented to Johann. Johann placed the hammer at his feet, and unrolled the scroll. He recognized this piece of paper immediately. He had seen it in the secret room of his uncle's shop. He squinted his eyes and wracked his brain but still couldn't make any sense of the seemingly random array of dots and lines. He glanced back up at the ghost, his eyes pleading for answers. "Uncle, what is this?"

"Look closer, Johann. What do you see there?"

Johann let out all of his air in one exasperated breath. "I might as well be reading a bunch of random ink stains! I don't understand this, or anything else I've seen. I—"

"I never wanted to involve anyone else in this risky venture, but it seems that now I have no choice. I cannot go to my rest until I make sure this is in the proper hands."

Brutus stepped closer and pointed to the scroll. He ran his pointer finger over the lines, tracing a pattern in the dots, humming softly to himself as he did. He glanced up at Johann with merriment in his eyes. "This, Johann, is music. These lines correspond to lines on the machine itself, and the dots mark where to place the raised pieces of metal that you saw in my workshop. When done correctly, it produces the most heavenly music imaginable. However, the song that I was working on is not merely to please the ear.

"It is a song of banishment!" he bellowed, his face clouding with increasing fury, "and the song is complete! If you can play it on the machine, the bane of the kingdom will never be able to reach this world again!"

For a moment, Johann sorely wished he could return to the time such a short while ago when his life was not entangled in complicated plots and intricate plans. "I wish to help, Uncle, but I can't read this scroll! I don't know where to go or how to get the machine playing—"

His voice trailed off, and Brutus picked up the train of thought. "Yes, but your father does. He wanted to teach you one day, but sadly, we've all run into . . . hard times." His eyes glowed bitterly as he briefly considered Peter, who was standing behind Johann. He muttered something poisonous under his breath and returned his gaze to his nephew. "Take these things to your father, Johann. He'll know what to do."

The form of his uncle started to blur, his outline becoming particularly indistinct. His face returned to its previous peaceful form. "Farewell, Johann," he spoke softly. "You shall make an honorable knight. May it suit you better than being a blacksmith's apprentice ever did."

His uncle's form faded until it completely vanished from sight, leaving Johann empty and languid. There had been so many other questions that he had wanted to ask, and other things to apologize for, but now it was too late. He lopsidedly sprinted with the hammer in tow to catch up with Peter, whose face reflected genuine annoyance. "So, he didn't make it. A pity, though I'm not terribly surprised."

Johann's face flushed red hot with indignation, but given the situation, he forced himself to bite his tongue. His head spun like the little toy tops he played with as a boy, but he still managed to keep his voice somewhat level. "Leave that for later. How is it that you can get us out of here?"

They came to the shaft that Johann had originally used and once again they imagined just how deep underground this adventure had taken them. Johann glanced at the ceiling. "Are we going up again somehow?"

Peter shook his head, bending down, and sifting his fingers through the dirt, humming softly to himself. He arose and glanced sidelong at Johann. "No, actually, I prefer the other direction."

He thrust his hand deftly into the dirt, twisting as he went. The dirt parted for him as the sea did for Moses, creating a tunnel large enough for the two of them to pass through. Peter stepped down into the hole and reached his hand up to Johann. "Grasp my hand, and do not let go. Make sure you have a firm grip on that hammer as well, because we are not going to be able to backtrack."

Johann grasped Peter's hand, holding his breath, completely unsure of what to expect. His stomach lurched as he shot forward faster than he thought possible. They disappeared into the tunnel in a split second, tunneling first downward for a moment before spiraling upwards. The hammer flailed out behind him like the blazing tail of a comet, sending clods of dirt and grime hurtling down after them. *I hate traveling like this,* Johann thought.

They burst into the sunlight, erupting from the ground in a geyser of mud and debris and landed in a tangle of hedges. Johann's vision swirled in a melee of dizziness and stinging pain. The harder he tried to extricate himself from the hedge, the more its thorns dug into his flesh. As he cried out in frustration, the bushes around him erupted in a flurry of motion as a blade slashed down on either side of him. All at once, he found himself free of the hedge's thorny grasp.

From his position on the ground, he glimpsed his father smiling down at him, brandishing a gleaming sword. Next to his father stood a frail-looking Siegfried, his eyes sunken back into his sockets. Despite his frail condition, the delight on his face was still evident.

"Johann!" they cried simultaneously, helping him to his feet. "We weren't expecting to see you come from that direction," admitted his father, casting a sidelong glance at Peter. "I'm sure you'll agree, it's more fun to be an eagle than a mole."

Siegfried slapped him on the back jovially with his arm. "Johann, I'm very pleased to see you were able to put our plan into action. I knew you had it in you!"

Johann grinned back, trying to ignore the pain that crawled all through his body. "What happened, Siegfried? How did they trap you?"

The old knight wrinkled his brow, staring off into space. "I'm not exactly sure, but I think somehow they tampered with my contact inside the castle. I was captured the moment I attempted to reach him."

Peter stood passively in the background, still coated with mud and keeping quiet. Johann's father turned to him, his gaze cool and collected. Silently, he held out a hand, nodding slightly as he did so. Peter hesitated, considering the offer, and slowly grasped Wilhelm's hand, pumping it up and down firmly. "I guess I can forgive your transgression," muttered Wilhelm. "It is true that you were literally not your best self."

Peter nodded, his eyes, though devoid of tears, filled with pain. "Thank you, old comrade. I have suffered much for it ever since, and I am glad that you do not see it necessary to inflict further punishment."

They released each other's grip and returned to the most important matters at hand. "We are only three," declared Wilhelm. "Brutus cannot join us. At a time as perilous as this, I only wish we could have him back, but also that we could retrieve our original member."

Johann cocked his eyebrows. He had no idea, to whom his father was referring. "Father, who are you talking about? I thought the knights have been the same from the beginning."

"Not quite," replied his father evenly. "The man who founded the knights was the most powerful of us all. He was a pensive man, who often spoke of his homeland, which he was very far from. We all thought it to be harmless reminiscing, but one day, he simply left, leaving only a short note telling us that he had returned home."

"We could use his power now," added Peter. "The Royal Knights were never as powerful as when we had him, and with only three members, we will be weaker still."

"Then what is to be done?" inquired Siegfried. "Are we to stand against him, incomplete as we are, and with the heirs so inexperienced? I am afraid we may not carry the day."

Wilhelm tensed, wanting to take the road of optimism, but was swayed forcefully by the path of pragmatism. Feeling that he could lighten the mood some, Johann decided to add what he knew. He extracted the scroll and held it out in front of the knights. "I believe that Brutus will help us yet," he announced.

He told the others of his recent conversation with his uncle. His father's stony expression softened as he considered possibilities. "It's decided then. Johann, you and I will delve back into the caverns below. Siegfried and Peter, you must protect the queen at all costs and fend off the Many-Named One and his minions until Johann and I can complete our task."

Wilhelm reached for Johann's sword and held it aloft. "As for this passenger, I think it best that he go with you, Siegfried. Who knows what advantage it may give us against the wizard himself? Are we agreed?"

The other knights nodded their heads while Siegfried crossed his sword with the one Wilhelm held out. At a few words from Wilhelm, the faint glow around Johann's sword transferred to the other sword. As soon as the transfer had been made, the three knights held their swords one by one out at arm's length, their tips converging in the middle. With a strange word that made no sense to Johann, they swiftly lifted the swords and plunged them into the ground in an ornamental gesture that Johann figured had to do something with their chivalric tradition. With a few soft-spoken words, the knights parted ways. Wilhelm escorted his son deeper into the gardens.

Johann could feel dread pooling inside of him, more intense and bitter than it had ever been in his life. It was as if he could glimpse the brewing storm clouds on the horizon, preparing to release their full fury on their unprotected heads.

Johann and Wilhelm entered the tunnels in the garden the same way that Johann had done just a short time before. They hurried through the passages below, not immediately meeting any resistance. Their luck, however, quickly disappeared as they reached the maze of mirrors, which was swarming with burly blonde-haired guards. Wilhelm deftly dispatched the first one they encountered, who cried in alarm, alerting the remaining guards. The maze transformed into a chaotic frenzy of sound and weapon fire. Father and son hurried for the entrance of the maze just as an enormous torrent of sound and motion rocked the complex and swept them off their feet.

They endured the ear-rending shattering of glass and the shrieks of those buried beneath it. They clawed at the ground, stumbling as quickly as they could as bits of the roof spilled onto the floor. "Johann!" yelled Wilhelm, straining over the commotion. "We'll have to try a different way!"

Finally getting to their feet, they dashed off in the opposite direction, just in time to see a section of the tunnel completely give way, barring their original path. Above them, the ceiling threatened to give in at any moment, but Wilhelm stopped short of the passage. Johann stared at him incredulously. "Father! We have to hurry! The rest of the tunnel is going to cave in on us!"

His father shook his head curtly. "We're not going that way."

Johann looked around, completely confused. The tunnel only branched off in two directions and a formidable pile of rubble already blocked one of them. He got his answer a few moments later, as his father bent down and picked up a metal grate from the floor, casting it aside in one heave. It clattered noisily on the stones just a few feet away.

Wilhelm glanced down quickly and began to lower himself into the gap. "I'll get down first, and then I want you to follow. Your legs won't touch the floor—I will be there to catch you."

Johann nodded, worry lines forming around the edge of his eyes as he watched his father disappear into the darkness. The tunnel continued to groan, like a Bengal tiger with indigestion, and he took this as a warning not to hesitate. Without a second thought, he crouched down and lowered himself into the pit. He let his legs dangle as far as they would reach until his father could brush them with his fingertips. He gave a count of three and then let himself drop. After a brief second of weightlessness, his father caught him smartly and lowered him to the ground. Johann brushed himself off and summoned a small spark to hover above his hand. "Thanks. Where to now?"

Wilhelm glanced tentatively in both directions before declaring. "It will be down this corridor. It's not far, but be warned. Things might get a bit cozy."

The two of them traveled in silence, and just as Wilhelm had promised, the corridor did indeed gradually become quite cramped to the point that they both had to drop on hands and knees to squeeze through the tight passages. Johann strained his ears as he thought he heard something in the distance. As they traveled on, the sounds grew louder, and Johann could no longer convince himself that he was hearing things. "Father, do you hear that?" he called forward. "Is it just me, or does it sound like—"

"Music," said Wilhelm. "It's coming from the direction we are headed. Don't ask me what a musician is doing down here. Maybe he's a prisoner. I've overheard that the Many-Named One has taken many. He takes them from their own worlds and replaces them with living statues so they will not be missed."

They continued on in silence, the music growing louder and louder as they advanced. Johann could make out the clear singing voice of a man, who accompanied his singing sporadically with a variety of instruments. At times, the muffled tones of an organ floated through the halls and at other times, the sounds of a string instrument, perhaps a violin.

They continued until the beautiful melodies seemed to originate just ahead of them. Johann's father halted and turned toward Johann as well as he could in the cramped space. "Our destination lies not more than a stone's throw ahead. I'm going to open the grate a bit to see if I can assess the situation."

Wilhelm lay flat on his stomach while Johann peered out over him through the slats in the grating in front of them. From what they could make out with their limited view, they could see a lively elderly gentleman with a swatch of graying hair adorning his head and a bristly moustache perched under his nose. He stroked a battered, old violin with the tenderness of a new father as he sung a strange tune, both melancholy and hopeful at the same time. The room held a large, rusting pipe organ near the rear while the edges of the nearly circular room were a smorgasbord of well-worn instruments, stacks of scribbled parchment and spent writing utensils. They both watched in fascination, both repeating their earlier question in their minds. *What is a musician doing here?*

As the man's song came to an end, he set down the bow and whirled around to face them, a congenial smile spreading over his face, causing his moustache to spread like a pair of wings. "Go on and show yourselves. It has been quite some time since I've had an audience."

Open-mouthed, they both practically fell out of the passage and into the grotto. "How did you know we were there?" Johann managed.

"You don't become a first-class, second-rate composer without having an eye for the details, no?" the man replied, arching his eyebrows. "But don't worry, I welcome the intrusion. To tell you the truth, it gets quite lonely down here. My name is Hart, by the way."

Johann and Wilhelm both rose to their feet and considered the man more closely. Nothing about his appearance seemed threatening, but even his mere existence seemed an anomaly. "Did you like it?" asked Hart.

"Did we like what?" Johann asked.

"The music!" Hart declared with a grin. "It's one of my 'Actual Four

Last Songs.' Before I came here, I wrote four songs that at the time I thought would be my last. However, the more I try to write my 'final songs' the more life tightens its grip on me. I must have written my 'Four Last Songs' at least a dozen times!"

Johann grinned and finally gathered the nerve to ask the question that had been nagging at him, now that he had been set at ease by the man's humorous demeanor. "What . . . what language were you singing in? I don't understand it, but it also seems like I've heard it before."

"Deutsch!" he replied, grinning broadly. "The language of my home-land and of the ancient queens. They say the first queen herself spoke an early form of it. The old manuscripts are proof of that."

It was then Johann realized where he had heard it before. "Brigitta! My friend Brigitta starting speaking that language when I found her lost in the woods. It was like she was in a trance, though, like she didn't know what she was saying!"

Hart stroked his chin, deep in thought. "It seems that she must have something to do with the queens. No one really speaks that language here anymore—not since the English queen came to power. She arrived in the kingdom from afar and could not speak the ancient language, and her influ-ence effectively abolished its common use."

His hands returned to his side. "But I'm sure you didn't come here for a history lesson. What brings you here to my humble studio? Are you 'guests' like me?"

Wilhelm shook his head. "Well, we're actually here to make a little music ourselves. Johann, show him the score."

Johann rummaged through his pockets and retracted the carefully folded piece of music. He unfolded it, taking care not to cause any damage, and handed it reluctantly to the composer. Hart's eyes widened, gulping up the manuscript like a sumptuous meal. He muttered incoherently while study-ing the score, holding it quite close to his face and pacing about. Finally, he set the manuscript down on one of his cluttered desks. "A truly superb piece of work," he announced, "and I must say, truly unique! I've seen dozens of these types of manuscripts before, many of them copies of one another, and I thought that I had seen all of them in existence."

He gestured broadly, indicating the stacks of parchment scattered across the various tables and desks. Johann looked around and realized that the majority of the sheets closely resembled the one that he had just given Hart, containing different patterns of line, dots, and notations. "Did you write all of these?" asked Johann incredulously.

"No," Hart admitted. "Mostly collected them, though I have tried my hand at a few compositions in this style." He picked up the one Johann had just given him. "The strange thing about this one is that it is not finished."

Johann arched his eyebrows in surprise. "Are you sure? It was given to me by my uncle and he did not say anything about it being incomplete. In fact, he claimed that it was complete!"

Hart nodded resolutely. "I am certain. It cuts off right in the middle of a phrase, in fact. It's a genuine shame. It doesn't seem that the composer had very far to go. It's like he stood up suddenly in the middle of writing and never came back." Johann stayed silent as he contemplated the uncanny nature of Hart's words.

"This presents a problem," muttered Wilhelm. "It will not work to play the song partially. The desired affect will only occur if every single note is in place. Otherwise, all we'll get is a pleasant tune."

Hart scrutinized the notes again for several moments, his face changing from concentration to resolve. "I can do it. Judging from the pattern of the music, it is only missing a few measures. From the rest of the score and from what I have learned from studying the other scores, I should be able to extrapolate the ending."

Both Johann and Wilhelm glanced at him nervously, wanting to believe him, but painfully unsure. "Are you sure?" inquired Wilhelm. "An educated guess won't do. It's got to be precise."

"Might as well give him a chance, Father. It's the only one we have," added Johann.

Wilhelm folded his arms, deep in thought. "I suppose you're right. Let us hurry, then. We should begin preparing the instrument while the music is being finished."

He turned his gaze to the direction he wished to precede and frowned. The dilapidated organ stood firmly in the way. He rushed over to it and tried to determine what was behind it with no success. He absently fumbled with several of the keys, which emitted a jumble of different tones. Hart stepped up beside him and with outstretched fingers, produced four large and dynamic chords, two long, followed by two short ones. He had to retract his hands swiftly as the organ slid off to the side and then into a slot in the ground, revealing the continuing passage beyond. Wilhelm raised his eyebrows in astonishment. "I guess there are things about this castle I don't know."

The three of them slipped through the passage and found that it only continued on a bit further before it opened up into a round stone chamber with smooth gray walls and only one feature—an antique marble fountain, devoid of water. Johann recognized it at once. Johann and his father placed their hands on the rim of the fountain, looking for Hart to follow suit. He hesitated.

"You need to place your hand on the fountain for this to work," reminded Wilhelm tensely.

"I know," replied Hart evenly. "But I have one . . . condition."

The smile vanished from Wilhelm's face. "Condition?"

Hart held a level gaze. "Yes," he continued deliberately. "It is not too much to ask under the circumstances. "

He rummaged in his pocket and extracted a much smaller, crumpled piece of parchment. It too had musical markings on it. "We play this song first."

Wilhelm scrutinized the paper warily. It had no writing on it or anything else to mark just what it was. "What is it?" he inquired, a controlled edge of frustration born of urgency entering his voice.

"I would rather not say," replied Hart shaking his head slowly. "But I will say that it is the culmination of years of work, and that it will not harm anyone."

Wilhelm considered the offer for only a few moments. "Fine," he blurted out with obvious anxiety. "Let's just go."

An instant later, Hart blurted the word of command that controlled the fountain, and they promptly found themselves dragged underground, whisking by at high speed. The trip finished sooner than Johann's first journey with the fountain but proved infinitely more twisted, causing his stomach to lurch uncomfortably. However, before they knew it, they had arrived, landing smartly in an austere room with smooth, gray, metal walls. It was almost the same dimensions of the room they had just left and contained nothing but the fountain and a metal door.

While the other two regained their composure, Hart simply brushed himself off and gingerly grasped the door handle as if the trip had been nothing more than a pleasant, leisurely stroll. As the door swung open, it revealed a narrow walkway, which led to a rectangular panel covered in a series of buttons and levers. The three of them stepped out onto the walkway, and Johann immediately drew in his breath in surprise.

The walkway spanned the length of an enormous cylinder riddled with hundreds of tiny mounds like the huts of an indigenous village. Hart stepped forward and fiddled with the levers for a few moments. A resolute click echoed as if they were in a cathedral as the levers fell into proper order. All lay still for the shortest of moments, and then the room erupted with the deafening din of metal grinding on metal. Johann watched in wonderment as the entire cylinder curved and flattened itself out until it lay like lumpy bed sheets strewn across the floor.

Now that it was a flat surface, Johann could distinctly make out the series of thin parallel lines spaced at even intervals across its length. "Those lines," he muttered in realization, "are just like those on the parchment!"

"Yes!" added Hart triumphantly. "You will find that they correspond exactly. That, and if you look along the edges, you will see there's no short-age of dots either!"

Johann glanced to the edge of the former cylinder and saw that these words were true. Stacks of the metal mounds formed waist-high columns along the sides, caked with possible decades of dust.

Hart stuck out his finger and pressed one of the large colored buttons on the panel, and with a similar but less deafening grinding of metal, all of the mounds drew themselves to either side, forming new columns and leav-ing a blank sheet of metal below them. Hart motioned for them to follow as he released the stop on a metal ladder, which led from the walkway to the ground.

Hart spread his arms, gesturing at the vast space. "Here is where we begin our work!" he announced. "It has been nearly impossible for me to do this alone . . . the device being damaged as it is and all . . . ."

Johann glanced around and saw that the eccentric composer once again had been right on target. The surface of the cylinder had suffered corrosion to the point that it left gaping holes, and many of the dots were so worn that they threatened to blend in with the rest of the surface.

As Johann bent down to examine a particular hole, he felt a strange tingling in his fingers. It started at the tips, but quickly spread like a million sparks of living electricity up his fingers, not fading in the least until it almost reached his elbow. On instinct, he reached for the open gash and instantly the edges of the metal rushed toward his fingers, repairing the gash so smoothly that he began to second guess himself as to whether it had really been there in the first place.

He retracted his hand, and the tingling momentarily ceased. However, as he bent down over another hole, the experience repeated itself, leaving him feeling more energized and alive than he had in a long time. "Father! I think you better take a look at this!"

The two others turned and watched intently as Johann demonstrated his newfound ability. To Johann's astonishment, his father put on a demonstra-tion of his own. Wilhelm extended his hand toward one of the lopsided metal stacks and quickly flicked his fingers toward himself. The top dot flew toward him and followed the pattern he traced in the air with his finger. His father finally lay the dot to rest across one of the lines, where it stuck fast.

"It is in our blood, Johann. It is our family heritage to be the keepers of music. Each one of us is endowed with certain gifts, and it appears that you have found yours. For that we are all fortunate." Wilhelm retrieved Brutus's hammer from his side and handed it to Johann. As it changed hands, it shrunk until it fit Johann's hands. "Here, take this. It will help you with the particu-larly dirty work."

Hart gazed on wide-eyed, positively bursting with enthusiasm. "Yes, marvelous. We must set to work right away. The machine has the remarkable ability to remember a variety of songs, so we'll get started on mine first so that you can fulfill your end of the bargain. Johann, you set about making repairs, and you, Wilhelm, start placing dots according to this pattern. I will begin my work with your song so as to be finished as soon as possible. Agreed?"

They both nodded silently as Wilhelm took the scrap of parchment from Hart's hand and set to work right away. Hart retrieved the unfinished parchment and began to pace, now and then marking additions. Johann studied the terrain for a moment and then decided on a direction in which the damage appeared particularly grievous. He leapt from hole to hole like a sprite with beating dragonfly wings. It was thrilling to see the bruised surface once again become whole, as if he was some miracle physician closing up even the grizzliest wounds with the slightest touch.

He quickly lost track of time, and when he glanced up to gauge the other's progress, he stopped cold. They were nowhere to be seen. "Hart! Father!" he called, his voice fading into the distance.

A thin mist had crept surreptitiously into the area, obscuring most of his view of what lay in the distance. Instinctively, he grasped his sword, his hands shuddering from a sudden cold. The more he wandered about, the thicker the mist became, and the more his apprehension grew.

Before him, the mists parted, revealing a hooded figure about his same height. The figure extended his hand, his palm facing ominously toward him. "Hello, Johann."

CHAPTER TWENTY-ONE

⚬

HEIR TODAY . . .

THE CANTICLE KINGDOM

In the midst of the darkness of the furnace room a gentle wisp of light floated down from the ceiling and rested on the sleeping queen. For a brief moment, her whole body glowed, and gradually, her pale skin resumed its healthy color. She stirred, slowly at first, her breaths coming more regularly and sounding less labored. Slowly, her eyes fluttered open, and she rose to a sitting position.

All her memories returned to her now, flooding back like the contents of a lake trying to enter through a single storm drain. The tumult sparked an immediate bout of dizziness, which soon passed. She gazed lovingly at the pristine statue in front of her, and ran her slender fingers over the surface, muttering in a soft sing-song tone:

> Awake, awake from stony sleep.
> For stones' eternal secrets keep.

In much the same manner as the queen, the color filtered back into the statue's features, softening and blending, peeling away until a fully revived Brigitta stood in front of her. Coming to her senses, Brigitta sighed loudly and flung her arms around the queen. "Oh, Gwen, ah, I mean Molly, it worked! I was so worried!"

The queen held her tightly, her own heart swelling with gratitude. "That was a very brave deed, Brigitta. They may not know it, but the entire kingdom has you to thank." *And Rufus, as well.* They released their embrace, and Brigitta glanced around frantically calling for Johann. He was nowhere to be seen.

She tried to remain calm but failed miserably. "Where could he be? Johann said that he wasn't going to go out of my sight."

"Maybe he found his father."

Brigitta sighed, trying again to collect her wits. "So what do we do now?

He could be anywhere!"

The queen nodded and wrapped an arm around Brigitta's shoulder. "I'm so sorry, Brigitta, but we have to go. We'll find him, I promise, but right now, we have to act quickly."

She reached into her pocket and extracted a shiny, metallic object. She displayed it to Brigitta, who saw that it was a miniature, highly polished mirror with a silver handle. "This is one of those objects I created that lets me travel to a certain place again. I've had it with me, but I did not remember its purpose until now, since my memory has been restored. Perhaps the time has not been right until now. Without at least some of my strength back, I don't think I could have survived the trip."

The queen held the mirror close to Brigitta's face. "I need you to look into your eyes in your reflection in the mirror . . . as soon as you are ready. I will follow just as soon as possible."

Brigitta gulped, trying not to let the emptiness in her heart reflect on her face. She nodded solemnly and brought her sad eyes to meet the ones of her reflection. Instantly, it felt as though a mighty wind was compressing her and driving her into the tiny space. Her entire field of vision blurred into white streaks of light, and for several breathtaking moments, her body rushed forward in a burst of exhilarating speed.

The journey ended almost as quickly as it began. With a jolt, Brigitta found herself in a lavish bedroom. A canopied four-poster bed with brilliant snowy sheets stood on one side, while a vanity and an ornate table with a chair occupied the other. Near the table lay a conspicuous pile of rubble, looking horribly out of place among the rest of the pristine surroundings.

With a thud, the queen also arrived in the bedroom. Glancing at the queen now, with her hair all out of sorts, her clothes and skin covered in grime, and everything in a general state of disarray, it was strange to think that she belonged in her current surroundings.

Wasting no time, the queen rushed to the side of the bed and stooped down. Brigitta followed her and gasped in astonishment. Next to another much smaller pile of rubble was an unconscious girl not much younger than Brigitta herself, with flowing chestnut hair and pallid skin. The queen felt the girl's skin and bent down, placing an ear next to her mouth.

Retracting her head, the queen nodded grimly. "She's still alive, thank heavens, though she needs some attention. Quick, help me lift her up onto the bed."

Brigitta responded quickly, and together they placed the girl under the bedclothes. Brigitta could feel that the girl's skin was quite warm to the touch, as if she were suffering a scalding fever. The queen quickly retrieved a damp cloth and placed it over the child's forehead. She did not stir.

Brigitta examined the girl's face, but did not even remotely recognize her. "Who is she?" asked Brigitta.

"Her name is Camilla," replied Molly. "She's my daughter."

"Your daughter?" cried Brigitta. "I didn't think the queen had a family."

Molly shook her head. "I don't, at least not officially. And technically, I'm not her birth mother, but I have been her caretaker for some years."

Brigitta squinted her eyes. "But . . . how did you keep others from knowing about her?"

The queen sighed. "Well, let's say that she was more like my pet than my daughter. I had to keep her identity hidden, for she is a very special girl. She is one of the heirs of the kingdom's royal knights. Officially, she was supposed to have died, but I made an agreement with her father to keep her here in disguise as my cat. Besides, the girl reminded the poor man so much of his wife, who actually was killed, that it was like reopening a wound every time he looked on her. May she rest in peace."

Brigitta's mind swam on hearing the strange account with questions flitting around like darting fish. "But . . . why bring her out of hiding now? It seems it is the most dangerous right now."

The queen nodded gravely. "The time draws near that the four heirs to the royal knights will have to step up to their places. The Many-Named One has returned and in addition to many other heinous deeds, he has stolen a very important possession, a powerful amulet. He first tried to steal it some time ago during the night, and afterwards, I placed a powerful spell on it, making it so that only children could touch it. I figured that then it would be safe, but somehow he still managed to get his hands on it."

A dense knot formed at the pit of Brigitta's stomach. She knew exactly what the queen was talking about, and exactly what role she herself had played in the account. Her face flushed with shame as she thought of how simple greed had driven her to such a reckless act.

With tears of shame scalding her face, she told the queen of her encounter with the amulet and her experiences in the forest and the castle garden. The entire time, the queen remained impassive, measuring the words with care. "Then you already know about my amulet. It's just as well. It isn't really mine anyway. It has always stayed with the queen, and for good reason."

She leaned in closely and whispered, straining to be heard over the sound of a distant crowd. "Brigitta, every living soul in this kingdom depends on my energy to sustain their lives. That amulet is called the Morgenstern, or in our language, the 'Morning Star,' and it is an incredible source of power that keeps this constant drain from killing me. Without it, I am slowly dying. The Many-Named One thinks that he can turn the amulet to work for him, but he's wrong. If there comes a time when there isn't a rightful queen on the throne, the amulet will stop working. When that happens, it will only be a matter of time before all life dries up here like a puddle in the noonday sun."

Brigitta looked about in alarm, realizing how close they had all come to imminent disaster. "What can we do then?"

The queen turned herself toward the sound of the crowd. Her face darkened for a moment, deep in thought. "We play along with his little game until he reveals himself. At best we should attempt to gather as many of the knights and their heirs to the castle. At any rate, we must prepare for the inevitable. As soon as we can get the Morgenstern back in our possession, we need to make provisions for someone to succeed me. If the kingdom is ever to be restored to its former state, it will need a new, healthy queen. To do that, we must play the correct song on the machine deep within the castle to summon a queen from the outside world."

Brigitta nodded in understanding, but furrowed her brow as she remembered one very important detail. "But I read the diagram of the music machine when we were down there, and I found out how it works. We might run into some trouble using it, even if we can find some way to fix it. It only works when the right people are in place."

"Perhaps," replied the queen. "I have thought about the possible candidates, and I think that I have two men in mind that could help the two of us activate the machine. We will worry about that when the time is right. For now, we need to keep a sharp lookout, and I think I know just the trick."

The queen stepped over to one of her cupboards and slid open the top drawer. Reaching her hand inside, she fiddled with the interior for a moment and then stuck her hand further in as another compartment clicked open. A moment later she retrieved an ornate colored glass flask with a stopper protruding out the top. The glass was exquisitely crafted in a slender pear-shaped design and shone with a full range of colors. The queen yanked out the stopper and headed over to the vanity, where she carefully tipped the flask and released a single drop in the porcelain basin in front of her. To Brigitta's astonishment, the basin quickly filled with a translucent fluid, which rippled and emitted a faint glow.

"This," began the queen softly, "allows me to see the royal knights wherever they are. It is a comfort as well as an item of strategy. This should give us an idea of how to proceed." The queen placed a single slender hand over the basin and whispered intensely. "Wilhelm, the first knight."

The colors rippled and swam, forming a clear picture on the surface of the liquid. It revealed two armored men against a vast white backdrop. Brigitta recognized one of the men as Siegfried, who leaned on another man, who looked strangely familiar. She gasped as a thought entered his mind. "Is that . . . Johann's father?" she asked in awe.

"Indeed," replied the queen. "Things are better than I thought, though Siegfried looks a little worse for wear. We'll have to take a look about where the other two are as well as their heirs if we . . . ."

A frantic voice spoke to them from behind. "Your Majesty! You are supposed to be out there in two minutes! What in the world are you wearing?"

The queen whirled about to glance a neatly groomed servant with highly styled blonde hair, wearing a festive tunic and tights in honor of the occasion. The servant's worry turned to horror as the queen turned about and he glimpsed her face. "Not even started on your makeup!" he wailed, waving his hands in the air as if grasping for a solution. "This is a travesty! I must stall the crowd to whom we have already announced your arrival! Oh, dear!"

Seeing no other choice, the queen launched into action and sprang toward the closet where she kept her gowns, apologizing profusely to the attendant. Seeing that the queen was at least now making progress, the servant's blood pressure dropped several notches, though nothing could be done about his incessant fidgeting.

With a glance toward the doorway, he leapt through it and out into the hall. "I'll stall them as long as I can, your grace," he called back nervously. "But please try to hurry!"

The queen shot Brigitta an awkward smile, already beginning to slip into one of her finer dresses. "Well, not exactly as I would have hoped, but I do not see that I have a choice. You stay here and look after Camilla. If she wakes up, give her something to drink from the flask by the bedside and keep her calm. It will be quite an adjustment to go from being a cat to a little girl again."

It took the queen a remarkably short amount of time to make herself ready for her upcoming appearance. She hustled about, applying makeup and articles of clothing until she resembled a china doll in a colorful mask more than the woman Brigitta knew. She could hardly conceive that this was the same woman whom she had found in the deep caverns below the castle.

Checking herself for the last time in the mirror, the queen pronounced herself ready and then turned to Brigitta, the same witty smile assuring her that it was still her friend under all the layers. "I will return as soon as possible. You know what to do."

Brigitta was about to protest that she really had not a clue as to what to do, but the attendant reappeared in the doorway looking beyond pleased, and the queen followed him out. All at once, Brigitta was left alone with the sleeping girl and her gnawing anxiety for company.

Immediately, she glanced back at the basin where the queen had summoned her liquid looking glass. Almost without thinking about it, her feet set her in motion back toward it. Peering over the side, she thought over what she should do. The queen had not given her any instructions to leave it alone, yet Brigitta could not help feel a bit uneasy and guilty gazing into it without the queen knowing.

However, a single thought nagged at her constantly, like a barking of a stubborn bulldog. When they had seen the image of Johann's father, Johann himself was nowhere to be seen. She simply could not stand the fact of not knowing where he was and if he was safe. Taking a deep breath, she stretched her hand out over the water as she had seen the queen do and whispered. "Johann, heir of the first knight."

To her delight, the water obeyed her commands and swirled about until Johann's face could clearly be seen on the surface. He was completely surrounded by darkness, fear and anxiety staining his face. He was crouched over some large object that Brigitta could not make out, and next to him was an armored man, whom Brigitta did not recognize,

"It must be one of the other knights!" she whispered, relief washing over her at the discovery that her friend was indeed alive, if not completely out of deep water yet. The image lasted only a few moments before fading back again to random waves and patterns. She was about to turn away, when her curiosity nagged at her once again.

She peered again into the water. Her curiosity begged her to find out who the other heirs were. If Johann was one of them, the rest of them could conceivably be people she recognized, and the secret would be too good to leave undiscovered. Taking a guess, she reached out over the water and whispered. "Show me the heir of the second knight!"

She gazed into the rippling waters as they bubbled and parted, but then suddenly became placid as a lake before sunrise. At first, she thought that something had gone wrong, because all she could see reflected in the pool was her own face. However, as she moved her face away from the pool, the reflection remained just as it was before, and not as one would ever expect. Brigitta stared awe-struck at the pool, not daring to believe what it might be telling her. As she watched, the image vanished.

Brigitta ran from the basin and fell to the floor next to the bed. Perhaps, she and Johann's friendship was not just a happenstance. Perhaps this was the way that things were always intended to be, for they shared one very important trait in common. They were heirs.

CHAPTER TWENTY-TWO

✦

A MURDEROUS MASTER

THE CANTICLE KINGDOM

Molly stepped out onto the balcony among a chorus of thunderous cheers. The crowd danced about and waved colorful banners, creating a rippling rainbow of color. The lavishly dressed queen, however, struggled to breathe, a dark foreboding looming over the scene in stark contrast to the merry mood. She observed the long, snaking line of the parade on its steady march to the castle and could not help thinking that this would be a prime opportunity for the dark wizard to make his terrible grand entrance.

Swallowing her fears, she stepped up to the very edge of the balcony and scanned the jubilant faces. To her surprise, while many of them seemed genuinely excited, she counted a great number whose excitement was mixed with profound fear. As she met their eyes, many of them shrank beneath her gaze, as if they feared she would strike them to the ground with her glance. This confused the queen to no end, as she did not consider herself as someone to be feared. She raised her hands and cleared her throat. A profound stillness fell over the crowd.

"My loyal subjects," she began, "I hope that you have enjoyed a bit of our royal hospitality today." She paused for a round of applause, which died down after a few seconds. "I stand before you as one very grateful to be alive, and I think that is something that we should all treasure. I know something of difficult times, which have not only befallen me but the entire kingdom. I am here today to pledge that things will change!"

Both gasps of surprise and shouts of approval soared up from the crowd. "But before I address that, I would that you should know of those who have given their very lives to make this change possible." Molly felt herself holding back the tide of bitter tears. "I shall begin with my chamberlain, Rufus . . . ."

ꙮ

Karsten's eyes scanned the parade as each group passed by. He couldn't help feeling uneasy, sensing a dark presence lingering frighteningly close but just barely hidden from sight. However, each group, starting with the royal guard and continuing on with the jester's guild, showed no sinister tendencies. Behind them followed the monks of the order of St. Molly's Cathedral. Karsten shook his head in disgust. *What could Edison possibly hope to find among so many people?*

Just as this thought crossed his mind, something caught his attention. Behind the lead monk, who had covered his head with a hood, followed a ridiculously short monk—a good head or two shorter than the others. The rest of the monks formed a regular pattern, while this one dwarf monk hovered around the leader at a very close distance. For some reason, this set off warning bells in his head, and he rushed ahead, keeping his eyes on the head monk.

A gust of wind brushed the monk's robe back, revealing an object that glistened briefly in the afternoon sunlight before disappearing again into his voluminous robes. Karsten whirled back around to find Capt. Edison, who was still scanning each face of the crowd in desperation.

"Capt. Edison!" he shouted. "Whatever you do, stay here. I'm afraid decisive action is needed."

Karsten leapt through the crowd, eliciting a round of loud protests. He leapt directly into the ranks of the monks and toward their leader. The monks scattered, recoiling with terrified faces.

The outburst quickly caught the attention of the guards, who rushed through the crowd brandishing their pikes and swords. Undaunted, Karsten plunged forward reaching the head monk and yanking back his hood.

The hood fell away, revealing a straggly mess of light brown hair, slicked back and greasy, which stood out in sharp contrast to the shaved heads of the others. The man had black, close-set eyes, bushy eyebrows and an unruly beard to match his hair. His pockmarked skin appeared clammy and withered, and although most of his features did not look familiar to Karsten, the man's eyes could not be mistaken. "Hello, brother," he muttered coolly.

The next few moments happened in slow motion. The monk grasped the shiny shape around his chest and held it aloft in no more than an instant. The man shrieked a command and immediately the object burst with light, scattering scathing rays like a miniature sun. The whole area swam with iridescent light, the air crackling with pure energy and exploding with the sound of a treacherous tornado. Karsten fell to his knees, futilely shielding his face with his hands. The chaos continued for a full minute, convincing Karsten that his rash move would soon cost him his life.

To his surprise, however, the havoc soon subsided, leaving an eerie darkness and calm. Timidly, Karsten raised his head, meeting the dark gaze of his twisted brother. The monk stared down at his cowering brother his face twisted in wicked glee. "Oh, Karsten, you've spoiled my entrance! Then again, you never did understand good theatrics."

"Jorgen," Karsten muttered weakly. "What . . . ."

His brother cut him off with a savage chop of his hand. "You will call me Saul," he ordered sharply, carefully accenting the name. "Jorgen is no more."

Karsten glanced about for the first time and gasped. Every living thing within sight had turned completely to stone. He stared about in crushing shock, his mind unwilling to accept the grizzly scene. "But . . . how? It couldn't be the—"

Saul held the golden amulet aloft, showcasing it like a war trophy. "Yes, Karsten, the Morgenstern. You of all people should be acquainted with its power. Though it was meant to give life, I have found that it can also take it away."

Karsten's face grew scarlet with rage. "I should have never consented to use it! This place should have never existed. We should have never brought it to life! But I never thought that even you could abuse it like this, taking advantage of our own creation!"

Saul raised the Morgenstern, which blazed again with searing light. "Wrong, brother! I have simply improved on our creation, and soon, both of our worlds will appreciate my remarkable genius! Behold!"

The swirling, gathering light from the Morgenstern burst forth, in an intense explosion of light and sound. "Awake, my minions! Come to your master!"

The light scattered in all directions, and for a moment, silence prevailed, though the sky remained a deep crimson. Suddenly, a gnarled claw punched up through the ground, near the place where Karsten was standing. More claws joined it as an entire army of creatures emerged from the ground. Others crept out from the surrounding forest, while even more slunk in from the town.

Karsten watched in express horror as each one of the knight statues that flanked the entrance to the castle stepped down from its post and joined the growing mob of grotesque and dangerous looking creatures.

The entire castle shuddered to its foundations, groaning like an ice shelf about to give way. Suddenly, the polished stones erupted as a giant misshapen abomination arose from the very center. It appeared to be an enormous conglomerate of creatures, a writhing mass of heads, horns, arms, wings and claws. The creature bellowed with rage, shaking furiously to dislodge the great chunks of jagged stone, which stuck out at wild angles from all over its great mass.

Saul sighed with pleasure. "You see, Karsten, I have finally outshined you. Now that this world belongs to me, I shall make our home world grovel on its knees. For what can it do against such workmanship?"

The crowd of creatures roiled and seethed like a boiling pot, their cries and screeches chilling Karsten to the bone. Saul's face remained as sheer as a cliff face. "I only have to give the word Karsten. I take no pleasure in disposing of you, but I'm afraid it must be so, lest you attempt again to thwart my plans as you've done so often in the past."

Saul raised his hand, preparing to give the signal to release his hordes, when an arrow soared through the sky, piercing Saul's hand clean through. Saul cried out in agony, and whirled about to ascertain the identity of his attacker. On the fringe of a mob stood Siegfried with a flaming arrow hovering over his one good hand. In the next instant, Peter burst from the ground like a trout leaping from the water, snatched Karsten, and dragged him back through the depths of the earth.

In a matter of seconds, the two returned and stood next to Siegfried, all bearing their fighting stance. "Peter!" bellowed the enraged Saul, clutching his injured hand. "You still bear allegiance to me! Take your sword and run Karsten through!"

Without the slightest hesitation, Peter snatched Siegfried's sword from its place and raised it over his head. "Yes, master."

Before anyone could react, Peter struck, stabbing the blade clean through Karsten. The old man gasped, and then with a groan, fell limply to the ground.

"Well done!" cried Saul with fiendish glee. "Your son should be proud of you!"

Saul nodded to the diminutive monk standing next to him, and he returned the gesture with a bow. The small figure of Bruno suddenly burst into motion, sprinting with superhuman speed toward the ruins of the castle and disappearing.

Saul returned to face his opponents. "Siegfried, old man, did you think that you would actually stand as a worthy opponent against me? How would you like to die? At the hands of your comrade, or at the hands of the mob? It makes no difference to me." Saul flicked his hands and a plume of flame erupted from the main head of the creature, which brooded over the castle. The flames ignited the castle gardens, reducing huge stretches of hedges to ash.

Undaunted, Siegfried lashed out with his own hand, allowing his arrow to fly. It struck one of the nearby creatures, which exploded in a shower of crumbling stone. "I choose neither! Life is a more honorable choice, regardless of the circumstances!"

Saul's eyes flashed with fury and with another flick of his hand, he summoned the conglomerate creature. "*Drachenherz!* Destroy!"

The creature known as Drachenherz unleashed a volley of three-foot spikes, sending a lethal hailstorm raining down on Siegfried. The old knight raised his hands to conjure protection but surprisingly was spared the need. A brilliant green globe of energy materialized in the last second, effectively deflecting the shards into the mob and wreaking havoc among the masses. They surged forward toward the knights, and surprisingly, Peter made no move to disarm Siegfried, but rather charged head on into the fray, slaughtering strange beasts with every stroke.

Siegfried's arrows flew, first taking down a black-furred Minotaur, then three praying mantis–like creatures with razor claws as they tried to hack at him. The minions spread out into the town and laid waste to everything in their path, clawing, pounding, incinerating, and bashing things down at every turn.

Karsten stirred. The unnerving sensation of having a sword stuck through him strangely did not bother him nearly as much as it should have. He opened his eyes, but did not stand. His blurry vision afforded him little view of the battle beyond, but at least it let him know one remarkable fact: he was alive.

As he lay there with the muffled action swirling around him, he became aware of a strange, distant voice. It started out as no more than a faint whisper, but steadily grew until it became intelligible. "Karsten, it's me, Jorgen."

Though he panicked at the sound at first, something inside him instinctively allayed his fears. This was the voice that he had known all those years ago. "Brother!" he called out in his mind. "How is this possible?"

The voice returned, insubstantial and hazy. "The sword, of all things. The other knights freed the goodness that had been separated from me and infused the sword with it. Peter knew what he was doing when he stabbed you with it."

Karsten groaned as reality sunk in, and the pain began to return. "What are we supposed to do now? How does this help us?"

"Much," the voice replied. "You will stand before my dark half and let me do the talking. When the chance presents itself, I will return to the sword and you will run him through. I will return to him, and we shall be whole again. Though I am the good, I am only half a person."

Arduously, Karsten rose to his feet and extracted the sword from his chest. The sickening sound nearly turned his stomach. *Then again*, he reminded himself, *that blow should have been fatal*.

He caught Siegfried's gaze, who was fighting alongside him. "I didn't sleep very well, if that is what you are wondering." His crimson blood dripped briefly from the blade and then vanished, leaving it clean, as if nothing had occurred. Karsten shrugged as he hurried past Siegfried.

"Where are you going?" yelled Siegfried. "You've just been stabbed!"

Karsten laughed heartily, as though Siegfried had just told a brilliant joke. "We Müllers are a hearty folk. It takes more than a sword to keep me down!"

The mob parted as Karsten approached his brother. His skin glowed as if he had ingested a swarm of fireflies, and even as he approached Saul, his appearance changed. His features shifted ever so slightly by broadening, and his hair darkened along with his eyes. He assumed a defiant stance in front of his brother, who still held the Morgenstern aloft.

As Saul met his brother's eyes, his countenance fell, as well as his hand. The color drained partially from his face. "What sort of trickery is this?" he gasped. "You are my brother, not my twin!"

"No," replied Karsten in a voice that was not quite his own. "Even better than that." Karsten swung the sword around, pointing it directly at Saul's throat. "Stand down. This is only the path to suffering."

Saul punched the amulet in the air, sending a shock wave through the ground. Karsten, however, remained firm as a granite column. "What's happened to you, brother? You were a noble man once, an artist—not a maniac! Step down!"

Saul snarled, bearing his teeth, yellowed and spider webbed with cracks. "Never! I *am* the ultimate artist. Haven't you seen proof enough of that? Soon, the whole world know it too!"

Saul barked a command, flailing his hands in the direction of the Drachenherz hovering above the castle. The creature reared back and spewed a fervent stream of fire directly into the sky that, instead of dissipating harmlessly into the air, tore the sky in two, ripping open a jagged white gash. Saul screamed the command over and over, but the monster made no difference.

Rage boiled up in Saul's face. The creature, though imposing, was obviously wounded. "It makes no difference," roared Saul. "It will only take a short time to recover! I can feel the draw of our world already through the fissure!"

Karsten gazed up at the fissure and immediately felt the dreadful truth of those words. Like the suction of a tornado, he felt himself and everything around him being drawn toward the split.

ᔕᕒ

Brigitta leapt to her feet as a shock wave rattled the castle. A moment later, the queen rushed back into the room from the balcony, snatching up Camilla from the bed and forcefully grabbing Brigitta's arm in one fluid motion. "No time to explain. Run!"

She dragged the two girls, sprinting as if trailed by a herd of stampeding cattle. Flying through the halls, she reached the balcony in record time.

Without thinking twice, she leapt over the balcony just as a second explosion rocked the castle. They plummeted to the ground, but as the queen held out her hand, a swash of green light surrounded the three of them, creating a protective cocoon.

They landed jolted but unharmed on the grass outside the castle. Immediately, Camilla's eyes popped open for the first time since her transformation. The sudden deluge of information around her proved too much of a shock, and she let out an ear piercing scream, which was largely lost amidst the rest of the turmoil.

Molly clasped the little girl in her arms, stroking her long hair affectionately. "Don't worry, sweetheart. I'm here. This is my friend, Brigitta."

Camilla glanced around, her eyes still seemingly feline. "What's going on?" she whimpered. "Is the wizard coming?"

Molly nodded, her eyes filling with sadness. "He's already here, darling, but I need you to be brave. We're going to take care of him for good, and we need your help. Understand?"

Camilla sniffled and wiped her nose on her sleeve. However, after she had done so, her demeanor took on an entirely new quality. She straightened up and looked Molly straight in the eye, her gaze confident and eyes dry. "What do we do? I'm tired of being a cat," she announced fervently.

Molly grinned broadly, patting her stepdaughter affectionately on the shoulder. "Now that's the tenacious little one I know and love."

Hiding within the rubble of the castle, Brigitta, Camilla, and Molly whispered frantically amongst themselves. "How much longer do you think you can keep that shield up?" whispered Brigitta to Molly.

"A good while longer," she replied, her voice full of strain. "I was able to absorb some of the energy when the Many-Named One used the Morgenstern. You two should concentrate on mounting an offense."

Brigitta nodded, while Camilla supplied her with another round of ammunition. She took careful aim and launched the sticky missile into the fray. It exploded with a satisfactory swash of black goo, bringing down two short bear-like creatures with golden fur.

Molly scanned the battlefield, and something caught her eye—something that one does not see often in a battlefield. Behind a huge, jagged boulder crouched a petite blonde-haired girl, frozen with terror. The queen squinted to make sure that her eyes were not playing tricks on her. "Look, both of you, behind that boulder. Do you see that little girl?"

Both girls leaned forward, and quickly retracted their heads. "Yes," replied Camilla in a mousy voice. "But I don't know what to think. It could be some sort of trick. That army is made up of all sorts of awful things."

The queen shook her head. "I don't think so. There is a good possibility that she's just a special kind of person. All the people around here who are from this world were turned into stone. Why not us? We were very close as well."

The girls could not come up with any answers. "Because," continued the queen, "there are certain people in this world who possess special traits. This happens because they are not from this world, not really, and thus the queen does not supply their life force. If that girl is one of them, we need her on our side."

Brigitta nodded, the importance of this girl immediately sinking in. "We have to get her over here. It won't be long before something else picks her up."

"I'll have to do it," remarked Camilla. "Brigitta can cover me, and you need to stay here to hold up the shield. It won't take long, and from what I've seen, Brigitta's a pretty good shot if something should come up." Camilla stooped down and fingered a stone in her petite hands. "Just use these instead, all right?" Brigitta nodded, and before anything else could be said to the matter, Camilla disappeared over the low wall.

Brigitta followed Camilla with her eyes. Luckily, her dress was dark enough as not to stand out as she scuffled along. A gangly creature, which looked like it had been an unusually tall person constructed completely out of light-colored taffy advanced on her from behind, grasping for her with its pliable arms. Brigitta took speedy aim and launched the stone straight through the creature's midsection. The creature swiveled its head around without having to change the direction its feet were facing, and was greeted with another expert shot in its gooey face. The stone imbedded itself deep so that it completely disappeared into the sticky substance.

After a momentary pause, it shook its head and continued its advance on the scampering child. Brigitta panicked, searching wildly for something to deter the flexible creature.

Blast, she thought bitterly to her self. *All I needed before were stones and seeds to do some damage!* She tore her gaze away from the creature in her search and quickly located what she was looking for: fire.

A small patch of brush lay smoldering only a few yards away. Snatching up a piece of wooden debris from the wreckage, she bounded over to the shrubbery and kindled the end of her stick. Rushing back, she arrived just in time to see the creature wrap a tendril-like arm around Camilla's skinny leg. Camilla screamed and fell on her face as the sticky tendril drew her in, dragging her slowly through the grass. Brigitta yanked back on her slingshot, realizing grimly that she only had one chance. She let the torch fly with a whoosh and crackle as it flew through the air. In the spur of the moment, her aim had not been as true as usual, and the torch landed not on the creature's back as intended but imbedded itself in his heel.

Brigitta watched first in horror and then in near amusement as the fire crept up the creature's legs and onto his body, which swiftly started to melt. The creature released its hold on Camilla and writhed, flailing about in a vain attempt to extinguish the blaze. Its movement only provided fuel for the fire, and quickly the once gruesome creature became no more than a puddle of slime on the grass.

Brigitta sighed in relief, being careful not to let her guard down. A host of grotesque reptilian flying creatures soon took notice of Camilla. They fluttered around her on mangy bat-like wings, their strange combination of scales and fur showing in black and silver patches all over their bodies. They lashed out with their tongues, which extended a ridiculous length and cracked like whips, flinging sparks through the air.

This time, Brigitta varied her assault, switching between chunks of rock and debris and the sticky black seeds, which effectively hindered the creatures' ability to fly. Luckily, these creatures responded much more negatively to being assaulted with flying seeds. Unfortunately, they proved persistent, despite their diminutive size, and it took all of Brigitta's strength to keep them at bay. She noticed through the onslaught that Camilla had reached the little girl and was speaking animatedly to her, using a generous amount of hand gestures. Encouraged by their progress, Brigitta returned to her task of fending off the creatures, with which she was having much more success. She recoiled in horror only a moment later as she glanced to where the two girls stood. The girls looked on helplessly as a dark figure emerged from behind the boulder and snatched them both up, one under each arm.

"Something's taken them!" Brigitta cried to Molly, who mirrored Brigitta's look of horror. Before Molly could reply, however, Brigitta had grabbed a handful of her diminishing ammo and bounded over the wall. She raced toward the direction of the dark figure at full tilt, ignoring the storm of flying creatures around her, which grasped out at her with their gnarled fingers. The few that were so unlucky as to come directly in her way quickly received a shot squarely in the chest from one of the sticky seeds. Occasionally, the claws ripped at her clothes and skin, but she ignored the pain and dashed on. As she rounded the stone where the little girl had been cowering, the stone itself reared up, revealing a beast of knotted and grinding stone. The beast roared, raising its melon-sized fists high above its head, readying a strike. The hammer fists drove into the earth, toppling Brigitta as if she had been no more than a feather on the wind. In an instant, the flying creatures were upon her, snatching and tearing at her skin.

Unable to scream, Brigitta felt herself nearly being torn limb from limb. Her vision faded as pain overwhelmed her. She thought of Johann, wherever he was, wandering through the darkness, and hoped silently that he would meet a rosier fate than hers.

Before she completely lost consciousness, she realized that her captors had suddenly decided to leave her alone. A burly man towered over her clutching a solid club in his hands, still swinging it side to side as if warding off potential opponents.

"Wow," the man cried. "I didn't think I had it in me. I guess all that time in the army kept me from going soft."

Brigitta managed to lift her head slightly and had to blink hard to get herself to believe what she saw. Two column-like legs were all that remained of the rock creature; the remainder of it laid as scattered debris in the grass. Several of the flying creatures lay prostrate on the ground, presumably also victims of the man's fierce bludgeoning.

At first Brigitta thought he might be one of the blonde-haired guards from the maze, but as she searched his face, he found none of the tense evil there, but rather a grim and righteous determination,

"We have to get you to safety," he whispered. "I am going to pick you up. Don't be frightened."

True to his word, Brigitta quickly felt herself being hoisted over the man's shoulders. She dimly saw Camilla leading, taking them back to where Molly was hiding. The other smaller girl followed close in tow, and they quickly reached their hiding spot.

Though Molly had been under no direct attack, she appeared the worst for wear out of all of them. Her blonde hair clung to her face, which dripped with sweat. Her eyebrows were knit together tightly, her brow furrowed with exertion. When she spoke, it was only with a wisp of her normal voice. "The attacks are getting worse. I'll fold under the strain if we don't do something quickly."

Brigitta observed the two knights locked in combat. Valiant as they were, they would not last long without the shield's protection, if merely on account of the overwhelming numbers against them.

"Then what do we do?" moaned Brigitta as her rescuer set her down on the uneven ground.

"We hope," he said.

Brigitta watched with growing apprehension as the gash in the sky grew wider and wider. She was not feeling particularly hopeful. Its draw attracted bits of debris from the wreckage, which spiraled upwards like an upside-down tornado. The creatures had spread out and were laying waste to the village in a horrific manner so that fires burned everywhere and smoke blanketed most of the sky. The ruins shielded them from the brunt of most of the Drachen-herz's showering attacks, but they all came frighteningly close. Though her face remained impassive, Brigitta could tell that the queen was about to buckle under the strain of sustaining the shield. The tall, blonde, strangely dressed man clung to the little girl, who was whimpering softly in his arms.

"What's going on?" he demanded. "What are we doing here?"

The queen spoke unexpectedly. "We're in a war, sir. From the looks of things you are no stranger to that."

The man nodded soberly. "I hate to admit it, but yes, though this is not like any war I've ever fought. How do we get out of here?"

"We can't" replied Brigitta. "If we even try to leave we'll—"

"Brigitta," the queen cut her off. "That might not be true. Where did you say that you were from?"

"Missouri," he replied hesitantly. "My name is Edison, and I'm a captain in the U.S. Army, but I don't expect that to mean much—"

He was cut short by a wail from the little girl in his arms. Capt. Edison stroked her hair and held her closer. "It's okay, little princess. Daddy is going to get you out of this."

Brigitta and Molly shared a glance of realization. "What did you just call her?" ventured Molly.

"My little princess," replied Capt. Edison testily. "She's my daughter, Kate. It's just a nickname. Why, is there a problem with that around here?"

They both shook their heads vigorously. "No, no!" Molly replied quickly. "Call her whatever you like. You just gave me an idea, that's all!" Without turning her head from the action, Molly addressed Brigitta, mustering as much excitement as she could manage in her voice. "Brigitta, do you still have the tiny music box? The one that I made for you?"

Brigitta nodded vigorously and produced the intricate device. Capt. Edison recoiled in surprise, forcefully shielding his daughter with both of his arms. "Get that thing away from me! Those things are cursed!"

Camilla stared at the box in awe, her charming smile like a rouge rose amid a field of scraggly dandelions. "What's wrong with it? There's nothing to be scared of. It's just a beautiful little music box."

Capt. Edison shook his head emphatically. "A music box of horror, more likely. One of those is what got me into all this trouble in the first place."

Molly ignored his strange outburst and continued her instructions. "Brigitta, wind the music box, but hold the key to keep it from playing. I won't be able to hold this shield much longer, but I would like to keep it as long as possible. I want all of you to stay close to me and when I feel like I'm about to run out of energy, I'll nod my head, and you are to let go of the key. Understand?"

Brigitta and Camilla quickly huddled close to Molly, while the other two kept their distance. "Aren't you going to join us, sir?" asked Brigitta. "The box doesn't bite or anything."

"I'm fine over here, thank you," he called back flatly, obviously looking around for some means of escape with his daughter, while backing slowly away from the rest of the group. His face reflected the desperation of a cornered animal, pathetic and desperate.

"Captain Edison," began the queen sternly. "I don't know what caused your irrational fear of music boxes, but unless you stand close when it starts to play, you won't have a chance of surviving. Now, swallow your fears, and get over here."

"No!" cried Capt. Edison. "Not a chance! One of those things took my daughter to begin with! I think I'll take my chances with this freak show."

As if to punctuate his sentence, a fiery rain of jagged rocks poured down around them, flying close enough to ignite their clothes. Frantically they dropped to the ground, rolling around to extinguish the blaze. Capt. Edison's face screwed up with frustration as he covered Kate with his own body.

"Are you convinced now?" cried the queen over the tumult, her voice cracking with strain. "Get over here!"

Capt. Edison gritted his teeth, his breath coming in greedy gulps. "Fine," he seethed, crawling toward them with Kate under his arm.

The queen nodded her head vigorously as she almost doubled over. "I can't hold it any longer. You've got to start playing, Brigitta. Release the key."

Brigitta released her hold on the music box key, and mechanism cranked into life, emitting a tune just like the one Molly and Brigitta had heard on the grand scale model. As the tune played, the air around them flickered with energy, buzzing and popping with fluorescent sparks. Capt. Edison stumbled forward with Kate tucked roughly under his arm. The air around them swirled faster, creating a light show to rival any firework display.

Capt. Edison dashed forward, his fingers drawing toward the outstretched hands of Brigitta and Camilla. "Sorry, princess," he reluctantly told Kate. Capt. Edison leapt forward with all his might. In an instant, the swirling light around the music box exploded with the force and sound of a lightning bolt, whisking its passengers deep underground.

They appeared a few moments later in the chamber beneath the castle that held the inner workings of the music box. They all took a moment to catch their breath while Molly explained everything she knew about the music box and the selection process of a new queen. Capt. Edison listened in rapt fascination, his cynicism giving way gradually to grudging acceptance.

When she came to the part about selecting a new queen, Capt. Edison interrupted. "You might have some trouble with that. The music box is lying in an abandoned room at the bottom of a hidden passage. There's probably no one else around except our tour guide . . . ." Capt. Edison's voice trailed off, his voice hesitant. "And my wife."

The queen peered pleadingly back at him. "Then we have no choice. She must become the next queen. If the box plays, she will be lead to it, no matter how well it may be hidden."

Capt. Edison rose up to his whole height, his fists clenched. "No way! We are getting out of here as soon as possible and dropping that awful contraption down the nearest well!"

All who were present reacted with shocked gasps. "With that sort of attitude, do you think we'll ever let you out of here?" replied Molly her voice rising sharply. "You simply cannot leave without our help! So sit down and start accepting the facts, or you will kill us all!"

Capt. Edison gritted his teeth but remained silently. He held his daughter closer, shielding her from view. Brigitta stepped forward offering a placating hand. "Please, sir. I know you are worried about your family, but we are worried about ours, too," she said, giving the man a gentle squeeze. "If we don't do something now, everyone I have ever known and loved will die. You'll be happy here with us, with your family, but we have to do this now. Once it's over, and if you want us to, we could probably even find a way to send you all back."

Capt. Edison sat down, the blood pounding in his temples. He had made split-second decisions constantly in the field of battle, but this one actually caused his heart to tremble. He pictured his wife's face, the one he had missed so long while he was at war and whom he was now missing again. They could not have any sort of normal life here, but then again, it was a strange and interesting opportunity. Maybe they did not want such a normal life in the first place. He met Molly's gaze, his eyes softening. "What do you want me to do?"

She gestured to the floor below where Wilhelm and Hart were hard at work, preparing the music box to play. "I need you to help them."

The queen leaned closer and continued her explanation.

CHAPTER TWENTY-THREE

ෆ෧

A Song of the Heart

The Canticle Kingdom

Wilhelm and Hart worked at a feverish pace, quite unaware of their surroundings. With their respective gifts, the task took a small fraction of the time it would have taken an ordinary person. Wilhelm fitted the final dot into place and glanced around. "Johann, are you finished with the repairs?"

Strangely, no one answered him. He strained his eyes, but could see no trace of his son. He called out several more times, but his cries were swallowed by the silence. Hart dashed up to him excitedly, thrusting the manuscript, ink still drying, in front of Wilhelm. "I think I've got it worked out! It's a beautiful piece of work, if I do say so myself. I'm just sad to say that I was not the author of all of it."

His smile faded as he realized that this great news was eliciting no reaction. Hart too glanced around, and immediately sensed the question on Wilhelm's mind. "Where's your son?" he asked warily.

Wilhelm stamped his foot in frustration. "He isn't here. I let him out of my sight while I was working. I figured he would stick close to us."

Hart's nervous smile first told Wilhelm that something was wrong. Hart began to speak, and then trailed off, muttering several times before he managed to cough up what was on his mind. "I'm s-sorry to say so, but I don't think we have time to look for him at the moment. We need to get this thing playing, or you might not have time for . . . your song."

As much as it galled him, Wilhelm saw the reason behind the musician's words. He sighed heavily through gritted teeth. "Fine. I trust you know your way as well to the main controls?" Hart nodded anxiously, rubbing his hands together in anticipation. "Good, let's go. Remember, keep a lookout for Johann," urged Wilhelm.

Before they left, Hart ascended the ladder and reversed the process that had flattened the cylinder, which rolled back together with much less grating than before. When everything was in place, the two men sprinted toward the far end of the room where the main controls were held. Taking the stairs two or three at a time, Wilhelm reached the control panel first and stopped cold as he realized what they had overlooked.

"Hart," he called as the musician came trailing up the stairs, huffing and puffing as he went. "One problem. We cannot activate the start panel alone. It has to be done with four people, and not just any people. I'm also sure that two of them have to be women."

Hart shrugged casually, wiping the sweat from his brow. "Sorry, as much as I would have enjoyed the company, I'm not hiding any women in my quarters." Hart moved toward the panel and promptly collapsed against it. "Though if I understand what I've garnered from all the old documents correctly, that setup is only necessary when—"

Hart did not get to finish his sentence, as a brilliant flash of light and sound caught their attention. They fell back, blinded and shocked by the suddenness of it all. Instinctively, Wilhelm gripped his sword with one hand and shielded his eyes with the other.

Fortunately, the outburst lasted only a few seconds before fading, revealing a small group of huddled figures. As the purple spots caused by the flash faded from Wilhelm's vision, he recognized several of the figures and began to laugh heartily. "Hart, good fellow, I think you'll get some company after all."

The queen looked up and met Wilhelm's gaze, a smile of relief flitting over her face. "It's as if you expected our entrance, good sir knight," she mused. "Can we be of assistance?"

"As a matter of fact, your timing could not have been more convenient. We were just about to try to activate the musical device, but we were short a few people."

"What song are you playing?" inquired Brigitta. "Depending on what it is, we'll have to use different people."

Wilhelm gestured at Hart. "He wrote it. He wants to play it first before we move on, shall we say, to the main attraction."

Brigitta wrinkled her brow. "For something like that, you would not have to be too picky. Any two men and any two women should do."

As if to demonstrate, Brigitta walked over to the first red panel and placed her hand on the surface. It glowed to life. Molly quickly followed suit, as did Hart and Wilhelm. As soon as the last panel had been lit, the cylinder sprang into motion, releasing a lovely lilting melody into the air. They all stood perfectly still, enchanted by the sweet strains of music.

ಐ

Further down the room, Johann's heart raced as he stared at the hooded figure. The hood flew back to reveal Bruno, his cruel eyes fixed on Johann.

"Wish I was in the mood to chat, but I've got other things on my mind," he spat.

Johann instinctively drew his sword bringing it into defensive position. "You mean, your new master has other things in mind," he retorted. "You just couldn't stay away, could you?"

Bruno's eyes flashed with rage as he brought one gnarled hand to bear, releasing a bolt of supercharged energy. "I said I'm not here for a chat!"

Johann writhed and staggered as the energy coursed through him, but quickly found his bearings once more and parried the next attack quite effortlessly.

Seeing his progress impeded, Bruno drew his own blade, which glowed ominously with black light. An instant later the two locked swords, sending a cascade of sparks in every direction.

"Bruno, stop this! Your father is alive, and he can help you! The wizard's reign will be short. He can't sustain the kingdom by himself. What will you do once he is gone?"

Bruno chuckled menacingly, his face contorting sinisterly. He appeared so different that it was as if a mask of evil had been draw over his countenance.

"Fool! I know he's alive, but he won't be for long! What do I need him for, anyway? He has never been there for me, and I don't see why I shouldn't return the favor!"

Both of them fell silent as the clashing of swords took over. Johann managed to parry the majority of the blows, but he could feel his strength slipping slowly from him. It was if his opponent leeched life from him with every stroke, even though none of the strokes actually caused any apparent physical damage.

Bruno's further attempts at magic were countered by the draw of Johann's blade, which glowed brighter with each attempt. Finally accepting this setback, Bruno fell back and changed his strategy. He let his sword hover over a pile of the metal dots, and they were drawn toward the tip as if it were magnetic. With a sudden jerking motion, Bruno swung his sword in Johann's direction, sending the metal hurtling through the air. Johann easily dodged the first assault, but had to dodge immediately again as another group of them whizzed toward him. The air twanged as a particularly large one ricocheted off the face of his blade and disappeared into the mist. Bruno drew up the mist around him and intensified his attack, making it nearly impossible for Johann to anticipate his opponent's next move.

Johann darted forward, weaving in a serpentine pattern across the floor to make him a difficult target. He yelped as a metal disk grazed his arm, drawing blood and sending a painful shock throughout his body. Undaunted, he lowered his head and charged headlong into the fray. He was hurtled quickly to the ground as another set of weapons slammed into his leg just below the knee. He resisted the urge to scream and further give away his position and continued to crawl, keeping himself low to the ground and gritting his teeth against the pain.

Though he had almost reached his goal, Johann did not see the danger until it was too late. Without warning, an arc of multicolored flames burnt through the fog and surrounded Johann. Though his sword took the brunt of the attack, the blaze burnt through most of his clothes and seared his skin. The pain hit so suddenly that Johann's brain scarcely had time to register it.

Bruno materialized from the mist and stood gloating over his fallen opponent. "I'll make this quick. Apparently my master believes that there isn't room for all you do-good knights in his new kingdom. Too bad, really. After you're gone, who will I have to push around?"

Johann only moaned in response, his hand still fingering the hilt of his sword. He had reached truly dire straights. His mind stretched to remember the command Siegfried had used to release the sword's terrible power. He also remembered what a drastic effect the sword had exhibited last time it was used and wavered on whether such a course of action would be wise in the first place. He attempted something that vaguely resembled a sigh. "Funny. And how much time before there won't be enough room for you either? You've seen what dark powers do to a person. You're just . . . a coward!"

He spat the last word like a venomous snake. Bruno clenched his hands with rage, flinging twisted fingers of energy, which fanned out and started crawling all over Johann's body. Johann tensed, unable to move any of his muscles, although the pain exceeded any that he had ever known. The force of the blast was such that the sword could never even begin to absorb it, and he surrendered himself completely to the attack. Before he blacked out, he felt his body being moved along at a rapid pace, and he heard something new on the air. It might have been the effect of the pain that had driven him crazy, but he was certain he heard the distant strains of muffled music.

When Johann opened his eyes, he was surprised to be alive. With some effort, he rose to a sitting position and found that his surroundings had changed drastically. The floor moved continuously in one direction and Johann could see that the sleek metal walls on either side of him curved up to meet each other high above his head. The walls vibrated constantly, emitting the same sweet music that had been his companion right before he passed out.

The realization hit him all at once. The cylinder had rolled back up with them inside of it and was now playing the old man's song. Warily, he glanced around and shuddered as he glimpsed Bruno crouched down a stone's throw away, his hood thrown back over his face. Feebly, Johann lifted his sword and pointed it in his opponent's direction, forcing his dry, cracked throat to utter a command.

Bruno raised a robed hand. "Save your breath. No magic works in here Do you think you'd still be breathing if it did?"

Johann's vision suddenly blurred, and he had to steady himself to keep from passing out. "Maybe I'm just not supposed to die today," he mused. "Had that crossed your mind? What makes you think you're on the right side anyway?"

Bruno drew back his hood, and Johann gasped at the transformed figure he saw there. Bruno's once brown hair now sported jagged white streaks across both temples, and his face held deep grooves which made him appear at least four times his age. His eyes peered out of hollow sockets, and his lip had become a cracked and jagged mass.

"It's too late to go back now," he croaked. "If I do, both sides will hate me! I have nowhere to turn!"

Johann scrutinized the pathetic, broken boy across from him and was instantly filled with pity for him. The feeling came somewhat as a shock to be having for the person who had just tried to kill him.

"I know it sounds crazy, Bruno, but that's not entirely true. We would take you in. The queen is supposed to have great healing powers, and I know that she would help you. From the looks of things, you need it pretty badly. I mean, what good is all this talk of power if you lose your body in the process? Just look at what it's done to you!"

Bruno stared down at his battered hands. Though they had once been smooth and young, they were now covered with calluses and soot. He gazed into the shiny surface of the metal, which reflected his contorted face. He recoiled in horror, refusing to believe the sight his eyes brought him. In a sudden peak of emotion, his hands flew into action, rending his hooded robe in two, leaving him only a thin leather tunic for protection.

He collapsed in a fit of anguished sobs, pounding his fists into the smooth metal. "Why can't I win, Johann? I try so hard, and I'm doomed to failure! I am useless. Worthless! And now I'm also hideous. The magic did this to me!"

"That's not true, Bruno," Johann said, trying to offer some sort of comfort. "You've made some bad choices, but so have I! I put myself where I shouldn't have been and now the people I love are in grave danger. We both have loads of things to be sorry for, and if we give up right now, it might be too late to fix the mistakes we've made. We need to get out of here and help the others."

"How?" sniffled Bruno, wiping his nose with his old cloak. "No doors or windows in this thing. *You* can't even get up."

Johann concentrated on the whirling metal until he spied a weak spot he hadn't managed to fix before being trapped. He waited until it rolled around to him and stretched out his hands, which immediately tingled with energy. He plunged them into the weak area, which instantly became whole. At the same time, however, the strangest thing happened—Johann also became whole. It was not the healing of the sore muscles or deep bruises that came to Johann, but the healing of his very soul. All the pent up frustration and anguish melted away like fleeting mist on a mirror.

ഗ

As the song came to an eventual halt, the entire party waited anxiously to see what would happen. For several moments, they waited in silence, until a small rectangle of light appeared at the far end of the room. It was in an upright position like a doorway, shining a white light for several meters in front of it. Hart jumped up and down excitedly at the sight, scarcely able to contain himself. "That's it! The door! Oh, I've waited so long to open it!"

Wilhelm scratched his head in puzzlement. "A door? We went through all that work just to open a door? I hope for your sake that its leads somewhere very worthwhile."

Hart nodded vigorously, gesturing in the direction of the door. "Indeed it does. It leads where I want it to. It's been sealed by a powerful magical lock the whole time I've been here, but now my song has undone the spell at last!"

Without another word, Hart dashed down the stairs and sprinted toward the rectangle of light. His arms were outstretched as if he were running to wrap someone dear in a loving embrace. Instinctively, Wilhelm followed him, growing even more uneasy. At their great speed, it took them only a few minutes to reach the far end of the large room.

As they approached the door, the light grew to a nearly blinding intensity. Wilhelm found that if he looked sidelong at the door itself, he could see flashes of colors, quick glimpses of faraway scenes and people. The door emitted a soft melodious hum, beckoning the weary traveler to come and find shelter. Hart stood directly in front of the door, basking in the light as if were straight from the throne of heaven.

Wilhelm raised a hand to his eyes. "Hart, what are you doing? How do you know what's beyond that door? It could kill you for all you know!"

Hart did not budge. "It is written of in all the old tales!" he cried. "A door to any place at any time! But it only stays open for a very short while, and so I am afraid I must bid you farewell."

Wilhelm stepped closer, reaching for the musician. "But where are you going? How can you be sure you'll arrive where you intend?"

Hart remained silent for a few moments and then continued, his voice resolute. "I am at the end of my life, Wilhelm. I know that and I welcome it. However, I do wish to behold one thing before I die. It is held in the world from which I come, and most people write it off as merely a legend. It is a magical instrument that lends the musician the ultimate creative ability! It can translate the player's very thoughts into actual music. Anything that I can imagine could come instantly into being! I must play it at least once, and then I can die in peace, knowing that I have documented all the music that was inside of me."

Hart turned briefly and nodded at Wilhelm. He then stepped through the portal and vanished instantly from sight. For a brief moment, a scene appeared of a dusty stone room in which two candlesticks provided the only source of light. They rested atop an antique organ with a vast array of keyboards. Each row shone a different vivid color, and Wilhelm caught a glimpse of intricate patterns etched into every key. As quickly as the image appeared, however, it vanished, leaving the space largely blank as before.

Wilhelm stood before the portal and stared as breathtaking possibilities crept into his mind. He inched closer and closer as the thoughts formed. "I could go back," he said aloud. "Back before all this with what I know! I could prevent everything!"

He gazed into the light, torn by indecision. He had no way of knowing how this would work, and if he failed, the consequences might be disastrous. As he gazed into the door, images began to form, but unlike earlier, these images were of things and people that he recognized.

First, the face of Peter appeared in his fox form, grinning and cackling like a banshee. The faces of the other knights swirled past, all wracked with pain and anguish. He saw dozens of people in distress and remembered bitterly how he could not help them. Finally, the image of his wife's tear-stained face arose before his vision, sobbing and moaning inconsolably.

Wilhelm stretched his fingers out so that they nearly entered the door. The light felt warm and inviting, and he could feel himself succumbing to its influence. He slowly set one foot in front of the other, coming ever closer to his fateful decision.

Suddenly, an obnoxious grating of metal tore him from his trance, causing him to whirl around. The cylinder had once again unraveled, revealing two crouched figures in the center of the floor.

"Johann!" he cried out desperately, all at once turning from the inviting light. "Johann, I'm coming!" In that instant, the rectangular form of the door scattered like a pane of breaking glass, sending shards of light scattering about the chamber. As Wilhelm glanced back, his vision blurry from the sudden intense light, he saw the opening had widened to an ugly gash, which curled open like a great maw about to swallow him whole. He willed his legs to propel him forward but made very little progress as the door exerted a pull of its own, now violently compelling instead of calmly inviting. Wilhelm gritted his teeth and ran full force against the pull. In a strange twist of fate, it was now he that needed assistance. "Johann!"

ༀ

Johann suddenly sat straight up as he found the world gradually unraveling around him. The song had finished not long before and the cylinder returned to its flat state. He first noticed the blinding patch of white light emitting from the other end of the room, and he could just barely make out the figure silhouetted against its radiance. He thought he heard his name being called from the direction of the light. Frantically, he turned his attention to Bruno, who held his face in his hands. "Bruno, I need to get out of here. Do you still remember that healing spell Siegfried taught us?"

It took several painful moments for Bruno to respond, and when he did, his voice was barely audible over the loud hum coming from the white light. "Yes, I remember it. Here."

Without even raising his head, he stretched out a finger in Johann's direction. A faint tendril of light snaked from his finger and rested on Johann's forehead. Johann closed his eyes as he felt the healing light wash over his body. He felt immediate relief, enough to raise him to his feet but not enough to return him to his normal vigor.

"Wow," he muttered, coming clumsily to his feet. "You really are a powerful wizard. To tell you the truth, I couldn't hold a candle to you. It seems that I've been going about things all wrong."

Bruno lifted his head slightly, craning his ear to the side. "How's that?" he asked cynically.

"I seen you as my rival, someone to overcome. It never entered my mind that I could really learn from you," Johann admitted.

Bruno slowly raised his head to meet Johann's gaze. His eyes registered a mixture of shock and deep-rooted pain. "I hadn't thought of that either. Though, I might have learned much from your swordsmanship."

Bruno also rose to his feet, glancing in the direction of the strange light. They both strained their eyes, unable to make out exactly what was happening. Then Johann heard his name called again, more clearly this time, and in desperation.

"Bruno, I think that's my father, and I think he's in trouble. I need to help him, but I'm going to need your help. Will you come with me?"

Bruno nodded silently, and they both dashed over toward the glow. As they approached, they found themselves carried along by an invisible force, which hastened their steps and drew them ever faster into the light. As they drew closer to the light, Johann saw that his father was trapped near the center of the light and floundering about ineffectually to escape.

Wilhelm saw the two young men approaching and yelled to be heard over the loud hum. "Don't come any closer, or it will drag you in! You must find something to drag me out!"

Johann studied the sweat-soaked brow of his father's face and knew instinctively that even his mighty father couldn't hold out for much longer.

"What is this?" called Johann. "What will happen if you fall into it?"

"I don't know exactly," Wilhelm yelled. "It happened when we played that last song, and Hart just disappeared into it, seemingly for good. We need to rearrange the notes to play the other song, and we need to do it soon, or the day will be lost! You need my help if we are to have any chance of completing the task on time!"

Bruno studied the brilliant light patterns for several moments, and then stepped forward even closer and raised his hands, bits of energy forming at his fingertips. His eyes took on the same wild glow as they had just minutes before as he had attacked Johann.

"What are you doing?" screamed Johann. "It'll kill you!"

"You fight fire with water!" replied Bruno. "As I see it, the only way to combat light, is with darkness!"

At his words, inky tendrils of black mist laced with deep purples and reds wafted from his fingers into the mass of light. At first the darkness melted into the light ineffectually, but as Bruno increased the intensity of the stream, the light began to ebb and wane, shrinking to a much more manageable size. The inexorable grip of the light also diminished to a point where Wilhelm succeeded in breaking free. He lunged forward and embraced his son, and they both glanced back, concerned for Bruno, who still spewed the mist at full force. As if reading their thoughts, Bruno stared directly at them and yelled before they could speak. "Go and do what you must! I will hold it as long as I am able!"

"But—"

"Don't argue! Just go!"

Johann staggered forward, his injuries momentarily crippling him with pain. Wilhelm thrust his arms under his son's and helped him along as they headed back toward the great metal sheet. "Patch up the holes in the sheet as much as you can, son. I'll do the rest!"

Johann grasped Brutus's hammer with one hand, plunged his other hand into the flaw, and felt the warm energy fill his body, lending him strength and courage as the gap mended. He could make out the sound of dots swiftly flying through the air as his father struggled feverishly to set them in their proper places, and he tried his hardest to keep up the breakneck pace.

They worked tirelessly; time blended together like the shades of a water-color painting. The gaps became fewer and far between, and Johann's heart soared at the prospect of finishing their task.

Just then, a great explosion erupted from the end of the hall where the white door had opened. The gap, which, through Bruno's efforts, had been contained to a space just smaller than a regular doorway, mushroomed out to fill the entire wall space. The once gentle pull became now an irresistible grasp, which, even at a distance, tugged Johann toward it. Stacks of dots shot into the air, creating a hailstorm of metal.

"Bruno!"

There was nothing that they could do. Johann kept low to the floor, crawling to the next flaw in the floor, expending almost all of his strength in the process. He could see his father working a far off, but for every dot he put down, two were drawn from their place, ripped off by the pull of the light. Johann rushed up to help his father. "We'll never make it at this rate! What do we do?"

"We're almost there! I just can't keep anything in place long enough! We need more help!"

As if on cue, a number of figures emerged from the chaos, running low to the ground. As they approached, they saw a muscular blonde man clutching a little girl in his arms, a woman in a fancy, yet tattered dress, and—

"Grandfather! Brigitta!" called Johann. "What on earth are you doing here?" Brigitta rushed forward and caught Johann up in a joyful embrace.

"I found him in his cell!" Brigitta laughed at the confused look on Johann's face. "It's a long story."

"Don't you ever scare me like that again!" chided Johann.

She slugged him playfully in the arm. "Speak for yourself. You've given me more than a few scares lately!"

Johann's grandfather gazed anxiously in the direction of the light. Sensing the need, he scrambled to pick up a dot. "You finally figured how to get this contraption to work! Where does this go?"

Capt. Edison handed Kate to the queen and stepped forward. "My name's Edison, and I'd like to help too, if I can."

Wilhelm nodded and motioned him to come forward. "Your help is gladly accepted. Okay, Johann, take your grandfather and Edison and let's get to work."

The queen stepped forward, taking Brigitta's hand. "Come, we'll stay by the control panel and see that no one can sneak up on us." With one last smile at Johann, Brigitta turned and followed the queen back in the other direction toward the control panel.

"Who was that?" asked a confused Wilhelm.

"The queen," answered Johann simply.

Wilhelm's eyes widened. He looked as though he had more questions but shook his head and set to work on the task as head. He gestured and yelled instructions, and all four scrambled around, as if working uphill on a very steep slope. However, with double the hands working toward their goal, they eventually began to make some headway. The rip, however, only grew worse, and the entire sheet of metal began its gradual advance toward the far wall.

"One of us has to rearrange the dots near the door, and another needs to get up on the platform to trip the lever as soon as we're finished!" cried Wilhelm over the din. "The rest of us need to maintain the ones we've already got! Who's volunteering?"

Those present answered with their actions. Though Johann tried to restrain him, his grandfather snatched the musical score from Wilhelm, dashed toward the door and commenced the work of rearranging the dots. Seeing no point in arguing, Johann dashed toward the ladder and positioned himself with his hand on the lever. He looked on in fascination at the uncanny speed and strength of the grandfather. All his life, Johann only saw him as a feeble shell of a man. His arms practically flew, setting the dots so forcefully that even the drag of the door could not budge them. Johann fixed his gaze steadfastly on his grandfather so as not to miss the second of completion.

That moment came quickly. His grandfather raised both hands over his head and shouted something that was lost in the din. Johann yanked on the lever, and the floor responded, hesitating slightly before overcoming the pull of the door. The massive sheet of metal reformed itself into a cylinder covered with the pattern of dots they had worked so hard to place.

Exhaling forcefully in relief, Johann glanced back to his grandfather, who had collapsed to the ground and was inching slowly into the shining, white door. Johann's breath caught in his throat as he scrambled down the ladder to be met by his father. He tried to dash after him but was restrained by a strong hand on his shoulder.

"No, Johann! We can't! Edison got trapped in the cylinder. That leaves only the two of us to start the song, and if we try unraveling the cylinder again, we might not get it back up! Come, now!"

Johann struggled against his father's grip. "But, it's Grandfather! We can't leave him! We'll never see him again!'

Wilhelm yanked harder, forcing his son around. "I'm sorry, Johann. It can't be helped!"

Reluctantly, Johann relented to his father's command and followed as fast as he could manage. His legs felt like putty under him, barely able to support his body. His head swam with a motley collection of light and sounds that threatened to overwhelm him. When they reached the wall by the control panel, he collapsed against it. Looking up, he realized their problems were far from over. "Father," he choked out. "I didn't think that they were invited."

A long row of blonde-haired, heavily armed guards lined the entire length of the control panel. They had ripped off the ladders, and all of them glared menacingly down at the weary knights, threatening to unleash death at any moment with their deadly, clawed prosthetics.

Wilhelm reacted instantly. Grabbing his son around the waist, he shot into the air and performed a flip followed by a corkscrew to keep them confused. Johann held his mouth as his stomach lurched at the sudden punishment. "Thanks," he muttered queasily.

The first attack from the guards flew narrowly past them and was followed closely by a plume of flame. Wilhelm flew farther away to stay out of range but toward the lighted doorway, struggling to keep control of his flight pattern.

"Father!" called Johann. "Why are we flying back into that place! It's already taken three people . . . we've got to fight them!"

"There's too many," came the response. "We need to try to lure them into the pull so they get stuck themselves, and do so without damaging the cylinder!"

The guards jumped down the ledge onto the floor as if merely stepping from one stair to the next. They rushed toward the cylinder, oblivious of the danger. The duo flew clear of the giant cylinder, and most of the attacks stayed away. Though the guards advanced appropriately, Johann and Wilhelm could tell at once that their plan was fated for failure. Without flattening the cylinder, the guards would never fall into the trap. If the cylinder was flattened, it would be trampled by dozens of feet and surely obliterated beyond repair.

Johann knew there remained only one option, dangerous but necessary. "Father, don't make any sudden moves."

Wilhelm grunted in response, staying as level as possible. Johann reached down and retrieved his sword from his belt. He closed his eyes and reached back through his memory to the word he had used to unleash the sword's power. "Father, fly right at that big group of them!"

"What? They'll shoot us out of the sky—"

"Just do it!"

Wilhelm changed course, flying at full speed into the largest group. In the instant they passed over the group, Johann released his sword, and the guards released a volley of fire. "*Hilfe!*" shouted Johann.

Johann plummeted to the ground, as the entire scene drowned in a sea of intense green light. The roar of the green, which rattled the entire chamber, masked the hum of the white light. The misty green light swirled and writhed for several moments and then disappeared. Johann hit the floor amidst a shower of dust and gravel. Coughing and sputtering, he flailed his arms and quickly discovered the reason why. The entire group of guards was now no more than an impressively lifelike band of statues, of which several were missing arms and shoulders.

Johann tried to move, but found that both his legs positively bristled with pain. "Father! Father, are you hurt?"

He stared through the jumbled forest created by the legs of the statues and saw his father lying face down a few meters off. A crimson pool grew slowly under him, streaming from a gaping wound halfway down his arm. Gritting his teeth, Johann crawled through the maze of statues toward his father. His muscles felt like they had been pulled taut and wrung out like a washcloth, leaving him weak and out of breath. However, he urged himself on, keeping his gaze fixed on his father. When he reached him, he could hear only very shallow breathing and could see where a cruel metal barb still clung to the flesh of his arm. He fought back his emotions as he gradually flipped his father over, the process causing a fierce moan of pain. All the color had drained from his father's face and his eyes stared blankly out into space.

"Father . . . stay with me. We need to start the song, and neither of us is in good enough shape to do so." Johann paused, swallowing hard. "I'm sorry I tried such a dangerous attack. I didn't think there was any other way . . . I'm sorry."

His father's eyes focused momentarily, locking on to Johann. "Johann," he groaned. "Just get me up there."

Johann sighed in frustration. "How, Father? I'm not you—I can't do what you can."

"Yes," muttered his father. "You can. You just haven't before. Take my hand—my good one."

Johann grasped Wilhelm's warm hand and felt his body growing lighter as it had before his mission to the catacombs. Assembling the pieces of his scattered mind, Johann imagined their bodies rising from the ground. He flew up and placed his father against the control panel. Wearily, Wilhelm propped his good hand up against the outline of a hand on the panel. It glowed brightly with a blue light.

Wilhelm coughed noisily. "Find the others."

Johann hovered just above the ground, careful to keep the pressure off of his injured legs. It did not take him long to find traces of the others. In the dim light, he spotted several strands of blond hair and one of the queen's shoes, which must have fallen loose during the chase.

He followed the trail that led to a pile of metal stacked up to provide access to a grate in the wall. Fresh blood stained the sharp edge of the entrance, causing Johann's stomach to lurch. "Queen Molly! Brigitta!" He yelled as he stared into the tunnel.

There was no answer. Johann shot into the tunnel with barely any room to spare. He followed a macabre trail of bloodstains, wincing every time his leg bumped against the walls on either side. He found Kate, Queen Molly, and Brigitta a few dozen meters into the tunnels, hunched together and shivering.

At first glance, Brigitta raised her slingshot, but soon realized he was not an intruder. Her eyes displayed a storm of worry that told Johann much, even before she spoke. "The queen," she whispered, "She's hurt badly. We tried to fight back against those brutes, but there were just too many of them. She tried to protect us. Thanks to her, I've only got a few scratches, and Kate here is unharmed. What about your father? Is he all right?"

Johann nodded solemnly, his lips forming a tight line. "He is. Those awful guards are gone, though we both have some wounds to show for it. Do you think you could help me move her?"

Brigitta nodded and set about the work on helping the queen into Johann's arms. Brigitta noticed for the first time that Johann was actually hovering over the floor. Her eyes grew wide and she allowed a fleeting smile. "I won't ask now, but sometime, you're going to have to explain to me how you do that."

"Deal," replied Johann with a fleeting grin of satisfaction. He started back the way they had come. "Follow me. We are going to need everyone if we want this to work."

They left the tunnels a few minutes later. Johann lay the queen down next to the control panel and took his place next the second blue hand.

A fierce grating of metal caused them all to glance up suddenly. To their horror, it was the cylinder whose metal protested loudly against the pull of the light, digging into the clasps, which held it in place.

"Hurry!" cried Johann. "The whole thing is going to give! How do we play the song to banish the Many-Named One?"

Brigitta placed one of the queen's limp hands on the display and frowned when it did not burst into light. "We have to have people who meet the right criteria! It's different for every song you play! Once they are in position, we need to pull the lever to get it going!"

Wilhelm muttered something, his voice drowning among the mayhem. Johann leaned in closer, straining to hear. "Have the little girl named Kate do it." Wilhelm wheezed. "This song . . . requires the heart of a child to function, the younger the better, and three others whose intentions are pure. The queen cannot participate without being conscious."

Johann looked inside himself to gauge his intentions. "I want to make our family safe so that my uncle did not die in vain!" He thrust his hand out onto the panel and it glowed brilliantly.

"For the queen," announced Brigitta, "and for our future!" She slapped her hand down, and the display burst into life. She beckoned the sniffling Kate to draw closer. Stooping down, she looked into the young girl's face.

"Where's my dad?" Kate whimpered through a plugged nose. "I want to see him."

Brigitta patted Kate's head with her free hand. "You'll see him soon. All you have to do is touch that picture of a hand over there. It's going to play some pretty music, and then you'll get to see your dad."

The little girl's eyes widened as she wiped away the last of her tears. "Really? Okay. I'll do it."

She scampered over the display and raised one hand back behind her head. "This is for my daddy." She brought her hand down with a thud.

Johann reached over for the lever and stumbled forward as the flying spell wore off. He cried out with pain but did not lose his hold on the hand or the lever. Holding his breath, he yanked it down with one determined motion and with a tremendous metallic hum, the music box sprung into action.

The cylinder turned, agonizingly slow at first, but as it built up speed, Brigitta flew into a trance and began chanting words in Queen Ellis's ancient language, just as Johann had seen in the forest. The words seemed to spur the cylinder on faster and faster until the song grew to its full, galloping speed. The light from the white door flickered and then went out, the passageway sealed once again.

Melancholy at first, and in a distinctly minor key, the song increased in tempo until the melody reverberated like cannon fire, rattling their teeth and jittering their nerves. The air rung as if charged with electricity, causing the hairs on their arms to stand on end and their muscles to twitch uncontrollably.

The song ended with a massive chord in which nearly the entire length of the cylinder was covered with dots. The force of the sound hit them like a tidal wave and sent them all sprawling back onto the floor. Then all was still and silent.

ꙮꙮ

The five people at the control panel recovered slowly. Brigitta rose first, and after staggering around, she found the lever. Remembering that it changed the songs, she returned it to its initial position and found that it glided much more easily than before. The dots swirled around the lines like an army of giant ants. Her task complete, she attended to the others. Both Johann and his father lay unconscious, as did Kate and the queen.

Camilla, who had been able to take better shelter, stood hunched over the queen, stroking her face and softly calling her name.

"It's no use!" she wailed. "She's dying, and there is nothing I can do."

"If she does not wake up, we can't play the song to bring in the new queen, and then we're all in trouble." Brigitta shivered in fear. "She hasn't shown any signs of life?"

"No, none!" cried Camilla "I can't think of what else to do! We need a doctor!"

Just then, Brigitta realized they had another option—one she herself had used just earlier that day. She turned to the little girl. "Camilla, whatever happens, do not be frightened. This may look scary, but it's necessary."

Brigitta grasped the queen's hand and recreated the feeling in her mind of becoming a statue in an attempt to give her own energy to the queen. At first her energy flowed only gradually, but the process quickly snowballed until Brigitta became hard as granite. Despite Brigitta's warning, Camilla yelped in fright but quickly stifled it as the queen woke up. She sat up with a gasp, still clutching Brigitta's stone hand. She looked sadly at her dear friend's stony face and instantly understood. She noticed her dear little Camilla and smiled.

"Sweetheart, it's finally time for a new queen to be chosen." The queen reached out and embraced her adopted daughter, tears welling up in both of their eyes.

"I'm going to miss you," Camilla managed between sobs.

"We'll see each other again, I promise. Now come with me, and we'll do this together."

Camilla helped her mother to her feet and they inched toward the panel, hesitating just before the buttons with the hands.

"Are you ready?" the queen managed, propping herself up on the panel, leaning all of her weight on it. When her daughter nodded, they reached out their hands and simultaneously pressed the panels. On the other side of the panel, two other hands found their mark as Wilhelm and Johann also rose to the task. The lights flared on, and the mighty cylinder burst into action once more.

This song, however, did not break forth like an avalanche. Instead, it wafted through the hall like the pleasant aroma of baking bread, starting out subtly but growing to fill the entire room. Its listeners enjoyed a growing delight, and a warm, comforting glow that permeated to their extremities, much better than a cup of hot cocoa, but not quite as good as falling in love.

As the last few strains of the song drifted off, the feeling lingered like a pleasant aftertaste. No one moved for several moments as the white light faded first to the size of a door, then smaller and smaller until it vanished. Sweet, enveloping silence filled the chamber for the first time.

A grin of delight on her face, Camilla leaned over to face her mother, but she was gone. In her place stood a woman with shoulder-length brown hair, dressed in the strangest clothes Camilla had ever seen. Kate jumped up and ran to the woman, flinging her arms around her.

"Mommy!"

CHAPTER TWENTY-FOUR

THE BREAKING STORM

THE CANTICLE KINGDOM

Above ground, the battle was not faring well. After the queen had let the shield down, the mob had rushed at the valiant knights, who were quickly tiring. To their relief, the growing fissure claimed many of the larger monsters such a giant, ape-like creature covered with matted white hair and a giant reptilian creature of mammoth proportions, which looked as if it belonged in a lake instead of on land.

As far as Siegfried could see, the queen had taken her leave, the ominous hole in the sky was growing larger by the moment, and Karsten and Saul were still grid-locked in conflict. Their war of words had escalated to one of blows, delivered at lightning speed with their respective swords. They whirled around in a deadly dance, oblivious to the fighting around them.

The only bright spot in their situation seemed to be that most of the creatures had diverted their attention from attacking and pillaging the countryside to avoiding the hole in the sky. Siegfried and Peter had already taken considerable punishment, and Siegfried figured if they did not regain control of the situation, they would quickly lose everything.

Siegfried squared his shoulders and called out to his companion. "Come, Peter! We should not leave Karsten to fight alone! Saul brought his friends, so I don't think it constitutes as an unfair fight!"

Peter heeded the call, quickly dispatching his skeletal opponent with a flick of his sword before using his magic to burrow into the ground, hurrying toward the main conflict. Just as Siegfried reached the fray, Peter exploded from the ground, placing himself and Siegfried between Karsten and his brother.

Saul studied the newcomers, threw back his head, and bellowed with sinister laughter.

"So, you just couldn't stay impartial in this . . . family dispute. No matter, I can just as easily take on the three of you. In fact, battling just one was getting a little boring."

With grim determination, all three knights squared up their stance.

"Good to have you at my side again, gentlemen," Karsten muttered, not drawing his gaze away from Saul.

"Likewise," the knights answered in unison as they lunged forward, striking as one.

Stalwart as the three knights fought, the power of the Many-Named One held them easily at bay. He ceased all conversation and now raved like a madman repeating the same names over and over again as he lashed out with evil magic. "Melchior, Caspar, Balthazar, Cornelius, Saul . . . ."

The knights struck mightily with their swords but could not land a single blow against the nimble sorcerer. He broke in his maniacal chanting only to goad the horrible creature above the castle to breathe fire into the sky.

"I suppose this is it, gentlemen," yelled Siegfried over the din, "and not just for us."

"Nonsense!" cried Karsten. "He thinks he's bested me, but that's where he's wrong. We just need a few more minutes!"

The wizard leapt straight at Karsten, who brought his sword to bear in time. The two swords locked with a metallic ding, and Karsten glowered into his brother's eyes.

"Too late," Saul hissed, thrusting his free arm into the air and releasing a jet of flame so intense that it stung their eyes. The flames dissolved into the sky, and instantly the barrier between the two worlds collapsed. Entire houses lifted from their foundations and trees from their roots, vanishing into the sky with a clamor that even the deaf could hear. The fallen stones of the castle swirled up like an odd tornado during a snowstorm.

Only the evil wizard remained unmoved. "You see, Karsten? I've won! A pity I must leave you know, but don't worry, I have a feeling you will be joining me shortly."

With a quick jerk of his sword, he laid Karsten on his back and glowered down at him. Raising his arms to the turbulent heavens, he began to deal a lethal blow. Only the sound of his maniacal laughter could be heard over the commotion around them.

Karsten paid no heed, preferring to look to the direction of the castle. "Play little music box. Play for your creator," he whispered desperately.

Above the clamor, Karsten heard the sweet sounds of their rescue. No one else heard it at first, and Karsten broadened his smile as if were a child with a secret to tell. Soon the sound grew much louder, forming a song of epic scope, ringing across the entire kingdom and bouncing back again.

Saul also took notice, clamping his hands over his ears as if the song was his own funeral knell. He writhed around in the air, as if each note stuck a sharpened needle into his flesh. Karsten seized the moment and brought his sword to bear. With a mighty heave and a keen eye, he launched the sword at his brother, impacting him directly in the center of his chest.

Saul gasped, his body snapping rigid and the color draining from his face. His face transformed, his eyes widening and darkening, his hair becoming bristlier and darker and his features younger. His body shifted as well, the gaunt muscles becoming the worn hands of a master craftsman. Even his attire changed. His robes became a cotton shirt and slacks with a worn leather apron. His still-rigid body floated softly to the ground and lay very still.

In an instant, the multitude of creatures vanished in a rather strange fashion. In a puff of acrid smoke, each of the creatures became a scrap of parchment or reverted to a tiny stone figurine. Above the ruins of the castle, the dreaded dragon vanished in a poof of smoke only to appear as a huge role of parchment, which quickly disappeared along with many of its companions into the white void in the sky, which, when the song ended, closed and faded into the clear blue sky. The statues of the parade guests that had not been carried away, in turn returned to the original forms, creating a crowd of confused denizens.

The three knights advanced on their former enemy and hunched over. As Karsten stooped down, Jorgen's eyes fluttered open, awash with pain. "I'm sorry, brother," he whispered. "You were right about my ambition. 'Twas a foolish thing."

Jorgen reached and slid the amulet from around his neck, offering it to Karsten. Karsten graciously accepted it and tucked it into his waist pouch for safekeeping. "Jorgen, we'll have plenty of time to talk because you're coming back with me. The shop is still there, you know. We could make a real fortune selling trinkets to American tourists."

Jorgen simply nodded, a faint smile forming on his lips. "Then let us go quickly. Perhaps it is not too late to undo what I have done."

Karsten nodded and glanced up toward the sky, which did not help to make him an optimist. "Siegfried, come with me. Peter, stay with my brother and keep him safe. Only the queen can undo this sort of internal damage and only if she has the power from this amulet."

With a short salute from Peter, the two other knights made for the ruins of the castle. Siegfried turned to Karsten and asked hurriedly, "What exactly did that song do? I've never seen anything like it."

Karsten answered, not taking his eyes from their task of scanning the area. "It's a song of banishment. It sends all evil back to where it came from and prevents it from returning."

Siegfried arched his eyebrows. "Then why didn't anything happen to Saul? He was here until you hit him with your sword."

"Indeed," replied Karsten. "Saul has been banished forever from this place, but when I struck him he once again became Jorgen who is actually good, for the most part."

Siegfried opened his mouth to ask another question, when Karsten raised hand for silence. He sniffed the air several times and prodded the ground with his shoe. After a few seconds, he nodded his head briskly. "This is the place. Looks like we'll need Peter's services after all."

Peter tunneled through the soil, his entourage keeping close. "Almost there!" he called back. "Careful! We'll be coming out of the ceiling!"

Without further warning, they burst through the ceiling of the control room and plummeted toward the floor, landing in a crumpled heap. Groaning, the unorthodox travelers rose to their feet and surveyed the room, grumbling and rubbing their sore spots.

"Peter," muttered Siegfried. "Remind me never to travel with you again."

Karsten, however, did not complain but instead located the one woman whose strange clothes and puzzled expression made her look more out of place than the rest of the group. Smiling, he offered her a hand. "Greetings your Majesty. I'm Karsten. I apologize for the abruptness of your trip, but I assure you there is nothing to fear."

Tentatively, the newly arrived queen shook Karsten's hand and retracted it. "Your Majesty? You must have me confused with someone else. W–what is this place? Where's my husband?"

"Closer than you'd think," chimed Wilhelm. "I'm sorry if he's a bit shaken."

Wilhelm indicated a man in the distance, staggering slowly toward them. Johann had flattened the cylinder to release its unwitting captive. He appeared a bit worse for wear but generally unharmed.

"That is why I never became a pilot," Capt. Edison muttered sarcastically to himself.

The woman called her husband's name, and Capt. Edison broke into a lopsided run, his steps like those of a man who has taken too many jabs to the jaw in a boxing match. Hastily, Johann located one of the battered ladders and propped it up again against the wall.

With some effort, Capt. Edison ascended the ladder and buried himself in his wife's arms. They held each other for a long time. "What's going on?" she whimpered, clutching her husband tighter.

"An adventure, sweetheart. A marvelous adventure." He stroked her hair and held her as the fear subsided. Then a sheepish grin crossed his face, and he struggled to meet her eyes. "Uh, honey? I don't know how to say this, but you know how you're always saying you want to be treated like a queen?"

CHAPTER TWENTY-FIVE

ෲ

THE IMPROBABLE PARENTS

THE CANTICLE KINGDOM

Capt. Edison tried to explain what was going on to his wife the best he could but found that he scarcely understood himself. While the reunions continued around them, Karsten approached Mrs. Edison and placed the amulet around her neck. Baffled, she studied the new addition to her wardrobe.

"Um, I don't think it really goes with what I have on at the moment," she protested. "Why give me such an expensive piece of jewelry?"

Karsten smiled knowingly. "That, your Majesty, is no ordinary necklace. I advise you to keep it on your person at all times. I apologize if this all seems overwhelming. You must have hundreds of questions, not the least of which is why I am referring to you as 'your Majesty.'"

She nodded, good-naturedly jabbing her husband in the side. "Well, it's much more than I ever get from him."

"Come, then. Let's get you three some place more comfortable where I can explain everything." Karsten gathered the little family and indicated for them to follow.

Brigitta stirred again for the first time and rose to stretch her stiff muscles. She found Johann laying flat on his back, staring off into space and groaning slightly. Stooping over him, she tousled his hair gently. "Hey, sleeping sounds like a good idea, but you might want to get home first."

Johann chuckled. "That is, if I still have a home. It's going to take ages to rebuild the town."

They sat in silence for a while, breathing deeply. "I'm glad you're all right, Johann. There were a few times I thought I would never see you again."

"Speak for yourself," Johann retorted. "I wasn't the one getting turned into stone . . . more than once."

Brigitta rapped him playfully on the head. "I know. I didn't make a very impressive statue. It's just . . . there were a lot of people who didn't make it." She defiantly wiped back a tear, and Johann rose to embrace her. Leaving all pretenses aside, they let loose their emotions and mourned for the ones they had lost during their strange adventure. They thought of Johann's grandfather, of Bruno, of Molly, and of Brutus.

At the thought of his uncle, something jogged in Johann's memory, and he abruptly let go of his friend. "Brigitta, there's something I have to tell you."

She wiped her eyes on her sleeve and stared, puzzled, back at him. "Go on. I just hope this is a good surprise for once."

"Oh, it is," Johann assured her. "What if I were to tell you that your father is still alive and that I know where he is?"

Brigitta cocked her head to one side. "First, I'd say you've probably hit your head too many times lately. Then, I'd ask you how in the world you would know something like that."

He glanced over his shoulder to look at Siegfried. "I can't explain how, but Queen Ellis—the Queen Ellis who ruled before Queen Molly—appeared to me in the catacombs deep beneath the castle." Johann fumbled in his pocket for a moment before withdrawing a single red ribbon. "She wanted me to give you this. She said it would help you and Siegfried remember."

He gestured again to Siegfried, nodding his head. "It's him, Brigitta. He's your father. And Queen Ellis was your mother."

For several moments Brigitta looked as though she had received a square punch in the gut. "But that's impossible! I'm the same age as you. They can't be my parents!"

"Brigitta, before we came to rescue you, Siegfried took me to a place where time flows very slowly. I felt like I stayed there for months and months, but when we stepped out, it was still the same day. I believe the story goes that they kept you there for some time to protect you. That's why you appear to be my age. I didn't think I'd ever have any royal friends."

Brigitta thought back as far as she could remember, but was met only with the usual shadows and riddles. She shook her head in frustration. "Ugh! I can't remember anything! He looks old enough to be my grandfather, for all I know . . . but I trust you, Johann. You wouldn't lie to me about something as important as this."

Just then, Karsten appeared in front of them, a mixture of elation and pain on his face. "Congratulations, you two. I've been told what wonderful things you have accomplished and I must say, you two put even my days as a knight to shame."

His face then turned serious as he withdrew his sword. "Johann, Brigitta, my time is short here. My name is Karsten Müller, and I was the first of all the knights to defend this kingdom. I must return with my brother to our world and fix the damage done to this one before it's too late. But before I go, I wanted to make sure that this world is safe from within." He raised the sword ceremoniously in front of his face. "Kneel in front of me. Both of you."

They did as instructed, Johann careful to keep the weight off of his bad leg. Karsten brought the sword around and tapped Johann once on each of his shoulders. "Johann Buchmuller, in honor of your heroic deeds and devotion to the kingdom, I hereby ordain you a knight of the Canticle Kingdom and charge you to continue to serve and defend it all the days of your life."

Johann bowed his head, accepting his charge. Karsten then turned to Brigitta and repeated the ceremony to the word. She looked up, feeling grateful and confused at the same time. "But sir, how is it that I am also to be a knight?"

Johann's words came back to her in full force, and at once, she realized that they were true. "You have the true lineage, young one. Since I am going away again, and because Peter wishes to search for his son, there are two vacancies, though I do hope you both live out the remainder of your days in peace."

He turned to go but paused as he passed Siegfried and Wilhelm speaking. He obtained Siegfried's attention with a quick tap on the shoulder and whispered briefly to him. Siegfried raised his eyebrows and cast a furtive glance to Brigitta and Johann.

Excusing himself hastily, he turned and approached the two. "Well done, my friends!" he boomed. "Karsten tells me there's something you wish to discuss."

Brigitta nodded slowly as a brief flash of memory washed over her like a leaf on the surface of a swiftly moving stream: a much younger face, but still Siegfried's, coupled with a beautiful woman's. They were singing to her, soothing her to sleep to a tune that sounded remarkably familiar. "Yes, Father. There is much I wish to discuss."

CHAPTER TWENTY-SIX

৫৫

REBUILT, REBORN

IDAR-OBERSTEIN, WEST GERMANY, 1945

An otherworldly glow shone brightly from the frosty windows of the workshop deep into the night. Once again, two men stood hunched over the workbench, lost in concentration and working furiously with their tools. They said nothing as the wood and stone figures took shape under their hands, forming a multitude of miniature buildings and people. They placed their creations one by one into the box, smiling as they did so at the new world coming to life below them.

At last, one of them placed the gleaming model of a shimmering white castle, twice as majestic and brilliant as before at the top of the hill inside the box, while the other man fastened a new crank handle onto the side of the box. With a cheer of excitement, they both stepped back to admire their handiwork. The old music box had been reborn with only a few minute scars attesting to its former painful existence. The castle glowed in the firelight, and a new, bustling town sprawled out beneath it. The trees, once hostile and imposing, now seemed to beckon with inviting warmth.

One brother slapped the other on the back jovially. "It looks even better than the first time. You've really outdone yourself."

"Ah, not so," countered Karsten. "It is you who have made the real contribution. It's a true masterpiece." They both walked around the table, examining their work from every angle.

"Do you think they'll make it?" murmured Jorgen. "I mean, I know evil has a habit of cropping up even in the most pleasant of places."

Karsten nodded solemnly. "Indeed it does. Even in the heart of a good man." He reached out and clasped the new winding mechanism. "Well then, brother, shall we give it a try?"

Jorgen cautiously backed up a step. "I'm not sure. Do we really want to chance it?"

Karsten grinned broadly, bringing his brother back with a friendly hand. "Not to worry, brother. I wrote this one myself."

He gently wound the box and let it go. Gentle music filled the room, simple yet profound. They waited in silence as the song played its course and stood still for some time after, neither willing to break the spell.

ෆ෨

THE CANTICLE KINGDOM

Time passed, and by the power of its original architects, the city returned to its former glory. The Müller brothers could not, however, fix all the wounds the kingdom had suffered, especially not those that its citizens kept locked inside themselves, but with time, even those dimmed and became nothing more than murky memories. Brigitta joined her father in the woods. Though the once wild woods were not perfectly tame, they held fewer terrors and kept in proper step with the weather. Together, they scoured the forests, looking for odd beasts and other strange happenings.

Brigitta and Johann still saw each other almost daily. Though they had been dubbed knights, they were not nearly as busy as their predecessors. Karsten's blessing had truly come into effect, and for years, peace reigned and the kingdom prospered. They constantly joked that life had become almost boring and they were growing soft.

The Edisons settled in better than expected. It took them all several weeks to adjust to the fact that they were not, in fact, dreaming. Little Kate could hardly contain herself at the prospect of living in a castle and getting to wear the beautiful dresses of royalty. Capt. Edison spent his time studying the lore of the kingdom and writing chronicles for future generations, while the new queen spent her time out among the people, listening to their cares and tales. She often commented that it was as if she had gone from having one child to thousands of children overnight, but that she could not be happier about it.

The Buchmullers took some time learning how to be a family again, though all acutely felt their grandfather's absence. Often Johann lay awake at night, wondering about his grandfather's fate as well as the fate of Bruno and the crazy musician who had nearly ruined everything by opening the mysterious door in pursuit of the ultimate musical instrument. The most ironic thing was that Johann couldn't imagine anything lovelier than the way the giant music box played—as it did often these days—and felt sorry that Hart couldn't hear it now.

ෆ෨

The days passed, and Johann grew restless. He would often sneak out from his house late at night and wander through the woods.

One night in the dead of winter, Brigitta caught up to him. "Hello."

Johann whirled about, his sword gleaming in the moonlight. At the sight of his friend, he lowered the sword, still breathing heavily. "Oh, it's you," he muttered sheepishly, sheathing his sword. "I guess an attacker wouldn't bother announcing themselves. Guess I'm just a bit jumpy."

Brigitta placed a gloved hand on his shoulder. "I don't blame you. It looks a lot tonight like it did back then . . . you know, the snow and all." The wind howled through the trees, filling the silence. "So," she began. "What are you doing here? I can't imagine you're making a snow angel."

Johann grinned at the thought, but shook it off. He parted the brush, to reveal a smooth panel of wood behind it. He knocked soundly on the wood to demonstrate its stability before replacing the brush. "We're boxed in, Brigitta. This one little town is all that we've ever seen. I didn't mind it so much when I didn't know what was out there, but now I do, and I just can't leave it alone. I've come here on so many nights, wanting to cross the boundary, but I just have not been able to make myself take the step."

He motioned for her to follow as he stepped several paces along the wall and again parted the brush. This time, it revealed not the solid wall, but a gleaming white opening, through which Siegfried had brought him into the Middlespace. Its unearthly glow reflected off the snow, glittering and glistening beautifully.

"That is," he added, "until tonight."

She stared at him with pleading in her eyes. "So, you're leaving," she finally whispered, her voice flavored with deep sadness.

"Only for a while," he added hastily. "I'll come back as soon as I find what I am looking for."

Brigitta raised her eyebrows inquisitively. "And that would be . . . ?"

Johann sighed and shook his head. "Whatever's out there. Siegfried told me once that the Middlespace is just that: a place between two different worlds. I've always wondered what he was talking about. Given the time differences, you might not even miss me all that long, but I have to do this. I can't stay here any longer."

He moved forward and embraced his old friend, keeping his face devoid of emotion. "Tell the others what you will, but just let them know I will be all right."

"I guess this means I can't go with you."

Johann nodded finally, once again parting the brush to reveal the passageway. With a final look back and a parting smile, he stepped through the barrier and vanished from sight.

At first, Brigitta moved forward, urging herself to follow him, but stopped just a step short of the opening. She couldn't bring herself to take another step, not with her father clearly in the twilight of his life. She could not bear to leave him with the chance of never seeing him again.

Slowly, she backed away from the place where Johann had disappeared and followed her tracks back through the snow. Strangely, she found her cottage home brightly lit when she returned.

As she entered, she found her father setting some warm drinks and snacks around the table. "Welcome back," he said, without looking up. "Just out for a midnight stroll, am I right?"

Brigitta sat silently and bowed her head. She remained silent as she began to sip at her drink. "He's gone," she finally muttered. "And he wasn't planning on saying goodbye."

Siegfried moved his chair closer so that he could place a comforting arm on his daughter's shoulder. "Brigitta, I knew this day would come. This usually happens to those who find out the true nature of our world. Perhaps that's why it's kept such a secret."

Brigitta looked up through blurry eyes. "I know . . . and I feel that we'll see him again . . . it's just . . . ."

Siegfried placed his hand on hers. "Go, Brigitta. Follow him. You are both still young and the kingdom is at peace. Who knows what such a journey may teach you? Perhaps you will learn what you need in order to defend the kingdom again someday."

Brigitta remained silent, torn by the choice presented to her. She looked up at the man whom she'd come to know and love as her father. "But what if I don't see you again? Who knows how long we'll be gone? How will we—"

Siegfried raised a quieting finger. "Do not worry, my child. If Johann has already gone, I suggest you leave quickly to find him before he gets too far ahead."

Silently, Brigitta obeyed, a hard lump forming in her throat. She hastily packed a small satchel of provisions and clothing along with her trusty slingshot and stood expectantly by the open door. Siegfried came over to embrace his daughter, and for several minutes she refused to let go.

"Brigitta," he whispered softly, "this place, this kingdom, is not the end for us, even when we die. If I am gone when you return, do not despair, for there is still hope of a joyous reunion. Never forget that, child." He released her and smiled broadly at her while opening the front door. "Now go with my blessing."

"I love you, Father," she whispered, taking a step toward the open door.

"And I you."

Brigitta stepped out into the snow and broke into a sprint, not pausing even to catch her breath. She reached the doorway to Middlespace and pushed back the brush. She smiled softly as she imagined her friend's mischievous face. "Johann, you old rascal," she called into the opening. "Did you really think you could go off on an adventure without me?

Not really expecting an answer, she drew in a deep breath and plunged into the opening. The whiteness enveloped her, and suddenly the entire forest scene vanished. It took her a moment to orient herself, but as her eyes adjusted to the brilliance of the Middlespace, she saw a figure standing only a few hundred yards away. Expectantly, she ran toward him and cried out to get his attention.

Suddenly the figure turned and displayed one of his signature grins. "So," he chided. "What took you so long? I tried to get a real head start, but apparently that wasn't meant to be. I couldn't run at all with my conscience eating at me."

She caught up with Johann and tackled him to the ground, catching him in a secure headlock and causing him to beg jokingly for mercy.

"Don't ever do that to me again," she scolded. "From now on, we stick together."

"Okay, okay, I get it," Johann protested. "Now let's get going. The new world awaits."

Brigitta arched an eyebrow. "The new world? What do you mean?"

Johann pointed silently, indicating an opening in the whiteness that afforded a panoramic view of a vast city with gleaming metal buildings, grander and more impressive than any they had ever seen. Hundreds of people milled about, carrying on their daily business.

Brigitta and Johann both stood still, awestruck by the scene for some time, until Johann offered an inviting hand. "After you?"

Brigitta obliged and broke first into a run. Johann trailed closely behind toward the new world that was waiting.

EPILOGUE

༄༅

Rufus found himself in a sea of exquisite whiteness. His body no longer ached, and he found that he could run and leap like he had not been able to since he was a boy. Looking down at his hands, he realized that he was, indeed, in the form of a child again, just as he remembered.

He could not say how long he walked along in the white expanse before he saw the girl. At first, she was only a hazy outline on the horizon, but as she gradually moved toward him, he could first make out her flowing blonde hair and then her playful blue eyes. As they approached each other, they ran faster and faster, as if drawn together like two halves of a magnet.

Finally, as she drew closer, he realized for sure who it was and caught her up in his arms. Her smile radiated like the first rays of sunlight tearing through the clouds after a bitter storm.

"Rufus, do you remember that day in the city? The day that you bought me that present?"

The boy's eyes widened in delight as the scene flashed across his mind. It seemed like an eternity ago, but it came back to him gradually, like an old friend coming to visit after a long absence: the snow-covered, cobbled streets, the crisp December air, the warmth of his bundles of winter clothing, and the magic of the lights and decorations in the store windows. As he formed the scene in his mind, the whiteness before them gave way to form a window to the same scene in front of them.

"Yes," he admitted excitedly. "Yes—it was magical."

The girl beamed, her eyes twinkling like sun on a new snowfall. "In more ways than one," she chuckled.

Rufus reached out and grasped her hand, the warmth of it filling him with breathless excitement. "Come then, Molly. Let's return together."

ABOUT THE AUTHOR

Michael is a graduate of Brigham Young University with a degree in German teaching and a minor in music. He lives in Utah with his wife, Jen, and his son, Jarem. Michael enjoys writing fiction, acting in community theater, and spending time with his family. He played for several years with the handbell choir Bells on Temple Square and is now a member of the Mormon Tabernacle Choir.